ASCENDANCY

By Sóng & Sól Skulkwithy

Arcana Elements

Library and Archives Canada Cataloguing in Publication

Title: Ascendancy / by Sóng & Sól Skulkwithy.

Names: Sóng & Sól Skulkwithy (Writing team), author.

Description: A novel presented as a found footage screenplay.

Identifiers:
Canadiana (print) 20260175218
Canadiana (ebook) 20260175226
ISBN 9781067450106 (softcover)
ISBN 9781067450113 (PDF)

Subjects: LCGFT: Science fiction. | LCGFT: Horror fiction.
LCGFT: Novels.

Classification: LCC PS8637.O533 A91 2026 | DDC C813/.6—dc23

Arcana Elements is an imprint of Arcana Creations.

This is a work of fiction. Any similarity to any events, institutions, or persons, living or dead, is purely coincidental and unintentional.

Cover design by Pat Bellavance.

Cover art by Danielle René Pecor with art elements under license by Sóng & Sól Skulkwithy.

Legal Deposit, Library & Archives Canada, May 2026

ISBN 978-1-0674501-0-6

www.arcanacreations.com

Acknowledgements

What a journey this has been to see this story from first draft to publication! Fraught with daunting challenges, but full of imagination and love. Without the support of some very specific people in our lives, this would have never been possible. To our loved ones whose faith in us never wavered, we are forever grateful. Our deepest gratitude to our generous and patient Kickstarter backers who believed in us by funding our efforts to finish and publish this story. Our heartfelt thanks to our brave beta readers, Samuel, Danielle, Marie, Stephanie, Taryn, Lily, Laura, and Michael, who believed in us by spending their precious time reading our story and giving insightful and invaluable feedback. To our technological rescuers, Alice Tiên, Loïc Tiêu Long, Thomas Lâm, Pierre-Hughes, Anik, Janik, Danielle, "Rawr", "O Captain My Captain", Vanessa, Isabelle, Marie, "Jatismara", Kimberly, Tony, Jessica, Andrew, John David "Hobbes", Erik, Maia, Andrea, Susie, "My Tutelary Witch", Brent, Scott, Artemis, Dale, Cassandre, Harold, and several anonymous givers, words fail to express how thankful we are for your incredibly thoughtful birthday gift. Replacing Sól's ten year old laptop which chronically crashed, froze, and lost files, with a top of the line gaming desktop so she can have access to all the power of creation she needs for years to come, is unbelievable. Suffice it to say, you left her speechless. Everyone's belief in us is humbling and has set us on the start of an exciting adventure with more stories to come!

-Sóng & Sól

For you who waited twenty years for me to come home. Your faith lights my way.

-Sóng

It is often said that writing is a lonely calling, but writing with you is the pinnacle of all that makes life worth living.

Dear brother, our unbreakable kinship has seen me through the most difficult of times. I cherish your friendship, love, and support. I'm blessed to have been born your sister and love you dearly.

As always, Mom, I dedicate my writing to you because you were my best friend and fellow writer, introducing my imagination to fantastical worlds and superhumans. I love you more than words can say. Take care of Circe and Arktos for me. Those little furballs loved you something fierce. I miss you and those lovebugs so much it's hard to breathe sometimes.

Dad, our relationship was complicated and full of heartbreak, but in the end, we finally came to understand each other, and forgiveness abided. Mom turned my gaze to might and magic, but you implored me to look to the stars. I hope you, Dingo dog, Cali cat, and all our furry friends before them are keeping you good company. I miss you all.

-Sól

PREFACE

Thank you for cracking open this book. Was it because the stunning cover captivated your curiosity? You know what they say about curiosity. Or was it because you uncovered its secret? Very clever. You're going to need to be clever. Whatever the reason, if you continue reading, I would ask that you suspend your disbelief until the end. Even I still can't believe what I'm about to tell you. Ignore the names this book is published under and the disclaimer that it's fiction. I'm the actual author, and publishing truth as fiction was the only way left for me to deliver it to the world.

There's no time to ease into this, so get ready for a cold plunge. After I spent five days and four nights in a theobromine-fuelled frenzy assembling recovered video footage into a documentary, a black ops team invaded my home. They stole my memory cards, hard drives, backup USB flash drives, and hard copy notes only hours after I had shared their contents with a private investigator. This hi-tech, clandestine operation coalesced from the shadows, raided everything, and then left me with a warning as they obfuscated back into the darkness. Tell anyone, and you and your loved ones will disappear.

I waited until just after dawn before calling the estate attorney I had on retainer. She had extensive experience in ensuring law enforcement followed procedures and property was not misused or lost. I asked her to confirm that the original footage was still stored in the Property and Evidence Unit at the local precinct. She knew that this was a mysterious, ongoing investigation, so she didn't question my request. Minutes later, she informed me that the officer on duty sounded baffled when his check-in showed that it had vanished without notice. With my heart in my throat, I immediately called the private investigator. He was the only legitimate, trustworthy expert in his field who had been willing to help me. He didn't answer. I rushed to his office with dread churning in my stomach only to find it justified. Someone had sanitized the site. He was gone and everything with him. I didn't know whether to feel furious, terrified, or guilty.

Sóng & Sól Skulkwithy

Although the footage is lost for now, the story itself remains. In their efficient frisking of my person with rough hands and probing sensory devices, my most precious belonging was discounted as it dangled from a chain around my neck. Inside the silver Nahui Ollin pendant, commissioned by my mom for my quinceañera, hid a nano flash drive holding a digital copy of all the writing I've ever done. My notes, outlines, and drafts stay next to my heart, my superstitious artist ritual to bring good luck to my projects. That's where this story remained safe while they rifled through my desk, bookshelves, and bags in a premeditated assault on our right to know the truth. The publishing of this book is my Civil Disobedience, and although it's painfully personal and incredibly dangerous for me, the truth matters more.

Once I exited the empty office, I purchased a burner smartphone with cash then made a hard copy of my contacts before destroying my personal smartphone. After initiating my own investigation and immediately realizing the magnitude of what I was up against, I retreated to a secure location. There, I began converting the screenplay into novel format. A few pages in, I realized what I was doing diminished the visceral impact of its very nature. This transcript of actual video footage captured by a courageous young woman deserved to be presented authentically. To honour her, I abandoned my attempt. What you now hold in your hands is the truest account of what happened to my dearest friend.

If you've never read a screenplay before, please don't let the idea alienate you. Designed for visual storytelling, it is inherently enjoyable to read and easy to follow. Immersive descriptions follow scene headings, which set the time and location. Character appearance and action show you their story, and dialogue is labelled by name. Visualize what you read, and let your mind become the screen on which this unbelievable footage plays.

For the safety of those involved, I have changed names and appearances and used fictitious locations. At this point, you might be thinking, "But how can we help you then?" If so, thank you from the bottom of my heart. You can help me by sharing this story with others so we can help save ourselves.

Luz creciente,
Amber Sierra Cárdenas Ibarra

FADE IN:

01 Interior Hospital Room
Thursday Night, April 28, 2022

A GoPro camera films from its tripod, revealing a modern, private hospital room painted in a warm Southwestern adobe palette. A plush sofa and matching chairs support and comfort their inhabitants.

ISABEL HALE, a slender woman in her early twenties with shoulder-length wavy auburn hair, pulls her charcoal cardigan sweater closed as she curls up on the empty hospital bed. The bedsheets match her gypsum skin. She cries to herself.

LOHAN HALE, a muscular man in his early sixties, slumps in the chair next to the hospital bed. His thick, silver-streaked brown hair, pulled back into a short ponytail, complements his freckled, fawn complexion. Wrinkles rumple his forest green polo shirt, which has wriggled its way free of his black tactical pants.

AMBER SIERRA CÁRDENAS IBARRA, a woman of average build and height, just shy of twenty, with a tawny complexion and dark wavy hair in a messy pixie cut, rises from her chair to kneel between the two of them. She wears a gamer-themed lilac T-shirt over a long-sleeved olive waffle shirt and black utility pants cinched by a black canvas belt. Her hushed voice sounds like she's addressing frightened children.

AMBER SIERRA

I know this is horrible. Something awful has happened to our loved one, and we couldn't stop it. Now as we regroup to figure out how we can best help her, I want to take a moment to honour her wish that we document her story. So I'm asking you to share your thoughts, if you can.

They each give Amber Sierra a faint nod.

She squeezes their hands, then gets up, goes off-screen, and moves the camera closer, pointing it in Lohan's direction. His daughter Isabel is still visible at the edge of the frame.

AMBER SIERRA (off-screen)

Mr. Hale?

Lohan looks around the room as he searches for what to say. His kind, hazel eyes fill with tears. Finally, he looks at the camera.

LOHAN

Charlie, I hope you know how much I love you. How proud of you I am. I'm so sorry that what I taught you wasn't enough to keep you safe. I know you tried hard, that you were listening even when you pretended not to be. You did everything you could, having made the decision you did. Now it's our turn. We won't stop until we find you and bring you home.

He draws in a deep, shuddering breath, his warm eyes narrowing, growing cold with promised violence. He points a finger at the camera.

LOHAN

And you! I don't know who you are, and I don't understand what you did to her, or why you did it, but you will answer for what you've done, you –

Tremors shake his powerful frame, then his face falls into a mask of despair.

LOHAN

--why did I let her go alone?

He turns away from the camera before he breaks down.

AMBER SIERRA (off-screen)

No one could have stopped her, Mr. Hale. Not even you. You know that.

He lets out a strangled laugh.

LOHAN

I'll be damned if that isn't the truth! Once her mind is set, there's no changing it.

She pans the camera over to Isabel.

AMBER SIERRA (off-screen)

Isabel?

Isabel rolls over just enough to look up into the camera with eyes like her dad's. Tears streak her delicate face and her voice is barely above a whisper.

ISABEL

Little Sis, I've always thought the world of you. I don't understand what's happened to you or why you're gone. I'm terrified to think about what you went through. About the possibility of having to go on without you. I love you so much.

She can't hold back a sob.

ISABEL

I already have to live without Mom. How do I live without you, too?

Her dad climbs up from his chair and pulls Isabel off the bed and into his arms. The two of them hug each other tightly.

Amber Sierra swings the camera over to the empty bed out of respect, then uses the opportunity to speak her mind. Her voice trembles with warring emotions, but above all, is filled with tenderness.

AMBER SIERRA (off-screen)

Querida, I understand why you did what you did. And of course, I forgive you. I should've been there with you. I was the one they wanted, and I should've been the one they did those things to, the one they took. Not you.

She lets out a shaky breath.

AMBER SIERRA (off-screen)

I wish you could know that I'm doing everything I can to take care of your family until we find you.

Charlie's dad gently corrects Amber Sierra.

LOHAN

We're your family, too, Amber Sierra.

Her voice catches for a moment.

AMBER SIERRA (off-screen)

Yes. Mi familia.

She stays silent for a contemplative moment, then continues.

AMBER SIERRA (off-screen)

Charlie, I'm documenting this and putting it with all the footage you captured, like you asked, for everyone, because the world needs to know. I won't let this be covered up or forgotten. Thank you for helping me do that by leaving notes. You thought of that even while you were terrified. Always wanting to help others, even if you're in trouble, too.

Amber Sierra moves around to sit on the foot of the hospital bed in front of the camera, her eyes fixed on the floor. She starts to confess something as she fights back tears.

AMBER SIERRA

I have so much I want to share with you.

She gives a slight shake of her head, deciding not to say it, but it costs her the battle, and she starts crying.

AMBER SIERRA

Lo siento. I didn't get there in time. I should've insisted that you call 911 and that I cancel my meetings and come straight to you. But from the time we first met in middle school, you've been such a mujer fuerte, independent and selfless. I should've known you were just putting on an Academy Award-winning performance to keep us from worrying.

She waits while tears drip from her face to the floor. Then she swipes them away and looks back up at the camera, her jasper eyes glistening like their namesake.

AMBER SIERRA

Te amo, Charlie. We will find you and bring you home. Te lo prometo.

FADE TO BLACK:

BEGIN TITLES

The vertical title Ascendancy hides in the darkness until a silvery light from behind the direction of the audience illuminates it, moving from the bottom letter Y to the top letter A and then vanishing back into the darkness in the same progression.

END TITLES

CUT TO:

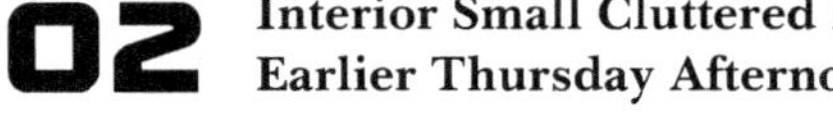

Interior Small Cluttered Home Office
Earlier Thursday Afternoon

Amber Sierra's Blackmagic URSA Mini Pro 12K camera records from its tripod.

Only a computer monitor and desk light illuminate the windowless, dark office. Stacks of books and piles of paper cover every surface possible, spilling out from mismatched shelves. Newspaper and magazine clippings, notes, photos, and posters litter the walls. They hang just far enough back in the shadows that the details are too difficult to make out. In their midst gleams a badge in the shape of a golden seven-pointed star, filigree leaves filling each point, outlined in royal blue, and an unreadable title around a centre ring of the same colour. The official seal of a governing body is crested inside like a gemstone.

SANI DURAND, a brawny man with a sepia countenance, sits with his broad back to his computer desk. A professional microphone peeks out from behind him. His long, black hair spills down his white shirt, embroidered with a geometric weave of turquoise, yellow, and black trim. His scarred knees poke through worn-out jeans pulled down over rugged work boots. He looks past the camera, his eyes as dark as the midnight sky and glittering with keen intelligence. The deep concentration lines on his face carve a sombre expression. His gentle intonation reins in the thunder of his baritone voice.

SANI

Thank you for reaching out to me. For what it's worth, I think you're doing the right thing.

Amber Sierra steps out from behind the camera into frame, wearing the same clothes she was in the hospital scene. She hands a flash drive to the man, then steps back behind the camera. Her voice holds a wary edge, its tone reserved.

AMBER SIERRA (off-screen)

Gracias, Sani. We'll see.

Sani nods as he takes the flash drive, his hair blanketing his shoulders.

SANI

You are. People have the right to know the truth.

AMBER SIERRA (off-screen)

How can they know it's the truth if it's too loco to believe?

She exhales a nervous breath from behind the camera.

He watches her struggle but waits for her to win her own battle.

AMBER SIERRA (off-screen)

My due diligence says you're legit. That's why I chose to come to you and not some conspiracy chiflado. You've worked with actual scientists, intelligence agents, and military veterans.

He spreads his hands out in front of him in acknowledgment, still holding the flash drive.

SANI

I may not be FBI, NSA, DHS, CIA, or other more secretive agencies, but I am a formidable detective with specialized training and decades of experience as a federal law enforcement officer. I have friends and contacts in the Missing Persons Unit at INTERPOL and in some of those agencies I mentioned, as well as others I haven't yet. I take my oath to protect and preserve to heart.

He holds the flash drive up as if to make a point.

SANI

You have hard data. You believe it, or you wouldn't be here. If we believe what we've experienced, others will start believing, too. But you have to trust yourself first before anyone else can trust you. That's why we have to speak out no matter the risk.

Her groan can be heard from behind the camera.

AMBER SIERRA (off-screen)

I'm trying.

He leans to the side and forward, as though trying to bypass the camera.

SANI

I've seen many things that you wouldn't believe. It's why I do what I do now.

Her smartphone chimes. She goes quiet, both with the weight of Sani's words and the unexpected interruption. Her finger pads tap against the touchscreen.

AMBER SIERRA (off-screen)

Perdón. I need to keep it on in case Charlie's family needs to reach me.

He tenses, watching, eyes narrowed and brows pinched together.

SANI

I understand. But for my safety, would you mind telling me who's texting you and why?

She lets out a sharp, breathy laugh.

AMBER SIERRA (off-screen)

An online gaming friend I know by the name of Toci.

He arches one eyebrow, giving her a disturbed look.

SANI

Toci? As in...?

She clears her throat, sounding a little embarrassed.

AMBER SIERRA (off-screen)

Sí, as in the Aztec deity. It's not her real name. She, Charlie, and I game online together in MMOs like WoW. It's her call sign, and it's her main toon, too.

He blinks, then continues to stare at her, raising his eyebrows.

She chuckles in anxious amusement.

AMBER SIERRA (off-screen)

A toon is a character played in massive multiplayer online games like World of Warcraft. Your main toon is the character you play the most. Usually, characters are pretty epic by nature, so her name is all good. I just forget sometimes that it could be seen differently in the non-gaming world.

He nods, still looking tense and a little confused.

SANI

Have you met Toci in person?

She hesitates before answering, her voice wavering with uncertainty.

AMBER SIERRA (off-screen)

No, and we've never exchanged real-life contact information. But we've gamed together for a couple of years, and in our online chats, we've shared some of our life goals. That led us to start planning to meet in person for a collaboration on a gaming documentary. But I doubt that will happen anytime soon if ever.

His eyes unfocus as he's listening, deep in thought.

SANI

Why do you say that?

AMBER SIERRA (off-screen)
I don't think our meeting would be safe.

SANI
I agree, at least for the time being. What about Toci first caught your interest, and what life goals did she share with you?

AMBER SIERRA (off-screen)
A ver, we bonded over something she quoted during our first WoW quest together right after she joined our guild. It was from one of my favourite sci-fi anime and turned out to be one of her favourites, too. Then that led us to start sharing about the work we do IRL--sorry, in real life--and I learned that she was an artificial intelligence gaming programmer who was developing a neural model driven AI gaming engine in her spare time. I pressed her about the ethical implications of it and was impressed with her awareness and sensitivity. She knew that it essentially eliminated the need for programmers, so she wanted to proceed carefully and morally. Our conversations about it fascinated me because the development of AI has world-changing implications, and that in turn, prompted me to discuss making a documentary about her process and journey.

He nods, absorbing all the information, then gives her a crooked smile.

SANI
What was the quote?

AMBER SIERRA (off-screen)
"The net is vast and infinite."

SANI
And how did that relate to the WoW quest?

AMBER SIERRA (off-screen)
Well, in the anime, the quote could be interpreted as a reference to the vast cyberspace network or the interconnectedness of the life and death cycle. At the time she said it, we were doing a quest in a zone that was like the afterlife for fae and nature spirits. Where they go after they die to rejuvenate until they're ready to be reborn.

SANI
I can see why you found her fascinating. Does your friend know where you are and why you're here?

AMBER SIERRA (off-screen)
She doesn't know where, but she knows generally why.

His eyes focus back on the camera.

SANI
I would advise you to be very careful about whom you trust, especially if you haven't met them in person and don't know much real-life information about them.

Her long silence hangs heavy in the air. When she does finally answer, her voice sounds tired.

AMBER SIERRA (off-screen)
The thing is, in the online gaming community, no one calls anyone by their real-life name because the whole point of a call sign is to protect your identity. Have you ever heard of Gamergate? Scary stuff. But you're right. I should've done due diligence on Toci, too, before sharing anything personal with her. I'll be more careful in the future.

He regards her for several seconds, his strong shoulders tensing beneath his shirt.

SANI
What was her text about?

She shakes off the weariness and her voice takes on its professional tone once more.

AMBER SIERRA (off-screen)
She's just checking in and asking for news.

SANI
And how did you respond?

AMBER SIERRA (off-screen)
I just told her I'd be in touch when I can.

His shoulders lower as he relaxes and sits back.

SANI
And your family? Do they know you're here?

After a slow breath out, she responds curtly.

AMBER SIERRA (off-screen)

No.

SANI

Why not?

AMBER SIERRA (off-screen)

They don't need to know.

He nods and drops his eyes to the USB flash drive in his hand.

SANI

Okay, back to why you're here. Thank you for being willing to share Charlie's experience with me. I've dedicated my life to finding people who've vanished under mysterious circumstances, so I know how dangerous it can be. Just how dangerous will be determined by the nature of who or what caused her to go missing. Determining that will guide our next steps.

He pauses, looking back up at her.

SANI

Regardless of what our investigation reveals, sharing our experiences is the only way to stop the suppression of the truth. It's a noble cause well worth the risk, in my opinion.

AMBER SIERRA (off-screen)

Espero que sí. I feel like I need to show this to el barrio global, you know?

He nods, recognizing the urgency in her voice, and without further hesitation, plugs the USB flash drive into his computer. He then opens the footage and clicks on play.

She zooms the camera in until the computer monitor fills the frame.

MATCH CUT TO:

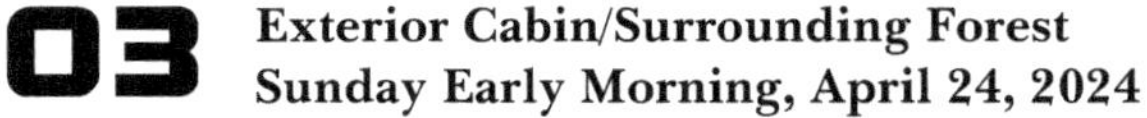

03 Exterior Cabin/Surrounding Forest
Sunday Early Morning, April 24, 2024

Amber Sierra hunches in front of her INNOVV motorcycle helmetcam, which she has set on a stump. A dark olive bomber jacket hangs open from her stooped shoulders. Shivers rattle her body as she stares past her helmet.

AMBER SIERRA

"After time adrift among open stars, along tides of light, and through shoals of dust..." I hope you're only on a pilgrimage, Charlie. That you'll return to us with enlightenment.

A grand, rustic cabin stands against the backdrop of a still, clear lake surrounded by ponderosa pine and Douglas fir. One Taos County Sheriff's mud-spattered, white Chevrolet Tahoe SUV sits in the gravel driveway next to a dusty, black Energica Experia electric touring motorcycle.

A tow truck driver finishes securing a cobalt blue Hyundai Ioniq EV to their tow truck, and a detective finishes taking notes in their department-issued notebook while supervising the scene.

Amber Sierra scrubs her hand through her short hair as she focuses back on the camera.

AMBER SIERRA

I'm Amber Sierra Cárdenas Ibarra, a documentarian, so I'm usually the one behind the camera. But Charlotte, or "Charlie" as her loved ones call her, is very important to me, and I want the world to know what happened to her here at--

Her face, tense with worry, softens as she thinks for a moment.

AMBER SIERRA

--Contemplation. I know things moved so fast we didn't even have the chance to decide what to name it, but I think she'd like it.

She blinks away tears that have snuck up on her and draws in a calming breath before continuing.

AMBER SIERRA

The world needs to know what happened to her. I don't have any hypotheses yet, because the initial evidence is confusing, and there hasn't been time to look at the footage she captured. I just hope it holds the key to helping her.

She purses her lips then motions with them back at the detective, her voice lowering.

AMBER SIERRA

I didn't want to take any chances with the footage, so I secretly made copies while the officer examined the area. I won't sleep until I've reviewed every second of it and assisted law enforcement in every way I can.

She looks over her shoulder when she hears the tow truck pulling away and the detective's vehicle door closing. The detective waves at her, and she waves back, then looks at the camera again, her eyes widening.

AMBER SIERRA
I shouldn't stay here alone.

She snatches up her helmet and puts it on then scrambles for her motorcycle.

FADE TO:

04 Interior Isabel's Spare Bedroom/Home Office
Monday Morning, April 11, 2022

Charlie Hale Webcam Vlog Episode #1

Papyrus-coloured brick walls, red wood flooring, and an industrial-style ceiling with exposed steel beams and pipes fills the webcam's view. It does a lazy rotation around until it settles on the person holding the laptop.

CHARLOTTE "CHARLIE" HALE, a young woman, not quite twenty, waves at the webcam, dark golden hair plastered against her moonlight skin. Her marbled eyes are the colours of maple leaves in various states of turning, and even puffy from insomnia, still sparkle with mischief. She lazes in bed as she sets her laptop down on her side table, adjusting it for the best angle. Her furry soulmate, a long-haired, brindle mini-dachshund snores softly next to her.

CHARLIE
Check out the spiffy digs. Too bad they're not mine, but so glad I'm allowed to stay in them after I voluntarily abandoned my much less fancy one! Good morning, everyone. I'm Charlie Hale, she/her pronouns, and this is my first vlog episode! Don't I look fabulous?

She musses up her curly hair.

CHARLIE
For those of you who haven't been following my blog and are just joining us now, you might be wondering what the heck is going on.

She motions to her disarrayed state and makes gestures with her hands.

CHARLIE
Let me catch you up. I work in a world of glamour and

kissing ass, of appearance versus reality, of smoke and mirrors. It gets exhausting, and I'm done playing their destructive game. The only games I'm interested in are of the geeky kind. So, with me, what you see is what you get.

She snuggles the sleeping beauty next to her who gives her kisses on the chin then rolls onto her back for belly rubs, four stubby legs sticking straight up in the air.

CHARLIE

I am not the only actor in the room! Don't you just know exactly how to be so adorable!

She obliges the request for belly rubs.

CHARLIE

Anyway, before I move on to the point of my vlogging, I want to tell you a little bit about myself and my spectacular rise to fame!

She gives a facetious snort.

CHARLIE

Let's see. I'm a failed teen actor, which was my first love. According to directors and producers, I'm not quite Hollywood material. But what do they know, huh? I could have been the next Jenna Ortega!

With a half-hearted laugh, she vogues for a moment, then pauses and looks over at her empty ring finger. Sighing, she holds it up for the camera, showing that she still has slight tan lines around where the ring once was.

CHARLIE

I'm also a failed fiancée. Apparently I'm not wife material either.

She waves it off, trying to appear like it doesn't bother her anymore.

CHARLIE

It was supposed to be a commitment to get married once we both graduated from the university. How was I supposed to know that he just considered us practice until he could get out into the world and find the real thing? I got the message loud and clear when I found out he cheated on me twice during his senior year in high school while I was attending the start of my sophomore year at the university. How he managed that during a pandemic lockdown is beyond me. Maybe I've got it all wrong, maybe my graduating from high school a year and a half earlier than him, but being the same age, might have been a blow to his ego and stirred up fears that some college frat bro might snatch me away? I guess I'll never know because he never said a word.

Her tight facial expression belies her attempt at humour and hints at her continued struggle to let go and move on.

CHARLIE

Hypotheses and insecurities aside, I'm too young to be getting married anyway! I need to explore life a little more before I settle down. I mean, there's no way you can find your soulmate at such a young age, right?

She gives a little shrug and an unconvinced smile.

CHARLIE

Finally, I'm a failed Hollywood screenwriter, my second love. According to the industry, my writing just doesn't quite fit their mould. Seems to be a recurring theme in my life.

Her eyebrows raise while she considers this revelation, then they drop back down as a wry smile takes over her bow-shaped lips.

CHARLIE

Despite these tragic shortcomings, I've managed to become quite a successful professional freelance writer and editor at an impressive young age in a remarkably short amount of time. I guess it's unheard of for someone who's not even in their twenties to have had some A-listers and big name game developers for clients. You heard me right, I did just say that I wrote for gaming companies, because my third love is for all things gaming.

Her eyes flash with excitement.

CHARLIE

My geekiness aside, this accomplishment has led to many of you, my eager Padawans, to request that I create an online tutorial for my secret to success. A sort of star chart for navigating your own way to stardom in this sector populated by numerous black holes and supernovas, but also boasting some wormholes, too. Because I've loved being in front of the camera ever since I can remember, but won't be getting any Hollywood gigs anytime soon, I decided it would be way more fun for me to make that star chart in the form of a vlog, which for the foreseeable future, will be replacing my blog. So thank you all for supporting me in this new endeavour! I'm so excited to be here with you.

She looks down at her biggest fan, who is watching her with adoration. She blows her a kiss, and then looks back up at the webcam.

CHARLIE

You, intrepid adventurers, who've already subscribed or will subscribe to my vlog and follow my course coordinates, will be rewarded with an epic freelance writer and editor voyage through space and time! I'll be focusing more on how to write good stories, so that you're more likely to be noticed, than on the business side of writing, though I will touch on that from time to time. You better secure your six-point harness because I'm opening the hyperdrive throttle wide!

For emphasis, she gives an evil laugh, but it gets overtaken by a yawn in short order. She covers her mouth with her hand, then once it passes, giggles, recomposes herself, and continues talking.

CHARLIE

Before our mission begins, I want to make a few things very clear. I am acutely aware of the AI threat on the horizon, but I'm hopeful that the combined power of the creative industries will be able to force regulation so that it's used as a powerful tool and not a replacement for humans. Because otherwise, what's the point of being human? What we can do as writers and editors is to be aware and to take part in pushing for ethical legislation by voting, writing to our local elected officials, joining advocacy groups, and spreading awareness through social media. Now, back to why we're here. Freelance writing and editing are thriving despite the pandemic, proving them to be the resilient resistance within the publishing empire that they are. Although success in this alliance of rebels does take skill and hard work, it also takes networking and luck. You can directly control the first three of those four factors, but even the fourth can be influenced by how well you do the third. Networking is key for getting connected with the right people, but it requires being adept at finding secret communication relays and satellites.

She flashes a mischievous grin at the webcam.

CHARLIE

You think I'm joking? I am in a way, but in reality, you have to be adept at something far more difficult! Socializing with people! Now this is often in direct opposition to most writers' and editors' personalities, as the majority of us are introverts. So how do we combat that? You either need to adapt and learn how to be extroverted for short periods of time or hire a professional public relations agent. If those options are outside your purview, try bribing an extroverted friend who has appropriate experience and skills and have them do the socializing on your behalf. That being said, the most important advice I can give you is to set time aside to write for yourself, whatever that entails. If you're already writing your ideas and getting paid for it, then you've made it even bigger than I have, and maybe you can hit me up so I can ask you to give me some advice?

Suddenly, the theme song for Doctor Who begins playing in the background. She glances down at her mobile phone, groans, and rubs at her eyes. Then she answers it on speaker, forgetting or not caring that the webcam is still recording.

CHARLIE

Hello, Trissa.

MANAGING EDITOR (off-screen)

Charlie, I just got a call from Mr. Avalos. He just finished going over your revisions. To say he isn't very happy is putting it mildly.

Charlie lets out an exasperated sound and mutters under her breath.

CHARLIE

Because he's disgusting--

TRISSA (off-screen)

--What's that?

Charlie snickers to herself.

CHARLIE

What? Oh, I was just talking to my dog. So, Mr. Avalos is unhappy, yet again. This is the fifth draft I've sent with his requested changes. What's the problem this time?

TRISSA (off-screen)

He says you're not making most of the changes he's requested, and that you're making lots of changes he hasn't requested.

Charlie rolls her eyes.

CHARLIE

That's because the changes he suggests either don't make sense or are far exceeding my moral boundaries. He needs to honour our morality agreement. The only reason I agreed to take him on as a client in the first place was because it would land your publishing company a lucrative contract, let me break into a grittier but substantial new market of True Crime, and tell a riveting story all without crossing serious moral boundaries. He needs to trust me. I'm the expert, he's not.

Trissa sounds bemused and irritated at the same time.

TRISSA (off-screen)

I understand that, Charlie, but he's the expert in what happened in his own life and the crimes he committed. Also, your years of expertise number in the single digits.

CHARLIE

I don't think you do understand. Knowing the details of your own life because you want to write an autobiography doesn't make you an expert in crafting it. As for years of expertise, you know mine are denser than most, or have you forgotten that? I mean, it sounds like it, so let me remind you.

Trissa starts to protest, but Charlie drowns her out.

CHARLIE

At age twelve, I attended my freshman year at the New Mexico School for the Arts where I specialized in stage and screenplay as well as creative writing and graduated in three years instead of four. After earning a perfect GPA and passing six advanced placement tests to put me a full semester ahead in college, I was awarded the University of New Mexico Scholars Scholarship and pursued a degree in English with a focus on Creative Writing. Again I graduated in three years, earning my final credits through an internship with the publishing house you work for. I didn't push myself to academic and professional excellence only to be told that I don't know how to do my job by a Drug-Trafficking-Black-Market-Arms-Dealer whose suggestions will not only make us look like idiots, but will bring our integrity into question!

Trissa gasps on the other end of the line.

TRISSA (off-screen)

Don't you think that's a little extreme? Our attorneys cleared his outline, he knows he can't stray too far from that. And yes, we're well aware of your impressive credentials, but they don't give you the right to rewrite a client's life.

Charlie's face starts flushing with anger.

CHARLIE

And you think I'm being extreme? Rewrite his life? I'm just trying to make it readable, palatable, and above all, ethical! Maybe your attorneys should advance their timeline for their next review of what he's asking me to change, and then see if they still agree it's ethical? I won't sacrifice my integrity or reputation for anything, Trissa! You, of all people, should know that.

Trissa's amusement and irritation crumble into strained concern.

TRISSA (off-screen)

Charlie, is it really that bad?

Charlie groans under her breath.

CHARLIE

I can send you our correspondence, but it's bad enough I won't repeat it out loud. Just the glamorizing that he insists on alone--

Charlie squeezes her eyes shut for a moment.

CHARLIE

--you know what? Just take my name off the project and credit the past edits to whoever doesn't care to have their name attached to this glorified filth. I don't want to be a part of this anymore.

Trissa sounds shocked.

TRISSA (off-screen)
You're breaking your contract with him?

Charlie's features harden, and she fixes the phone with a steely gaze.

CHARLIE
Absolutely. He's repulsive.

TRISSA (off-screen)
W-wait, we'll have our attorneys look at everything, and then if what you say is true, we'll bring him back into line for you.

Charlie lets out a scornful laugh.

CHARLIE
If what I say is true? If? You talk about trust? You're questioning the word of one of your most reliable freelance writers and editors over the word of a criminal? You're lucky I'm not breaking my contract with you right now!

Trissa backpedals, trying to do damage control.

TRISSA (off-screen)
No, I misspoke, that's not what I meant. Of course we believe you, we just need to convince him into compliance by going through our attorneys, okay?

Charlie shakes her head, her curls, like waves of honey, flow over her symmetrical face, obscuring her delicate features.

CHARLIE
I don't have the energy for this crap anymore. Just remove me from the project.

Trissa sighs.

TRISSA (off-screen)
Okay. I'll let Mr. Avalos know, but after what you've just told me, I think he's not going to take this very well. Are you sure you want to risk that?

Charlie swipes her hair out of her face, which is becoming redder by the second.

CHARLIE
What are you insinuating exactly? I can't tell if this is a veiled threat or a subtle warning?

Trissa struggles to sound sincere while still controlling the narrative.

TRISSA (off-screen)
A warning. Like you said, nothing is worth putting your safety at risk, but at this point, quitting might be more dangerous than continuing.

Charlie glowers, her voice tight with barely contained anger.

CHARLIE
Yeah, that sounds more like a veiled threat, Trissa. I won't let anyone bully me into doing anything. He can go to hell, and so can you if you don't stand up for me.

Trissa lets out an involuntary gasp.

TRISSA (off-screen)
I am standing up for you, Charlie! I just have to get all the facts, and I'm worried about you, that's all. I'll submit your resignation as soon as we get off this call. Now let's get you started on another project. Also, we need to talk about your resistance to using AI to help you in your work. In the coming years, your work output will be left in the dust if you don't use it.

Charlie grimaces and makes a disgusted face.

CHARLIE
The only way I'll be using AI is for internet searches, checking for typos, grammar, and spelling, and to detect AI generated writing.

TRISSA (off-screen)
Well at least that's something. We can revisit this later. So, there's that wonderful food security piece that focuses on agroecology that we talked about previously. I think you should take a look at it and see if you want it to be your next project.

Charlie hesitates then gives a weary reply.

CHARLIE
That piece sounds amazing, and I'm looking forward to it, but I'm so burnt out, Trissa. I think I'm going to need to take a break for a while.

Trissa goes quiet for a long moment.

TRISSA (off-screen)
There's a queue of at least ten clients who needed you yesterday.

Charlie rubs her thumb between her eyebrows.

CHARLIE
I'm a crispy critter. They can either wait for me, or choose to go with someone else, as sad as that would make me.

TRISSA (off-screen)
How much time are we talking?

CHARLIE
At least a couple of weeks if not an entire month. I haven't taken a vacation in the almost four years since I signed a contract with you!

Any warmth in Trissa's voice drains away.

TRISSA (off-screen)
We can't afford that, Charlie. A few days, maybe even a week, but--

CHARLIE
--And I can't afford to not take more.

TRISSA (off-screen)
Then we're going to have to remove you from the top of our pool. And that means you'll lose priority when they hire from the pool for the next in-house writers and editors.

Charlie clenches her jaw.

CHARLIE
You've lost your mind! I'm one of Dardanos' most lucrative freelancers!

TRISSA (off-screen)
When you're writing and editing, yes. But time lost is money lost. We'll have to raise someone else to take your place. You can start your ascent with us again once you return from your sabbatical.

Charlie hisses her words through her teeth.

CHARLIE

You mean start at the bottom again?

Trissa sounds detached now.

TRISSA (off-screen)

Not from the bottom, of course, but somewhere in the middle. You know that's the way it works in this business, Charlie. Keep in mind that a lot of other publishers are going to have a hard time believing that a nineteen-year old can write like you do. We took a chance on you, knowing you were young, but that's only because you lied about your age in your application for internship. Had we known you were barely sixteen at the time--

CHARLIE

--If the industry didn't have such prejudices, I wouldn't have had to. My work speaks for itself. You can take your empty threats and shove them someplace unpleasant!

She jabs at her phone screen, disconnecting the call. She sits for a few moments, calming down by stroking her snuggle bug's fur. Then she straightens her oversized grey T-shirt and smoothes down her hair, shaking off disarray caused by the combative conversation. It's only then she seems to remember the webcam is still recording.

CHARLIE

I'm almost twenty, damn it!

She thinks for a minute then laughs at herself to disperse her anger, putting on a brave smile as she speaks with an uplifting tone.

CHARLIE

That sure wasn't the way I intended to start our space odyssey together! But you know what, it's apropos for the first course coordinate I wanted to give you, anyway. Don't ever compromise your integrity. The moment you do, you lose your credibility, and then you'll just become one of the bucketheads. And while it's true that I've just lost an invaluable source of clients, there are other reputable, albeit smaller, publishing houses as well as honest individuals who'll want to hire me because I was true to myself. I can live with that. What I can't live with is someone telling me who or how to be. So, I think that's enough drama for my inaugural vlog episode. Hopefully you found it interesting, riveting even, and you'll stay with me for the entire saga.

Her hypnotizing eyes look back and forth for a few moments.

CHARLIE

And that Trissa or Dardanos won't sue me for recording our conversation. Maybe I should edit this out... Nah, who am I fooling? I'm a rebel at heart.

She becomes very serious then, putting on a sage-like expression.

CHARLIE

See you soon, and "may the Force be with you, always."

She holds her pose a moment then gives the camera a crooked smile, though it doesn't quite reach her eyes.

FADE TO:

05 Interior Isabel's Living Room Tuesday Morning April 12, 2022

Charlie Hale Webcam Vlog Episode #2

Charlie sits on a black plush sectional sofa with an empty Tardis mug in one hand and her laptop in her lap. She has a charcoal cardigan draped over her shoulders. The sofa acts as a divider between the living room and the kitchen and dining areas.

Her faithful hound lies next to her, ears perked, listening to the bustling morning activity and hoping for either treats or belly rubs.

CHARLIE

So after yesterday's career blowup, I was contemplating over my empty coffee mug--

Isabel, Charlie's older sister, walks into view from the left hallway, still wearing mismatching pyjamas. Her shorter, darker hair sticks out in random directions, having not yet been brushed. She goes behind the sofa, and bonks Charlie on the head with a folded newspaper.

ISABEL

--And what are those divinely fragrant fair trade coffee grounds predicting? Anything interesting?

Charlie laughs and rolls her eyes.

CHARLIE

Yes, in fact, they're predicting that you should mind your own business or you'll be late for your dream job any nerd would be jealous of!

Isabel sticks her tongue out at her then heads into the kitchen.

Charlie looks back at the camera with an amused smile.

CHARLIE

That hot mess is my big sis, Isabel. She works for Sandia National Labs as a Robotics Engineer, which explains why she's being nosy. She has to know how everything works! I can't complain too much though. She's been nice enough to let me stay in her unit of the duplex she and my dad share until I get things figured out. Let's face it, trying to rent or buy in the city during the pandemic is pure madness.

She raises her voice to be sure her sister can hear her.

CHARLIE

I do love her, even if she's annoying!

Isabel can be seen preparing breakfast in the background. A wide centre island and generous counter space with dark grey granite tops and all stainless steel appliances adorn the kitchen. A black modular table with matching chairs and hutch dignify the dining room. The entire residence shares the same industrial-style ceiling and red wood flooring. As she pours herself some coffee, taking a moment to inhale, she replies in a sing-song voice.

ISABEL

I love you, too, you ingrate! Ooh, and I love the jasmine aroma of this smooth, medium-bodied Arabica coffee!

Isabel takes a sip from her Borg cube mug.

ISABEL

Mmm, complexity for the win, starting with a floral flavour and finishing with a citrus tang! It's like sunshine in a mug!

Charlie snorts with laughter.

CHARLIE

Coffee snob! Anyway, where was I?

Isabel takes another sip and shouts from the kitchen with a mischievous grin.

ISABEL

Fortune telling!

Charlie groans, still laughing.

CHARLIE

Would you just go away?

Isabel giggles as she walks back behind Charlie, giving her bunny ears.

ISABEL

But I'm making you breakfast!

Charlie pointedly ignores her sister despite the threat of going breakfastless.

CHARLIE

I was contemplating what second course coordinate I should give to you, my faithful Companions, when I realized that I haven't taken one of the most important pieces of advice I've offered you. Although it's a passion of mine to help others create their stories, I need to start creating my own again. And finish them! I've never had the time to finish a single one. It's criminal!

Isabel rests her chin on Charlie's shoulder, her loving smile fading into a serious expression.

ISABEL

Yes it is.

Charlie squeezes her sister's face between her shoulder and head.

CHARLIE

That made me start asking myself, how did, or rather, why did I let this happen?

ISABEL

'Cuz you're a sucker.

Charlie makes a face at Isabel.

Isabel kisses her sister's head, picks up the attentive dackel from next to her, exclaims how adorable she is, then walks back into the kitchen while snuggling her. Then she sets her down and starts throwing tidbits to her. The back of the sofa hides the results of each toss, although the clacking of excited toe bean nails resounds on the hardwood floor, suggesting victory.

CHARLIE

I'm the sucker?

Isabel giggles from the kitchen as she starts giving commands along with the tidbits.

ISABEL

Come on, girl, prove your mama wrong!

Charlie shakes her head.

CHARLIE

It's a hopeless cause! She doesn't believe she has to earn her keep.

Isabel gives her little sister no heed.

Charlie lowers her voice and leans in to the camera.

CHARLIE

I guess I am. But don't tell her I admitted she's right. I'd never hear the end of it!

She pulls her long hair over one shoulder then glances over the other shoulder, making sure Isabel hasn't heard her.

CHARLIE

I'm sure there are several interrelated reasons that I still have to figure out. Guess I'm taking you on a journey within a journey, an inner-space one, and then, if you find yourself in the same place, you have my evacuation plan as an example. With this revelation in mind, I have my second course coordinate for you. Find the balance between helping others and yourself. Nurture your own creativity and allow it to be expressed, otherwise you'll end up a burnt out shrivelled husk like me, and I'm not even twenty, yet.

She chuckles and smooshes her face with her hands for a moment, giving herself wrinkles. When she releases her face, her eyes, though tired, hold determination.

CHARLIE

From here on out, I'm no longer going to sacrifice my own stories to help others develop theirs. Like both my sister and my best friend have advised, I need to try and look at being unemployed as an opportunity and not a failure.

She chews on the last word, spitting it out, then moves on to more palatable thoughts.

CHARLIE

I have a lot of savings and a safe place to live for free, so I have no excuse not to take a chance.

Isabel shouts her two-cents from the kitchen.

ISABEL

Penny-pincher!

Charlie scrunches up her nose.

CHARLIE

Profligate!

Isabel cackles, which echoes in the spacious kitchen, causing a rather eerie effect.

Charlie tosses her hands in the air, giving up the battle with her sister, then continues her thoughts.

CHARLIE

If no one wants to give me a shot at writing my own screenplay or taking a starring role, then I'll have to take my own shot. I'll write one, cast myself as the main protagonist, and produce, direct, and film it! We all need to be our own champion, so we can find the wonderful stories within and bring them out to inspire others. It's about damn time I take my own advice and rediscover what my imagination holds.

One side of her mouth quirks up, mischief dancing in her eyes, and she raises her Tardis mug.

CHARLIE

I assure you, "it's bigger on the inside."

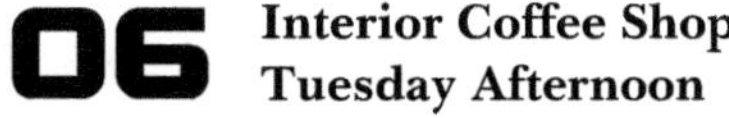

Interior Coffee Shop
Tuesday Afternoon

Charlie Hale Webcam Vlog Episode #3

Charlie lounges in the corner of her favourite coffee house at a mosaic-topped table, picking at the remains of her tofu scramble breakfast, frowning, and staring over her screen. The sage of her mandarin collared shirt brings out the stunning green in her eyes as they glitter in the sunlight.

CHARLIE

Apparently it's a lot bigger.

She puts her face in her hands.

CHARLIE

It's hard to choose just one idea. I want to explore something deep and inspiring that fascinates me, but that I don't know a lot about and requires interesting research in order to come to understand it well. It's my favourite part about writing, learning new things. Those parameters, of course, kind of give me countless possibilities. I guess it's a much better problem to have than writer's block!

Her fingers spread out, and she peers through the spaces in between, her eyes looking like embers smouldering, waiting for a breeze to ignite them.

CHARLIE

Some would be quick to remind me that a limiting factor is that it needs to be marketable. And while they're talking about the Big Five of both the publishing and motion picture industry's definition, which is making them large amounts of money, I would argue that it could be redefined for self-publishers and self-producers. I would define marketable as a piece that a large enough niche audience would love. And when I say large enough, I mean that the amount they buy from you is enough to sustain your daily living expenses as an author and both you and your production crew's as a film production company. Believe me, your living expenses are a fraction of what the Big Five of either industry expect to make off of your hard work. With this perspective in mind, it makes this factor not as limiting as it might sound. Instead, it assures that you'll write and produce a good story. Think of the word marketable as a synonym for well-crafted with a large enough audience to sustain you.

She rubs her face with her hands, then runs her fingers through her silky hair, her captivating eyes now flaring with inspiration.

CHARLIE

And that is the key to deciding which of your ideas is worthy to be forged into a story that you plan to sell! In that light, let's think about what elements make a story well-crafted.

She organizes her thoughts for several moments then starts dividing the food remnants on her plate for each element she counts.

CHARLIE

First, the story needs to be something the writer wants to tell with all their heart, one they believe needs telling. Second, they need to understand the nature of their idea and its themes, this means a lot of research both before writing begins and all throughout the writing process. Third, those first two need to be expounded on in an outline of characters, plotlines, and scenes. Fourth, they need to know their characters, their wants, needs, and flaws. Fifth, they need to start their story in the middle of something engaging. Sixth, they need to leave out anything that doesn't move the story forward, especially mundane activities, thoughts, and conversations. Seventh and finally, they need to keep their audience wanting more by not giving them too much all at once and by not making things too easy to figure out. Okay, now we're getting somewhere!

In celebration of the small victory, she scoops each portion of leftovers into her mouth until she looks like a gerbil. Her eyes roll from side to side as she tries to look demure while chewing with a full mouth. Then she remembers she's in public and finishes chewing while snickering to herself and finally swallowing.

CHARLIE

Since I only have a month to create a story that can fulfill all of those elements, I think it might be a good idea to choose something I've already put some work into and already done most of the research for.

She sighs with a groan.

CHARLIE

That means I'm going to have to dig through my files and figure out which of the legion of story ideas I have the most completed. More time spent not writing, but hopefully that'll be made up by the writing that I already did! I must confess it's not helping that the internet is eating my brain every time I turn on my laptop. You would think there would be less ridiculous news with the Reality TV President finally out of office, but he continues to star in the headlines. The hardest part is not to sneak glances at job listings!

A surly voice, laced with mordancy, speaks from behind the laptop screen.

AMBER SIERRA (off-screen)

I told you that looking for a job was off-limits for the

foreseeable future.

Charlie looks to the voice, her face lighting up when she sees who it is.

CHARLIE

Amber Sierra! What are you doing here?

Charlie turns the webcam toward Amber Sierra.

Amber Sierra strikes a heroic pose, hands on hips, bomber jacket making her look like a military pilot.

AMBER SIERRA

"I'm here to set things right. Also? To look dashing. That part's less difficult."

In the background, a small crowd buzzes with activity. Everyone is interested in their own conversations and the food in front of them except for a wiry thirty-something STRANGER. Their long, dark hair is pulled into a ponytail that disappears inside the collar of their black leather jacket. They watch Charlie with hard, bistre eyes that match their lean, chiselled face. They dart their eyes away when they realize they're on camera. Neither Amber Sierra nor Charlie appear to notice them.

Charlie turns the webcam back around and grins with a slight flush to her cheeks, her fingers toy with one of the silver stud d20 earrings in her ears.

CHARLIE

Channeling Lord Pavus and his rizz, are we? You've been playing way too much Dragon Age Inquisition!

Amber Sierra laughs.

AMBER SIERRA (off-screen)

O sí! You can never play too much Dragon Age! I'm glad to see you like the earrings I got you for your birthday!

Charlie drops her hand back down to her side, looking shy for a fleeting moment.

CHARLIE

What's not to love about these ubergeeky earrings?

AMBER SIERRA (off-screen)

That's what I thought when I first saw them! Anyway, your sister might have hinted that you're feeling frustrated with everything that's been going on and needed to see a friendly face. Besides, I need to ask your advice on something.

Charlie's delicate features draw into a playful scowl.

CHARLIE
I'll have to hold a tribunal for her later for leaking classified information! You look tired. Is everything okay?

Charlie doesn't wait for an answer and pats the seat next to her.

CHARLIE
Come sit down next to me so I can formally introduce you to everyone, and then we'll talk.

AMBER SIERRA (off-screen)
Ni tonta! You know I like to stay behind the camera!

Charlie reaches out and tugs at one of her hands, mischief crinkling her eyes.

CHARLIE
Come say hi for me. Pretty please?

She bats her irresistible eyes.

An off-screen sigh and a moment later, Amber Sierra comes into view, shrugging off her jacket and squishing in next to Charlie. Her face matches the colour of her baseball shirt's gamer logo. A red star inside a red circle slashed through twice by the white body of the shirt. The black sleeves act as a frame displaying the bold symbol.

AMBER SIERRA
Hola.

Charlie claps her hands with glee.

CHARLIE
Let me introduce you to my best friend, badass gamer chick, and only reason I ever get any acting gigs, Amber Sierra Cárdenas Ibarra. She's one of the youngest award-winning documentarians in the world, and is currently working on bringing one together about climate change that might involve two of her favourite acclaimed documentarians and their production company! Take a bow!

Amber Sierra gives an awkward nod to the camera, then reaches down to comb her fingers through her messy, short hair.

AMBER SIERRA

Anda ya! You've just had bad luck and too much integrity. Besides, I'm the one making bank from the whole arrangement. I get a professional actor for cheap!

Charlie hugs Amber Sierra tight and kisses her cheek.

CHARLIE

I'd do it for free if you'd let me!

Amber Sierra's blush reaches her silver earring-adorned ears, and she stiffens in Charlie's arms.

Charlie looks back and forth between the camera and her red-faced bestie, oblivious to Amber Sierra's discomfort.

CHARLIE

Oh, guess what the name of her production company is? It's just so perfectly perfect! You'll never guess! They'll never guess, Amber Sierra, so you need to tell them.

Amber Sierra looks like a squirrel who has just realized she's been spotted by a hawk. It takes a moment for her to answer.

AMBER SIERRA

Ombers.

Charlie giggles so hard she has to catch her breath.

Amber Sierra relaxes, now looking more like a squirrel who finally found her stash of nuts.

CHARLIE

For those of you not from our green and red chile loving state, that term was used when we were kids, in an ominous tone, when someone was going to get into trouble for doing something they weren't supposed to do. I love so much that in the same instance she's paying homage to her home state, she's also disclosing the purpose of her production company in the most clever and adorable way.

Charlie beams at Amber Sierra.

Amber Sierra starts squirming in Charlie's arms.

AMBER SIERRA

So anyway, can I go back to sitting on the other side of the camera now?

Charlie snickers then releases her from the embrace.

CHARLIE

Oh, you're all cantankerous today! Not, yet. Tell me what kind of advice you need?

Amber Sierra frowns at Charlie then chooses her words with care.

AMBER SIERRA

You know how we've talked about me needing a spacious place where I can live, film, and edit while I'm creating a documentary? One where you can come and stay and have writing retreats in? I think that's going to be necessary much sooner than we expected, because it looks like my climate change initiative is going to happen.

CHARLIE

I do, and that's fantastic news! But will you elaborate for my now deeply invested audience, who I know will ream me if I don't ask you to?

Amber Sierra arches a warning eyebrow to Charlie that she knows she's being set up but is playing along for now.

AMBER SIERRA

Since it means possibly reaching a wider audience, I will. So you know that two of my esteemed colleagues reached out to me about my initiative. But did you know that they produced a documentary about Africa's Great Green Wall? It's an astounding collaboration of over twenty African countries working together to reverse land desertification and degradation that spans eleven countries across Africa. They're holding the line against the creep of the Sahara desert as well as overgrazing and deforestation. Climate change documentaries like the one my two peers' did about initiatives like the Great Green Wall demonstrate tangible, inspiring results that can move members of world governments to action where scientific reports and presentations can fail.

Adoration gleams in Charlie's eyes as she listens.

CHARLIE

I knew they captured your attention for a good reason, but I didn't know it was that incredible. And now you've captured theirs! Tell us more!

AMBER SIERRA

Bueno pues, scientists have formulated the mitigation strategies that the world needs to employ. They have the data to back it up. Yet some world governments still resist committing to international cooperation and implementation within their own borders. So I want to demonstrate each mitigation strategy by matching it with the most appropriate documentary that currently exists. Then I would break that complementary documentary into sections that illustrate the objectives, tactics, and actionable plans of the mitigation strategy. Once that's done for each one, I'd have an educational climate change series that I believe could reach even the most resistant minds. Now that I possibly have two famous documentarians on board, it is much more likely that many others will agree.

CHARLIE

Because both of us have been so busy, we didn't have the chance to go into this much detail. I'm floored by the insight and intricacy of your idea, and I understand why you need the cooperation of other documentarians like yourself. You're going to have to dig deep for investors, I'm afraid.

Amber Sierra shrugs then curls her lips into a subtle smirk.

AMBER SIERRA

I just found out they're backed by a scientific research foundation. We're going to need a home base.

Charlie's jaw drops.

Amber Sierra shakes her head with disbelief.

AMBER SIERRA

I'm still mystified, since I'd just put feelers out a couple of weeks ago on a few of the relevant documentary networks. But anyway, Toci's been helping me research, saying I should do it sooner rather than later, and she doesn't even know about my initiative. So, what I need to talk to you about, in private, is a recurring dream I've been having related to everything I just said. But I'm not discussing something like that on your vlog.

An evil smile crosses Amber Sierra's face.

AMBER SIERRA

But since you don't mind that so much, why don't you tell me what's got you so frustrated?

Charlie gives Amber Sierra the side eye.

CHARLIE

I see what you did there. Let me finish my vlog episode, and then we can talk about everything, off camera. I better start stepping up my game or Toci's gonna take my spot as your bestie! I guess it shouldn't surprise me since her main toon is a paladin, always looking to help anyone in need. I promise I'll start looking for options, too, as soon as I'm done here today. I know this has been a dream of yours, and that it might become a reality soon is unbelievable! Possibly being backed by a scientific research foundation is unimaginable!

Charlie's smile brightens then a sheepish look passes over her face.

CHARLIE

I never realized you had actual recurring dreams about this. We should always pay attention to those. They're where some of my best story ideas have come from. I'm sorry I either missed you telling me that, or you didn't feel like I had the time for it. I really suck.

Amber Sierra looks a little smug but more relieved than anything else.

AMBER SIERRA

No one could ever take your spot, Charlie. Not even our chida guild leader. And you only suck a little.

Charlie leans her head on Amber Sierra's shoulder for a moment.

CHARLIE

Thanks. You're kind to say that. Even so, I'll always strive to be worthy of that spot. It's one that should be coveted.

Amber Sierra's face, almost back to normal, bursts with colour again, and she looks away from the camera, pretending to see something interesting in the crowd.

Charlie doesn't appear to notice as she goes back to addressing the webcam.

CHARLIE

Don't worry. I haven't forgotten about you, my brilliant

Cadets! Thank you for listening to my whining while I figured out how to move forward after finding myself stuck, but also, I'm delighted you got to hear my bestie's amazing news. Spread the word! Now on to course coordinate number three. Choose a subject that not only interests you, but challenges and thrills you! Don't be afraid to write about things you don't know or understand at first. Part of the perk of being a professional writer is getting to research, explore, and learn about all kinds of interesting things. I mean how many people can go adventuring and write it off as a job expense? If your brain is engaged with what you're writing, you'll be less likely to be distracted by outside influences. So, expand your horizons and stretch your mind!

Her brow furrows as she takes on a contemplative expression. She tugs down on her shirt then gives a command.

CHARLIE

And "boldly go where no one has gone before!"

She nods once to the camera then looks to Amber Sierra, obviously expecting some kind of reaction.

Amber Sierra is still staring off into the distance until Charlie elbows her. Her face pinches with feigned pain then flashes a cheesy grin for the camera.

Charlie laughs and shakes her head while mouthing the word, hopeless.

07 **Exterior Park**
Wednesday Morning, April 13, 2022

Charlie Hale Webcam Vlog Episode #4

Charlie props herself up on her elbows while lying in the grass of a well-tended park. She has pulled her mass of curly hair back into a loose ponytail, which trails down over her dark brown crisscross blouse and charcoal cardigan. She hides in the shade of a weeping willow tree, sprinkled with yellow blooms, while her leashed hot dog lazes in the sunlight next to her. She smiles, a travel mug of coffee in hand, her puffy but wistful eyes wandering over the golden yarrow and dusky lavender bordering the grass. Birds chatter in the trees and bees mumble as they go about their business.

CHARLIE

Spring is such an auspicious time for me to be coming back to life. I can feel the energy of rebirth vibrating all around me, in the bright burst of colourful blossoms--

She draws in a deep breath through her nose.

CHARLIE
--and their delicate scent, in the hum of bees on their quest for pollen, in the tweets of birds socializing, and in the cool breeze heralding brief showers and bright sunlight.

She looks thoughtful for a moment, a peaceful smile on her face.

CHARLIE
Wow, suddenly I'm an enlightened poet because I'm sitting outside in a park. Maybe there is something to this communing with nature thing! I used to do it all the time with my family when I was little. I guess I always forget how much I miss it until I get a taste of it again.

Her peaceful smile fades and her eyes grow distant.

CHARLIE
It's been hard to go back to it after my mom passed away. She was always there, and it felt wrong to be there without her.

She blinks back tears with a sigh then pushes the memory away and tries to focus on the task at hand.

CHARLIE
Well, as you can see, I've gotten away from the brain devouring internet. And after a deep-dive with my bestie, I've settled on an old idea resurrected by our discussion about her rather oracular dreaming. I'm not gonna lie, it's a little unsettling, and we've agreed to explore it together in the future as a documentary, because there's something powerful about dreaming that modern society seems to have forgotten about. Case in point, my old idea came from the fact that I used to be a vivid dreamer, before mom--

She grimaces and shakes her head like she's trying to clear it.

CHARLIE
Let's just say everything changed after she left us, and we've all been trying to centre ourselves again. Anyway, for now, I think I gave my bestie some good advice about it. Creative minds need to pay attention to dreams because they can

provide inspiring insight and guide us to revolutionary ideas. Are you listening, Circe?

She looks down at her little love with a smirk, who is lost to sunbathing, laying on her side, not a care in the world. Her brindled fur looks like tiger's eye sparkling in the sunlight.

CHARLIE

I guess I can't compete with a good sunbeam. But even though she's not listening, I know you are, my dauntless Special Agents. On to course coordinate number four! Contemplate your dreams, both figuratively and literally. Practice exploring them with intent. Lucid dreaming is an invaluable skill and incredible resource. It's helped me create inspired ideas like the one I'm using for my new story.

She draws her eyebrows together, looking off into the distance, then speaks in a soft, low tone.

CHARLIE

"I've often felt that dreams are answers to questions we haven't yet figured out how to ask."

Sadness seeps into her eyes as she sips coffee and rubs her sweet pup's belly, who stretches out in encouragement of more attention.

CHARLIE

If only I'd believed in them more all this time, who knows where I would be now?

She re-focuses on her recent triumph, which helps her shrug off the melancholy.

CHARLIE

Well, here is where I am now, and as I was saying, talking things out with my bestie helped me uncover an old idea I loved but had abandoned when I took the editor's fork in my writer's journey. After reviewing my notes and outlines with her, I shook the dried up seeds from the glume and soaked them in the water of my imagination, planted them back in the soil of my mind, and started cultivating their growth again with my words. My head didn't hit the pillow until the false dawn, because I was brainstorming plotlines and characters for most of the night. Thank goodness for this sweet elixir we call coffee!

A yawn wrestles her to her back, and she surrenders, flopping into the grass.

CHARLIE

Now I just have to keep tending them so they grow and blossom into a magical landscape for my characters to discover. I have to admit it's been a little overwhelming because for the last few years, I've been working with other people's ideas and materials. But when it comes to generating my own, I'm feeling like forgotten gardening tools that have been left out in the elements over the winter.

She takes in a deep breath and lets it out over several seconds, then makes a guttural sound of appreciation.

CHARLIE

Mmm, lavender! The scent is helping me stay outwardly calm even though I'm panicking a little inside over the first few scenes I managed to eke out last night. I tried different structures to order my scenes in the most effective way possible and to start constructing an intricate plotline that's hard to predict. The best result I got was using a combination of the Fabula-Syuzhet and Oneiric structures. I think I'm on the right track, but something just isn't clicking.

She reaches out and scrubs the irresistible, soft ears of her woolly weeny, whose luxurious fur makes her ears look even longer than they are.

CHARLIE

I think it's the characters who are giving me trouble even though I've also used Snyder's beat sheet, which is character centred and designed to make character creation a natural process. But for some reason, the characters just aren't coming to life. Their dialogue is stiff, and their reactions forced.

She bites at her plump lower lip.

CHARLIE

I don't understand why it's so hard for me now. Maybe because I've been doing more biographical and non-fiction work recently? I'm just out of practice, I guess. When I was little, I used to play make-believe and have entire conversations between multiple characters with an evolving plotline I couldn't have planned even if I wanted to. It flowed without effort.

Her autumn eyes look far away, lost in reverie, then a sudden realization dissipates her daydream and whisks her back to the present.

CHARLIE

Wait a minute.

She taps the webcam.

CHARLIE

You're the answer!

She wiggles her smartphone out of her pocket and makes a call, putting it on speakerphone.

Amber Sierra answers in a playful tone.

AMBER SIERRA (off-screen)

Hey, guapa, did you miss me? What can I do for you?

Charlie sits up and blushes, looking confused at her reaction for a fleeting moment, then makes a flustered recovery.

CHARLIE

Goodness, if you're going to answer my phone calls like that from now on, I may have to call you more often! Also, you're on speakerphone, and I'm filming my vlog.

Amber Sierra's flirtation turns to indignation with a dash of defensiveness.

AMBER SIERRA (off-screen)

Pues, I wouldn't mind if you called me more often than you do. And you better edit this out!

Charlie looks down, her voice quieting.

CHARLIE

I'm sorry, cariño. I just haven't been good company these last six months or so. But now you're gonna to see so much of me, you'll be sick of me in no time! And I make no promises about editing this out.

Amber Sierra makes a sound of dismay.

AMBER SIERRA (off-screen)

Nunca! That could never happen. And since you're refusing to edit this out--

Before Charlie can reply, Amber Sierra manages to find her swagger again.

AMBER SIERRA (off-screen)
--what's got you all excited, besides hearing my voice?

Charlie squeezes her eyes shut with a laugh, but doesn't take the bait. Instead, she looks at the webcam, her expression still a bit flustered, but her voice steady and sure.

CHARLIE
I need to borrow a camera or two.

Amber Sierra sounds both disappointed that Charlie doesn't bite and intrigued by the subject matter's change in direction.

AMBER SIERRA (off-screen)
Oh? Cuéntame! Because the production company I'm negotiating with just sent me a cutting edge drone. I think it's their way of showing off and proving their serious interest in my initiative. You should see it! It's all sick!

Charlie's eyebrows raise, and she pauses a moment to take it in before she winks at the webcam.

CHARLIE
Of course they're already investing in you by giving you a high-tech contraption. They know how valuable you are! Anyway, me realizing the answer to getting my writing to flow again is your fault, really.

AMBER SIERRA (off-screen)
How typical of me!

Charlie laughs as she reaches to close her laptop.

08 Interior Isabel's Dining Room Wednesday Night

Charlie Hale Webcam Vlog Episode #5

Charlie sits at the black modular dining room table with her back to the bay windows. Behind her, thirsty cottonwoods line the banks of the Rio Grande, drinking their fill. She's wearing black yoga pants and a lavender moisture wicking tee shirt. Her face glows with excitement, her eyes bright and her smile wide. She has devoured her plate of food to the last crumb. Table clearing and dishes being put in the dishwasher make a clatter in the background.

CHARLIE

The answer's been sitting right in front of me all along! I just need to be a kid again and film as I create. Then I can run it through a video-to-text program like the one Amber Sierra uses and edit it into the proper format. I'm a Meisner Technique actor, for crying out loud, so of course I'm a Meisner Technique writer!

She flails her hands in the air with the epiphany then laughs and settles down.

CHARLIE

This profound yet simple revelation brings me to course coordinate number five. Find a writing method, my resourceful Witchers, no matter how unconventional, that works for you! Maybe there's more than one. Maybe you'll need to use several.

In the blink of an eye, she puts on a disarming scowl and speaks in a gruff voice.

CHARLIE

But whatever it takes, remember, "Only myths and fables do not know the limits of possibility."

Her dad, Lohan, leans into frame, a few dishes in hand, and kisses Charlie's cheek. A silver streaked lock of hair escapes from his ponytail and tickles her face.

LOHAN

My insightful and brilliant, if not a bit odd, youngest daughter, everyone!

She gives him a teasing side eye and wipes at her cheek as he heads back to the kitchen. Despite her antics, she responds over her shoulder to him in a loving voice.

CHARLIE

That's sweet, Dad, thank you.

She looks back and addresses the webcam with a giggle.

CHARLIE

Nothing like your dad unintentionally embarrassing you by interrupting your professional vlog episode to gush about you. He and my big sis bought a duplex together, so he's always lurking about.

Something behind her laptop catches her eye, and she starts laughing. Without explanation, she spins her laptop around.

Her dad has pulled the hood of his navy blue sweat jacket over his head and is creeping around like a vampire in the night, crossing in front of the black brick fireplace. After a moment, he gets back to work, and returns to the kitchen.

She turns the laptop back to her, shaking her head.

CHARLIE

See what I have to deal with? Anyway, now that I've figured out the best method for me, I've borrowed two video cameras from my bestie, one of which is a GoPro that can attach to the drone she's lending me! That's right, that's how awesome she is! I get to play with her new state-of-the-art drone before she does.

Isabel appears in frame upside down as she leans over Charlie's laptop. Her turbulent hair fills the screen. She does her best impression of a news reporter.

ISABEL

Amber Sierra, while not yet old enough to legally drink, owns her own equipment and production company. She's already won several awards at film festivals around the world, and someday she and my li'l sis are going to rock Hollywood as Tinseltown's next power couple.

Isabel disappears out of frame almost as fast as she appeared.

Charlie feigns annoyance.

CHARLIE

Hey! I was getting to that.

Their dad yells from somewhere in the far reaches of the house.

LOHAN (off-screen)

When is she coming over for game night? It's been forever! Tell her that her chosen family misses her!

Charlie's expression softens as she calls out.

CHARLIE

Hopefully soon. I will. She misses you, too!

She focuses back on her webcam.

CHARLIE

My scene-stealing sister is totally right, though. Amber Sierra is the only reason I've ever had any decent acting work or know more than just the basics about cameras for that matter.

Her eyebrows pinch together as she realizes what her sister implied.

CHARLIE

Wait a minute! Power couple?

Isabel shouts from the kitchen.

ISABEL (off-screen)

Two successful people in their own right who wield influence in society?

Charlie groans.

CHARLIE

I know the definition of a power couple, but aren't you leaving something out?

Isabel makes an exasperated sound.

ISABEL (off-screen)

Nope, why can't you just let me dream? Buzzkill! I'm just saying that when you're famous, Amber Sierra will have this footage to make a documentary about you!

Charlie scoffs with a breathy laugh.

CHARLIE

Hey, I'm more fun than a series of escort missions, okay? I've just been in a slump for a few months. Anyway, my dream come true would be making a documentary with her about my journey so far! But she's got way more important things to document than my sorry butt, and since no one else wants to, I'm just doing it myself! I've already tried getting her to appear in it, but she remains resistant. I'm still plotting on how to draw her in, because let's face it, she would give it star power!

Isabel slides into frame next to her little sister, her voice full of conviction.

ISABEL

If anyone can make their dreams come true, it's you two, and I'm sure she would say the same thing about you.

Charlie stretches her arms up in surrender.

CHARLIE
I'll just take my wise big sister's word for it and try not to let anyone down!

Charlie frowns and looks at her sister as she circles back to her previous teasing.

CHARLIE
But seriously. Why a power couple?

Isabel tilts her head down and raises her eyebrows at Charlie.

Charlie lowers her arms with a confused look.

Isabel sighs and rolls her eyes.

Charlie splays her hands out in front of her in a shrug, but when her sister still doesn't respond, she dismisses her with a wave of her hands.

Isabel shakes her head and disappears from the camera's view.

Charlie ponders silently, her golden locks falling around her face, then looks down and leans over out of frame.

CHARLIE (off-screen)
Come here, you little beggar. Do you know what my sister's going on about?

She comes back into frame holding her ever hungry beastie who has no answers for her except a few licks to her chin.

09 **Interior Isabel's Spare Bedroom/Home Office**
Friday Morning, April 15, 2022

Charlie Hale Webcam Vlog Episode #6

Charlie hides beneath her cozy bed covers, a white synthetic down comforter over a bamboo brown fleece blanket. She peeks out, the shadows under her eyes deeper, the lines of worry on her face more pronounced.

Her lazy furball is buried next to her.

CHARLIE
This isn't working. It's been almost two days since my last

vlog episode, and I've deleted all the scenes I've recorded. They're horrible.

She gives a pitiful groan.

CHARLIE

I can't concentrate with the constant temptation of the internet and social media. The numerous phone calls and texts, that while I appreciate, still interrupt me. And the din of the big city noise outside permeates my every thought. I have this intriguing concept about the power of dreams and a good foundation built to make a paranormal mystery, but I can't give it the focused attention it demands. I can feel this opportunity slipping away, and I don't know how to hold onto it.

She puts a pillow over her face and screams into it, then after a moment, addresses the camera.

CHARLIE

I'm sorry I don't have a course coordinate for you, yet. I guess even the Navigator can get lost.

10 Interior Isabel's Spare Bedroom/Home Office Later Friday Morning

Charlie Hale Webcam Vlog Episode #7

Charlie hasn't moved from bed. Her attempt at cheering for Amber Sierra's arrival sounds more like she's about to cry.

CHARLIE

Yay! Bestie to the rescue! I've been drowning in my sea of bed covers, unable to face the day, so I sent up a distress signal text.

She listens and waits. After a few moments, the sound of doors opening and closing then footfalls breaks the silence.

Amber Sierra's hand appears in the frame of the webcam as she stretches it out to Charlie.

AMBER SIERRA (off-screen)

Rise and shine, chula.

Charlie pulls the covers over her face with a whimper.

AMBER SIERRA (off-screen)

I did not just cancel my World of Warcraft raid night for nothing! Toci and our other guildmates send their get well wishes. Ahora, ándale!

Charlie yanks the covers down to her chest, staring at Amber Sierra in disbelief. Then she sets the laptop on the other side of her so they're both on screen.

Amber Sierra stands with her hands on her hips, wearing granite grey carpenter's pants and a black t-shirt with the woman symbol in white but altered at the top to look like a power button.

CHARLIE

You what? Aww! You're the best! Tell Toci and all our guildies that they're sweet, and I'm so sorry! She's right, you know, about sooner being better than later.

Amber Sierra arches an eyebrow at Charlie.

CHARLIE

Well, she is! Anyway, tell her I'll make it up to them by getting back in game and catching my druid up soon. I miss playing with you all.

Charlie reaches out and takes Amber Sierra's hand as emotion overwhelms her.

CHARLIE

And you, you must really love me.

Instead of getting up as requested, Charlie pulls Amber Sierra into bed with her.

Amber Sierra lets out a surprised grunt then tumbles down next to Charlie.

Charlie buries her face against Amber Sierra's chest and starts crying.

Amber Sierra's neck erupts with a blush that travels up and into her face. She looks helpless for a moment then puts her arms around Charlie. Her gruff tone softens.

AMBER SIERRA

Oh chiquita, it's going to be okay.

Charlie's concerned companion wriggles her way out from under the covers, fur sticking out every direction with static. She watches them with a worried expression, her doggie eyebrows raised and eyes soft.

Charlie sniffles.

CHARLIE

I've got to get out of here. I need some peace, but I don't know where to go! If I had the money, I'd buy that cabin for you right now. Then we could both use it. But I had to go and lose my job. I feel so lost.

Amber Sierra nods, rubbing Charlie's back.

Charlie's loving pup licks her arm a few times then rests her head on her leg.

Amber Sierra leans down and kisses the top of both their heads.

AMBER SIERRA

You need a writer's retreat. How about I pay for one as your early birthday present?

Charlie sighs against Amber Sierra and fidgets with her Nahui Ollin pendant, which has slipped out from inside her shirt.

CHARLIE

That would be amazing! And you're even more amazing for wanting to give that to me. But it's almost impossible to find places at the last minute, and even if we did, I'd need at least a month there, which would run into the thousands of dollars. Neither of us can afford that right now.

AMBER SIERRA

Maybe not, but I'd do it anyway. If the other documentarians and their production company decide to team up with me on my initiative, money won't be a problem. Like I said, they've got the funding. I just don't know how long that will be, and I don't want you to have to wait any longer. How about a writer's residency?

A groan rumbles up from Charlie's chest.

CHARLIE

That would be heaven, even though I'd miss you tons. It's still a no-go, because I'd have to apply first, and then wait to get accepted, and that can take forever if it happens at all. I need something now. I just don't know how.

Amber Sierra's face burns bright red before her expression changes from tender to determined. She takes in a steadying breath, her voice gentle.

AMBER SIERRA
"If our lives are already written, it would take a courageous woman to change the script,"

Charlie sighs with appreciation.

CHARLIE
Oh, that's a good one. Alan Wake has always been one of my favourite games. I know, kinda cliché for a writer.

Amber Sierra nods with a small smirk.

AMBER SIERRA
Lo recuerdo.

Her smirk fades from her face as she contemplates something.

AMBER SIERRA
You're both right. I'm going to do it.

Charlie raises her head for a moment.

CHARLIE
Do what?

Amber Sierra's voice takes on a teasing tone.

AMBER SIERRA
Buy the cabin, since you and Toci have been all bossy about it. Besides, it's that or rent one for you, and that's a waste of money if I need to buy one anyway.

Charlie pushes herself up and hovers over Amber Sierra, eyes searching and lips parted.

CHARLIE
What?

AMBER SIERRA
How can I overlook the fact that both of you decided on the

same cabin separately from one another? The very same cabin I was literally having recurring dreams about. Dreams in which we're making incredible films together. Pero, I never even told you what it looked like! After all that discussion about how powerful dreams can be, it's a sign from the universe I can't ignore, right?

Charlie shakes her head, spirals of her hair sliding from her back to brush across Amber Sierra's neck.

Amber Sierra swallows hard, like something is stuck in her throat. Then a pained look flashes across her face as she tucks her pendant back inside her shirt.

Charlie is so wrapped up in her thoughts she doesn't appear to notice it.

CHARLIE

I'm a little freaked out about that, to be honest. But yeah, it feels like destiny. I mean, you know I believe in Bigfoot, ghosts, and aliens, so who am I to argue? I'm just worried that you haven't even seen it, yet. And the artist community name that it's a part of is a little strange, too. Governing Dynamics? It doesn't exactly fit the theme of the area, even if it does have some apropos implications. And for the record, we're only bossy about it because you deserve it!

AMBER SIERRA

You deserve it, too! You, Toci, and I have gathered all the data to make an informed decision. I agree that the name seems a little out of place, then again, there's a community of earthships not too far away, so maybe not. I actually like the name. It's thought-provoking and progressive, which is the whole point of my projects, so it kind of feels like you said, like destino. The time is right, and you and I both need this. I can't keep working out of my tiny apartment!

Amber Sierra slides herself back and up against the wall, out from under Charlie.

Charlie's pastoral eyes glisten with tears as realization dawns on her.

CHARLIE

So you're going to go for it before knowing for sure that your initiative will be funded?

Amber Sierra nods, a smile creeping across her face.

AMBER SIERRA

Creo que sí.

Charlie rises up on her knees, looking conflicted for a brief moment, then tackles Amber Sierra down into bed.

Charlie's deft doggo, used to her heart humans' shenanigans, dodges out of the way and watches with curiosity from a safe distance.

A mix of shock and bliss ripple across Amber Sierra's face as she wrestles with her silly, best friend.

The laptop bounces around on the bed, accompanied by trills of laughter and breathy giggles for several moments, then is righted again.

Amber Sierra's ruddy face fills up the screen then Charlie's rosy one appears next to hers.

Charlie's eyes have regained some sparkle.

A smirk tugs at Amber Sierra's mouth.

AMBER SIERRA

Since it appears we're not going out after all, let's order some Thai for lunch and dust off one of these games I installed for you that you've been neglecting.

CHARLIE

Yes! I'm so hungry. I haven't eaten since yesterday morning. Ooh, either Control or Outlast. Hmm... I pick Outlast. I really want to play it, but it's too creepy to play alone!

Amber Sierra chuckles and leans her head against Charlie's.

AMBER SIERRA

There's nothing to be scared of. Estoy aquí contigo.

Charlie closes her eyes at the affectionate gesture.

Amber Sierra looks at Charlie from the corner of her eye and opens her mouth like she wants to say something, then shuts it and looks away.

11 Exterior Isabel & Lohan's Duplex Sunday Early Afternoon, April 17, 2022

Charlie Hale GoPro Vlog Episode #8.

Charlie stands in front of her dad and sister's duplex, an elegant building with gold and brown toned brick and mortar walls, its generous windows framed in blackened steel. Gleaming solar panels crown their modern castle. A GoPro perches on the hood of Charlie's cobalt blue Hyundai Ioniq EV cater-corner from her. As she walks toward it, her eyes glimmer above her dazzling smile. She carries her wiener dog with one arm like a football, supporting her hips in the crook of her elbow and her chest in her hand, and a few bags with the other. She has on a comfortable blue and grey plaid flannel shirt and faded black jeans over charcoal wool barefoot clogs.

CHARLIE

What a difference having hope can make, huh? Amber Sierra made a bold move and put in an offer on the cabin. The owners accepted right away! It's a long-term investment that I know will pay off big time. It'll take a month to close, but apparently, the current owners are really chill. They know our situation and insist that we can start using it right away!

She dances with her fluffy friend for a moment then opens the door, leans inside, and starts strapping her into her special car seat. The GoPro is positioned so that it just catches her actions through the windshield.

CHARLIE

It's astonishing, even a little disturbing at how easy it's been so far! But who am I to stand in the way of destiny? Instead, I'm going to embrace it and make every moment count even if I am a bit wary!

She shrugs with a carefree smile then double checks that the straps are secure.

CHARLIE

I've offered to help make mortgage payments, but she says she won't accept any until after I sell my first screenplay. She's way too good to me, and I'm so lucky she loves me!

She kisses her little frankfurter on the head then snuggles her for a moment, muttering into her fur.

CHARLIE

I'm even luckier that you love me so much.

She steps back and closes the car door.

CHARLIE

My brave Fellowship, I leave you with course coordinate number six until I'm done with my exciting journey and can upload again. The footage I'll share with you then will be a mix of the official blogs and my writing sessions, as well as my journey to and arrival at the cabin. The rest will just be a video journal for me. But I digress.

She looks through the camera, wistfulness and sadness swirling in her composite eyes.

CHARLIE

When you feel like giving up, talk it over with someone you love. They can help give you perspective and remind you, that while "you can only come to morning through the shadows," they will always be at your side.

She stretches her arms up toward the sapphire sky, draws in a deep breath, then lets her arms come back down to her sides as she exhales.

CHARLIE

This is my chance, and I'm not going to let any kind of darkness keep me from it!

12 Exterior Isabel & Lohan's Duplex
Moments Later Sunday Early Afternoon

Charlie's dad and sister are out at her vehicle to see her off. Both look a little worried.

Lohan hugs Charlie with one arm, while the other remains behind his back. His favourite attire, an olive drab polo shirt tucked into belted, black tactical pants over black tactical boots, makes him look like a combative arts or firearms instructor.

Isabel hangs back, giving her dad his moment, her bold bohemian style in direct opposition to his. A fringed raspberry and teal poncho-style blouse flows over her thin shoulders in a mesmerizing pattern spiralling down toward her slate palazzo pants, which drape over black faux-leather side gore boots.

Charlie hugs her dad back, then tries to release him but he hugs her tighter for a few more moments.

When he finally lets go, his face is drawn with worry.

LOHAN

Be careful and call if there's anything you need.

Charlie is touched by his concern, but teases him to reassure him.

CHARLIE

Dad, you're acting like I'm going away to war or something.

A ghost of a smile forms on his lips.

LOHAN

In a way, you are, dearheart.

She scrunches up her face then nods.

CHARLIE

I suppose I am.

He finally reveals the small duffle bag he has hidden behind his back.

LOHAN

I want you to take these and set them up as soon as you get there.

Charlie looks confused, takes the bag, and unzips it, finding two security cameras inside.

Isabel takes in a sharp breath then steps forward and admonishes him, her flowing pants swishing around her legs.

ISABEL

Dad! Paranoid much?

Isabel looks relieved despite her disapproving reaction.

Charlie sighs and shakes her head.

CHARLIE

I'm not going to need these. You've got to let your special forces and detective mentalities go. You're retired now, remember?

Her dad frowns at her, his usually gentle hazel eyes flaring with heat.

LOHAN

You're barely an adult, and you're going to a cabin in the woods alone after pissing off a violent felon cartel boss, and there's nothing I can do to convince you otherwise. Take it. Don't argue. Also, my 1911 service pistol is in the side pocket with two extra full magazines.

Charlie's eyes widen, almost enveloping her face.

CHARLIE

Dad! He's got way more pressing matters to contend with than his book editing ghost writer quitting, like trying to stay alive in maximum security prison?

Lohan's expression darkens, the worry lines between his eyebrows deepen.

LOHAN

And when he's not doing that, he has all that time to plot revenge on anyone who's slighted him. If you think just because someone's in prison means they can't make things happen on the street, you're mistaken. I guarantee you he still runs his drug and black market arms empire, and if he wants to, he will come after you. It might just take a little time. Or it might not.

Charlie looks like she's reconsidering the gravity of what her dad is saying.

Isabel sighs and shakes her head.

ISABEL

Aren't you taking this a little too far?

LOHAN

Isabel. Don't. I'm trying to give Charlie agency even though I'm a protective papa bear. Charlie, just take the bag, or I'll find a way to make it so you can't go at all, or better yet--

He crosses his arms and smirks.

LOHAN

--I'll come along with you.

Isabel imitates her dad, crossing her arms and making a face at him.

Charlie puts one hand up and pretends to wave a white flag, takes the bag in hand, kisses her dad's cheek, and then tugs on his ponytail to lighten the mood.

CHARLIE

I love you too Dad, but no offence, I wouldn't get any work done with you around. Look, I know my ex-client fairly well at this point, because I've had to scour through his notes and outlines ad nauseam. He's got a long list of people ahead of me who he's hell bent on going after. Besides, he's probably relieved he doesn't have to work with a snot-nosed kid anymore, anyway. So don't worry. I'll take the bag, and I promise I'll be careful.

Lohan makes a heart symbol with his hands.

LOHAN

Thank you, Charlie. I love you.

Charlie laughs, sounding a little forced, then turns to hug her sister.

Isabel laughs along with her and hugs her close.

ISABEL

You know he won't sleep the entire time if you don't. Now go, stay safe, and come back soon. I love you.

Their dad scowls at them both, though his loving eyes betray him.

Charlie and her sister laugh harder while still hugging.

Charlie smoothes down her sister's unruly hair.

CHARLIE

I know. You're right. I love you too. Wish me luck.

Charlie kisses her sister's cheek then releases her.

Her dad waves off the notion.

LOHAN

You don't need luck, you've got skill.

Isabel rolls her eyes at her dad then smiles at her little sis.

ISABEL

Good luck.

13 Begin Montage - Multiple Locations Sunday Afternoon

All scenes use the GoPro.

A) The GoPro sits in the dashboard holder, pointed toward Charlie and her furry child, encompassing the full back window of her car and beyond. A black, off-roading Jeep Gladiator drives a few car spaces behind her. The low sun casts long shadows inside her car as she drives northbound on Interstate 25. She dances and sings along with the music she has blasting while her inquisitive pooch looks out the window. They pass through and skirt the opulent Santa Fe National Forest, ride the edge of the high desert grassland of the Pecos National Historical Park, and cross into the Wild West of Las Vegas by late afternoon. During this time, the Jeep Gladiator disappears from and returns to view multiple times, sometimes with a car or two in between them. She oohs and aahs at the authentic historical buildings as they enter the city, windows lowered for better viewing and sniffing.

CHARLIE

I feel like we've traveled back in time and any moment I'll see stagecoaches, outlaws on horseback, and a sheriff keeping the peace! I'm glad I decided to take the long scenic route so I could see this and have dinner here. It's sad I've never been here before. Maybe Amber Sierra and I can stop in Cimarron on our way back! That's another Old West town I've never taken the time to see. I've really been short-changing myself.

She glances over at her adorable co-pilot.

CHARLIE

Are you hungry, my little love?

Her curious canid is too busy sniffing out the open window to answer the question.

She laughs and starts looking for a place to stop for food.

B) Charlie and her feisty furball sit in the pristine Plaza Park of Las Vegas. They chow down on dinner, a green chile veggie burger for the pilot and chicken, rice, and vegetables for the co-pilot. The three story, red brick, square-topped Historic Plaza Hotel stands proudly behind them. Once they finish eating, they pack up and walk through the park beneath the shade of generous cottonwood trees until they enter the historic district on Bridge Street and saunter along its sidewalk. The various shops and offices look like they are from the set of a Wild West movie. Finally they deviate onto University Avenue and stroll past southwestern style stone and adobe buildings of higher learning until they reach the parking lot where her car is charging. The Jeep Gladiator can be seen parked across the street in another parking lot, a figure watching them from inside.

C) She drives north out of the anachronistic Las Vegas on a NM State Road through more of the lush Santa Fe National Forest, sliding into the breathtaking Carson National Forest as it's starting to get dark. She looks a little unnerved, but is oblivious to the fact that the Jeep Gladiator is once again behind her, varying its distance from her over the course of an hour.

CHARLIE

It's times like these that you realize how screwed you'd be if your car broke down.

Behind her, the Jeep Gladiator's lights fluctuate. The video footage zooms in to show it veering off the highway and coming to a stop, lights flickering off. The video footage zooms back out.

CHARLIE

Why is it now that my brain decides to summon all the scary local legends? It's strongly advised not to talk about them because it can attract their attention. But does thinking about them count? Maybe it's time for an audiobook.

She reaches out and turns her audio system on.

D) She drives many more miles north on a US Highway through the awe-inspiring mountain vistas bathed in the dying light with no other vehicles behind her. A dark body of water glitters in the distance off to her east, reflecting the last rays of the sun's descent behind the horizon. She listens to an urban fantasy audio novel while her fuzzy friend sleeps in her doggie car seat.

E) She rolls up the gravel road that leads to the cabins of the Governing Dynamics Artist Community lining the small, private lake. About a quarter of the way around the shoreline, she pulls into a driveway cut between a copse of evergreen trees.

CHARLIE

We're here, my little love! Would you look at this place? It looks even more amazing in person!

Her adventure buddy barks, her tail wagging so hard her whole body wiggles.

CHARLIE
I know! I can't wait to explore it all either!

F) The GoPro has been rotated to look outside the windshield. Her headlights illuminate a stately, rustic cabin.

End Montage
Sunday Evening

14 Exterior Amber Sierra's Cabin
Sunday Evening Twilight, April 17, 2022

Charlie hops out of the car with an enthusiastic smile that takes up most of her face. She holds the GoPro on a selfie stick, but it's dark and her surroundings are hard to see. She walks down the short stone path from the driveway to the cabin, her voice tight with excitement.

CHARLIE
It's so regal! And you can't be more lakeside than this!

She starts to pan the camera around.

CHARLIE (off-screen)
I'm going to have to convince Amber Sierra to go halfsies! I think I'll be wanting to be here like, all the time. It's stunning, except for that you probably can't see that right now. Hang on, she told me she had this GoPro camera modified to see into the near infrared and ultraviolet part of the electromagnetic spectrum. Basically it can see in the dark. But in order to do that, I have to flip the cut filter off. Cut filters block out IR and UV light so that digital cameras only film in light our eyes can see.

She fidgets with the camera, switching it to full spectrum mode, illuminating the dark world with a wash of Tyrian hues. Then she starts her camera pan over again. A three level post and beam timber frame log cabin stands before her like a bastion in the dark. The lake behind it, nestled against a hearty coniferous pine and fir forest, ripples in the light breeze. Cabins of varying styles peek out from the tree line along the shore.

CHARLIE (off-screen)
There we go. Much brighter! Is this what the world looks like through rose-coloured glasses? Eerie and strange?

She laughs and walks back to her car. She retrieves a small bag of trash, crosses the driveway to the square latching trash can, and tosses it in. Then she flips the GoPro's cut filter back on so it only films visible light.

CHARLIE (off-screen)
I'll take more shots tomorrow in the daylight. You'll just have to take my word on how beautiful this is at dusk.

In the distance, a spine-chilling fracas arises, sounding like the maniacal laughter of asylum patients running amok in a horror film.

Her breath catches for a moment as she listens. The camera shakes a bit in her hand as she lets out a nervous laugh.

CHARLIE (off-screen)
Those are just coyotes, Charlie. You're not in The Wrong Turn series.

Despite reassuring herself, she begins rushing to unload her car.

15 Begin Montage - Interior Amber Sierra's Cabin Sunday Later That Evening

A) Charlie has brought her luggage, cooler of groceries, and dashing dachshund inside the tidy foyer. To her right, rough-hewn log stairs lead up to a loft and down to the basement, both blocked off by pet gates. To her left, a spacious coat closet with inlaid shelves and boot rack beckons visitors to stay awhile. Next to it, an expansive bathroom with a free-standing copper bathtub and capacious shower tiled in tawny sandstone and colourful Mexican raised relief ceramic welcomes weary travelers.

CHARLIE (off-screen)
What do you think, ma'am? I guess the previous owners had a child or dog and already blocked the stairs off. Someone's got to keep you little goofs from hurting yourselves, especially you and that long back of yours!

As she steps past the bathroom, the open-floor plan makes the cabin appear larger than it is, connecting the soaring great hall to the sprawling open-concept kitchen. The primary bedroom loft above crowns the social spaces below. A floor to ceiling, ochre-toned, Chacoan masonry fireplace splits the great hall's massive windowed view overlooking the lake. Its tawny blocks of sandstone continue into the flooring, becoming flat tiles extending throughout the entire ground level. Above its grand mantle hovers a seventy-five inch 4K OLED TV anchored deep into the stone. On the other side of the glass stretches an extensive Ipe deck decorated with matching outdoor furniture, a brushed nickel four burner barbecue grill, and a fire pit made from the same sandstone as its big sibling.

As she moves into the great hall, she spins around for a view of the loft above, its wall trimmed with the same timber as the frame, and the warm decor of the Southwestern culinary space below. White cabinets and a kitchen island cradle brushed nickel appliances, their countertops made from the same sandstone as the tile floor. The maize yellow walls set off the backsplash above the range and copper sink, which matches the masonry of the fireplace but painted in mixed shades of cobalt, cerulean, turquoise and copper. Copper pots and pans hang from a brushed nickel ceiling rack above the kitchen island, which holds a smaller copper sink and space for six people to cozy up to the cook on mesquite stools. A hearty table for six, consisting of long planks of mesquite held up by solid trestle legs and skirted by matching high-back chairs, competes for attention as the best place for feasting.

She points the camera at her silly sidekick who runs around, investigating every square inch she's allowed.

CHARLIE (off-screen)

I know, my little love! This is unbelievable!

She turns the camera to herself, her cheeks flushed without her realizing it.

CHARLIE

Yep, I can see myself not wanting to leave, ever. Especially if Amber Sierra was here!

She sweeps the camera around to the right corner of the great hall.

CHARLIE (off-screen)

I'm going to put the Blackmagic camera over there so I can get a wide angle view and not have to move it.

She aims the camera at a padded black duffle bag holding the Blackmagic camera.

CHARLIE (off-screen)

That's Amber Sierra's baby, and I'm shocked she insisted on me using it! I'm almost afraid to, because I can't afford to replace it if something happens to it. She said it was going to become the permanent studio camera here, so I might as well bring it with me and use it! Plugging it into its portable hard drive will allow it to hold days of 4K footage. The GoPro I'm using isn't too shabby either with almost 9 hours of recording time, and it has another Amber Sierra modified feature of a timer for recording.

B) She films down from the loft, giving an aerial view of the artist haven below. She aims the camera at the immense blackout curtains pulled back from the great hall's monumental windows.

CHARLIE (off-screen)

Those are going to come in handy. I'll be closing them and all the other window curtains when it gets dark so I don't imagine scary things watching me from the spooky, dark forest outside.

She spins the camera around to show where artists go to dream. More blackout curtains line the slants of the ceiling, ready to be unlatched and unfurled for privacy and sleep. Sturdy wooden bookshelves run along the top of custom-built storage closets and dressers, framing the four-poster king-size bed. Strands of LED lights dangle over the tester, ready to generate soft light for a sensual mood. A plush comforter, draped over the doughy memory gel bed, calls to the weary, promising a deep and comfortable sleep.

She lets out a long sigh, her voice sounds wistful.

CHARLIE (off-screen)

Can you imagine being cozied up with your S.O. in that? It's so romantic I can't stand it!

C) She poses in front of the Blackmagic camera in the great hall, which is now set up on a tripod. The entire open concept cabin behind her makes an inviting backdrop. Next to her, two plush, chocolate recliners flank a matching sofa, which she has pulled the hide-a-bed from to create a makeshift bedroom and base of operations. She unpacks two silky, burnt sienna puffer camp quilts and snaps them together then tucks her pillows inside.

CHARLIE

Since I'm reconnecting with nature, my first priority is to make sure I'm warm and comfy so I can get good sleep. Yeah, I know, I'm sleeping inside a cabin right now, but I plan to do some backpacking with Amber Sierra once she's here. Toci helped me research the most versatile, weather resistant, packable, and warm sleep system available. She's super good at doing research for stuff, so I always ask her opinion. And once again, she totally delivered! This fits every requirement, and it has the cutest name. Introducing the

Puffle! I bought one with an expander for when I'm solo, and an extra one so that if I ever have someone to snuggle with again, we can snap them together.

She looks down at her ringless finger and sighs then shrugs off the momentary melancholy and gets back to setting things up.

Her low rider has claimed one of the recliners and supervises from there.

Charlie grins at her and bends down to open the leg rest half-way, acting like a ramp for the shortie. She then pushes the convertible coffee table to the side of the unoccupied recliner and extends it to use like a desk. She holds a remote control up for a moment then sets it down in the recliner's cup holder.

CHARLIE

So from here, I can capture anything I want, and I can control it from wherever I am with this. I'll just keep it running when I'm working so I don't miss anything.

She points her thumb over her shoulder.

CHARLIE

While I could sleep upstairs in the primary bedroom or downstairs in one of the two secondary bedrooms, I'm feeling--

She pauses to think about how she's feeling, sadness shadowing her face for a moment then chased away by the excitement of where she is.

CHARLIE

--lazy. It would be a pain to have to go up and down stairs with a camera, so I'm going to crash here. Besides, I have everything I need on this level!

The cabin's cordless landline phone rings from the foyer, startling her. A knowing smirk settles her surprise, and she walks over, answering it on speaker phone.

CHARLIE

Hi, Amber Sierra.

AMBER SIERRA (off-screen)

Hola, chica. So did you just get there or are you all settled in, or what?

Charlie sounds a little sheepish as she walks back over toward the great hall.

CHARLIE

I'm just starting to settle in.

Amber Sierra chuckles.

AMBER SIERRA (off-screen)

Abuelita.

CHARLIE

Yeah, yeah, I drive slow, but at least I'm here safe.

Amber Sierra still sounds amused.

AMBER SIERRA (off-screen)

I am thankful for that, at least. So, what do you think? You know I'm dying to know!

Charlie looks all around her before plopping down in the recliner.

CHARLIE

It's perfect! I'm actually feeling even worse that I got to be here first. You should be here with me.

Amber Sierra makes celebratory sounds on the other end of the phone.

AMBER SIERRA (off-screen)

Órale! That makes me so happy! Don't feel bad. I'm sorry I've got stuff I need to finish before I escape with you, but I can't wait! It looks like it'll be about a week if that's okay?

CHARLIE

I wish you could come sooner, but I understand.

AMBER SIERRA (off-screen)

Me, too. Have fun, but not too much without me! Call me tomorrow night so I know everything's good?

CHARLIE

I will. Thanks for keeping everyone updated.

AMBER SIERRA (off-screen)

The whole point is for you to have as little distraction as possible, so no problema.

Charlie smiles.

CHARLIE
Good night, cariño.

AMBER SIERRA (off-screen)
Bueno-bye, guapa.

Charlie hangs up then starts looking around at what still needs to be done and decides to get up and start putting groceries away.

D) The GoPro films from the small foyer table while Charlie slides her now full hydration bladder into her safety-cone orange backpack. Once it's secured, she reaches into one of the utility pockets and pulls out a head lamp, straps it on, and then hangs the backpack up on a hook in the closet. She's changed out her wool clogs for calf-high, black, barefoot hiking boots and has her jeans rolled up just above their edge. She looks at the pile of duffle bags near the door and picks up her personal one and the one her dad gave her and puts them in the closet on the middle shelf. She pauses and shakes her head at her dad's duffle bag. Then she turns back to the huge, heavy-looking duffle bag, but leaves it at the front door, and instead walks to the camera and crouches in front of it.

CHARLIE
I've always wanted to do this ever since I studied the classic movie Joe Versus the Volcano for a screenwriting class. In his hero's journey, he ends up caring for his love interest while they are adrift at sea on a raft made from his steamer trunks. The night sky above him glitters with more stars than he's ever seen in his life, then an impossibly large moon ascends from the horizon, reminding him of just how beautiful life is. So I decided that my first night here, I would take this raft I bought--

She points over her shoulder to the duffle bag still at the door.

CHARLIE
--out for a midnight float on the lake. It's a new moon, so I won't have the same experience he did, but a moonless night means the stars will appear brighter and more numerous. Also, I saw in the news that the Lyrid meteor shower is peaking at the end of the week, so I might catch some shooting stars, too.

She picks up the camera and walks over to her first mate who is curled up in the recliner, resigned to being left behind.

CHARLIE (off-screen)
And you are staying here to guard the cabin. I know how you are in boats.

The usual suspect tilts her head to one side as if she has no idea what her captain is talking about.

CHARLIE (off-screen)
Don't play innocent with me! And you better behave yourself and use the recliner footrest as a ramp, or I'm bringing out the one I bought for you! You need your back to stay healthy so you can continue to take walks under your own power, you hear me?

She laughs then puts the camera down on the coffee table and looks into it.

CHARLIE
You know what? I've been so self-involved I never introduced you to my heart dog, Circe. She is the little love of my life and has been with me through everything, the best and the worst times. Especially the hardest one. Without her...

She blinks her eyes, clearing the tears starting to form. She moves over in front of the recliner and takes a treat out of her pocket.

CHARLIE
Let's show off for the camera, Circe!

Circe's ears perk, making her look like she has a brindled lion's mane. After a moment, she gets up and obediently walks down the ramp made by the footrest being in its lowest position then looks up at Charlie with anticipation.

CHARLIE

Sit.

Circe sits.

CHARLIE

Good girl! Down.

Circe lies down.

CHARLIE

You're so cute! Roll over?

Circe stares at her then sits back up.

CHARLIE

Twirl! Shake! Play dead!

Circe's lips start to curl up like she might let out a bark.

CHARLIE

Yeah, I know you think those are extraneous requests. How about, beg?

Circe raises her two front paws up and sits back on her haunches like a groundhog.

CHARLIE

That's her default mode when she wants food or needs my attention for something. And if I wait too long, well, she'll perform the speak command without my prompting! You can see she's already preparing to.

Circe finally barks with frustration as if illustrating Charlie's point.

Charlie giggles, gives Circe a treat, and waits for her to finish it. Then she picks her up, hugs her, and gives her lots of kisses and snuggles.

Circe returns all of the love, mostly with her tongue.

CHARLIE

Oh my goodness you're so soft and so adorable! They may not think you're movie star material either, girl, but gorram I love you to the frelling moon! I would take you with me, but it's too dark to keep a proper eye on you. But don't worry, I'll be back in a little while. And I promise we'll go together when it's light outside.

She lowers Circe back down onto the recliner seat then walks to the coat closet where she grabs her black hoodie and puts it on. Then she turns the outside lights on and starts to open the front door before realizing she forgot the camera. She giggles and dashes over to grab it.

End Montage
Sunday Night

16 Begin Montage - Exterior Lake
Sunday Night

A) The GoPro is attached to its selfie stick and films in full spectrum mode as Charlie walks around the cabin and down the dirt path to the lakefront, casting everything in the signature heliotropic wash. She sweeps the camera from shore to shore. Nestled within the sparse edges of the evergreen forest, her neighbours' cabins peer out toward the picturesque lake.

CHARLIE (off-screen)
Looks like everyone's asleep already. I don't see any lights across the lake, or to either side of us. I guess people go to bed early out here in the middle of nowhere.

She sets the camera up on one of the many granite rocks scattered across the gravelly sand of the lakeshore, then takes her nerdy headlamp out of her pocket and puts it around her head and turns it on. She unpacks her raft and fills it with air using a rechargeable electric pump. The high-pitched whine against the still night makes her wince.

B) She lounges in her raft, headlamp off, her long hair laying in waves about her shoulders as she gazes up at the stars. She's attached the GoPro to an octopus tripod and wrapped it around one of the raft handles to get the right angle. She stretches, getting a mouthful of orange life vest, makes a face at it as she spits it out, and then draws in a deep, satisfied breath.

CHARLIE
I can't believe I'm really doing this. I don't think I've ever been anywhere so quiet and calm. The air smells unbelievable! Filled with the scent of water, pine trees, and wild flowers. How do we breathe at all in the city?

She manoeuvres the tripod so the camera points skyward. It displays many more stars than the naked eye could see, catching even the faintest satellites and other moving objects. Through the middle of the screen blazes a nebulous amethyst cloud sprinkled with pulsating lights.

Awe hushes her voice.

CHARLIE (off-screen)
You live in the city too long, you forget just how much is out there above your head. Look at that Milky Way, Mom. You would have loved it out here.

She sinks into reverent silence, absorbing the significance and beauty of the moment before speaking again.

CHARLIE (off-screen)
It's so ethereal in full spectrum mode.

She leans over and removes the camera from the tripod, then flips its cut filter back on. She turns it toward herself, and all that can be faintly seen of her is her light-toned skin, the white of her eyes, and her white teeth. Darkness obscures the rest of her.

CHARLIE
Amber Sierra said that unmodified GoPros see well in the dark as long as they have some light, but I don't think she said that with stargazing in mind. I'm not sure how well this will work, but it's worth a try so I can share what I'm seeing with my own eyes. It's like freshly poured cream rising up from the depths of dark coffee.

She attaches the camera back to the tripod and points it skyward again, but it captures only a fraction of the stars.

CHARLIE (off-screen)
I bet I have to change the settings to low light or something. Hang on, let me figure it out.

C) The fathomless night sky, pricked with countless pinpoints of light, fills the GoPro's field of view. A shimmering, silvery haze arches and swirls through its centre, diffusing from a bright white core out into misty wisps. Bands of darkness spiral through it like creeping vines up a trellis.

CHARLIE (off-screen)
There we go. That's more like what I was seeing. Breathtaking, isn't it? I just wanted to share it with you before I switch back to full spectrum mode, which is the only way you'll be able to see me while I vlog. There's little to no light pollution, which is amazing for stargazing, but not so much for filming anything else.

Several black shapes whoosh overhead with a flurry of croaks, blotting out the starscape as they pass through it. Their chatter quiets as they land in the tops of the tallest pine boughs nearby.

CHARLIE (off-screen)
Were those ravens? What are they still doing awake? I can't wait to see what they looked like on film!

She waits for several moments more before switching the cut filter off, then adjusts the camera so it points at her. Even in the strange magenta hues, her eyes reflect bewitching striations, full of dreaming.

CHARLIE
Don't worry, I won't torture you with watching me vlog for too long. I promise I'll return you to the stars soon.

She stretches languorously then yawns, looking like a leopard lazing in a tree.

CHARLIE
This must be what it's like in heaven. It's exactly what I needed. The only way it would be more perfect is if I saw one of those meteors right about now.

A few seconds pass by.

CHARLIE
Come on shooting star! I want to make a wish before I start my vlog.

Except for the normal night sounds, crickets chirping, cicadas buzzing, owls hooting, and the soft lapping of the water at her raft, everything is quiet as the camera watches her stargaze.

Only a minute later, she gasps, and her face lights up with an ear to ear smile.

CHARLIE
I saw one! It was bright orange and lasted a whole second!

She closes her eyes and whispers.

CHARLIE
Please let my wish come true.

After a moment, she opens her eyes and wiggles her eyebrows at the camera.

CHARLIE
Can you guess what it was? I'll never tell, because they say if you do, it won't come true!

With a grin, she returns to admiring the expanse above her, appearing to have forgotten that she is supposed to be filming her vlog. The video footage fast-forwards for several minutes, catching other delighted facial expressions, each a little less enthusiastic than the last, until her eyes flutter shut. The video footage resumes play as her breathing transitions to the deep, slow pattern of sleep. For several minutes, only the chitter of cicadas, chant of spring peepers, and lament of loons fill the quiet night. Then her arm shifts and bumps the camera, causing it to slip and rotate down toward the mirror-like water, which reflects the starscape in all its eerie amaranthine beauty.

A few minutes later, a soft, low thrum in the distance joins the rhythmic eventide music, growing louder with each passing moment. A radiance seeps into the edge of the camera's view, growing more intense in time with the sound. As it brightens, the gloaming chorus goes quiet, and her hair rises and stands on end like someone has rubbed a balloon against it. The glow dances on the edges of the screen, its movements matched by the direction of the thrum.

The video footage fast-forwards as she continues to sleep despite the disturbance. The reflected constellations creep across the sky as an hour goes by within seconds. It resumes play when the radiance and thrum start withdrawing and end abruptly with the sound of two splashes echoing nearby. Her sudden movement of waking up shakes the camera. In the moments that she comes to, her hair settles back down into place and the denizens of the dark return to their serenade.

She turns her headlamp on and looks around, breathless with an adrenaline surge.

CHARLIE (off-screen)

Who's there?

When she realizes the light from her headlamp doesn't let her see very far, she grabs the camera. She uses its viewscreen to look around, but there's nothing to be seen except the rippling water and the nature around her. After a few more seconds, she seems satisfied that she can't see anything, even though she still looks spooked. She reattaches the camera and positions it so that it's pointed at her again then turns off her headlamp.

CHARLIE

Holy crap, that scared me! What was that? I didn't see anything, but I sure heard it. There must be some monster fish in this lake or something!

She takes in a deep breath and lets it out slowly, steadying herself.

CHARLIE

I can't believe I fell asleep! I guess it just shows how exhausted I've been.

A yawn overtakes her words.

CHARLIE
I dreamed I was on a train, running from something evil.

She freezes as though she's heard something, then looks around.

CHARLIE
I better get back to the cabin. I-uh-need to write the details of my dream down, and I-uh-don't want Circe to miss me too much.

She starts paddling back to shore.

End Montage
Sunday Night

17 Exterior/Interior Amber Sierra's Cabin
Sunday Night

Using the GoPro in full spectrum, Charlie films walking up the beach path around the cabin to the front door, a flutter of wings and corvid susurration accompanying her. She raises the camera to capture her uninvited guests only to see empty treetops.

CHARLIE (off-screen)
Where did they go? It must just be the wind that's started picking up, soughing through the pine boughs and carrying their gossip from the beach where I saw them nesting.

She focuses back on the front door and opens it and peers inside, sounding sheepish.

CHARLIE (off-screen)
Circe, I'm back. I know you were worried, because I never leave you for that long.

Two glowing eyes stare at her from just above the sofa.

The view startles her, and the camera jumps.

CHARLIE (off-screen)
Whoa, you look creepy in full spectrum.

She closes and locks the door behind her, turns the lights on, and puts the cut filter back on the GoPro.

CHARLIE (off-screen)
There, that's much better. You no longer look like a demon dog waiting to eat my soul.

Circe continues to stare at her for a moment, her nose the only thing moving as it sniffs the air. Then she runs off the bed onto the recliner and down the improvised doggie ramp to greet Charlie, hopping up and down on her hind legs like a kangaroo.

Charlie puts the camera down on the floor, lies down, and wrestles with Circe, giggling the whole time.

CHARLIE
I missed you too, girl. Thanks for keeping watch.

18 Exterior/Interior Amber Sierra's Cabin Sunday Late Night

Charlie Hale Webcam Vlog Episode #9

Charlie is in bed, oversized grey tee shirt and sloppy sweatpants for pyjamas, with Circe lying next to her. She leans in for a close-up of her own sleepy eyes.

CHARLIE
I promise I didn't forget you, my fellow Tau'ri! I just wanted to get comfortable before really filming my vlog. Despite falling asleep stargazing, having a nightmare that I'm now actually considering using for my story, and spooking the crap out of myself, today was an amazing beginning to what I truly believe will be a productive journey. I can't wait to get up and get started. But first, sleep, which is going to be course coordinate number seven. Get plenty of sleep! It renews your body and mind, and dreaming refreshes your creative energy. Problems can be solved during sleep. New ideas can come from dreams. I'm living proof of that. If you have writer's block, get more sleep!

She scrubs at her hair, teasing it until it fluffs out like an '80s hard rock star. Then she takes on a serene expression and speaks as though she has the wisdom of the ages.

CHARLIE
Of course, you'll probably ignore this course coordinate because "the very young do not always do as they are told!"

She giggles and winks at the webcam then closes the laptop.

19 Interior Amber Sierra's Cabin Monday Morning, April 18, 2022

Charlie Hale Webcam Vlog Episode #10

Charlie sits in her recliner, basking in the morning sun streaming in through the large windows. Her eyes gleam with anticipation. Her oversized tee shirt hangs from her shoulders. A mug of steaming tea sits in the drink holder, and next to it, a plate holding a cream-cheese smeared bagel and slices of apple.

Circe has wedged herself down between Charlie's leg and the armrest, content to be squished.

CHARLIE

Who would have thought that one night away from the big city, surrounded by nature, would have me wake up feeling so energized and rested? And that's despite the continuation of my nightmare once I went to bed! Why didn't I do this sooner? I'm going to chalk the intense dreaming up to all of this repressed creativity! I wrote everything down as soon as I woke up, because it's better than what I came up with before I got here. It's exciting to feel so inspired on my first official morning here at--well, Amber Sierra and I will need to choose a fitting name for it--and to welcome my Monday morning instead of dreading it like I have for so long. I can feel this opportunity vibrating with potential. Everything is set up and ready to go for a day of writing in a cabin in the woods. As soon as I finish my vlog, it begins. Thank you for being here with me for this special moment.

Charlie reaches to the side of her laptop and picks up her pair of sunglasses and puts them on. She slows her speech down, enunciates each word, and lowers her voice.

CHARLIE

Now, my restless ones, do you want to know what course coordinate number eight is? It is all around us, even now in this very cabin. You can see it outside, feel it when you go about your day. The mundane tasks of the world have been wielded against you to distract you from the truth and hold you in a prison for your mind. Sadly, no one can tell you what the ritual is that can free you. You have to discover it for yourself. The blue pill will return you to the mundane world never the wiser. The red pill will lead you to fully harness your imagination.

She flips her sunglasses up over her head, pulling back her hair from her face, which erupts with a grin.

CHARLIE

Obviously I chose the red pill, and that means that I developed a ritual to shield myself from the mundane and welcome in the fantastical. Having a ritual before writing is crucial to setting the stage for your creative mind to act upon. In my case, as you see, I find a comfortable and quiet place. Then I procure coffee or tea and some delicious fare I can nibble on. Finally, I practice box breathing while I meditate for a few minutes.

She demonstrates her meditation technique, closing her eyes, taking in a deep breath, holding it, slowly releasing it, holding it again, then taking in another deep breath. She looks content in a way that she hasn't until now.

CHARLIE

Because this is a ritual I always do before writing, it signals my body, mind, and soul that it's time to withdraw from the outside world, enter my imagination, and write.

She opens her eyes again.

CHARLIE

Your ritual doesn't have to be like mine, it just has to be one that works for you.

She stirs her tea with a spoon, then looks at it, thoughtful. She opens her eyes wide and innocent and speaks in a soft voice.

CHARLIE

Remember, "there is no spoon," because "it is not the spoon that bends, it is only yourself."

She smiles at the camera then sips her tea.

20 Begin Montage - Interior Amber Sierra's Cabin Moments Later Monday Morning

The Blackmagic camera rolls during Charlie's writing session.

A) Charlie sits in bed with Circe snuggled next to her as she taps furiously away on her laptop and pours over her notes. The footage fast-forwards for the next hour while she diligently works at capturing her nightmare into a scene breakdown and beatsheet. Finally, she grins from ear to ear, lighting the room up brighter than the sun streaming through the enormous great hall windows.

CHARLIE

I've got it! I think falling asleep beneath the open sky allowed me to relax in a way I haven't since I was a kid, and it collapsed the walls I built to protect myself from painful things. It felt so good to dream so vividly again, even if it was a nightmare.

B) She connects her laptop to the enormous flat-screen TV over the fireplace mantle. The laptop sits on the coffee table that she has pushed a few feet away from the recliner. She grins up at the camera.

CHARLIE

Dialogue is the aspect of writing I have the most trouble with, but improv acting is something I'm a natural at. This new writing method will capture the spontaneous dialogue and reactions that occur between characters in an organic setting. I can take the dialogue straight from film to paper, and I can watch the reactions and then describe them. To keep the flow of the scene, I'm going to narrate the setting and character reactions and actions then act them out along with the dialogue. The coolest part about this whole experiment is that I'm not following a script. I'll literally be making it up as I go, guided only by the outline of the scene. I'm so psyched! Now, enough stalling. Let's go!

She draws in a settling breath then looks at the big screen and reads her notes for the scene before beginning. Her voice takes on an edge.

CHARLIE AS NARRATOR

Interior Helen's Bedroom / Dreamscape - Night. A malevolent presence watches, hovers, waits, taunting and teasing. The air hangs thick, throbbing with dark desires. I'm afraid to close my eyes because it's waiting for me, and I've grown so

> weak, I'm not sure I can stop it this time. I haven't told anyone else about my nightmares; not since I told my closest friends and they started avoiding me. They told me that dreams couldn't hurt me. So how come I keep waking up with bruises? My heart hammers against my ribcage, labouring under the influence of too many stimulants. Anything to stay awake. But my eyelids are so heavy. Darkness is inevitable.

She looks like she's fighting to keep her eyes open, and within moments, they flutter shut. Her face twitches with troubled sleep. She peeks through one cracked eye as she continues to narrate.

CHARLIE AS NARRATOR

> This time I find myself on a train traveling across a black and barren desertscape. The clickety-clack of the tracks is hypnotizing; the sway of the train itself designed to lull me.

Her eyes fly open in fear, and she gasps as she leaps out of bed, examining her surroundings like a caged animal.

Circe looks startled for a moment, then settles back down, being used to her silly human's antics.

CHARLIE AS NARRATOR

> After looking around in desperation, I find I'm alone, as usual. If only I'd just stop fighting, it would all be over with. But these are not my thoughts. My eyes dart to the possible entrances and exits. Its laughter echoes around me, through me, chilling me to my core. Its speech is a sneer made of shattered glass.

One moment she's looking up at the ceiling in terror, the next, her face contorts with scorn. Her voice empties of warmth, lowers, and becomes raspy and cutting when she speaks as the dream monster.

CHARLIE AS DREAM MONSTER

> You can't escape, Helen. Though I do so enjoy it when you struggle.

She clasps her hands over her ears, screaming.

CHARLIE AS HELEN

> Leave me alone!

Mocking laughter rises from her chest.

CHARLIE AS NARRATOR

I can see its ominous silhouette, a fathomless shadow, through the sliding door window. It's coming my way from an adjacent train car. I dart up from my seat and race down the aisle toward the opposite end. I slap the button to open the door, my heart stuttering as I half expect it to stick. But it hisses open, and I scramble through. The frigid air in the vestibule between cars makes my rapid breaths into puffs of steam. I slap the next button, and as the second door opens, I slip through and sprint down the length of the car. It takes me several heartbeats to realize that somehow it has gotten in front of me. I stumble with a shriek and fall to the ground.

She flings herself to the ground, letting out a scream.

CHARLIE AS NARRATOR

It grins at me, a leering, hungry smile. I can feel its hot breath against my face, smell the spicy tang of its mouth, as it puts its forehead against mine. Some calm, logical part of my mind thinks how it really isn't very scary looking. Coiffed, short sandy hair frames a youthful face. A prominent nose beneath chocolate brown eyes, round cheeks, and pouting lips make for a wholesome appearance. These were not supposed to be the features of a monster. But they are. Suddenly they have hold of my hair and drag me up onto one of the reclined train seats.

She grasps at her hair then scrambles backward, dragging herself up onto the recliner, almost toppling the laptop.

CHARLIE AS NARRATOR

The arm of the chair rakes into my ribs and takes my breath away. I kick and punch, but my blows bounce off their wiry frame. They pin me to the chair by my wrists, holding both of them in one hand over my head. Then taking their time, they force my legs open with one of their knees.

She lets out a gasp then kicks and punches. She flings her arms up over her head, crossing them at the wrists.

CHARLIE AS NARRATOR

I think how strange it is that they could be so strong and yet so slight of build.

CHARLIE AS DREAM MONSTER

Don't like what you see? I know you think you like women,

but once you feel what a man can do, you'll thank me and be begging for more.

CHARLIE AS NARRATOR

He grinds his groin against me. I clench my eyes shut and scream. He backhands me across the face. It burns like fire. Bright white stars dance beneath my eyelids. A soft whimper escapes my lips.

She fights as though her legs are being pried open. With a wince, she shrinks her hips away, then clenches her eyes shut and screams again. Her head whips to the side, and she whimpers, blinking back tears.

CHARLIE AS HELEN

Get off of me! Get off!

CHARLIE AS NARRATOR

The sharp nip of spiced tobacco fills my mouth as his smothers mine. The taste of him is more than I can stand, so I do the only thing I can think of to make him stop. I sink my teeth into his tongue.

She makes a muffled sound and tries to pull away, baring her teeth and clacking them together.

CHARLIE AS NARRATOR

He howls as he rocks backward away from me. The sound of it is something inhuman, calling up goose bumps across my skin. I try to shove him off, but he's far too strong. He smashes his fist into my mouth, and copper replaces tobacco.

She flips herself over in the recliner, now looming over it. Her head jerks backward as she lets out a disturbing howl. Her voice drops into a low growl.

CHARLIE AS DREAM MONSTER

You like it rough, little girl? You haven't seen rough, yet.

CHARLIE AS NARRATOR

I believe him.

She collapses into the recliner, rolling onto her back, then her body starts twitching.

CHARLIE AS NARRATOR

He rips at my pyjamas like a ravenous animal tearing at the flesh of his prey. But that gives me the opportunity I've been waiting for. I throw my weight over the arm of the chair and manage to take him to the ground with me. His head strikes the floor hard, and I take that opportunity to scramble away.

She hurls herself over the arm of the recliner into a crouched position then scurries away.

CHARLIE AS NARRATOR

The door seems impossibly far. But I can't give up now. I run faster than I ever have, but tendrils of shadow chase after me, tripping me up time and again. After a stumbling eternity, the button on the door comes within my reach. I strike it and roll through. The icy metal floor bites at my skin. He crawls toward me, cursing and spitting. I tug on the door, fending off lashing shadows, trying to make it shut faster. I beg it to close, and to my surprise, it slams shut.

She makes a fist and punches the air, then does a martial art roll. She spins around in place and starts tugging at the imagined door until she lets go and falls backward onto her haunches.

CHARLIE AS NARRATOR

His voice, like the wind in winter trees, surrounds me. He speaks as though we are the most intimate of lovers.

CHARLIE AS DREAM MONSTER

There is always tomorrow night, my little vixen.

CHARLIE AS NARRATOR

I drag myself to my feet, ready to continue racing through the darkened train cars, but as I take my first step, a tear in the darkness opens and I fall into the light.

She takes a deep breath in, falling out of character, and collapsing to the floor.

CHARLIE

Wow, that was intense. Not a lot of dialogue, but I caught the essence of Helen's desperation and will to fight as well as the pure vileness of the antagonist.

She pumps her arm in victory.

C) She lies on the floor and looks up at the ceiling, having not moved from where she collapsed. Her hair fans out around her and shimmers like gold in the sunlight.

Circe hides within the camp quilts like a crocodile, only her snout and eyes visible.

D) She sits in the recliner scrubbing at her thick hair and pretending to pull it out.

Circe naps next to her, oblivious.

E) Circe wanders down the half extended recliner leg rest and over to Charlie as she's starting the next scene. After a moment, she sits up and begs like a weasel, her fluffy ears perked.

Charlie's lips draw into a charming smirk as she drops out of character.

CHARLIE

What, you want to be in this scene?

She bends down and picks Circe up, then makes her talk like a puppet.

CHARLIE AS CIRCE

Why, of course! I'm your best furry friend, aren't I?

CHARLIE

You're right! How rude of me! But there are no dogs in this screenplay just yet, and if there are any, they'll only have a supporting role. How about I write one just for you where you're the star?

CHARLIE AS CIRCE

But I wanted to be in this one! Oh well, I guess I can wait if I get to be the star.

Charlie blows softly on Circe's face.

Circe starts licking at her chin.

Charlie giggles and kisses her on the side of her face.

CHARLIE

I'm glad you forgive me. Now let's go do what you were really begging for, a potty break.

F) She sits in her recliner and makes faces across the bed at Circe, who's sitting in the other one.

CHARLIE

Okay, I think I've recovered enough to go on. Now where was I? Come on, help a girl out!

Circe sneezes at her.

Charlie bursts out laughing.

CHARLIE
Oh, but of course! How could I forget?

G) She frowns down at her hand as it rests on the coffee table, which is now stacked with several small piles of books surrounding her laptop. She is kneeling in front of it as if someone is across from her.

CHARLIE AS NARRATOR
Interior Domingo's Bookstore - Next Day, Afternoon. The moment the kind bookstore owner's hand had touched mine, I couldn't move until the memories stopped rushing from me and our intimate connection ended. Now he whispers in what I'm certain is Castilian Spanish.

She moves to the other side of the coffee table then closes her eyes and whispers.

CHARLIE AS DOMINGO
Dios mío, un depredador de ensueño.

She returns to the previous side of the table, looking scared and upset.

CHARLIE AS NARRATOR
From the pure horror I hear shivering through his voice, I know then that he had lied to me. I stare at him, both frightened and angry, and I demand answers.

CHARLIE AS HELEN
You said it would only be like watching a movie! Why did you touch me?

CHARLIE AS NARRATOR
But I already know the answer.

CHARLIE AS HELEN
I didn't want him to hurt anyone else! Why did you touch me?

CHARLIE AS NARRATOR
He steals his hand away into his pocket then switches to English, still wrapped in his Castilian accent.

She switches places then closes her eyes. She jerks her hand away and her eyes fly open, levelling an intense gaze.

CHARLIE AS DOMINGO

Helen Zorbas, you must go to my wife for help. You must! I thought I could help you, but this, this is beyond me.

Sliding to the original side of the table one last time, she gasps and looks like she's searching for answers behind someone's eyes. Then she looks out across the room with an empty gaze.

CHARLIE AS NARRATOR

I gasp at the sound of the name I had not given him, and I start to ask how he could know, but again, I already know. The unsolicited story that had come spilling out from him when he first saw me, before he took my hand in his, held all the answers. I look deep into his eyes and find myself staring into pools of molten gold. They're warm with caring, drawn with concern, and hold something that my friends' had not. Belief. For the first time since my nightmares began, I no longer feel so wretchedly alone. My anger at him drains away like rain through parched earth. I reply in a voice that sounds miles away.

CHARLIE AS HELEN

If anyone could help, it would be your wife, Aisling.

CHARLIE AS NARRATOR

My response has an immediate effect on him, and I watch as the tension uncoils itself from his shoulders. It takes me a moment to realize that he hadn't thought I'd accept.

H) She carries Circe around in one arm like a baby, cooing at her and kissing her snout as she mutters to herself about what comes next.

I) She makes Circe fly like an airplane around the cabin, delaying the inevitable.

J) Circe lies on her back snoozing, all four short little legs sticking up in the air.

Charlie watches her for a few moments with a loving smile on her face, then starts her next scene.

CHARLIE AS NARRATOR

Exterior / Interior Tomlan Hall - Late Afternoon. A massive monolith of wavy concrete and unending glass looms over me as I recheck the address to be sure I'm in the right place.

The 3210 Tomlan Hall noted on the paper in my hand matches the address plaque, which also informs me that this is the Graduate School of Education. This isn't making any sense to me, but I trust Domingo, so I wander inside to find a directory.

She acts out her narration, looking perplexed at what she's seeing, then walks around until she stands in front of the wall nearby. She puts one hand up with an extended finger as she reads the imagined directory.

CHARLIE AS NARRATOR

Room 1650 is listed under the Psychology Department. I read it over and over, and soon it sways before my eyes. The tips of my fingers and toes begin to tingle. Without a care to any onlookers, I turn and lean my back against the wall. My breath comes in short gasps and quiet sobs. I slide to the ground and pull my knees to my chest, burying my face in my arms so no one can see my tears.

She turns around and slides down the wall, knees pulled to her chest, head hiding beneath her arms. Sobs shake her body.

CHARLIE AS NARRATOR

After a few moments, a voice with a soft, lilting accent carefully asks after me. It's accompanied by a light touch on my shoulder.

She stands up and leans over where she had been sitting, reaching down with a gentle hand.

CHARLIE AS AISLING

Whatever is the matter?

She sits back down, head still lowered.

CHARLIE AS NARRATOR

I can only shake my head, unable to look up.

After shaking her head, she gets up and frowns down at where she was.

CHARLIE AS AISLING

I suppose this isn't the best place to converse, is it? Why don't you come into my office and tell me what's wrong while I make you some tea?

CHARLIE AS NARRATOR

The light touch becomes a gentle grasp around my upper arm. I feel myself being lifted to my feet. Not wanting to seem even more foolish than I already do, I stand up and blindly follow where the hand leads me. After traversing a dazzling maze of corridors, I'm deposited upon a plush chestnut easy chair and handed a few tissues.

CHARLIE AS AISLING

There now, tell me what's troubling you, Miss?

She relocates to the closest recliner, dabbing at her eyes.

CHARLIE AS NARRATOR

The scent of blended black teas soothes my senses. I can hear the tinkle of bone china teacups and the rustling of clothes as I stare at the floor trying to remember my own name.

She rubs at her downcast eyes then mumbles.

CHARLIE AS HELEN

Helen. Helen Zorbas.

CHARLIE AS NARRATOR

The room falls silent, and I feel myself being closely regarded. I drag my eyes up from the intricate pattern of the hand-woven throw rug to look at my rescuer.

She looks up, her face going slack with awe.

CHARLIE AS NARRATOR

I feel the barbs of shock prickle through my body as I meet the woman's gaze. Eyes, not quite blue nor quite grey, not quite light nor quite dark, somewhere in between, like storm clouds building on the horizon. Open pages to her heart like a book of self-poetry. A cascade of curls glistening as red-golden as a California sunset, frame a darkening face. I look down at the woman's hands to confirm my fears. A bronze ring, in the shape of tree roots ensnaring petrified wood as its gem, clings to the woman's right ring finger. I should have recognized the Irish accent right away, but it's fainter now than how Domingo had described it when he shared their strange love story with me. I can only watch her, my mouth agape.

CHARLIE AS AISLING

Miss Zorbas. I made tea, if you'd like some.

She stands up, picks up a cup of tea from nearby, and turns to loom over the recliner, eyebrows raised, waiting for a response.

CHARLIE AS NARRATOR

I take the offered tea and sip at it so I can speak, but just swallowing is a struggle because the Sahara has spread into my mouth.

CHARLIE AS AISLING

Miss Zorbas?

She plops back down in the recliner and continues to stare up.

CHARLIE AS NARRATOR

I cough, then manage to whisper.

CHARLIE AS HELEN

Aisling.

She rises and turns to face the recliner, taking a step backward.

CHARLIE AS NARRATOR

Aisling's jaw clenches. Her voice comes out tighter and her accent stronger.

The muscles in her jaw flex as her expression becomes serious.

CHARLIE AS AISLING

Do I know you, Miss Zorbas?

She curls up in the recliner, shrinking away.

CHARLIE AS HELEN

No, no you don't.

Standing up again, she starts fidgeting with her right ring finger, scowling.

CHARLIE AS AISLING

Then how do you know my first name?

CHARLIE AS NARRATOR

Caution seeps into Aisling's once gentle tone, the kind smile on her face fading as her eyes narrow. Her fingers spin the ring around and around. I feel uneasy as I watch Aisling's countenance change. I have to think of something and quick, so I put my hands up in a helpless shrug.

She sits in the recliner then shrugs as though she's holding a cup in her hands.

CHARLIE AS HELEN

Your name is listed on the wall directory?

She pulls herself out of the recliner to loom over it.

CHARLIE AS NARRATOR

Aisling's eyes turn the colour of steel and pierce through me like a needle.

CHARLIE AS AISLING

My name is listed as Research Professor A. Fergus, and Aisling, would hardly be anyone's first guess. Anna, Amy, April, even Ashley, but Aisling? Try again. You'll have to find something more convincing if you're not going to tell me the truth.

She flattens herself against the back of the recliner.

CHARLIE AS NARRATOR

I feel like an insect pinned to a board. I squeak a reply and try not to spill my tea.

CHARLIE AS HELEN

Your husband sent me.

She stands back up, turning toward the recliner, going rigid.

CHARLIE AS NARRATOR

As I speak, Aisling's entire body stiffens, and her face goes blank. Perhaps it was a play of light, but I watch her eyes turn the colour of rich soil, burying all emotion beneath it. The eerie transformation chills my blood.

She steps away from the recliner and shakes her limbs out. Then she winks at the camera.

CHARLIE

I think I'll leave you at this little cliffhanger for now while I mull over what Aisling's response will be. Poor Helen.

K) She lowers herself into the recliner with a big grin and a bowl of soup.

Circe lays in the centre of the bed, stretched out and asleep.

CHARLIE

That was good work! I can't believe I dreamed this and how easy it is to remember! Usually my dreams fade fast when I wake up. Anyway, I don't want to overwhelm myself by doing too much on my first day, though. I want to ease into it. Time for lunch, a nap, and then a w-a-l-k.

Circe's luxurious ears twitch, and she lifts her head to give her heart human the side-eye.

Charlie giggles.

CHARLIE

Are you learning how to spell? Figures. You've always been too smart for my own good. Anyway, I'm going to join you for a nap after I eat Dad's squash bisque, then we can go for a hike.

Circe's nose works at identifying the food Charlie has and whether it's worth getting up to beg for it. After a moment, she lays her head down and returns to snoozing.

Charlie savours the lunch made with love and gazes longingly out the windows at the natural beauty waiting outside.

End Montage
Afternoon

21 Begin Montage - Exterior Amber Sierra's Cabin
Late Afternoon

A) Charlie has the GoPro on the selfie stick and pointed at the thirty-two gallon, outdoor, latching trash can. The lid has been flung open, and the very few pieces of trash that were in it are laid out on the ground in a methodical way.

CHARLIE (off-screen)

Circe and I took our nap and didn't hear a thing. I would say that a bear figured out how to get into it, except I don't think a bear would have been so neat about it.

She gets a close-up shot.

CHARLIE (off-screen)

It was probably just someone looking for cans or food or something, right? Or maybe someone casing the joint? It is a pretty sweet joint.

She sounds a little nervous as she scans the camera around looking for other signs.

CHARLIE (off-screen)

Glad I brought my very effective alarm system who barks at the slightest squirrel sound, but would snore through a home invasion.

She points the camera at Circe.

Circe perks her ears, the sunlight bringing out the brindle of her mahogany fur, and gives Charlie a hopeful stare.

Charlie chuckles.

CHARLIE (off-screen)

Yes, yes, we're going to take that walk anyway and worry about this when we come back.

Circe dances around when she hears the word walk.

Charlie points the camera at herself and looks a little concerned.

CHARLIE

I can't believe I'm saying this, but I guess I'm also glad for Dad's pistol, which I am now bringing along, just in case. I hate that he was even a little right. Please know that my whole family and I believe in gun control. I'm trained in how to use it properly, have been through courses for conceal carry, am licensed, and know that using a firearm of any kind should be a last resort and only to save you or others from grievous harm or death. Alright, enough of the grim stuff, I didn't come here for that. I came here for this!

Charlie swings the camera to the cabin. Its strong, red pine timbers hold aloft a majestic pitched gable roof made from steel and painted verdigris.

CHARLIE (off-screen)

I promised to get a daytime shot. Gorgeous, isn't it? Look at all that roof space where solar panels and a satellite dish could go! That's right, Amber Sierra, I'm already making plans for your place!

B) From the shore, she pans the GoPro across the placid lake surrounded by a verdant forest dominated by ponderosa pine and Douglas fir and smattered with juniper, oak, and aspen. The lake surface hosts several diving and lounging platforms belonging to the various neighbouring cabins.

CHARLIE (off-screen)
And this is what the lake is like during the day.

Circe, who is leashed, goes to examine the water's edge. It laps at her, and she jumps back when the cold water touches her feet.

CHARLIE (off-screen)
Be careful, girl, most of the fish in that lake are bigger than you!

Circe ignores her warning and continues investigating.

Charlie shifts the camera from one distant neighbour's place to another.

CHARLIE (off-screen)
It's strange. I'm not sure I have neighbours at all even though there are cabins next to me. That one over there--

She points the camera to the south of them at a massive A-frame with a river-stone hearth and chimney splitting it down the middle.

CHARLIE (off-screen)
--has been quiet with no sound, light, or activity. Of course, it is spring, so maybe it's still a bit too early for people to be visiting or living in their cabins.

She then points the camera to the north of them at a smaller bi-level cabin of Scandinavian design.

CHARLIE (off-screen)
This one hasn't had any signs of life either. Not even a flutter in the drawn curtains. I mean, I guess it's good that I won't have anyone around to distract me, but still, it's kind of unsettling.

C) She jogs along a shaded trail, letting Circe stretch her stubby legs. A bee hums by the camera, which shakes with every footfall.

CHARLIE (off-screen)
I guess I should have prepped the drone and given it a practice run. Sorry if I'm making you sick! I'll make sure I have it ready for my next outing, I promise.

D) She focuses the GoPro on Circe, who digs furiously into a burrow in the rocky soil near some tree roots. Neither of them appear to notice a figure in the distant background peering out from behind a tree. The footage zooms in on the figure, becoming too grainy to make out any details, then zooms back out.

CHARLIE (off-screen)
What are you after, Circe?

She draws closer to get a better look.

CHARLIE (off-screen)
Is that? Is that a snake hole? No, Circe! Get away from that!

She pulls on Circe's leash until she gets her to move away.

CHARLIE (off-screen)
That's the last thing I need to happen! Have you get bitten by a rattler! I can't blame you, though, this is what you were bred for.

Circe barks and pulls, trying to get back to the snake hole.

CHARLIE
That's enough excitement for today, I think. Come on, girl, let's go home and make some early dinner.

End Montage
Early Evening

22 Interior Amber Sierra's Cabin Night

Charlie Hale Webcam Vlog Episode #11

With the day's work and play behind her and a full belly, Charlie lounges in her recliner, mug of tea in hand.

Circe, ever loyal, lies next to her, gnawing on a dog chew.

Charlie's laptop sits on the coffee table, angled to include them both. She looks uneasy.

CHARLIE
I just finished talking with Amber Sierra. I didn't reveal anything about how my story is taking shape, other than it's

going well, because I want to surprise her with it when she gets here. I want to read it to her and see her reactions. It will be so cool! I also didn't mention the trash can incident, because she'll just worry, but I did ask her about her non-existent neighbours. She said she didn't know anything about that, that neither the owners of this cabin nor her realtor ever mentioned it. Can you believe that, Circe?

Circe's tail thumps a few times at the sound of her name.

CHARLIE

She said she'd ask her realtor to do some research about that.

Charlie reaches out and scrubs Circe's ears.

CHARLIE

Neighbours or not, I got more done today than in all the time since I started this vlog! That's both sad and exhilarating. So here's to my first productive day at the cabin, and I didn't think I'd ever say this, but I hope I have a continuation of the nightmare about Helen and her paranormal struggles!

She raises her mug and toasts herself then sips some of her tea.

CHARLIE

Now, my dear Warehouse Agents, my ninth course coordinate is simple.

She takes on a snarky but humorous tone.

CHARLIE

Don't be like Pete, who's "a smart guy, but only when he's not thinking about cookies or boobies." Keep distractions to a minimum. This increases production and improves creativity.

She chuckles then becomes more serious again.

CHARLIE

If I pick up the pace more each day, I might be done with my first draft before my bestie gets here, and then we can have more play time! But in order to do that, I've got to make sure I sleep well and enough. I hope you do, too!

23 Interior Amber Sierra's Cabin Just Before Midnight

Charlie Hale Webcam Vlog Episode #12

The only light in the cabin comes from the laptop. It illuminates Charlie's spooked face, the whites of her eyes showing, her hair flying around her head with static electricity like a halo. A low thrum pulses in the background. Her voice is a whisper.

CHARLIE

I just heard something in the rafters or maybe on the roof, and there's a weird humming sound, like electricity through a transformer or... I don't know exactly how to describe it or if you can hear it, too.

She pauses a moment to listen.

Circe barks and growls intermittently, her ears perked at the sounds, their fur floating all around them.

The low thrum continues on, accompanied by a creaking in the rafters above.

CHARLIE

See?

She hushes Circe and listens a little longer, but the sounds of movement die down, leaving only the thrum.

CHARLIE

It's just forest critters, right? And the hum is probably from faulty wiring or the system being taxed by all the tech and rechargeable batteries I have plugged in. Maybe I didn't notice it because I was so excited and doing so much.

Circe's attention is directed up toward the rafters near the loft.

She follows Circe's gaze and listens for a few moments, then produces her headlamp from the coffee table and shines it up at the ceiling, revealing dusty, cobwebbed rafters.

Circe growls and huffs, ready to defend Charlie from danger.

Charlie frowns as she continues to look around, then she thinks about it for a moment and laughs at herself.

CHARLIE

I don't see anything, and if Circe is barking, it's probably not my ex-client's hitmen coming to take me out. Funny how creepy normal sounds can be when you're by yourself in the middle of nowhere. Anyway, I'm going to check the windows and doors to make sure they're locked, and then I need to take notes before the details of this continuing nightmare saga slip away. It was so realistic and intense, it took me a moment to realize I was awake when I woke up, which is probably why I felt so freaked out by everything going on. Once I'm done with that, I need to try to get more sleep. I've got a big day ahead of me.

As she reaches over to close the laptop, she finally notices her hair and attempts to smooth it down, but it just floats right back up.

CHARLIE

What is going on with my hair? I look like I touched a Van de Graaff generator. Or like lightning is about to strike me! But I'm protected inside the cabin, right? It was a clear night when I went to bed, so I don't think there's a storm going on outside.

The audible thrumming fades away over the next minute as she gets up and looks outside the nearest window. When she comes back into frame, her hair has settled back down.

CHARLIE

I see stars outside. The electrical sound is gone, and now my hair is back to its normal sleep-mussed mess. I've heard if electrical wiring isn't properly shielded it can make people feel sick, but if it's bad enough to cause a static build up, that sounds dangerous. I think I better unplug some things while I'm up and only have what I need drawing power. We'll definitely need to get an electrician in here.

She frowns, shrugs, rolls out of bed, then turns the webcam off.

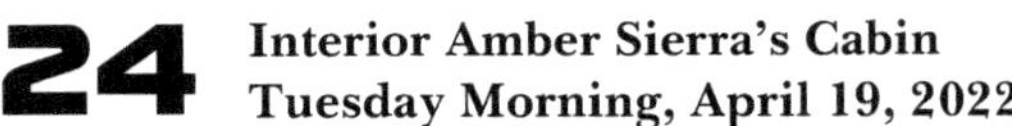

24 Interior Amber Sierra's Cabin
Tuesday Morning, April 19, 2022

Charlie Hale Webcam Vlog Episode #13

Charlie looks sleepy and has the hint of circles under her eyes. Her dark golden hair holds more tangles than curls. She sits in her recliner, one knee pulled to her chest, and stares right past her laptop. Hot coffee wafts steam into the air from the cup holder next to her. She's wrapped in a silver workout jacket and black yoga pants. With a wistful sigh, she takes the coffee mug in hand and brings it close to her nose, inhaling.

CHARLIE

Mmm, much like country air, coffee smells divine. And it's desperately needed this morning. I know a lot of animals are nocturnal, but I guess I didn't realize how loud they could sound in all this quiet. I know I shouldn't have gotten spooked, although the electrical issues are quite scary. I haven't heard it anymore since I unplugged some things, so I think it's okay. You're probably laughing at me right now. I guess that's what I get for being a city girl.

She shrugs with a sheepish smile and takes a sip of coffee.

CHARLIE

I think for my peace of mind I'm going to set up the GoPro with full spectrum mode on to see if I can capture the culprits in action. I'm guessing raccoons, but just in case it's critters of the human kind...

She yawns and stretches, showing off the lithe form she works hard to maintain.

CHARLIE

I'm afraid if I stay in the cabin this morning, I'll be too tempted to crawl back into bed. I've got to keep momentum going, so I'll spend today outside by the lake. Circe will love that! Especially since we're going for a stroll first. One thing that's so nice about this property is it's right up against national forest, so there are all kinds of hiking trails! I haven't used the w word yet, so she doesn't know the good news.

She turns her laptop and points the webcam at Circe who's snuggled under the camp quilts on the bed, only her face peeking out.

Circe watches her through half-closed eyes.

Charlie turns the laptop back to herself, smiling.

CHARLIE

Now before I drag myself out of this comfy chair, I give to you course coordinate number ten, my weary Hunters, don't allow room for excuses.

She squints her eyes and pouts her lips as she speaks in a low, serious tone, her voice hoarse with intensity.

CHARLIE
"No matter how much it hurts, no matter how hard it gets, you gotta keep grinding."

25 Begin Montage - Exterior Amber Sierra's Cabin/Surrounding Forest/Lake - Morning

A) Charlie films with the GoPro on the selfie stick and aims it down the driveway. She does a pass over the outdoor trash can and her EV car.

CHARLIE (off-screen)
Glad to see the prowler hasn't been back.

Circe barks at her, her retractable leash vibrating with her excitement.

CHARLIE (off-screen)
What is it, girl? Do you want this?

Charlie holds up a small doggie frisbee in front of the camera.

Circe barks again.

Charlie turns and tosses the frisbee, just past her car in the driveway to the gravel road beyond it. It falls within reach of the long retractable leash.

Circe chases it, ears flopping in time with each surge of her little legs.

CHARLIE (off-screen)
Get it, girl! Now bring it back.

Circe brings it halfway and drops it with an expectant tilt of her head.

Charlie points the camera at her face for a moment, chuckling.

CHARLIE
She's never quite gotten the concept of bringing it all the way back. I guess that's better than running away with it!

They play this game several times as they walk northwest along the gravel road now skirting both the lake and the national forest where numerous hiking trails, picnic areas, and campgrounds branch off.

CHARLIE (off-screen)

I know I promised to have the drone up and running before our next trek, but after last night, I needed to get my blood pumping to my brain before taking on a tech-heavy task. I'll do it when we're down on the lakeshore after the walk. Look at how many trails there are--

She stops mid-sentence and points the camera at a pine tree, along the gravel road, adorned with a metal band around its trunk about a foot wide and four feet off the ground. It looks like it's made from gold.

CHARLIE (off-screen)

--What is that?

She walks over to the tree, keeping the band in frame. Then she sweeps the camera to the other naked trees.

CHARLIE (off-screen)

I've seen tree bands for insect control before, but they don't look like that, and they're usually on all of the trees affected. I've also seen metal bands to keep animals from climbing them or clawing them, but they're always much wider than that. Maybe it's a fancy trail head marker? Maybe I should go to the visitor's centre and get a trail guide at some point.

She steps closer to the tree and reaches out to touch the band, her hand coming into frame. She recoils a bit.

CHARLIE (off-screen)

Whoa! That feels strange. Hot? Cold? Electric? I'm not sure.

She turns the camera to herself, her pretty face pinched in confusion. She reaches out and touches the band again, testing the surface.

CHARLIE

It's not sticky at all, in fact it's super slick. I wonder if it's like a cutting-edge anti-insect band they're trying out or something to help a sick tree?

She brings the tree back into view, focusing on its healthy looking buds.

CHARLIE (off-screen)

It doesn't appear to be sick, but what do I know? In the big city, they often mark trees with paint if they need to be cut down. If I see a forest ranger, I'll ask, otherwise it'll have to wait until I get around to the visitor's centre. I guess I should see if Amber Sierra's realtor knows.

She drops the camera down to ground level to catch Circe begging at her, frisbee in her mouth.

She reaches down and gets the frisbee from Circe.

CHARLIE (off-screen)

Sorry, girl.

She throws the frisbee again then spins the camera toward her, one eyebrow arched.

CHARLIE

I don't remember seeing this one, or any on our walk yesterday, and we went the same way.

She shakes her head and chastises herself.

CHARLIE

Come on, Charlie, you're just being paranoid. You're writing a paranormal thriller alone in a cabin in the woods and creeping yourself out. Simple as that.

Circe gives a frisbee muted bark.

CHARLIE

Let's go see if there are any more, Circe!

She reorients the camera ahead of her and leaves the road, cutting north into the forest.

B) The GoPro points at another gold band around a fir tree.

CHARLIE (off-screen)

So, here's another one, which blows the trail marker hypothesis because we haven't found a trail to follow for this one, yet. It's sparse enough here that we don't need to, though I can tell we'll have to find one soon as the forest thickens.

Circe strains against her leashed harness.

They start walking again, and then Charlie breaks into a run.

CHARLIE (off-screen)
I'll race you to find the nearest trail, Circe!

Circe keeps up with her despite being height-challenged.

C) She points the GoPro at yet another gold band around an aspen tree.

CHARLIE (off-screen)
So this is the third one I've found. This one is only a couple of minutes away from the last one, kind of like the second one was from the first. Different species of trees, too, whatever that means.

She twirls the camera around to face her.

CHARLIE
It's gotta be some kind of system used to record something, though I don't have any idea what. I probably didn't notice them yesterday because I was just so excited to be here. Anyway, as fascinating as this is, I've got work to do, so solving this mystery will have to wait.

She points the camera down at Circe.

CHARLIE (off-screen)
Come on girl, next time we'll find a trail to follow. That way we can go longer without the worry of getting lost.

Circe reluctantly turns around and follows after her.

D) She scans the shoreline of the lake with the GoPro, coming to rest on her raft, which is up on the bank nearby, oars and life vests stashed inside it.

CHARLIE (off-screen)
Good to know the hooligans who messed with my trash aren't into rafting. I figured the chances of someone stealing it were low, and I don't want to waste time inflating and deflating it and hauling it in and out of the cabin every time I want to use it. If I get some good scenes done, I'll reward myself with an afternoon lounge on the lake.

She rotates the camera to look at Circe.

CHARLIE (off-screen)

And you can come with me this time if you want to. God help me.

Circe barks and wags her tail.

End Montage
Morning

26 Exterior Lake Late Morning

Charlie has the GoPro set up on a rock using the octopus tripod. It faces the back of Amber Sierra's cabin, showcasing the extensive back deck. She sits in a camp chair enjoying the shade cast by the grove of pine trees that extends from the front yard almost to the shore. Her laptop sits on a folding side table nearby and her backpack beneath it where she draws out a small black hard shell case.

Circe lazes next to her on a plush dog bed, her retractable leash hooked to a stake driven into the ground.

Charlie unzips the case, revealing a silver drone no larger than her hand. Its design, a sphere housed inside a triangular frame with three gimballed thrust propulsion engines at each point, resembles something from a sci-fi movie. She takes it into her hands with care, examining it, then looks up at the camera, mystified.

CHARLIE

Where are its rotor blades?

She searches the case to no avail.

CHARLIE

There aren't any! How does this thing fly? I guess I should read the instruction manual.

She places the drone back down in its protective foam, slides a booklet from a zipped compartment in the lid, and squeals with delight as she opens it. She reads silently for several moments, her lips moving with the words, her eyes growing wider by the second.

CHARLIE

Ion engines with atmosphere-breathing electric propulsion systems? An electromagnetic plasma anti-gravity field generator? A nuclear battery that only has to be recharged every century? A USB-C cord to keep whatever camera is attached charged? Whoa, Amber Sierra wasn't kidding when she said that the company who's courting her gave her some cutting-edge tech!

Her expression becomes troubled as a frown settles across her brow and lips.

CHARLIE

I hope she knows what she's getting herself into. This drone looks like it belongs in a secret military installation, not in my civvy possession. But I guess if you're really going to have a chance at combating climate change, you're going to need some advanced technology!

She reaches into her pocket and draws out her smartphone, using the camera to scan the QR code in the manual.

CHARLIE

I'm not sure how this will work without a mobile phone signal or internet, but it says I only need a Bluetooth connection. It probably has an onboard AI system.

She waits a few moments, then her eyes light up when the connection establishes.

CHARLIE

Oh! It connected and installed a drone control app. I was wondering about that since there's no controller in the case. It's also warning me to always use the included launch pad when powering it on, which is stored under the foam.

She lifts the drone back up and digs under the foam, pulling out a slender, rigid, grey woven material. She moves over to a flat rock nearby and puts the material down then sets the drone on top of it.

Realizing Charlie is going somewhere without her, Circe stretches and hops from her bed to investigate. She gets within a few feet of the drone, as close as her leash allows, nose working and ears attentive.

CHARLIE

The moment of truth!

Charlie taps at her phone and suddenly the drone flares to life with a faint hum, going from resting to hovering in an instant.

Circe jumps away from it, startled, then barks chidingly at it for daring to surprise her.

CHARLIE

This is amazing! I can control it manually or set parameters for it to follow a target from almost any distance.

Charlie turns her phone sideways like a gaming controller and places her thumbs on the screen and slides them around. The drone obeys the movement inputs flawlessly. Within moments, she has it flying around Circe, who bounds after it, trying to snatch it from the air like a frisbee. Charlie giggles, but doesn't tease Circe for very long, setting it back down on its landing pad after a few revolutions.

CHARLIE

Okay, I've had my fun, and so have you, girl. All I have to do now is figure out how to attach the GoPro to the landing gear skids and how to set it to follow me, both of which look pretty straight-forward. We'll be all set for our next adventure, Circe!

Circe barks in frustration at not being allowed to reach the drone and strains against her harness.

Charlie shakes her head with a smile and brings the drone over to her for a sniff.

It takes several moments before Circe is satisfied that it's not a frisbee to chew on, then she trots back over to her bed.

Charlie puts everything back in the case then addresses the camera, her eyes shining with enthusiasm.

CHARLIE

It's exciting that this drone will let me be more mobile with my writing, which I know Circe will be happy about. So far, I've gotten some wonderful results using this new method of writing, and I can't wait to see where it will take me. Now it's time to get back to work!

27 Begin Montage - Exterior Lake Late Morning

The GoPro rolls during Charlie's writing session. She holds the laptop in one hand so she can refer to her notes while she's acting out her scenes.

A) Charlie stands in front of the empty camp chair looking grim with narrowed eyes and tensed mouth. Behind her lies the drone launching rock that she has dragged into place to act as a second chair.

CHARLIE AS NARRATOR

Interior Tomlan Hall - Late Afternoon. Aisling speaks in a flat voice, her accent more noticeable.

CHARLIE AS AISLING

Why am I not surprised? Call me Ms. Fergus, please, as we are not even acquaintances, yet. Why did my husband send you here?

She pulls back into the chair, shoulders hunched and head downturned.

CHARLIE AS NARRATOR

I shrink away from her and study the elegant Celtic knotwork decorating my teacup before glancing up and stuttering between chattering teeth.

CHARLIE AS HELEN

I'm sorry, Ms. Fergus. He said you could help me.

She rises and looks down, her strained face relaxing.

CHARLIE AS NARRATOR

Aisling's hard gaze softens at the sound of my distress. She moves over to sit in a matching easy chair across from me. As she sinks into it, she lets out a long sigh but doesn't utter a word.

She moves over to the rock and sits down, remaining silent for a moment before getting up and returning to the chair.

CHARLIE AS NARRATOR

After several moments pass, I can no longer stand the silence.

CHARLIE AS HELEN

I appear to have upset you, Ms. Fergus.

She moves to the rock and sits, touching the pads of her fingers and thumbs together.

CHARLIE AS NARRATOR

Aisling steeples her fingers and regards me with eyes that cool from smouldering earth back to their original storm clouds.

CHARLIE AS AISLING

No, you haven't. My husband has. You are but his unwitting instrument.

She rises then slumps back into the chair, looking defeated.

CHARLIE AS NARRATOR

The chill creeps deeper, and all I want to do is leave.

CHARLIE AS HELEN

I think I should go. Thank you for the tea.

She stands up and deposits the imaginary cup then almost topples over before leaning against an invisible wall.

CHARLIE AS NARRATOR

I set my teacup down on the antique black marble table next to hers and the tree of life themed teapot. I rise too fast and almost fall, dizzy with the tempest of emotions raging inside me. Aisling reaches out to steady me. It is then that I realize how very small I feel next to the statuesque woman. I pull away and lean against the wall, almost bumping a painting I recognize as Waterhouse's Boreas, the very same that hangs on my bedroom wall. In that moment, I feel the kind of connection Domingo had described in his story. It is a bizarre sensation since in the same instant I feel completely alienated.

She turns to the empty chair and extends her hand in a pleading manner.

CHARLIE AS NARRATOR

Gentleness returns to Aisling's voice.

CHARLIE AS AISLING

Please wait, Miss Zorbas. Wait, Helen, please. I would like to try and help you if you'll tell me what's wrong.

She steps away from the chair and offered hand, her face contorted with pain.

CHARLIE AS NARRATOR

I can't hide the hurt. I've been hurt enough. I feel more angry now than afraid. I'm so tired of being afraid.

CHARLIE AS HELEN

Look, I don't like upsetting anyone, Ms. Fergus. I don't want your help if it means I'm doing that. Please tell Domingo that this was a cruel joke. That he's hurt me more than that monster has.

CHARLIE AS NARRATOR

Before she can respond, I head for the door, nearly knocking over a wispy youth who is trying to enter. I mutter a brief apology to them, then rush down the hall.

Crying in quiet sobs and sniffles, she wanders around the lakeshore as though she's trapped in a labyrinth.

CHARLIE AS NARRATOR

Hot, angry tears slide down my face and blur my vision as I try in vain to find my way out of the maze of corridors. How ironic that a psychology department would be as complex and confusing as the mind. I nearly give up when I hear a voice speak like leaves brushing against one another in the wind.

CHARLIE AS LAB ASSISTANT

If you'll let me, I'll show you the way out.

She stops then turns around, swiping her arm across her eyes.

CHARLIE AS NARRATOR

I pause, then turn to face the soothing voice's owner and find the same person I had nearly run over. I have to look up at them to meet their inquisitive, loam eyes. I hesitate between being thankful and being insulted. I wipe at my tears and try to salvage what little dignity I have left.

CHARLIE AS HELEN

Yes, please. I would appreciate that.

CHARLIE AS NARRATOR

The person nods, their thick long black hair shiny under the fluorescent lights.

CHARLIE AS LAB ASSISTANT

Of course, follow me.

CHARLIE AS NARRATOR

Without another word or glance, my rescuer traverses the corridors, leading me outside.

CHARLIE AS LAB ASSISTANT

Here we are.

She looks down at the ground, suddenly shy.

CHARLIE AS HELEN

Thank you. Sorry to have bothered you.

CHARLIE AS LAB ASSISTANT
It's no trouble at all.

She falls quiet, contemplating something.

CHARLIE AS NARRATOR
The person hesitates a moment, looking as though they want to say something more, but closes their mouth and turns to leave instead. Their hesitation gives me a chance to inquire about Domingo's enigmatic wife.

CHARLIE AS HELEN
Do you know Aisling very well?

She hugs herself and lets out a breathy laugh.

CHARLIE AS NARRATOR
They stop just inside the doorway, folding their arms around themself, and giving a soft laugh tinged with bitterness.

CHARLIE AS LAB ASSISTANT
Does anyone? Definitely not me. I'm only her lowly lab assistant. Why?

She cringes and takes half a step back.

CHARLIE AS NARRATOR
I hadn't meant to run headlong into a feud, but I've come this far and have never been so humiliated, so I need to know.

CHARLIE AS HELEN
I was just wondering what it is exactly that she does? I mean, she's a psychologist, right?

CHARLIE AS NARRATOR
Amusement replaces the lab assistant's bitterness, and they shake their head.

CHARLIE AS LAB ASSISTANT
So, before you continue giving me the third degree, my name is My San, she/her pronouns, and more accurately, I'm one of Aisling's research team members.

CHARLIE AS NARRATOR
My San looks expectantly at me. Her name makes me wonder about its origins, but shame overshadows my curiosity. I'm

mortified to think of the scene I've made inside, and now I haven't even bothered to ask the nice woman her name.

CHARLIE AS HELEN

I'm so sorry. I'm Helen. She/her.

CHARLIE AS NARRATOR

My San nods, her smile wry but her expression still concerned by the draw of her brow.

CHARLIE AS MY SAN

Much better. Now, to answer your question, Helen, she's a research psychologist who specializes in dreams. Her current research project is an extensive dream study to see if there's some kind of switch--

Her eyes take on a distant look, and she starts to wobble, then collapses in slow motion.

CHARLIE AS NARRATOR

My San's words cut off, and suddenly she is dashing toward me. I wonder why she's reaching for me even as I feel myself sinking. My San manages to grab one of my arms.

She straightens back up then dashes forward, clutching at the air and then acts like she's steadying someone. She looks a little freaked out.

CHARLIE AS MY SAN

Are you okay?

She returns to a half-fainted position.

CHARLIE AS NARRATOR

I sag against My San, barely able to stand back up. My San steadies me. I start to give her a pat answer, but when I meet those deep, dark eyes, I feel compelled to tell the truth.

CHARLIE AS HELEN

No, I'm not.

CHARLIE AS NARRATOR

As soon as I admit it, I feel self-conscious and pull away from My San.

She pauses for a moment then looks straight at the camera and sighs.

CHARLIE

I'm not quite ready for the rest of this scene. I already screwed up my own love life, I don't want to screw up anyone else's, even if they are only characters.

B) She sits with her knees to her chest and tosses pebbles into the lake.

Circe looks like she wants to chase them, but barks at them instead.

C) Circe digs a hole, her back hunching like an inch worm while her front paws imitate two backhoes working overtime.

Charlie lies flat on her back on a yoga mat, watching clouds instead of doing yoga.

CHARLIE

Circe! That one totally looks like a kitty!

Circe pulls her sand encrusted muzzle from the ever deepening hole to look for the invading feline. When she doesn't see one, she runs around with her nose to the ground determined to find its hiding place.

Charlie giggles.

CHARLIE

I'm such a jerk.

D) She stands in front of the camera, looking past it as if she's studying something nearby, conflicting emotions warring on her face.

CHARLIE AS NARRATOR

Exterior Domingo's Bookstore - Early Evening. The vibrant colours and elegance of Domingo's bookstore hadn't struck me till I stood across the street from it now. I had been too singularly focused on what was inside to notice what was outside. Though maybe it was the unconscious deciding factor that had made me go into his store and not some other, as aesthetics have always swayed my decisions. I linger long enough to marvel at the form, material, and palette of the architecture. He has taken great care in designing his bookstore and has created a unique look that blends into the Haight Ashbury's eclectic tastes. Low-pitched gables with a terracotta roof stretches out over the storefront. As the sidewalk approaches the arched entrance way, it bleeds into ceramic tiles the same colour as the roof and continues on inside. A gradient of glazed cobalt to deep aquamarine tiles fan out around the archway and disperse into the coral stucco walls. Two small wrought-iron banisters lead up a few steps to elegant olive wood double doors boasting gorgeous wood grain patterns and wrought-iron rings for handles. Two enormous arched windows flank the magnificent entrance way allowing the diffused autumn sunlight to spill in and sparkle across the tiled floor. I feel as though I'm looking at the front of an exiled Mediterranean villa. Just another eccentricity of his that calls to me. So why am I resisting the call? It is not my wonder keeping me from crossing the street. I am torn inside about what to do next. My emotions have been on a roller coaster ride, and I'm not quite sure the ride is over yet. Part of me wants to throw open those doors and march inside and demand an explanation. But the other part of me is scared what his answer will be. I feel as though I am both betrayed and betrayer. In my haste I had abandoned trust, assumed too much, and discovered that my mistrust was not well-founded. As I loiter there, I wrestle with these things. If it hadn't been for Aisling's chilly reception and my own shame, I might have crossed the street.

E) She pulls her chair closer to the lake and splashes her toes in the water, squealing with the cold.

Circe's head pops out from one of the several holes she's peppered the shore with then disappears again once she's sure her heart human isn't being eaten by a lake monster.

F) She breaks out her packed lunch to eat.

Circe begs as usual, sitting up like the prairie dog she's pretended to be all morning.

Charlie protests and then gives in, tossing Circe tasty morsels.

CHARLIE

Damn your doxie mind tricks!

G) She relocates her camp chair, flat rock, and Circe's dog bed with her in it, out of frame.

CHARLIE AS NARRATOR

Interior Helen's Bedroom / Dreamscape - Night. He's here. I can tell the moment I cross the threshold between waking and sleeping. Like the chill of a fever coming on.

She adds rasp to her voice and speaks in a low tone as the dream monster.

CHARLIE AS DREAM MONSTER

Darkness means inevitability. Can you feel it? It's so comforting. To know that no matter what, this particular thing will occur. It makes it so much easier to give in, to resign yourself. So much easier than fighting.

She grabs at her head, tangling her fingers in her curly honey-gold hair, her face a mask of conflict.

CHARLIE AS NARRATOR

His voice slithered like ice across metal. His thoughts, my mind, our dream. How could I fight someone who could get inside my head? Was that my thought or his? It was getting harder and harder to tell. So tired, I was so very tired. It would be easy to give up. He wasn't going to stop invading my dreams until he invaded me completely. Maybe if I begged.

Her eyelids look heavy as she starts to drop to her knees.

CHARLIE AS DREAM MONSTER

That's right, beg my little vixen. Get on your knees and beg.

She jerks herself back to her feet and opens her mouth wide with a snarl then casts frantic glances around as tears slide down her cheeks.

CHARLIE AS NARRATOR

I let out a wordless scream, filling it with the emotion of what I couldn't say. Then I felt something strange. Did he just flinch? It was all the reminder I needed to know that I still held power here. I would cling to the very last shreds of it before I would give in. He roared his fury into me, first sounding like he was in distant places, then growing in intensity as he manifested himself into my dream. My blithe meadow scene, filled with marigolds and dandelions, shimmered around me. I watched as the vibrant trees at the edges twisted and shrivelled, their leaves rotting even before they hit the ground. The dandelions matured into white puffballs and simultaneously burst, filling the air with thousands of dancing white seeds. The marigolds withered until they were nothing but blackened husks. The grass fell to ashes beneath my feet. A moonless night replaced the sunny day like a derecho roiling in, leaving me in darkness. I trembled at his might in this place, my place. It wasn't right. I looked down at one of the marigolds, grieving its desecration, and a few of my tears dripped down onto it. At their touch, it sprang back to life. Do not give up, it begged me, but his mocking laughter drowned it out. He was very close now, his sigh like the wind rustling the dry boughs of the dead trees.

She speaks in the same low, icy voice.

CHARLIE AS DREAM MONSTER

What a pathetic display. Do you really think you can save yourself from me? How amusing. But it ends now. I wouldn't want any more surprises.

She gasps then falls to the sand like she's been tackled, setting the laptop on her belly.

Circe leaps out of her bed and runs over to her, worried.

Charlie falls out of character, sweeps her onto her chest, and reassures her with snuggles and kisses. After several moments, she sets her back down.

Circe scampers off to her bed, but continues to watch with concern.

Charlie slides back into character without effort. She groans and winces as though someone were on top of her, then flails around, trying to escape.

CHARLIE AS NARRATOR

I felt his dark presence rush toward me. Before I could even think, he was upon me. His hands formed from the darkness and shoved into my shoulders, sending me crashing to the ground. Then he crouched over me while I lay there gasping for breath. He placed one knee on my hip while he drew out a long, slender blade. I was too stunned from the fall to move, and I could only squeak when I felt roots swarm up from the ground to bind my sprawled limbs. He whispered into my ear as he leaned in to slice open my shirt.

CHARLIE AS DREAM MONSTER

How powerful do you feel now, my little vixen?

She hisses at where the knife would be then mouths a silent scream.

CHARLIE AS NARRATOR

He pressed the tip of the blade against my collarbone. A rivulet of blood seeped from my wound and soaked into my shirt. The pain helped me catch my breath, and I screamed, finding my words this time.

CHARLIE AS HELEN

Get off of me, you monster!

She struggles to get free once again, but each passing moment she succumbs more.

CHARLIE AS NARRATOR

I tried to buck my body, but the bindings held me fast. He laughed in my face, and then smothered my protests with his mouth. I couldn't breathe or move or even think. This was it. He had won. I screamed again, defiantly into his mouth. That's right, Helen, I've won. Fill me with your fear, your rage. Yes, that's it. His thoughts had become mine at last. It was over. He'd won.

She stays a few moments longer on the ground, composing herself, then she sits up and takes the laptop in hand.

CHARLIE

Acting these scenes out is way more taxing on me than just writing them, plus I already lived through them in my sleep. The results are so worth it, but I need to take a break. I'm going on that raft ride with my furry child.

A thought crosses her tormented face, and she sucks in a breath of air then laughs.

CHARLIE

I avoided actually screaming so I wouldn't disturb anyone since I'm outside, but I got so lost in the scene I didn't think about how I might look. Like I'm nuts, I'm sure. I just hope because it's an artist community, they're used to artists expressing themselves in... unconventional ways.

H) She has attached the GoPro to the drone's camera mount and figured out how to make it track her. It faces her at chest height, hovering a couple of yards away. She wears an orange life vest, which, paired with her silver jacket and black pants makes her look like she's ready for Halloween. Her smartphone, tucked inside a clear dry bag, dangles from it by a carabiner lanyard.

CHARLIE

I can't believe this tiny drone can carry a GoPro at all, let alone still move like a silent hummingbird! It's so badass! The app on my phone lets me set its tracking mode either generally or quite specifically. I thought this would be a great time to test it out.

She leans down to Circe, who's patiently waiting, and dresses her in a shark-finned doggie life vest. Once the buckles are secured, she lifts her by the convenient back handle and lowers her into the raft where she tethers her leash to a handle. Then she unties the raft's anchor rope from a nearby log, tosses it into the raft, and climbs in after it.

Circe hops up on the edge of the raft and perches there like she's the captain while her first mate rows. The drone stays at a perfect distance, and the GoPro's wide angle shot captures everything within frame.

Once they are away from the shore, Charlie starts relaxing.

CHARLIE

I think everyone should have a lounge on the lake every so often. It's good for the soul.

Circe stands up and balances on the edge of the raft, looking down into the water at something that's caught her attention.

Beneath the surface of the clear water, several trout with back dappling and red throats and bellies dart past the raft as though they are fleeing from something.

CHARLIE

Careful, girl, or you'll fall in! Of course, it wouldn't be the first time, and it won't be the last!

Circe ignores her and continues to balance on the edge, the small waves and her excitement almost dumping her several times.

Far below the raft in the darker water, a shadow rises toward them.

Circe's body trembles as she starts barking, and as predicted, she falls in.

The disturbance of the water masks the shadow's sudden retreat into the darkness.

She shrieks when she gets splashed then laughs at her canine captain's misfortune.

CHARLIE

I knew you couldn't be trusted!

Circe swims around, shark fin jutting up from the water, and tries in vain to get back into the raft.

CHARLIE

You are the cutest shark ever! A bit colder than you expected, huh?

She reaches over the edge and hauls Circe back in.

CHARLIE

So much for a relaxing raft ride! That's okay, I still love you, you goof.

Circe shakes, spraying Charlie.

Charlie shrieks again.

CHARLIE

That's how you repay me for rescuing you? I see how it is!

Charlie wrestles with Circe, who mouths her hands with playful growls while trying to get back to her perch, still captivated by the presence she sensed below. Charlie finally relents, letting Circe hop back up on the raft's edge to continue her vigilant watch, then joins her in observing the lake's fascinating aquatic life.

End Montage
Late Afternoon

28 Interior Amber Sierra's Cabin Late Evening

Charlie holds the cordless landline to her ear, her hair pulled back into a messy bun. Everything is a little too bright, making her face gleam. She fidgets with the Blackmagic camera, which she doesn't realize is recording. Amber Sierra's voice can be heard on the other end.

CHARLIE

Hey, sorry to interrupt you with this, but I think I messed up the frakking white balance on your Blackmagic camera. It's my first time using it at night, and it was filming kind of dark, so I was trying to fix it. If you have the time, can you walk me through it, please?

Amber Sierra snickers at Charlie.

AMBER SIERRA (off-screen)

Con gusto. It's good to hear from you whatever the reason. I know the technical part of our courses in filmmaking weren't your favourite, huh?

CHARLIE

They weren't, but I regret not paying better attention so I don't have to bug you all the time.

AMBER SIERRA (off-screen)

You don't bug.

Charlie teases back.

CHARLIE

Well, it is what I keep you around for! That and the acting work you give me.

AMBER SIERRA (off-screen)

I'll take what I can get, guapa.

Charlie blushes the same colour as the red light on the camera that finally catches her attention. She swallows a giggle and doesn't let on.

CHARLIE

You might get more than you bargain for once you're stuck here with me for a week or two.

AMBER SIERRA (off-screen)

Órale! I'm willing to take the risk.

29 Interior Amber Sierra's Cabin Fifteen Minutes Later

Charlie still has the landline held to her ear when she starts recording with the Blackmagic camera again.

CHARLIE

Okay, I think everything's good now. I'm recording our conversation to see how things look after. Thanks for being so patient. I can't believe how hard that was!

AMBER SIERRA (off-screen)

You gotz to have skillz to make things look good on filmz.

Charlie snorts.

CHARLIE

That's another reason why I keep you around, you know.

AMBER SIERRA (off-screen)

Because I'm silly?

Charlie's fingers reach up to fidget with one of her dice-shaped earrings.

CHARLIE

Yes, that, but also because you're clever. I know your dreams are going to come true. Together we'll write amazing scripts that you can direct and film, and I can star in. And they'll make us rich and famous on top of saving the world.

Amber Sierra chuckles on the other end of the phone.

AMBER SIERRA (off-screen)

I suppose that's a good enough reason. Though I keep you around for many others as well.

CHARLIE

Hard same. I'd be heartbroken if not!

AMBER SIERRA (off-screen)

Me, too.

Charlie smiles, but it doesn't quite reach her hypnotic eyes. They gaze inward, and what they find leaves her unsettled.

CHARLIE

Well then, let's not break each other's hearts.

She frowns, almost surprised at what she's just said. Then she clears her throat and changes the subject.

CHARLIE

Now, I have a couple more questions for you, and then I'll let you go.

Amber Sierra doesn't let her off the hook, literally or figuratively. Her voice softens from its usual sardonic, guarded tone.

AMBER SIERRA (off-screen)

I'm in no hurry. I love talking to you.

Charlie squirms, rubbing at her forehead and tangling her fingers in her hair.

CHARLIE

You know I do, too. It's just that the longer I keep you on

the phone, the longer it will take for you to get here.

Amber Sierra's voice returns to normal.

AMBER SIERRA (off-screen)
Good point. Get on with it, then, mujer!

Charlie laughs, breaking the tension, her face lighting up with relief.

CHARLIE
Did your realtor say anything about the whole no neighbours thing?

AMBER SIERRA (off-screen)
He hasn't gotten back to me, yet. I'm sure he's just busy, though, so we might have to give it a day or two.

CHARLIE
Yeah, I guess so. Oh, and something else, I heard a humming last night, like electricity through poorly shielded wires, or a surge or something. I think all this extra technology plugged in is taxing the system and we should get the wiring checked and maybe even updated.

AMBER SIERRA (off-screen)
I guess that's what I get for buying sight unseen, no? But that's okay, the price was right, so we can definitely get everything inspected and updated.

CHARLIE
True, and the cabin was built in the late 1960s, so I guess it's to be expected. I've got another question for you to ask him, though it's not actually related to the cabin, but more the area. He might not know, but can you ask him about the metal bands around some of the trees? I was just curious what they were for.

AMBER SIERRA (off-screen)
Weird, there was never any mention of that. I'll have him look into it.

CHARLIE
Right? Anyway, thanks for checking on those things, and I can't wait for you to be here!

AMBER SIERRA (off-screen)

Thanks for noticing them. I want the place to be perfect, so let me know if you find anything else. I can't wait to be there, either! We're going to get up to no good, I promise. So there's a chance I could arrive a little sooner than anticipated, but only if you don't think it'll mess with your vibe?

Charlie grins and shakes her head.

CHARLIE

Come as soon as you can! I know your presence will jibe with my vibe!

Amber Sierra groans.

AMBER SIERRA (off-screen)

That was bad.

Charlie makes a face.

CHARLIE

Hey, I learned from the best!

AMBER SIERRA (off-screen)

That's fair, and I wouldn't have it any other way. Okay, call me mañana. Dulces sueños.

CHARLIE

I will. Sweet dreams, to you, too.

Charlie looks at the camera askance for a moment.

CHARLIE

Oh yeah! I forgot I was recording. Let's see how it looks.

30 Begin Montage - Interior/Exterior Amber Sierra's Cabin Night

A) Charlie Hale Webcam Vlog Episode #14

Charlie sits in her recliner, back in her oversized grey tee shirt and sweatpants, firelight dancing across her face. She looks longingly at her sofa bed.

Circe snuggles against her hip.

Charlie lets out a big yawn then addresses the camera.

CHARLIE
I've gotten everything from today down in writing. All of this effort is starting to look something like a screenplay.

She smirks.

CHARLIE
Now if I can get some uninterrupted sleep tonight, I'll be able to get even more accomplished tomorrow!

Her eyes grow large as she realizes something.

CHARLIE
Speaking of which, I forgot to get the GoPro set up!

B) Charlie Hale Vlog Episode #14 continued via the GoPro with the cut filter off.

The GoPro points toward the driveway with the trash can at the centre of the frame and about one third of her car at the edge of the frame.

CHARLIE (off-screen)
There. That looks about right. Here's hoping I don't catch anything except some cute woodland animals!

C) Charlie Hale Vlog Episode #14 continued via the Webcam.

She holds her laptop in her hands as she sits back down into the recliner. She giggles when she realizes Circe has curled up in the middle of her pillow on the bed. She tilts the laptop toward Circe to get a close up.

CHARLIE (off-screen)
Are you trying to tell me something?

Circe opens one eye and peers at her.

Charlie shifts the laptop back to herself while she watches her dog with loving eyes.

CHARLIE
I'll come to bed soon, my little love. But first I must express some ponderings.

She redirects her eyes to the camera. They sparkle with mischief.

CHARLIE

I was curious if you, my amazing Abnormals, have wondered about some things in my story? Obviously it's a paranormal thriller, but what might you have deduced and what questions might you have? Pause this video if you want to write them down. Then play it again when you're ready to hear mine.

She waits for a moment then continues.

CHARLIE

Welcome back. Here are my thoughts as I process the unfolding story. Why is our protagonist seen as an object to be conquered, dominated, and owned by the antagonist? Is the antagonist actually another being who's violating the protagonist in her dreams or is it only in our protagonist's mind? Is what she's dreaming really affecting her physically? Why does the bookstore owner care so much? Why is his wife so angry that he sent someone to her for help? Will her lab assistant become important to our protagonist later?

She leans in closer to her webcam with a warm smile.

CHARLIE

I hope these ponderings and many others have gone through your head as you've watched, and I hope it makes you want to know more. I wish I could hear your thoughts, right now, but alas, I'll have to wait. Now before I crash for the night, here's course coordinate number eleven. Write about things that fascinate you, that ignite your imagination, that let you learn, and that allow you to address matters that are important to you. The more invested and challenged you are, the better your writing will be. Good writers play it safe.

She pulls away from the camera, tugging at her bun and letting her wild shock of hair flow down around her shoulders. Her eyes fill with a burning confidence, and she speaks in a singsong voice laced with a British accent.

CHARLIE

"The great ones dare to believe in the unbelievable."

End Montage
Night

31 Interior/Exterior Amber Sierra's Cabin 3AM Wednesday Morning, April 20, 2022

Charlie Hale Webcam Vlog Episode #15

Charlie lies in bed looking scared with wide eyes and shallow, rapid breathing. Her dad's pistol sits on the arm of the recliner. There's no sound but the sound of her breaths and movements.

CHARLIE

Something woke me up, and I haven't been able to go back to sleep.

She shakes her head.

CHARLIE

I know this is going to sound stupid, but I don't think it's because I'm hearing things. I think it's because I don't hear anything at all. I haven't heard a cricket chirp or an owl hoot or a coyote howl. This is so much creepier.

Circe barks from under the camp quilts and scares the wits out of Charlie who chokes back a scream.

CHARLIE

Oh God, Circe, that wasn't funny!

Circe gives a low growl and starts to slither her way out.

Charlie's brows draw together as the low thrum, like a transformer full of electricity, becomes just audible, cutting through the silence. Her hair starts to become statically charged as it grows louder.

CHARLIE

That sound again! But I've been careful with what I've got plugged in. What is that?

Circe's head pops out, her ear hair afloat in the air, and she continues to growl, hackles raising.

Charlie shushes Circe and listens. A few soft, undefinable sounds muted by the thrum and accompanied by a faint glow of light and a few rhythmic flashes, disrupt the quiet over the next couple of minutes. Then the glow goes dark and a thudding noise outside makes Charlie jump. She reaches over and grabs her dad's pistol.

CHARLIE

Okay, I'm totally wrong, it's still creepier hearing things outside the cabin at night! This would make for a great story if I wasn't actually in it right now.

After a few moments, the thrumming fades away and everything goes quiet again.

Circe relaxes a bit, her hackles and floating hair laying back down.

Charlie takes a deep breath, her hair settling around her shoulders. Then her thoughts tumble out in a stream of consciousness.

CHARLIE

Come on, Charlie, get it together. You've got plenty of protection. I mean what are you going to do, go outside and go all Jack Reacher? Besides, it's just creepy raccoons playing bass kazoos while they do whatever raccoons do. Do raccoons even have lips to play the kazoo with? They can't open locked doors, can they? Maybe they were trying to get into the trash can or my car or something. Guess I'll find out in the morning, if I'm still alive then.

She closes her eyes and takes in a deep breath then lets it out over several seconds.

CHARLIE

You'll remind your bestie in the morning to talk to her realtor about the cabin's wiring and the surges it seems to be having, because that's my story and I'm sticking to it, and I hear aluminium wiring isn't super safe, and he needs to do something about it yesterday!

She rubs at her forehead, opens her eyes, then looks at Circe.

Circe looks back at her, ears sill alert, nose sniffing the air.

Charlie tries to lighten the mood and teases Circe.

CHARLIE

But besides all that, everything's fine, Circe. Go to sleep! I mean, sheesh! Why are you keeping me up?

She reaches over and cuddles Circe close who tries to comfort her with licks.

32 Interior Amber Sierra's Cabin Late Morning

Charlie Hale Webcam Vlog Episode #16

Charlie is still in bed and yawning. Her laptop sits on the extended coffee table, turned toward her. Her mussed hair half hides her face. She smiles with sleepy eyes.

CHARLIE

So last night sucked, because after the weird stuff going on outside, I finally fell asleep again and had yet another continuation of the same nightmare. Now I'm more tired than when I went to bed, but I didn't die, so that's good. I'm still spooked, too, so I'm going to watch the footage now so I can prove to myself it's just wildlife, and I can stop worrying and get to writing!

She blows her hair out of her eyes with a frown then looks pensive.

CHARLIE

I'm really tapping into something special in this magical place. I've had dreams about stories I've been writing before, but never the other way around where I'm dreaming about the story first and then writing it. Especially not four in a row! I've rarely felt so inspired! Now let's see if I can inspire Circe to get out of bed.

She pulls back the camp quilts to expose her little love, who's still snoozing next to her. She blows softly on her.

Circe's tongue lashes out at the air.

Charlie lets out a tired giggle.

33 Interior Amber Sierra's Cabin Late Morning - Moments Later

Charlie Hale Webcam Vlog Episode #16 continued

Charlie sits in her recliner and has retrieved the GoPro and downloaded the video footage.

CHARLIE

So nothing looked disturbed when I went outside, and nothing attacked me. So there's that, at least. Ugh! Nine hours to watch. I'll just fast-forward to the time I woke up, first, and if nothing shows up around then, I'll slog through the rest.

She uses the touchpad on her laptop to reach the correct timestamp.

CHARLIE

Okay, here goes.

CUT TO:

34 Exterior Amber Sierra's Cabin
3AM Wednesday Morning, April 20, 2022

Video footage plays from the GoPro in full spectrum mode with the cut filter off, giving the scene a deep lilac overlay. The trash can and a little less than half her EV car are in view. A shadow darts from off frame, where the roof would be, jumping into a tree on the edge of the frame near the trash can. The dense branches and needles of the fir tree obscure the creature's form as it climbs out of frame. Minutes later, a low thrumming begins in the distance from behind the cabin then grows louder. Suddenly the driver-side car door can be heard opening, and after a few moments, the engine turns on with a whine and the headlights illuminate the forest across the gravel road. A second later, the windshield wipers activate, followed by the window on the passenger side rolling down and back up again a few times. Then, the passenger side turn signal starts flashing and the brake lights flicker, stay on, then go out. After several flashes, the turn signal turns off, and the windshield wipers stop. Finally, the motor and headlights shut off, and the sound of the driver-side car door closing with a thud can be heard. Everything is quiet except the low thrumming, which fades after a few more seconds.

BACK TO:

35 Interior Amber Sierra's Cabin
Late Morning

Charlie Hale Webcam Vlog Episode #16 continued.

Charlie has her hand over her mouth, her eyes wide with shock.

CHARLIE

What the hell jumped from the roof into the trees?

She pauses the footage on the shadow.

CHARLIE

It's a blur. It moved too fast for the camera, which is

impressive and disturbing considering the GoPro is an action camera. It looks too big to be a kazoo playing raccoon, so it has to be a bear, right?

She stares at her laptop screen.

CHARLIE

And someone totally broke into my car and played around with it. I'll check the rest of the footage later to see if they come into frame and show their face.

She reaches for the cordless landline laying on the arm of the recliner, not caring that the camera is still recording, dials a number, then puts it on speaker phone.

AMBER SIERRA (off-screen)

I'm that irresistible, huh?

Charlie's concern cracks for a moment as she lets out a chuckle.

CHARLIE

Without a doubt!

Charlie pauses, not sure how to broach the troubling topic.

Amber Sierra sounds concerned at Charlie's silence.

AMBER SIERRA (off-screen)

Charlie, qué onda?

Charlie clears her throat.

CHARLIE

Something happened last night that has me a little shook.

AMBER SIERRA (off-screen)

How bad are we talking? Like I can leave now and be with you as soon as possible, or I can call the cops for you and then come right after.

CHARLIE

You're sweet, but no, I'm okay. I do think there's someone messing around outside your cabin at night, though.

AMBER SIERRA (off-screen)

En serio? Did you call the sheriff's office? And it's our cabin, try to get that right next time.

Charlie smiles at Amber Sierra's insistent correction, then her face tightens again with worry.

CHARLIE

Unfortunately, I am serious. I'll call after I get off the phone with you.

AMBER SIERRA (off-screen)

You should have called them first, Charlie! Hang up with me right now and call them! Then call me back.

Charlie cringes.

CHARLIE

It's not that big of a deal.

AMBER SIERRA (off-screen)

Terca! Call them now!

CHARLIE

Okay, okay!

Charlie hangs up, dials a number, and puts the speaker phone on. She looks at the webcam while it rings and makes a face.

CHARLIE

I entered all the numbers I might need into the phone's memory, but only because I could hear both my dad's and my bestie's voices lecturing me in the back of my head.

After multiple rings, the voice mail picks up.

VOICE MAIL

You have reached the Taos County Sheriff's Office, if this is an emergency, please hang up and dial 911, otherwise, please leave us a detailed message with your contact information, and we will get back to you as soon as possible.

Charlie rolls her eyes and waits for the beep.

CHARLIE

Yes, this is Charlotte Hale. Last night someone broke into my car while I was asleep. I need an officer to come check things out and take my statement, please.

She gives the cabin's address and phone number, then hangs up and redials Amber Sierra.

AMBER SIERRA (off-screen)
When will they be arriving?

Charlie takes in a deep breath.

CHARLIE
I had to leave a message.

AMBER SIERRA (off-screen)
You need to drive yourself to the sheriff's office so you're not alone and have the officer accompany you back. Call them again and tell them that's what you're going to do.

Charlie hesitates.

CHARLIE
I don't think that's necessary. What happened was hours ago, and there was no one around when I went out to get the GoPro. I'll keep calling and leaving messages until they get back to me. I'll be careful, I promise.

Amber Sierra heaves an angry sigh.

AMBER SIERRA (off-screen)
You are so infuriating, sometimes, chica! So you put the GoPro outside? Why didn't you use the security cameras your dad so prophetically provided?

Charlie looks like she's going to go crawl into a hole somewhere.

CHARLIE
You wouldn't have me any other way, right? Look, I'm already carrying around the pistol he gave me anytime I leave the cabin.

Amber Sierra lets out a choked laugh.

AMBER SIERRA (off-screen)
Ajá! Can't let him be totally right, huh? Not like he's trained his whole life to sense danger or anything. Put those damn security cameras up, Charlie.

CHARLIE

I do hate it when he's right. But yeah, I should.

AMBER SIERRA (off-screen)

You better. Now the phone line has call waiting, so you'll hear a beep when the sheriff's office calls you back. Just tell me everything.

Charlie lets out the breath she's been holding, and her words come out in a rush.

CHARLIE

My first morning here, I found the outdoor trash can picked through. But that thing latches so animals can't get in! I've been hearing noises at night that I was hoping were just from wildlife like raccoons. But last night, I put the GoPro outside with full spectrum mode on to see if I could catch anything, and obviously, I did. First, it looks like we have an adolescent bear that likes to climb on our roof. Then someone broke into my car, started it, played with all the controls, then turned it off and left. I didn't have my car totally in frame because I was focused on the trash can, so I don't think I caught anyone on video. I have like nine hours of footage to go through, so maybe whoever it was walks into frame at some point.

Amber Sierra lets out a breath of frustration, her voice rising with fear.

AMBER SIERRA (off-screen)

Híjole! Why didn't you say something about the trash can when it happened? I would've had the police there in a heartbeat, and I would have been there as fast as speed limits allowed!

CHARLIE

I was so excited and so wrapped up in my writing that I didn't think about it.

AMBER SIERRA (off-screen)

Did you check to make sure your car still works so you can get the hell out of there, if you need to? If someone was able to unlock it and start it, they either stole your key fob or they hacked it.

Charlie gasps at the possibility that hadn't occurred to her. She leans over and looks down at her backpack, which rests on the floor against the recliner.

CHARLIE

Oh hell, you're right! I'm not really awake enough yet to think things through. My keys and key fob are still attached to my backpack next to the zip ties my dad always insists on me having, and he has the spare key fob. I probably left it unlocked, to be honest. I'd rather thieves steal what they want out of my car without damaging it. All of that aside, how do you even hack an EV car and start it?

Amber Sierra's voice lowers as she goes from near panic to the kind of calm needed during urgent situations.

AMBER SIERRA (off-screen)

You know your dad has an eerie knack for knowing what you might need. I don't know why you always resist him. Anyway, I'll research hacking EV cars while you investigate further. Take the pistol with you and be careful. I'll stay on the phone so if you yell for help, I can hear you and call 911.

Charlie looks frightened, her pupils dilated and her jaw clenched.

CHARLIE

I guess it's my way of denying that the world is a much more dangerous place than I want to believe it is. Okay, I'll go check. I'll be right back.

She tells Circe to stay on the bed, then gets up and walks out the front door, 1911 service pistol in hand. A moment later, the barely audible whine of her car starting and soft rumble of the virtual engine sound system can be heard. Everything goes silent when she shuts the motor off. Then she comes back inside, looking confused, and returns to sit in front of her laptop.

CHARLIE

It's so bizarre! There's no sign of a break-in, and it started fine. I'm convinced I left it unlocked, but I'll make sure from here on out that I always lock it.

Amber Sierra sounds relieved when she hears Charlie's voice but pissed off at what she says.

AMBER SIERRA (off-screen)

I can't believe you leave your car unlocked on a regular basis! Someone could hide inside and carjack you. Your life's not worth keeping your car from getting damaged, Charlie!

Charlie's expression and tone become sheepish.

CHARLIE

I said I'd lock it from now on, okay? Now did you find out how someone can hack the onboard computer system, or what?

Amber Sierra calms down a bit after a huffed breath.

AMBER SIERRA (off-screen)

I did. And you're not going to believe what an epic fail of security it is. All you need is a fracking USB cable.

CHARLIE

To plug from the dashboard into a smartphone or tablet?

Amber Sierra scoffs.

AMBER SIERRA (off-screen)

No, just the USB cable. You pop the steering column cover, dismantle the key slot, then put the USB cable connector over the ignition tumbler and turn it. It starts the car and unlocks the steering column.

CHARLIE

That's all it takes? That's not even hacking!

AMBER SIERRA (off-screen)

I know, right? Disappointing. Did they take anything?

CHARLIE

Nothing at all.

AMBER SIERRA (off-screen)

Why didn't they just drive off in your car, then? And why would someone play with your trash?

CHARLIE

I don't know why anyone would go to all that trouble and not steal it. And the trash, it's like they were looking for something. Unless they were literally just trying to scare me.

AMBER SIERRA (off-screen)

What would they want from your trash? And why would

anyone want to scare you? You just got there. You haven't had time to make any enemies, yet.

Charlie narrows her eyes at the dig.

CHARLIE
Very funny. But you know I would never dream of taking that pleasure from you.

Amber Sierra snickers.

CHARLIE
Besides, like I said, I haven't even seen any of your neighbours let alone encountered one. But what you said actually makes me wonder.

Charlie thinks for a moment.

CHARLIE
This is an eclectic artist community. Maybe one of them takes a piece of trash from each newcomer and adds it to their art project?

Amber Sierra doesn't sound convinced.

AMBER SIERRA (off-screen)
I might buy that if it was the only incident. How do you explain your car break in?

CHARLIE
Well, maybe one of them is a creep? I won't know until I meet one of them and can ask what the community is like.

AMBER SIERRA (off-screen)
That's all we'd need, is some stalker living nearby. I should've thought of checking into that.

CHARLIE
I have no doubt you'd put the fear of God into them once you got here.

AMBER SIERRA (off-screen)
While that's definitely true, I'm not there right now, and you're just too damn linda to scare anyone.

Charlie puts her hands on her hips and scowls, failing to look any less cute.

CHARLIE

I am not! I'm fierce and fearsome!

Amber Sierra gives a faint laugh.

AMBER SIERRA (off-screen)

I mean, you are on the inside, for sure. But outside? No one would believe it. I really think--

Charlie sighs and squeezes her eyes shut like she knows Amber Sierra's going to say something she doesn't want to hear.

CHARLIE

--I'm not ready to leave yet. I've started remembering my dreams again, and I've gotten way more accomplished in two days than an entire week, and you know how stubborn I am. I've got security cameras, a pistol, and most importantly Circe, who senses things before I do. You know I can take care of myself, because my Dad taught you the same things he taught me and my big Sis. You're not the only one who can kick ass and take names.

Amber Sierra makes a growling sound in the back of her throat.

AMBER SIERRA (off-screen)

A la ve! I'd feel the same way you do if I were in your place, but if you were in mine, you'd do exactly what I'm going to do. I'll be there in about three hours. Then you can tell me all about your dreams. I've missed that.

Charlie smiles at first, then looks horrified, having to think fast.

CHARLIE

I knew you'd say that, but a little birdie was singing to me before I left the Burque.

Amber Sierra lets out a low growl.

Charlie winces but continues.

CHARLIE

She told me last week that you're supposed to leave on a very important trip this morning to New York. Something about it being to solidify the deal on your amazing project with those documentarians you have a crush on and their fantastic production company that you basically worship? You must have forgotten to mention it to me.

Amber Sierra fumes on the other end of the line.

AMBER SIERRA (off-screen)
It can wait. They'll understand that my best friend needs me. We can reschedule--

CHARLIE
--I know that this could actually help save the world, so I can't let you do that. If anything else happens, I'll evacuate and then call you.

AMBER SIERRA (off-screen)
I'm actually sitting in the parking lot at the airport. I didn't want you to hear where I was, so I didn't go inside, yet. Tell me which little birdie sang to you, again?

Charlie shakes her head and chuckles.

CHARLIE
Nice try. I didn't actually say! Gotta protect my informant! Though obviously they're a double agent.

Amber Sierra groans, her voice breathy and desperate.

AMBER SIERRA (off-screen)
Your sister, la pícara, is in a lot of trouble next time I see her! So, there's this climate change symposium my documentarian peers are attending Friday through Sunday, and they invited me to attend, thinking it would be an excellent opportunity to meet face to face. It would allow us to work together during the symposium and expedite deciding on whether we want to join forces or not and make my initiative an official project. Originally, I was going to be having virtual calls with them on their breaks to share projects and data. Then once they were back home, we were going to have a debrief about the symposium and discuss how and if we wanted to move forward. That would have taken much longer to conclude than this new plan. I didn't want to tell you in case it fell through. It's one of those things that feels too good to be true. And yes, this could be very important for the world as well as both of us and our careers, but nothing is worth risking your life for, Charlie!

Charlie's brow furrows, her eyes pained but determined. She cradles the phone almost as if she were holding her bestie. She takes in a deep breath.

CHARLIE

You're right. I don't know what I was thinking. I'll leave now and go back to la pícara's and wait for you to get back. Then we'll take a road trip together, okay?

Amber Sierra lets out a relieved breath.

AMBER SIERRA (off-screen)

Thank you for not forcing me to do something drastic. I'll be back Sunday evening, and we can go that night if you really want to.

CHARLIE

No, no. We can wait until Monday afternoon. You just concentrate on making our dreams come true.

AMBER SIERRA (off-screen)

You got it. I do have a good feeling about this. Like we'll have a reason to celebrate when I get back. Please call me once you have reception. I'll already be in the air, so leave me a message. I'll call you back when I land.

Charlie chews on her lip, nodding to herself.

CHARLIE

Yes, yes. Now stop worrying and go catch that plane! I'll talk to you soon, and I'll see you in a few days. Have a safe flight, cariño.

AMBER SIERRA (off-screen)

Yes, talk to you in a few hours! Be careful, querida!

Charlie's cheeks flush, and she smiles at the term of endearment.

CHARLIE

I promise.

AMBER SIERRA (off-screen)

Okay, Charlie, but I swear, if anything happens to you...

Charlie sounds confident.

CHARLIE

I'll be fine.

AMBER SIERRA (off-screen)
You better be. Bueno-bye.

Amber Sierra hangs up.

Charlie turns her attention to the laptop.

CHARLIE
I guess I should skim the rest of the footage.

She groans.

CHARLIE
No, that will take forever, and there's probably nothing else to see. It's time I could be spending writing down this story the universe is sharing with me.

36 Exterior Amber Sierra's Cabin Late Morning

Charlie has set up the Blackmagic camera on the cabin's deck overlooking the lake. It ripples with the light breeze, glittering like crystals in the sunlight.

Circe sniffs around, tail wagging with excitement at a new place to explore.

Charlie has her dad's pistol and the cordless phone on the round outdoor dining table nearby. A mug of coffee and the camera remote rest in the arm cup holders of the lounge chair she's sitting in. She's dressed in indigo hiking pants and her black hoodie. Her freshly washed hair hangs in a loose ponytail. She has the same pained expression on her face as she did when she last spoke with Amber Sierra.

CHARLIE
Don't hate me. I know what you're thinking. I just lied to my bestie. But it's for a noble cause, I swear! She's way too protective of me to let me stay here under these circumstances, and I'm way too stubborn to be bullied into leaving. The hell if I'm going to let either of us lose out on incredible opportunities because of some eccentric artist or stalker asshole!

She gives a resolute nod then contemplates the ramifications of her choice to lie.

CHARLIE
And yes, someday she'll find out because it's all on video, and because I can't keep anything from her for long. But she'll

forgive me. She'll understand why, and she'll forgive me. She has to.

Her raised eyebrows make her look sceptical.

CHARLIE

Anyway, the footage didn't catch anyone on video, so that isn't helpful. Also, I called the sheriff's office again right after I finished reviewing it.

She scrunches up her face.

CHARLIE

I had to leave another message. So, I'll be waiting around here for a return call while I write. Despite my teasing, Circe is an excellent guard dog. She'll let me know if anyone's around, and then she'll bite their ankles off, making them fall to the ground so she can lick them to death.

She motions to the pistol.

CHARLIE

Needing to have this around is seriously pissing off my Muse.

She rolls her shoulders to loosen the tension in her muscles.

CHARLIE

But as you know by now, I am not one to give in to intimidation, and as any actor worth their salt would say, the show must go on.

37 Begin Montage - Exterior Amber Sierra's Cabin Moments Later

The Blackmagic camera rolls during Charlie's writing session.

A) Charlie stares off into space, deep in thought, when suddenly she hears a noise. She jumps up, snatching the pistol from the table, finger off the trigger, and moves toward the cabin, out of frame.

Circe chases after her.

When Charlie returns, she's shaking her head.

CHARLIE

Poor squirrel! I scared it half to death! It was digging around in one of the planters outside the kitchen window looking for its buried treasure.

B) She holds Circe in her lap and rubs at her soft, fluffy ears.

CHARLIE

Come on girl, how about you act out a scene for me? That way I can keep watch.

Circe licks her chin.

C) She paces around while Circe is curled up in the lounge chair watching her. She walks the perimeter of the deck, looking over the railing, then she leans against it and sighs.

CHARLIE

Stop. Being. Paranoid.

She closes her eyes.

CHARLIE

And stop feeling guilty.

She puts her hands over her face.

D) She scrubs the barbecue grill grates with a bristle-free grill brush.

Circe helps by lounging in the sunlight nearby.

After several moments, she lets go of the brush with a disgusted sound in her throat.

CHARLIE

What are you afraid of? You've got the higher ground. You'll have plenty of warning if anything goes down. Now come on, you're at a triumphant moment. Let that fill you with courage.

E) She has moved into the more open area between the grill and the fire pit..

CHARLIE AS NARRATOR

Interior Helen's Bedroom / Dreamscape - Night. A familiar voice comes from seemingly nowhere.

She cups her hands around her mouth, her voice resounding with power, carrying a strong Irish brogue.

CHARLIE AS AISLING

I would do as she commands, if I were you, you monster!

She takes a few steps then crouches as if she were on top of someone.

CHARLIE AS NARRATOR

My attacker jerks upward and backward off of me as though he were a marionette obeying his master's hands. He doesn't stop moving until he is several feet away from me, and even then he remains still, his joints frozen at strange angles. Only his face twists into a fierce snarl, and he lets out a primal growl.

She acts like a puppet on strings, her voice losing its accent and becoming low and gravelly.

CHARLIE AS DREAM MONSTER

Who are you?

CHARLIE AS NARRATOR

Aisling coalesces from the darkness right behind him.

She straightens up and stands tall in an imposing stance that would make a paladin proud.

CHARLIE AS AISLING

I am aislingeoir. And if you don't know what that means, then you are a fool.

Her hand makes a dismissive motion, then she returns to the position of the antagonist and flings herself backward, falling to the deck.

CHARLIE AS NARRATOR

She flicks her hand at him, and he goes flying several feet to the side, crumpling to the ground. I can only gawk, still bound by the earth itself. Aisling's fiery-golden hair floats about her shoulders, as if a wind were stirring all around her. It blends into a long, dusky dress that flows to the ground where it trails behind her. The monster picks himself up, gingerly testing each limb to see if it still works. Aisling makes a cutting motion with her hand, this time toward me. The roots obey her silent command, withdrawing back into the ground, setting me free. Aisling floats over to me and offers her hand. I stare up at her, still too stunned to move. She presses her hand in mine. I sense the cool ring against my skin, taste rich soil on my tongue, smell the clean odour of trees and grass, and feel as though I am being held and lifted by a mountain. Aisling draws me up to my feet, but doesn't stop pulling until she wraps me in her arms. I feel like I am tucked inside the protective walls of a cavern. The monster swears under his breath, his voice now a frenzied whisper.

CHARLIE AS DREAM MONSTER

No one does this to me.

She makes fists with her hands and looks like she's ready to attack.

CHARLIE AS NARRATOR

His hands clench. His eyes burn like two suns inside his head. Though he looks like he is going to launch himself toward us, he does something strange instead. He takes one step backward, then another, till he turns and flees into the darkness.

She takes a few steps back then sprints away the length of the deck. Then she returns and spits out a single word.

CHARLIE AS AISLING

Coward.

She looks like she's going to say more, then her shoulders droop and she drops out of character.

CHARLIE

I just can't concentrate enough to finish this scene. I have butterflies in my stomach about talking to Amber Sierra. I'm waiting for a phone call that might not come today at all. And I'm waiting for more shenanigans to happen that might force me to leave. If everything remains calm this evening, I'll try to write more. Anyway, I should give Amber Sierra a call now before she lands and finds I haven't called her yet. She'll totally know I'm still here by her caller ID. She's going to be so mad at me.

She rubs at her temples then sits down in the lounge chair and picks up the phone and dials Amber Sierra's number.

CHARLIE

Hey there. Just checking in. I'm doing fine. Call me back when you land.

She hangs up then looks at Circe.

CHARLIE

Once Amber Sierra calls me back, we're going for a walk near the cabin, okay, my heart dog?

Circe recognizes the word and rolls from her side to her paws, a feat easy for one with stubby legs, and tilts her head in anticipation.

Charlie reaches over and picks her up, rubs her ears, and kisses her nose before putting her back down. Then she gets up and goes back to cleaning the barbecue grill while she waits.

F.) About ten minutes later, just as Charlie is done cleaning the grill, the phone rings.

She looks at it like it's a snake ready to strike, then picks it up.

CHARLIE

Hey.

Amber Sierra sounds confused and afraid, teetering on the edge of upset.

AMBER SIERRA (off-screen)

Why are you still at the cabin?

Charlie puts a hand up as if to ward off the coming storm and keeps her voice calm and casual even as she squeezes her eyes shut against yet another lie.

CHARLIE

Because a deputy called me back from the sheriff's office, and then he dropped by to check things out.

Amber Sierra goes quiet for a moment, then her tone rises out of the anger it was sinking into.

AMBER SIERRA (off-screen)

Qué suerte! That's a relief, but we'll discuss that in a minute. First, shortly after take-off, something terrifying occurred to me!

Charlie's eyebrows raise, and she opens her eyes. Her tortured expression slides into worry.

CHARLIE

What's that?

AMBER SIERRA (off-screen)

That shady culo for a client you dumped, he could be responsible for this!

A hint of fear flashes through Charlie's eyes.

CHARLIE

I hadn't given that much consideration.

Charlie shakes her head like she's dismissing the idea.

CHARLIE

I'm pretty sure he's got more important things to worry about.

AMBER SIERRA (off-screen)

But what if he's the petty, vindictive type? What if he thinks he told you too much?

Charlie goes quiet for a moment as she gives it some thought.

CHARLIE

I don't know. I was very careful about what questions I asked and what information I told him about myself. I mean, from the very start I made it explicitly clear that I didn't want to know anything that I'd have to report him for. Even if he is petty or vindictive, I'm sure I'd be last on his list, you know? Besides, it wouldn't be easy to know where I am now, either, right? Like, only you and my family know.

AMBER SIERRA (off-screen)

Maybe you wouldn't be first on his list but you've embarrassed him publicly, so you're probably not as far down as you think. That also makes it easier to find you, guapa.

Charlie frowns, confused for a moment, then covers her mouth when she realizes what Amber Sierra is referring to. True fear flares in her eyes.

CHARLIE

My vlog.

Amber Sierra's voice becomes stern.

AMBER SIERRA (off-screen)

Charlotte Elise Hale, pack your things and come home right now, sheriff or not!

Charlie's shocked face becomes stony with determination, her voice to match.

CHARLIE

He's a seventy-something year old man rotting in prison until he dies. He probably doesn't even know what a vlog is, Amber

Sierra Cárdenas Ibarra! I've never written so easily and so well since coming here. I'm not going to let a remote possibility scare me off!

Amber Sierra makes a strangled groaning sound.

CHARLIE

Look, the deputy assures me he hasn't seen any signs of anyone trying to get into the cabin, and he searched the surrounding area but didn't find any traceable evidence of anyone being around. We checked the footage, and no one shows up on video. He told me to call 911 if anything comes up at all, that I'll get an answer right away. He's also going to send an officer to patrol the area once a night for a few nights.

AMBER SIERRA (off-screen)

I'd feel the same way if I were you. But I can't just leave you there by yourself. If you won't let me cancel my trip, at least consider letting your dad or sister come? Or another friend?

Charlie shakes her head vigorously.

CHARLIE

My dad can't hear about this! He'd swoop in and destroy my perfect creative environment with his well-intentioned paranoia! If I ask my sister to come, he'll want to know why, and she can't lie to him. My friends? Half of them don't talk to me anymore because I let Jaime alienate them, and they won't accept my apology, and the other half are workaholics like us, so they don't have any free time.

Amber Sierra's voice goes guttural with anger.

AMBER SIERRA (off-screen)

Screw Jaime and the carnals who've abandoned you! They don't deserve someone as beautiful as you! Yeah, he may have felt neglected because you had to work so much to achieve your dreams, but you were building a secure future for you both, and you tried your best to spend quality time with him, so much so that you didn't have time for anyone else. And if he needed more time with you in order to continue being with you, he should have expressed that and given you the chance to change things instead of cheating on you! Twice! And those who haven't had time for you, and this goes for us as well, need to seriously find some work-play balance. If they can't find the time to be there for you when you need them the most, especially when you've always been there for them even at the cost of your sleep, then they don't deserve you either!

Charlie's eyebrows raise at Amber Sierra's outburst, and for a moment she's speechless. Then she tries to calm her down by teasing her.

CHARLIE

Stop holding back! Tell me how you really feel?

Amber Sierra's voice grows quieter in response, but she is not amused.

AMBER SIERRA (off-screen)

I don't like this, or how you're blowing it off, that's how I feel. But you're an adult, and I can't make you do anything you don't want to, I learned that a long time ago. Just know that I'll be worried sick about you until I'm there. At least I'm coming sooner than I first thought I could.

Charlie chews on her lip, a war of emotions on her face.

CHARLIE

You don't have to be, I promise I'm okay.

Amber Sierra lets out a sigh of defeat.

AMBER SIERRA (off-screen)

Yes, I do. You'd do the same. Por favor, ten quidado, don't go far from the cabin until I get there. Call me every few hours. And try to somehow continue your writing process despite all this mierda.

Charlie puts on a determined smile.

CHARLIE

I will. At least I have this huge sun deck, which will let me be outside while still staying safe. Thank you for understanding, Amber Sierra. It means a lot to me that you do.

AMBER SIERRA (off-screen)

Of course I do, tonta.

CHARLIE

I am silly. Guilty as charged. Now go dazzle them with your brilliance!

Amber Sierra snorts.

AMBER SIERRA (off-screen)
For you.

Charlie blushes then shakes her head.

CHARLIE
No, for us.

Amber Sierra doesn't reply, and after a long moment of uncomfortable silence, hangs up.

Charlie frowns with worry, hanging up the phone and smoothing back her tangled ponytail. She looks down at Circe.

CHARLIE
She will forgive me, right?

End Montage
Afternoon

MATCH CUT TO:

38 The Recorded Footage Displays On a Computer Monitor
Interior Small Cluttered Home Office
Thursday Evening, April 28, 2022

The Blackmagic camera zooms out from the monitor to reveal Sani's small cluttered home office.

AMBER SIERRA (off-screen)
First impressions?

Sani rubs at the bridge of his nose.

SANI
First of all, I don't think that Charlie was their initial target. I think you were.

Amber Sierra makes a mystified sound.

AMBER SIERRA (off-screen)
Why would her ex-client be targeting me?

He tilts his head, remaining silent.

She sucks air between her teeth.

AMBER SIERRA (off-screen)
Wait. You don't even suspect her ex-client at this point? What about that vato who was watching her at the coffee shop? Probably the same one in the black jeep following her?

He looks down for a moment, his hair spilling around his face. When he looks back up, he gives her a small knowing smile then tucks his hair back over his shoulders.

SANI
I suppose it's possible that all of this is his doing. His MO suggests that if he was afraid she knew too much, she would have never left the Duke City, and if he felt she had embarrassed him, she would have already been abducted.

AMBER SIERRA (off-screen)
You know his MO?

SANI
I do. Mexican cartels make a habit of disappearing people that know too much and torturing to death anyone who makes a fool out of them. That's why the person surveilling her is concerning. They could be one of her ex-client's foot soldiers sent to do either of the things I just mentioned. But if that were true according to her ex-client's MO, why didn't they make their move just after the coffee shop? Why would they try and follow her days later to a cabin in the woods?

AMBER SIERRA (off-screen)
Good question. What do you think the answer is?

He pauses a moment, frowning.

SANI
The seemingly obvious one is that they could have been sent to intimidate her into working for their boss again. But I don't think that's true. I think they were actually sent to torture and kill her.

She takes in a sharp breath.

AMBER SIERRA (off-screen)
But you said you didn't think her ex-client was responsible for the things happening to Charlie? I'm confused.

SANI

I did say that because I don't think Charlie's would be attacker made it to the cabin at this point. I think whoever went through her trash and hacked into her car also sabotaged their Jeep. Now, maybe that just slowed them down, and they'll show up later. But the fact that an opposing force interfered with her ex-client's efforts to have her followed to the cabin means they probably interfered with his efforts to have her abducted from the coffee shop.

AMBER SIERRA (off-screen)

Damn, you're off to a good start. Okay, what would make you say I was their initial target?

He regards her with sharp scrutiny.

SANI

The dreams.

She sounds like her deepest, darkest secret has been uncovered.

AMBER SIERRA (off-screen)

The dreams... wait, you mean Charlie's, or mine?

SANI

Yours, though we'll get to hers in a minute. You think this is all your fault. You think they were after you, not her. And you already have a general suspicion of who they are, even if you don't want to believe it.

AMBER SIERRA (off-screen)

A la maquina, I didn't even get to ask the question, "Who are they?" Maybe I do, but then I'd be loca, or no? What do you hypothesize so far?

He strokes at his clean-shaven chin.

SANI

The only conjecture I could make at this time is that they want to use you to reach the many, to what end I'm unsure. You have the equipment and training and connections, but are not high profile, yet.

AMBER SIERRA (off-screen)

Why does it matter that I'm not high profile?

SANI

High profile means too many eyes on your day-to-day life. They want to remain unseen for now, and that means that whoever they abduct can't be missed too much.

She goes silent.

He watches her, his face changing from detached to concerned.

SANI

I apologize if that's a sensitive topic for you. I didn't mean to insinuate that you aren't important to anyone. Quite the contrary. It's just that people go missing every day who have many loved ones. They just aren't rich or powerful or popular enough for anything to be done about it. In my opinion, having even one friend who loves you as much as Charlie does is a treasure to be cherished. Most people don't ever have the privilege of experiencing that.

She sighs.

AMBER SIERRA (off-screen)

She is a treasure, and I do cherish her. It's all good. You didn't know.

He looks at the floor for a moment then looks back up.

SANI

I should have. I usually know everything I can about my client, but I didn't have enough time, all things considered. Do you want to talk about it?

She sounds uncomfortable.

AMBER SIERRA (off-screen)

No, but thanks. So are you saying they can control dreams somehow?

His mouth twitches.

SANI

I'm not saying anything with confidence, yet. But however ridiculous it might sound, thoughts and dreams can be influenced. Mentalists have been doing it for centuries, and scientists for decades. If they've been watching you and spying on your communications, then they already knew you had a desire to build a film studio in the middle of nowhere. They just manipulated what was already there so that you'd choose where they wanted you to be.

Her voice waivers, sounding disturbed by this revelation.

AMBER SIERRA (off-screen)

I get the mentalist part. I was talking at length with people I only knew by reputation, so they may have influenced me. But how could scientists do it?

SANI

From what I understand, they use quantum sensors to interact with the electromagnetic-quantum field that your brain contains. They could have used Transcranial Low-Level Laser Therapy and Optogenetics or even technology I'm not aware of, yet.

AMBER SIERRA (off-screen)

When would they have been able to do that without me knowing?

SANI

While you were sleeping or they may have even abducted you, and you don't remember.

AMBER SIERRA (off-screen)

Neta, while I was sleeping? Abducted, but I don't remember? How is that possible?

He shifts in his chair.

SANI

Many ways. I suspect you already know some of them because you saw them do it to Charlie.

She growls under her breath.

AMBER SIERRA (off-screen)

That means they could still be manipulating me. How do I stop it?

SANI

Not by using a tin foil hat. You're talking about a Faraday cage which shields the interior from electromagnetic radiation like lasers and light. It has to enclose your entire body to be effective, though, so that's difficult to do in everyday life. The best way is to know yourself well so you can sense when a thought or dream is not your own and act accordingly.

AMBER SIERRA (off-screen)
Claro. Socrates. Simple, but profound. If they were watching me, doing these things to me, then they knew how important Charlie is to me.

SANI
Yes, and then they probably started watching her, too, to see if she was useful.

Her voice softens.

AMBER SIERRA (off-screen)
Which she is. She's a phenomenal actor and writer.

He nods, his jaw clenched.

SANI
And they probably knew that the two of you worked well together. They may not stop until they have you both.

She covers up her fear with bravado.

AMBER SIERRA (off-screen)
Vente! Let them try. So, let's say they manipulated me into buying the cabin. They stopped a dangerous criminal from hurting Charlie two times, which would suggest they're protecting her and probably me, too, because they want to use us. They expected me to be there first or at the same time as Charlie, which means they would have been doing these things to me or to us both.

SANI
And maybe that's why they're manipulating her dreams as well.

AMBER SIERRA (off-screen)
What do you mean?

SANI
By inspiring her with a story, they're giving her a good reason to stay even if she's experiencing weird things. They're helping her achieve what she came there to do.

Her tone oozes sarcasm.

AMBER SIERRA (off-screen)
How kind of them.

He raises his eyebrows at her.

SANI
Better than the alternative.

AMBER SIERRA (off-screen)
Órale. So if they want to make sure she sticks around, why would they pick through her trash and mess with her car?

He looks at the computer screen then back toward Amber Sierra, his expression contemplative.

SANI
Have you heard of psychometric testing?

AMBER SIERRA (off-screen)
Like testing your mental toughness for certain career fields?

He gives her an appreciative smile.

SANI
Yes. It's a technique for psychological measurement. As you said, it's often used for career aptitude testing, but that's not its only use. I can tell you already know that. You probably also know that through that measurement, knowledge, abilities, attitudes, and personality can be quantified. I get the feeling you've done some work involving law enforcement and security or covert agencies before?

AMBER SIERRA (off-screen)
DEA, US Special Forces, and a Mexican drug cartel made solely of ex-military members all in one documentary. It was intense.

He whistles with new-found respect.

SANI
I can only imagine. So like all of those agencies, this one is running her through their kind of psychometric testing, and they're observing and recording her every reaction. It would have been easy to explain away the trash can being tampered

with as just wild animals doing what they do. But when the trash inside has been meticulously laid out, not something wild animals typically do, it should trigger some kind of reaction. By tampering with her car but not actually being seen on video, they set the stage for the worst kind of fear.

AMBER SIERRA

Fear of the unknown.

SANI

Exactly. They could observe how she would react to having her property invaded and her safety threatened without ever revealing themselves.

AMBER SIERRA

What about the sounds on the roof and the strange thrumming?

SANI

It's impossible to tell what jumped from the roof to the trees, but logic would dictate that it was an animal such as a young bear or even a bobcat. The electrical sound could be explained by faulty wires, but if that were the case, where did it come from when she was in a raft away from all electrical wiring? How about when they tampered with her car? It's either a part of the testing, or it could be drones they're using to observe and manipulate her, or both. And I don't mean like the drone you gave her. Speaking of which, I would appreciate being allowed to see it, if you have it.

She laughs half-heartedly then speaks in a mechanical, emotionless voice.

AMBER SIERRA (off-screen)

"At the Enrichment Centre, we believe that a highly motivated test subject can carry out rather complex tasks while enduring the most intense pain, so in case you don't make it through the testing, goodbye."

He gives her a confused look.

She shakes her head.

AMBER SIERRA

Forget it. It's a reference from a hilarious and challenging video game.

He looks disquieted.

SANI
An eerily appropriate one.

AMBER SIERRA (off-screen)
Too appropriate. Anyway, I did bring the drone with me, because I thought you might want to see it. It's in my backpack. I'll get it for you in just a minute, but first, what do you think about the lack of neighbours and the bands around the trees?

SANI
Thank you, anything related to this case is valuable. It is disturbing that Charlie hasn't knowingly encountered any neighbours. But let's not forget the possible neighbour watching her from the nearby tree line. Charlie is definitely not alone.

AMBER SIERRA (off-screen)
Nothing gets by you.

SANI
It's part of the job description. Even with the evidence that Charlie has neighbours, whatever agency this is has most likely acquired all the cabins in the area so that no one but their own agents are around to discover what they're doing. As for the tree bands, I haven't seen or heard of anything like that. They may be some kind of signal boosters or relays or maybe a sensor grid around your property and surrounding area. I need to see more before I can give further analysis and conjecture.

AMBER SIERRA (off-screen)
I'm not sure how, but what you've said makes sense. Let's see what you can do with the rest after you examine the drone.

He grimaces with something unsaid, then shakes his head and holds out his hands for the drone case she hands him.

After he takes it, she zooms the camera in on the monitor.

MATCH CUT TO:

39 Begin Montage - Surrounding Forest/Lake Afternoon

A) The GoPro-carrying drone hovers a few feet away from Charlie and Circe, who sit on a log beside a hiking trail beneath the shade of a large aspen.

Charlie finishes the last few twists of her braid, tying it off, then picks up and stashes the remnants of their picnic into her bright orange backpack.

CHARLIE

I can't believe how gorgeous this area is. We've been hiking for about an hour now. I know, I know, I said I wouldn't go far from the cabin, but I kind of lost track because I was busy appreciating all this beauty! It's been very quiet, I promise, and we'll probably turn around soon. This hike is making me fully realizing how important it is to commune with nature. From this day forward, I swear to do it at least once a week no matter where I am. It really helps you to recharge and find some serenity.

B) Using the controls on her smartphone to direct the drone, Charlie shoots a scenic vista from a wild flower-peppered meadow. A cinereal, jagged, snow-capped mountain range rises like a tsunami over the vibrant forest.

CHARLIE (off-screen)

Would you look at that? Breathtaking! I'm so glad we kept hiking!

She does a slow pan back around toward the evergreen-shaded hiking trail that led them to the meadow. Behind them in the distance, a figure is watching them for a moment, then vanishes from sight.

The video footage pauses, rewinds, then plays at a quarter speed. Again, the figure who is watching them is seen briefly, but this time it is apparent that the air around them shimmers before they vanish.

The video footage zooms back out and resumes play.

She sets the drone to follow five feet to the side of them and a few feet above her head level. Then she draws in a deep breath, appreciating the floral scent of the mountain air.

CHARLIE

The wild flowers smell amazing! I think I see purple aster, geraniums, and some sort of red and golden yellow flowers. Now I know where to come when I need inspiration. I'll have to show Amber Sierra! If she ever talks to me again, that is.

Circe is busy sniffing everything she can. Her long ears fly in the breeze like little, fluffy wings.

CHARLIE

Give me a few minutes, Circe, then we'll head back home.

Circe doesn't seem concerned by this at all.

C) The drone now follows them from behind, avoiding tree branches on the sides of the trail back to the cabin. Ahead of them, a figure stands with a water bottle to their mouth, then slides it into a hip holster and starts hiking away from them.

CHARLIE

Hey! I think I see a hiker! Hopefully they're a resident here, so I can ask them some questions.

She picks up the pace, her barefoot hiking boots silent on the pine needle-mottled ground. She shouts.

CHARLIE

Hey! Wait up! Can I talk with you for a minute?

The figure stops and waits for Charlie.

Charlie speaks in a low voice over her shoulder to the camera.

CHARLIE

Don't worry. I'll keep my distance and be careful.

She approaches the figure and stops about half a dozen feet away, beneath a subalpine fir tree.

CHARLIE

Hey! Thanks for waiting. I'm, Charlie, she/her. I just need to get some water for Circe and me really quick before I ask you a couple of questions.

The person nods, their movements a little stiff, their tone a bit flat. They don't appear to be surprised or impressed by Charlie's high tech drone.

ITZEL

Hello. I'm Itzel, and I use she/her pronouns also. Please take your time, I can wait.

Charlie sticks the bite valve from the hose of her hydration bladder into her mouth and takes along draw while she reaches into her backpack for Circe's water bottle and portable bowl. She sets the bowl on the ground, fills it, then stashes the bottle back in its place.

Circe looks torn between drinking the offered water and meeting the stranger, then decides the stranger can wait and starts lapping up water.

Charlie positions herself in a ready stance, putting her far hand behind her back to rest it on the handle of her dad's pistol. Her other hand holds onto Circe's leash, which she extends in a wave.

CHARLIE

I always forget to drink water when I'm hiking, and seeing you drinking yours was the perfect reminder.

ITZEL

I'm glad I could inadvertently be of assistance. What else can I do for you?

Done drinking her water, Circe runs up and starts hopping up and down against Itzel's leg.

Itzel bends down and pets Circe with a careful, open palm.

Charlie smiles and relaxes a little, dropping her hand down away from the pistol's handle to her side.

CHARLIE

I was wondering if you could tell me about the area and the community of cabins? My friend and I just moved into one, and I haven't met a single neighbour yet!

ITZEL appears to be an athletic middle-aged woman with straight, dark-brown hair cut just above her shoulders. Her charcoal cargo pants, matching rain jacket, hunter green tee shirt, and hip pack with water bottles on each side suggest she is a hiker. She stops petting Circe, stands back up, and looks off in the distance for a moment. She smiles, but it doesn't quite reach her dark terracotta eyes.

Circe starts investigating nearby flora, satisfied that the newcomer is not a threat.

ITZEL

You're not the first new neighbour to notice that. We don't get new neighbours very often. Our community is a quiet one where we respect each other's need for space and privacy. We're composed entirely of artists who like to keep to ourselves.

Charlie's stance relaxes more.

CHARLIE

I understand, and I'm sure my friend and I will appreciate

that aspect of the community. Are there some cabins that are vacant right now? The ones to each side of mine seem to be.

Itzel's smile fades as her face becomes pensive.

ITZEL

Which cabin are you in?

CHARLIE

I'm in the tri-level post and beam timber frame between the A-frame and bi-level Scandinavian cabins on the east shore. I think that's what they're called.

Itzel nods in recognition.

ITZEL

Ah, yes, the one that appears abandoned used to belong to a lovely photographer who passed away a few years back. Apparently his family is fighting over the cabin, so no one has come to claim it yet. Your other neighbour is on vacation in the Bahamas at the moment. She'll be back in a few weeks.

Charlie squares her shoulders to the hiker, no longer wary.

CHARLIE

I'm sorry to hear about the photographer. I hope that gets all sorted out soon. And I look forward to meeting my other neighbour when she returns. Which cabin are you in?

ITZEL

I'm in a more modest single level post and beam timber frame across the lake from yours..

CHARLIE

Well it's wonderful to meet you!

ITZEL

Likewise.

Itzel nods politely and turns to continue on her way.

Charlie motions for her to wait.

CHARLIE

One last thing before you go. Do you ever have any trouble with trespassers? I had someone go through my trash and my car.

Itzel pauses, her expression remaining neutral.

ITZEL

Every now and then we do, just like any community. Usually vagrants passing through. I'm sorry to hear there's one in the area. You should contact the sheriff's office.

Charlie leans down and picks Circe's water bowl up.

CHARLIE

I did. No one answered, so I had to leave a message.

Itzel shrugs in empathy.

ITZEL

The sheriff's department here is small, under thirty officers, so that happens far too often, I'm afraid. I'm sure they'll get back to you, soon. In the meantime, as much as it pains me to say, keep your doors and windows locked, and be careful.

Charlie nods.

CHARLIE

I kind of figured, and yes, I already am. There isn't an artist who likes to collect items from other artists for their art projects, is there? Or maybe someone who likes to create found art? That might explain my trash incident.

Itzel looks up into the clouds.

ITZEL

Could be. There have been a couple of projects like that in the past, but those artists usually asked first before taking anything. If I see anyone else, I'll ask them and if they know anything about it, I'll stop by your cabin and let you know.

CHARLIE

Great! Thanks for all the info, and I hope you have a lovely day.

Itzel looks back down at her and smiles politely again.

ITZEL

You also.

Itzel continues on.

Charlie watches her go for a few moments, turns her head toward the camera with a look of puzzlement, then dumps Circe's water bowl out before returning it to her backpack.

CHARLIE (off-screen)

Well that was an interesting conversation. I guess I feel a little better about things.

End Montage
Late Afternoon

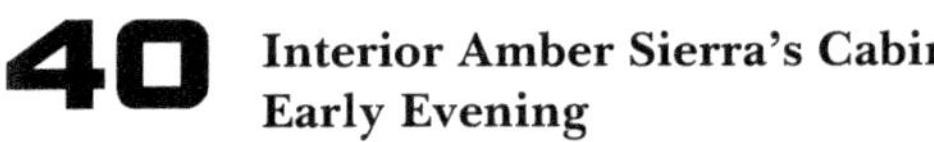

40 Interior Amber Sierra's Cabin Early Evening

Charlie Hale Webcam Vlog Episode #17

Charlie looks a little dishevelled from her hike, tufts of hair escaping her braid and smudges on her face. She sits in the recliner with her feet up and Circe passed out next to her.

CHARLIE

That hike was exactly what I needed, and I walked way faster and longer than I expected. Like even though I feel tired from lack of sleep, I have tons of energy! I had to carry poor little Circe part of the way back. Something about this mountain air, I guess! I saw a few more banded trees within the first half hour of the hike, but no more after that, so it must be a very localized thing going on. My conversation with Itzel didn't really help explain anything except the lack of neighbours, which I'm glad to know at least, but I'm frustrated with myself for forgetting to ask her if she knew anything about the tree bands. I have to admit, she did weird me out a little, but I have to keep in mind she's probably an eccentric artist. I probably weirded her out a little bit, too.

She nods with pursed lips toward the cordless phone laying nearby.

CHARLIE

No phone call back from the sheriff's office, yet, so I'll call again in the morning. I'm just trying to drum up the courage to check in with Amber Sierra.

She sighs, picks it up, stares at it for a moment, then dials. She gets Amber Sierra's voicemail.

CHARLIE

Cariño, all is well. I've had a productive day, and now I'm making dinner. No more signs of trouble. Give me a call later when you're free, if you want, but just know I may be passed out because I want to get an early start tomorrow! I'll call you in the morning if I don't hear from you tonight. Have an amazing night with your new friends!

She hangs up the phone and breathes out with relief.

CHARLIE

Now I need to do something to chill out so I can refocus and maybe write later tonight. And what better way than another night out under the stars in my raft, and this time I won't fall asleep! Although it was probably one of the most profound naps I've ever had, I don't feel safe enough to do that this time. Honestly, I shouldn't go out after dark at all till Amber Sierra gets here, but that night sky, though.

Circe stretches, looks to Charlie, then sits up and starts begging.

Charlie looks at her.

CHARLIE

I'm hungry, too. Let me catch up on my vlog, then we'll go scrounge something up.

She looks back at the camera with an intensity burning in her eyes.

CHARLIE

My deepest apologies for my negligence, my Hidden Ones. I'm just trying to make sure I'm not being stalked by a psycho, and if I am, that I'm ready for them. I'm sure you understand, so thank you. For my twelfth course coordinate, I want to talk about something that we all battle on a daily basis, fear. Fear comes in many forms and from many sources. It worms its way into our heads and our hearts, especially as writers. And that can stop us from writing at all. Whenever you're facing fear, write about it, and you'll find the act gives you courage and power over it. Then use your new-found might to write about whatever the hell you want to, and you'll most likely find it's better than you imagined it could be. "Sometimes the face we show the world needs to be one of strength, despite the chaos we harbour beneath."

41 Exterior Lake Night

Charlie holds the GoPro in full spectrum mode on her stomach by the octopus tripod it's attached to. She looks content, but she sounds sad.

CHARLIE

If my career as a professional writer and my numerous futile attempts at breaking into the film industry had allowed time for this, maybe I could have made Jaime happy.

Anger creeps across her face.

CHARLIE

Who am I kidding? Nothing I could have done would have made him happy. He just used that as a convenient way to excuse his behaviour and move on. Like my bestie keeps saying, I deserve to be with someone who loves me just as I am and wants to be with me because they adore me. I have to start believing that or I'll just keep ending up with Jaimes instead of the one I deserve.

She sighs then a wistful look brushes her anger aside.

CHARLIE

I can only imagine how beautiful making love on the water beneath the stars would be. I guess I could still get to experience that someday.

She clears her throat and changes the subject.

CHARLIE

I'm going to have to be sure I come out here early Friday morning to see the peak of the Lyrids meteor shower. I'll keep my fingers crossed that Amber Sierra's flights are on time and that she can make it here for Sunday night. Maybe we can watch it together then since it will still be near the peak.

She sighs with a smile.

CHARLIE

I swear after the time I've spent here, my life will never be the same.

She flips the cut filter back on then points the camera skyward. Countless celestial bodies glitter in a cosmic light show. A bright, golden haze cuts a swath through the spectacle, diffusing into an indigo glow that flows into a cobalt bloom. She watches for several moments before murmuring.

CHARLIE (off-screen)
I've never seen so many stars before coming here. I always wondered why they named our galaxy the Milky Way when all I'd ever seen was a wispy cloud barely visible against the light pollution. Now that I'm beneath dark skies, I understand. It's a mesmerizing manifestation, and the more time you take to appreciate it, the more vibrant it becomes, revealing its true stellar palette. What you see starts matching what the camera captures. It reminds you of just how little you are in the scheme of things, which is comforting, because it means the Universe has endless secrets to share if you just pay attention.

42 Exterior Lake
Half An Hour Later

Charlie has wrapped the octopus tripod around one of the raft handles and aimed the GoPro back toward her. She looks extra geeky with the headlamp on her forehead.

CHARLIE
I'm going to finish that scene I left hanging. Since it's all dark and spooky out here, it's perfect for Helen's current emotional state. I'd be worried about the neighbours thinking I'm crazy, but I don't have any, so...

She closes her eyes, centring herself, then opens them and begins her writing session.

CHARLIE AS NARRATOR
Interior Helen's Bedroom / Helen's & Aisling's Dreamscape - Night.
I tremble against Aisling as she stroked my hair. Several minutes pass before she finally speaks.

CHARLIE AS AISLING
Are you alright?

CHARLIE AS NARRATOR
I answer in a ragged voice.

CHARLIE AS HELEN
I think so.

CHARLIE AS NARRATOR

Aisling slowly releases me.

CHARLIE AS AISLING

Good.

CHARLIE AS HELEN

Where did you...? How are you...? Why...?

CHARLIE AS NARRATOR

I fail at finishing a single sentence, so instead, I give Aisling a sidelong glance. The imposing woman holds out her hand in response.

CHARLIE AS AISLING

Now is not the time for questions and answers. You are desperate for undisturbed sleep. I can feel your exhaustion, and that won't do at all. Come.

CHARLIE AS NARRATOR

If I hadn't just survived a vicious attack, I might have felt like fighting for answers. Instead I relent, taking Aisling's hand.

CHARLIE AS HELEN

I've hardly slept for weeks, why would I be able to sleep now?

CHARLIE AS NARRATOR

Aisling speaks with a coldness in her voice belied by the concern in her eyes.

CHARLIE AS AISLING

Even if he does come skulking about, I'll be here to send him scurrying away tail tucked between his legs.

CHARLIE AS HELEN

But I'm too afraid to sleep.

CHARLIE AS NARRATOR

A whimper escapes my lips despite her reassurance. I feel thankful for her hand in mine even though she is a stranger I've just met.

CHARLIE AS AISLING

I won't let anyone or anything hurt you tonight.

CHARLIE AS NARRATOR

Aisling squeezes my hand. Then in an instant, we travel from my devastated dreamscape to one that emanates safety and comfort. I can't describe what it looked like, because before I could see it, Aisling wraps me up again in her protective embrace, placing a kiss on the top of my head.

CHARLIE AS AISLING

Close your eyes now, and sleep. We'll talk on the morrow.

CHARLIE AS NARRATOR

I start to say something, but feel a heaviness settle through me. I fight to keep my eyes open, but they flutter shut, and what I want to say escapes me. The night's terror fades into a peaceful bliss, and I sleep deep and long.

She draws in a slow breath then lets it out over several seconds.

CHARLIE

I hope I get to sleep like that tonight. But first, more stargazing.

43 Exterior/Interior Amber Sierra's Cabin 1AM Thursday Morning, April 21, 2022

Charlie carries the GoPro by the octopus tripod, still set in full spectrum mode. She walks up to her car and examines it, using her headlamp to look inside.

CHARLIE (off-screen)

All locked up. They'd have to be a superspy to get in now without smashing a window.

She walks to the cabin door and examines it for any signs of tampering.

CHARLIE (off-screen)

Looks undisturbed.

She flips the GoPro's cut filter back on and laughs.

CHARLIE (off-screen)

I don't want to scare myself again with Circe's glowing demon eyes.

She opens the door, turns on the lights, and turns her headlamp off.

CHARLIE (off-screen)

I'm back, my little love.

She closes and locks the door behind her then walks through the kitchen and dining areas into the great hall, shrugging out of her backpack and lowering it to the floor. As the recliners and sofa bed come into view, they are devoid of any balls of fur curled up on them.

CHARLIE (off-screen)

Circe?

None of the suspicious lumps beneath the camp quilts move in response.

Whispers of panic rise in her voice.

CHARLIE (off-screen)

Circe, where are you, girl?

She sets the GoPro down on the coffee table, and begins a systematic search around the cabin.

CHARLIE

Circe, come! Circe! Come here, girl!

Several panicked minutes go by as Charlie checks everywhere on the ground level, then runs up the stairs to the loft and back down into the basement, before dropping to her knees in the middle of the kitchen and crying.

CHARLIE

She's not here.

She takes a moment to get a hold of herself then explodes into action, springing to her feet, grabbing her backpack and drone case, putting her headlamp back on, and picking the GoPro up from the coffee table. She connects it to her smartphone and flips the cut filter off as she mutters to herself.

CHARLIE (off-screen)

Thank God this has infrared and ultraviolet capabilities. I'm going to find you, you little escape artist! It has to be that, because otherwise, God help anyone who took you from me!

She slings her backpack over her shoulders, which still has water and snacks in it from her hike. She digs the drone out of its case and switches the GoPro from the octopus tripod to the drone. Drone in hand, she rushes outside, closing and locking the door behind her. Immediately, she sets the drone down on the walkway and launches it into the air, manually controlling it as she uses it to scan the area.

CHARLIE

Circe! Circe, come! Where are you?

She calls out and whistles for her beloved furry friend a few more times, listening in between for any response. When she doesn't hear or see anything, she starts heading around the cabin.

CHARLIE

I'll look down by the lake first, do a few rotations spiralling out around the cabin, and then retrace our hike.

44 Begin Montage - Exterior Lake/Surrounding Forest Predawn Hours

Charlie spends the next several hours looking for Circe without any heed to her own safety.

A) Her shouts and whistles echo across the placid lake as she scours the rocky beach and then around the cabin and surrounding area using the drone. When the eerie sound of the first coyote howl starts followed by the yips of his partner, she decides it's time to widen her search. Soon other nearby coyotes join in the primal chorus. The worry in her voice is heartbreaking.

CHARLIE

I can't let the coyotes get her!

B) She races down the beginning of the forest trail in a full-blown panic, crying out for her little lost love. The drone catches glimpses of banded trees here and there. Then the dim light of her smartphone blinds her just enough for her to run into a low hanging pine branch. It strikes her across the top of her forehead, and she goes down to her knees. She brings the drone around in front of her to examine the bleeding gash on her forehead just above her headlamp. Rivulets of blood run over the band, down her face, and into her eyes. She presses her sleeved forearm against it for a few moments, and when she draws it away to check, it's already stopped bleeding. She wipes up the rest of the blood, then climbs back to her feet, sets the drone to follow her from above and behind again, and continues her frantic search.

C) She bursts into the meadow, panting with effort and emotion. She has to catch her breath before calling out and whistling for Circe several times. When she doesn't hear a response, she sends the drone up higher for an aerial view, starting at the outer rim of the meadow and flying in concentric circles until she reaches the middle. She watches for eyeshine and sends the drone in for a closer look anytime she spots some. After spooking a few rabbits, a fox, and a pair of coyotes, she starts jogging across the still field of wild grass and flowers.

D) The drone spots eyeshine on the trail up ahead. She calls for Circe multiple times as she approaches it, but before she can reach it, it disappears. Once she reaches where she saw it, she pauses and sends the drone up above her for another bird's eye view. The drone watches her from above as she sinks to the ground and breaks down crying for a few moments before finally managing to send the drone out for another search. It soars up above the forest giants, and almost collides with a spotted owl, which clacks its beak at the sudden danger. After settling from the near miss, the drone shows the thick weave of branches blocking most of the ground view. She lets out a frustrated roar before bringing the drone closer to the forest floor. She looks like a gamer navigating a sci-fi battle as she zips the drone through the maze of branches and trunks.

E) An outcropping of boulders looms over her as she searches beneath them tearing through brush and bushes, the drone hovering just behind her, capturing it all. After failing to uncover anything but a few scared deer mice, she collapses and rests for a few moments before getting back up and continuing on her desperate quest.

F) She rounds a bend in the hiking trail, drone trailing behind her, and sees a strange violet glow on the horizon filtering through the trees. Fast-moving water chatters nearby. Her voice sounds hoarse.

CHARLIE

What in the Nether is that?

She guides the drone back to her and flips the cut filter on. The glow disappears. She flips the cut filter off, and it reappears. She moans.

CHARLIE

I don't have time for a mysterious light on the horizon that I can't see without a special camera!

She goes quiet for a minute, her panicked breathing louder than the water. Then she murmurs.

CHARLIE

But maybe that's where Circe went because she sensed a disturbance? Dogs are able to sense stuff we can't, right?

She sends the drone five feet over her head and behind her, sets it to follow her, and then starts sprinting for the strange radiance. Roots and rocks clutch at her feet, but she evades them with little effort. She darts through the forest like a wolf on the hunt before realizing that she's about to run headlong into a rushing stream. Unable to stop in time, she decides to launch herself from the bank as far as she can, perhaps in the hopes that she will make it past the deepest part and not get swept away. From the drone's perspective, it looks to be at least thirty feet across if not more. She sails through the air for an impossible amount of time, then lands with both feet well on the other side of the riverbank where she pauses in disbelief.

CHARLIE

How did I--

She looks back and forth from one bank to the other.

CHARLIE

--it just looks further than it is. Focus, Charlie. There's only one thing that matters right now.

She continues on her hunt, vaulting over fallen trees and thick brush. As she draws closer, calling out to Circe over and over, the light flares up on the screen then vanishes. She freezes, waiting for something more, but everything remains dark and quiet.

CHARLIE

Where did it go?

She pans the drone around, calling out to Circe a few more times in a trembling, pleading voice.

CHARLIE

Circe, come here! Where are you? Please come back to me! Circe!

When she doesn't find any eyeshine or movement, she sets the drone to follow behind and above her again. She searches the area for dead wood to mark the spot she's in and the direction of where the violet light was emanating from. As she's doing this, an orb of white light streaks through the trees in the distance with a low, barely audible thrum. She pauses and listens, spinning around to try and echolocate it to no avail. She gives up with an exasperated breath of air and proceeds to lay a giant arrow out on the ground. In a voice ragged with fear and sorrow, she explains.

CHARLIE

In case I get the chance to come back here and investigate with my little love, once I find her. I don't think I can do any more searching tonight and still make it back to the cabin. I have to sleep a little before I can do more.

She chokes back tears and starts heading back toward the cabin by following the stream, looking for an easier way to cross. A fallen pine tree a few hundred feet away spans the stream, and she crosses it as easy as a squirrel could then hops to shore. Before moving on, she slips her pocket knife out and opens it. She bends down next to the log and carves a shape into the rough bark, a cone made of rising horizontal slashes, its base an upslanted triangle. Satisfied, she continues on her way. As she retraces her steps, now and then, she bends down to stack rocks in a cairn to mark her passing until she gets back to the trail she came from.

G) She sounds numb as she turns her head and speaks to the drone that has been faithfully following her.

CHARLIE

I'm so tired I can hardly take another step. I'm shocked I haven't passed out by now. I might even have a concussion and need stitches.

Dried blood, scrapes, dirt, and tears streak her face. She looks like a warrior who's survived a fierce battle.

CHARLIE

I got lost for a little while, but I'm pretty sure I know where I am, now.

She gets choked up.

CHARLIE

I just need to know where Circe is. I haven't heard or seen anything that would indicate where she could have gone. The only thing I can do now is hope she's found her way back to the cabin. Oh God, I can't think about her being out here all alone. I just don't understand how she got out. I can't believe this is happening! There are so many animals out here that could eat her like those coyotes or even mountain lions! I'm not giving up until I find her, I just need a little sleep before I continue.

She lets out a shuddering sob.

CHARLIE

Please let her be safe, please!

End Montage
Just Before Dawn

45 Interior Amber Sierra's Cabin Morning Twilight

Charlie Hale Webcam Vlog Episode #18

Charlie lays in bed alone with her laptop on her lap. She is a mess. Her eyes are bloodshot and swollen from crying. Angry welts and scrapes mar her beautiful face.

CHARLIE

I called the sheriff's office and left another message, one that is much more insistent. I may have thrown in a curse word or two. Apparently break-ins aren't important. We'll see if a dognapping catches their attention. Probably even lower on their priority list.

She moans and clenches her fists.

CHARLIE

If I had known any of this would happen, I would have never come here. I've searched everywhere in the cabin, and there is no way she could have gotten out. Unless someone took her, it's impossible that she's gone!

She holds back tears.

CHARLIE

But she's gone.

She rubs at her eyes and smoothes back her tangled hair, taking in a deep shuddering breath. When she speaks, her voice has an edge to it.

CHARLIE

Someone's been messing around with me since I got here, and I'll never forgive myself if it's my asshole ex-client. And, I'll never forgive myself for not taking Amber Sierra's advice.

She takes a few more deep breaths in, trying to calm down, but more anger roils up from inside her.

CHARLIE

Whoever it is, they must know how much Circe means to me. If I find them...

Her body shakes with fatigue and emotion. She draws in several deep breaths and closes her tired eyes for a few moments. Then she opens them again and speaks in a faint voice.

CHARLIE

I'd call Amber Sierra, but I'm not going to ruin this life-changing opportunity she has. Besides, she's not going to be able to do anything for me tonight that I haven't already done, except for maybe hold me.

Sobs wrack her body, and she swipes at her tears with her bloody sleeve, then attempts to get a hold of herself again.

CHARLIE

I'll call her after the sun is up and see what she thinks I should do, maybe drive to go see the sheriff's office in person after I do another search, or maybe I need to go there first. I wouldn't survive losing Circe. I'm not leaving here without her!

She pats the empty space next to her and shakes her head. Tears creep from her eyes again.

CHARLIE

I'm so sorry, Circe. I should have never left you alone. I'll never leave you alone again.

46 Interior Amber Sierra's Cabin Just After Sunrise

Charlie Hale Webcam Vlog Episode #19

Charlie lies in bed, camp quilts mostly unsnapped and flung off of her, still in the clothes she wore the night before. Her puffy eyes stare off into space, clean streaks beneath them from the tears that cut through the dirt and crusted blood. She sounds heartsick when she speaks.

CHARLIE

I was hoping it was all just another nightmare, and when I woke up, everything would be okay. Instead, I had another dream continuing my story, only this time it wasn't bad, it was sweet and comforting. I'm thankful for that, because I'm not sure I could have handled anything else, when I'm waking up without my little love. I'll try to remember it in case I ever write again. Until I find Circe, I'm not going to be able to write another word.

Her forehead furrows, as though she hears or senses something, then she shakes her head in dismissal.

CHARLIE

I can feel her laying near my feet like she does when she gets too hot under the covers.

Her pupils dilate with surprise.

CHARLIE

Did I just feel movement?

She scoffs at herself.

CHARLIE

It's just your imagination refusing to accept the truth.

She starts to tear up, then frowns and props herself up on one elbow, her braid, now looking more like a frayed rope, falls over her shoulder.

CHARLIE

There it is again!

She holds her breath and peers over the top of her laptop. The moment she can see past it, she lets it out in almost a scream.

CHARLIE

Circe!

She flips the laptop around and sets it on the arm of the sofa so she can sit up and lean forward toward her heart dog.

Circe lays against Charlie's feet, staring at her with a serene expression.

She pats the bed next to her, her hand shaking.

CHARLIE

Come here, my little love! Where have you been?

Circe gives Charlie an unconcerned look, but doesn't move.

Charlie rubs at her eyes and turns her head to the camera.

CHARLIE

Am I hallucinating? She's really there, right?

She looks back at Circe and pats the bed again.

CHARLIE

Circe, come.

Circe doesn't move a muscle.

Charlie sounds almost hurt.

CHARLIE

I know you can be stubborn when you don't want to come, but aren't you happy to see me, Circe? Why are you acting strange? Normally you'd have smothered me by now.

Realization lights her darkened eyes, then fear flashes through them like a lightning strike. She reaches back behind her and grabs her pistol from under her pillow.

Circe watches her without reacting.

Charlie gets out of bed, chambers a round, and systematically moves about the cabin with her pistol in the low ready position, finger off the trigger. Sometimes she's off-screen and can only be heard. After clearing every room on every level, she returns to Circe who has followed her movements with her eyes.

She kneels down in front of Circe, placing the pistol on the bed, and checks her out, running her fingers over her fur from head to toe.

CHARLIE

I thought maybe your dognapper brought you back, but there's no one here. Maybe they just left you? But why? And how did they get in? Or maybe you escaped them and came back? But how would you have gotten in? Are you all right, my little love? What's wrong? Did they drug you?

Circe remains still except for her rhythmic breathing, watching without reaction.

She snuggles Circe to her, kissing her head and face. Circe doesn't respond at first, but after a few moments, she snaps out of her torpid state and starts licking Charlie's face.

Charlie lets out a ragged laugh, burying her face in Circe's fur.

CHARLIE

Maybe you've been here all along? If so, why didn't you come when I called you?

Circe starts hugging Charlie with her whole body and licking her as fast as her long tongue will allow.

Charlie curls up on the bed with Circe in her arms, crying tears of relief. Then after she settles down, she ponders out loud.

CHARLIE

What would scare you so much that you'd hide without a sound and not come to me for comfort? Or did you somehow get out because you missed me, and then you got lost, but then finally found your way back home again? If so, how did you get back in? Why didn't I hear you? I just don't understand.

She hugs Circe tight against her.

CHARLIE

All that matters now is that you're here and safe with me, and that sometimes nightmares can have happy endings.

She reaches over to close her laptop when there is a loud knock on the door. She almost jumps out of her skin.

Circe doesn't give warning barks, but instead, wags her tail as if with anticipation.

CHARLIE

You've got to be joking! Stay here, Circe.

She deposits Circe down into the plush camp quilts, then picks up the pistol in one hand, the laptop in the other, and heads for the door. She places the laptop on the entrance way table facing the door, minimizes the vlog window but doesn't stop it from recording, and opens up her writing. She peeks outside the window then mutters to herself.

CHARLIE

It's about damn time.

She tucks the pistol in her waistband holster behind her back, pulling her black hoodie down over it, then opens the door.

DEP. SHERIFF GABALDON

Charlie Hale? I'm Deputy Sheriff Gabaldon. I'm responding to the messages you left.

Charlie struggles to keep her voice civil.

CHARLIE

That's me. Thank you for coming, finally, Officer Gabaldon. Please come in. What are your preferred pronouns? Mine are she/her.

She steps aside and motions to one of the high-back chairs sitting around the broad dining room table.

DEP. SHERIFF GABALDON

Thank you. I'm good with he/him.

DEPUTY SHERIFF GABALDON, a fine-boned, fit man stares at her for a moment then steps through the doorway and walks toward the dining area. His sheriff's uniform, dark olive drab pants and a desert brown button down shirt, looks rumpled and dusty, as though he hasn't been off duty in a few days. His well-worn, tan cowboy boots clack against the sandstone tiles.

She picks up her laptop and follows after him, casually setting her laptop down at just the right angle to capture them both.

He removes his matching cowboy hat, exposing his medium length, wavy black hair, and places it on the table next to him. He sits down, then motions to her face with his hand. His vocal cadence sounds a little stiff.

DEP. SHERIFF GABALDON

Are you injured? Do you need medical attention?

She frowns, confused for a moment as she drops into the chair across from him, then realizes he's talking about the dried blood on her face.

CHARLIE

I think it's just a bad scrape and a few welts. I hit my head on a branch last night. I was too tired to shower when I got back, and I just woke up a few minutes before you arrived.

He nods, scanning her face with his keen, dark eyes.

DEP. SHERIFF GABALDON

Sorry to take so long to get back to you, and that it's so early, but I didn't want to make you wait any longer. I was on an investigation at another small community nearby for a rather serious matter. I'm relieved to see you're safe and found your dog.

Circe peaks over the back of the sofa at them.

Charlie leans against the table like a deflating balloon.

CHARLIE

Me, too. You have no idea. Anyway, thank you for explaining, and please forgive my last impassioned voice message, but having someone go through my trash, break into my car, make commotions at night, and either spook my dog so bad she hides for almost twelve hours or steals her and then decides to return her, is rather terrifying when you're alone in the woods.

Deputy Sheriff Gabaldon takes out his department issued notebook and pen.

DEP. SHERIFF GABALDON

Of course, Ms. Hale. Again, my apologies. First I'd like to take a statement from you and get all the details. Then I'll take a look around.

She nods.

CHARLIE

Sure, no problem. Also, I'd like your opinion on whether you think it's safe for me to remain here for the duration of my vacation or if I should leave.

He starts writing notes.

DEP. SHERIFF GABALDON

Of course, Ms. Hale. I'll do my best to give you an informed opinion. Now start from the beginning.

47 Interior Amber Sierra's Cabin A Few Minutes Later

Charlie Hale Webcam Vlog Episode #19 continued

Charlie holds the laptop in one hand and watches the sheriff through the window as he examines the area around her car. Then when he heads for the door, she scurries over to sit down after putting the laptop in the same spot. She waits for him to come inside and join her.

CHARLIE

So, what's the verdict?

Deputy Sheriff Gabaldon looks relaxed for someone investigating a crime.

DEP. SHERIFF GABALDON

I haven't found any evidence of anyone trying to break in to your cabin, which is a very good thing, ma'am. As for your car, there's no damage, so I think you're right. You must have left it unlocked, which meant they didn't have to actually break into that either.

CHARLIE

But why wouldn't they at least steal something from it if not the car itself? I mean why turn it on and play with the lights and windows as if you're making sure everything works if you're not going to steal it?

DEP. SHERIFF GABALDON

Did you have anything of value inside?

CHARLIE

No, not really. I brought everything inside.

DEP. SHERIFF GABALDON

So why would they bother once they realized that? As for stealing your car, maybe they contemplated it then decided it wasn't worth going to jail over. Maybe they just wanted to see if they could do it. Maybe they were tempted by how much they might be able to sell it for, but then realized they wouldn't be able to find a viable buyer. Sometimes people do things for the thrill, and they don't think things through.

Her shoulders hunch up and her hands clench.

CHARLIE

But what if someone is just trying to scare me? I mean, what they did with my trash was pretty sus! And what if they're just getting started?

He folds his hands together.

DEP. SHERIFF GABALDON

Unfortunately I have no surveillance footage of the person in question nor any physical evidence to try and track them down with. I dusted for fingerprints and will run what I have through the database. Hopefully I'll get a hit on someone other than you. I've already searched the area and didn't see anyone, and the only fresh tracks I saw belong to you and your cute little dog.

She reaches up to massage her scalp in an effort to calm herself.

CHARLIE

What about the noises keeping me awake at night on my roof and in the area around my cabin? What do you think that shadow was that jumped into the trees?

He gives her a patronizing smile.

DEP. SHERIFF GABALDON

Raccoons are very intelligent, curious, and determined creatures and are probably responsible for the disturbances. I agree with you that the shadow you saw was either a juvenile bear or a bobcat. You'll need to get used to wildlife noises if you're going to live in the wild. It might take a little while, but you will, I promise.

She scowls, hovering between being indignant and embarrassed.

CHARLIE

So there's nothing you can do?

DEP. SHERIFF GABALDON

I've done everything I can at the moment, but, I'll see to it that there's a patrol once a night around the lake just to have a presence. Hopefully that will deter any more trouble. Personally, I don't think you're in any danger.

She sinks into her chair like the balloon she's been imitating.

CHARLIE

Thank you for that, at least.

He nods, takes his cowboy hat in hand, then stands to leave.

CHARLIE

Wait, before you go.

He waits, his face neutral.

CHARLIE

Do you have any idea what that glow was on the northern horizon last night?

He gives her a quizzical look with the tilt of his head.

DEP. SHERIFF GABALDON

How did you manage to see that? I only saw it because my dashcam switches to IR when it gets dark.

CHARLIE

I was out looking for my dog all night. I took my drone with my full spectrum GoPro camera attached to help me see and look for eyeshine.

His face returns to a neutral expression.

DEP. SHERIFF GABALDON

That was a smart idea, though you shouldn't have been walking alone in the woods at night. There are mountain lions bigger than you out there. Anyway, was your drone able to spot the source?

She sits back up, indignance rising to the surface along with a little fear.

CHARLIE

I wouldn't have had to if someone wasn't playing games with me! Before I could get anywhere close, it had vanished. How about you?

He clears his throat.

DEP. SHERIFF GABALDON

Same for me. It was probably a phenomena called ball lightning that we do see around here from time to time. With the high occurrence of iron in the surrounding rock and geothermic activity in the region, we sometimes get electromagnetic anomalies even when there are no storms around. That said, there's supposed to be thunderstorms early this evening.

She starts calming down as she listens to his scientific-sounding explanation.

CHARLIE

So you've seen something like that before?

DEP. SHERIFF GABALDON

Several times, actually. I never have been able to prove what it is, but when I've seen more than just a glow, it appears as a ball of plasma.

CHARLIE

That's true, ball lightning is plasma. But if it was that, shouldn't

I have been able to see it without my full spectrum camera?

DEP. SHERIFF GABALDON

Oh yeah, the ball lightning itself is, but we were only seeing the infrared heat it was giving off.

She scrunches her nose, not quite sure she buys the explanation.

CHARLIE

I guess that makes sense.

DEP. SHERIFF GABALDON

Now, if you're satisfied with my investigation and conclusions, I'll be going. I have a lot of work to do today.

CHARLIE

For now, I suppose. Thank you again for coming, sir.

He nods and puts his cowboy hat on.

DEP. SHERIFF GABALDON

If at any time you feel unsafe again, I would suggest that you call 911 and then just leave and not come back unless you're with companions.

She gives him a Vulcan salute.

CHARLIE

Yes, sir.

Deputy Sheriff Gabaldon watches her for a moment, like he's trying to figure out the gesture, then turns and leaves the way he came in.

Charlie gets up and heads off-screen to close the door behind him, then returns and looks at the camera after the door closes.

CHARLIE

Why do I feel like he's not being totally honest with me?

Her exhausted demeanour brightens up a bit as she lets the feeling go.

CHARLIE

At least I feel somewhat vindicated for what I told my bestie. Talk about a self-fulfilling prophecy! I mean, I really had the feeling that's the way things were going to go once an officer actually came and took a look around.

Her small smile fades as she realizes something, then stands up and heads toward the coffee table in the great hall. She picks up the landline phone, which has a little red light blinking on it.

CHARLIE

Frell! I didn't realize Amber Sierra called and left a message last night! I told her I might be sleeping, so I hope she didn't worry.

She walks back toward the camera and sits down again. She cringes as she puts the speaker phone on and starts the message.

Amber Sierra's voice resounds with rare excitement.

AMBER SIERRA

Hola, Charlie. Sorry, I was in the pitch meeting with the production company, and from their reaction, I rolled a frakking natural twenty on my persuasion check. And chula, they're larger than life! I'd never met either of them before and only seen them in pictures or on video, you know? Jorunn Ulberg, the producer, is a tall, Norwegian woman with punk hair that's all sick, gorgeous Urnes style tattoo sleeves, and eyes like two blue stars! Usian Mugendi, the director, is an even taller Kenyan man with an impeccable fashion sense, an eternal smile, and these russet eyes that gleam with an inner fire. I felt so insignificant next to them, but despite their intimidating stature, I really like them both, and not just because I'm a fangirl. They're pragmatic and down to earth but also visionaries and dreamers. It's a charming balance that's the reason they're so good. I'm really starting to think this could work out, and I can't believe it, because they are way out of my league! Bueno, I've babbled long enough. Thanks for leaving me a message so I know you're okay. Now I won't worry, as much. I hope you sleep well. Call me when you wake up. I may not be able to answer, but I'll call you back as soon as I can. Adiós.

Charlie lets out a relieved breath in a whoosh of air that vibrates her lips.

CHARLIE

I was so worried I had screwed things up for her. This is the best news ever! It'll fuel my day for sure, and I'm going to need it! I've never felt so exhausted both physically and emotionally in my life! I know I need to call Amber Sierra right away, but I need some coffee first or I'm going to fall asleep on the phone.

48 Interior Amber Sierra's Cabin A Few More Minutes Later

With steaming coffee in hand, Charlie dials Amber Sierra's number and puts the phone on speaker.

AMBER SIERRA (off-screen)
The night owl has become an early bird. It's, what, seven thirty in the morning there? I'm impressed!

Charlie chuckles, making a face at the camera, then using her honed acting skills to sound sincere.

CHARLIE
That's what happens when I get a good night's sleep!

AMBER SIERRA (off-screen)
I'm so glad. You deserve many more of those.

Charlie fidgets with her coffee mug.

CHARLIE
You know, I got to talk with a deputy sheriff this morning. He was checking up on me. Everything's been quiet, and he agrees that though I should be careful, I'm relatively safe here.

Charlie holds up one finger.

CHARLIE
Now before you protest, hear me out. I think you should attend all the meetings you planned to. Even then, you'll be here in just over forty-eight hours.

Amber Sierra is quiet for several moments then groans.

AMBER SIERRA (off-screen)
Oh chica, I don't know.

Charlie wipes at her face with one hand, using the webcam as a mirror.

CHARLIE
I'm fine. I promise. This is literally your moment! Carpe diem!

Amber Sierra lets out a frustrated breath.

AMBER SIERRA (off-screen)
Our moment. Híjole, Charlie! I was all settled about this and now--

Charlie's lips curve into a tired smile.

CHARLIE
--you go and seal the deal, and then we'll celebrate the start of an amazing chapter in our lives once you get here!

AMBER SIERRA (off-screen)
Yeah, it's looking that way.

CHARLIE
Go on, go dazzle them some more!

AMBER SIERRA (off-screen)
Are you sure?

Charlie lets out a deep breath, a smile in her voice.

CHARLIE
I've never been more sure about anything.

Amber Sierra growls then relents.

AMBER SIERRA (off-screen)
Okay. Call me this afternoon?

CHARLIE
Without fail.

AMBER SIERRA (off-screen)
Charlie?

CHARLIE
Yes?

AMBER SIERRA (off-screen)
I...

Amber Sierra hesitates for a moment.

AMBER SIERRA (off-screen)
I can't wait to be there with you.

Charlie looks down at the floor, somehow looking both guilty and pleased at the same time. One of her hands goes to her ear, and she brushes one of the icosahedron earrings with her fingers.

CHARLIE

Me, too.

MATCH CUT TO:

49 The Recorded Footage Displays On A Computer Monitor Interior Small Cluttered Home Office Thursday Evening, April 28, 2022

The Blackmagic camera zooms out from the monitor to reveal Sani's small cluttered home office.

AMBER SIERRA (off-screen)

Before I ask any questions about what you've just seen, tell me what you think about the drone now that you've examined it.

Sani's eyebrows raise, like he's impressed.

SANI

It's quite the feat of reverse engineering, and quite a generous gift. Did they say where they got it from?

AMBER SIERRA (off-screen)

Yes. A private foundation called Design by Ethics. The same one that funds my peers' production company and now my initiative in collaboration with them. I suspect they gave it to me to impress and entice me, making it clear they were really interested in a potential partnership. Drones changed the documentary and independent filmmaking game, so we covet any advancement that might give us an edge. But you're saying that Design by Ethics didn't create it?

SANI

The technology you possess is only theoretical in the scientific community at large. That means that Design by Ethics is either the best kept secret in the world, rivalling highly restricted facilities such as Area 51, Area 52, the Trinity Test Site, and the Utah Test and Training Range, or--

AMBER SIERRA (off-screen)

--they stole it from one of those places? So they're just a bunch of pirates.

He quirks his mouth to one side.

SANI

They stole it from someone, or someone gave it to them, or they're not who they say they are.

AMBER SIERRA (off-screen)

Hui, that would explain why the person watching Charlie pulled a Predator and vanished into thin air.

He chuckles, though his gaze is grim.

SANI

An insightful observation. Now the question is, did Design by Ethics provide that tech to said Predator impersonator or a different agency? Who does Charlie's ex-client have connections with?

She makes an appreciative sound.

AMBER SIERRA (off-screen)

You know how to ask all the right questions. Unfortunately, I haven't had time to research her ex-client. But now that I have the documentary done and in your hands, that should become a priority. I really need to know those answers.

SANI

It's a necessary skill, one I'm confident you possess as well, given your profession. I promise that we'll search for these answers together. Now, I've seen unclassified footage of that type of cloaking more than once, and it's always been caught by accident.

AMBER SIERRA (off-screen)

It wouldn't be very effective cloaking, otherwise. You say, unclassified. Have you seen classified instances?

SANI

I have, and they don't measure up to this level of technology.

AMBER SIERRA (off-screen)

So despite Design by Ethics' penchant for piracy and possibly espionage, they at least have the ability to improve on stolen technology, eh? That's good to know. In all the cases you've seen, what's the science behind the cloaking effect?

SANI

There are many hypotheses. One is the natural ability of an organism to mimic their surroundings like chameleons, cuttlefish, or octopi and squid. Another is that inherent weaknesses in our sensory system are exploited. The rest are technologically based like bending light with metamaterials, optical camouflage, or electromagnetic manipulation. The US's national laboratories have prototypes of some, but none that work this flawlessly and with no visible equipment. What we need to know in this instance is, does this work with all wavelengths of light or just in the visible light spectrum? Can it be seen by technology that detects other wavelengths on the electromagnetic spectrum? For instance, LIDAR has been known to identify figures or shapes that weren't caught on film.

AMBER SIERRA (off-screen)

So we might be able to see through the cloaking you're describing with something like a full spectrum camera, right?

SANI

Possibly, depending on the technology or biological function being used. Near and far infrared as well as ultraviolet digital cameras can detect things that unmodified digital cameras can't. For example, the Milky Way appears brilliant and has hints of colour when seen through a normal digital camera and vibrantly colourful when seen through a full spectrum digital camera, where the human eye only sees a faint cloud of grey and white. I must say I was surprised at what Charlie claimed she was able to see the second time she went stargazing.

An uncomfortable silence settles over the room.

AMBER SIERRA (off-screen)

Let's skip the doublespeak. Give it to me straight.

He draws in a deep breath, regarding Amber Sierra for a long moment, then lets it out.

SANI

I know you've been hoping this entire time that I've been speaking only about human agencies, but you know--

AMBER SIERRA (off-screen)

--you're not. And that sounds completely loquísimo.

He sweeps his hair back over his shoulders, squares them, then challenges her with his eyes. His once gentle tone, like the rumbling of distant thunder, becomes taut and sharp.

SANI

I'm not crazy.

The camera jiggles as she comes around it into view. She moves to one side of him, leans over, and searches his eyes.

AMBER SIERRA

Yo sé. That's why I'm here.

He watches her for a moment then slowly relaxes, dropping his gaze to the Nahui Ollin pendant that's escaped from her shirt and dangles from her neck.

SANI

What does that mean to you?

As if by reflex, her hand reaches up, clasps the pendant in her fingers, and tucks it back inside her shirt.

AMBER SIERRA

A reminder for me to keep my life in balance.

He lifts his head and locks his gaze on hers.

She meets it but isn't able to hold it for very long. She lets out a breath of air with a sardonic smile on her lips as she looks away.

AMBER SIERRA

It was a gift from my parents for my quinceañera. It symbolizes the day I stood up to them and chose to never hide who I am again.

He nods, his gaze never wavering, his voice returning to its good-natured tone.

SANI

We can't take our rightful place in the cycle of existence if we aren't true to ourselves. So it also symbolizes your courage. The same courage that it takes for me to speak out about this subject matter, and for you to have stepped foot in my office.

She nods, her brow furrowing as she struggles with emotion.

AMBER SIERRA

Gracias, Sani.

She retreats back behind the camera.

AMBER SIERRA (off-screen)

Is there anything else can you tell me about the footage?

SANI

Several more things. Whatever agency they are, they have ramped up their testing, and Charlie's acing it. She hasn't been scared off, adapts to changing situations, and doesn't give up easily. What their end goal is, yet, we don't know. The vanishing person Charlie caught on film is an example that supports the hypothesis that many species in existence are using cloaking abilities or that some agencies have much more advanced technology than the public knows. It lines up with footage I've analyzed and authenticated in the past where the cloaked figure was the size of a child and another one where it was two feet taller than the average man.

AMBER SIERRA (off-screen)

So like Homo habilis and what, Sasquatch?

He flashes her a wry smile.

SANI

Nice try. Homo- habilis died out over a million years ago. And believe it or not, there are hypotheses that Sasquatch can cloak themselves similarly, which would explain how they're so elusive. However, both of those examples are terrestrial, and you know I'm referring to extraterrestrial species.

AMBER SIERRA (off-screen)

I plead the fifth, your honour. So, what are the implications?

He chuckles then dry rubs his hands together and thinks a moment.

SANI

From most likely to least likely: That nature has already perfected this technology we think we've invented, when really we just borrowed the idea, like so many things. That we did invent it or we reverse engineered it from a non-human source, and it's being used by or tested on humans and other terrestrial species. That it's extraterrestrial and could either be a naturally occurring ability or a technology we don't yet understand. And of course, it could be a combination of any of these.

She makes a noise of affirmation.

He runs his fingers through his hair, working to untangle the ends as he hesitates to say more.

AMBER SIERRA (off-screen)
What are you holding back?

His face darkens.

SANI
I think you know.

She draws air through her teeth.

AMBER SIERRA (off-screen)
That jump she made, a la--

SANI
--could have probably broken a world record.

AMBER SIERRA (off-screen)
How is she suddenly a superhuman athlete?

SANI
I have some ideas, but I'll keep them to myself until I see more.

She gives an irritated huff.

He puts his hands up in apology.

SANI
Sorry to make you wait, but I have to be sure before I say anything. Now, the neighbour and deputy sheriff were definitely acting strange. I mean, Itzel didn't even react to the incredible technology hovering in front of her when Charlie first encountered her, and the deputy sheriff had just the right answers to settle Charlie down. This makes me believe they are probably agents of whatever agency this is. Either humans under their control or appearing human. The information they gave sounded rehearsed. It was tactically executed to reassure her that she was safe and to maintain the appearance of her being free to leave any time

she wished, even though she was most definitely not.

AMBER SIERRA (off-screen)
Agreed, that's the feeling I get, too. They gave her a false sense of security and freedom, which is all her obstinance needed. And the glow?

His lips give a fleeting smirk but then scrunch up in scepticism.

SANI
Ball lightning is a good cover up. It's obvious to me they didn't mean for her to be aware of it at all. They didn't predict that she would think of a way to see beyond visible light. Your friend is smart, and like them, I'm impressed she thought to use the camera and drone that way.

AMBER SIERRA (off-screen)
Yeah, she is. Too much for her own good sometimes. Okay, so are you saying that if they had predicted she would use the GoPro and drone and their capabilities, they wouldn't have let her go that way or they would have stopped doing whatever it was that they were doing?

SANI
I don't think they would have done anything different. I just think they would have been more prepared to respond to her query about it instead of being caught off-guard and giving a perhaps less than convincing reason.

AMBER SIERRA (off-screen)
Because they're gauging her reactions to different stimuli, right? Okay, if it wasn't ball lightning, what do you think it was?

SANI
It could've been several things. I'm not ready to conjecture, yet. The only thing that's clear is whatever they were doing, it was in a spectrum of light that human eyes can't see, because they didn't want to be seen by casual observers. It indicates they don't believe they're under actual surveillance.

AMBER SIERRA (off-screen)
So they must feel confident that no one knows about what they're doing in the area. That's disturbing. How about what happened to Circe?

He stares at the floor for a few moments while he thinks.

SANI

More testing. They needed to measure the strength of her loyalty to someone she loves but also her response to fear and stress at extreme levels. And for Charlie, losing a family member is certainly the highest stressor on that list. They've done something to her dog so they can exert some amount of control over her, perhaps so she won't alert your friend to their presence anymore.

She sounds sad.

AMBER SIERRA (off-screen)

I think it's a permanent change. She still isn't acting totally normal, and she's so lost without Charlie.

His face matches how she sounds.

SANI

I'm glad she has you to be with her through this. When you're able, maybe adopt a companion for her?

AMBER SIERRA (off-screen)

I feel the same about her. Your suggestion is thoughtful. I was thinking the same thing and already asked Mr. Hale if he could look into that. It would be a good distraction for us all.

She draws in a shuddering breath and goes quiet.

He looks like he wants to get up and give her a hug, but instead turns back to the screen.

SANI

You never told her, did you?

She lets out a soft gasp.

AMBER SIERRA (off-screen)

Excuse me?

He doesn't take his eyes off the screen.

SANI

You never told Charlie how you felt.

She doesn't reply.

He turns back to look at her.

SANI

I'm sorry, I shouldn't have asked. It's none of my business.

Irritation overcomes her sadness.

AMBER SIERRA (off-screen)

You're right on both counts, but I suppose you can't help yourself. It's your job to be perceptive.

He nods with an apologetic expression on his face.

SANI

It is. Thank you for understanding, and for forgiving me when I have to ask hard questions. Here comes another one. I know your production company's name and what it means, but what's theirs? It could hold valuable clues and help me determine whether or not--

AMBER SIERRA (off-screen)

--Do you think my documentarian partners know the nature of the foundation they're dealing with?

SANI

That's the million-dollar question. They may be as unaware as you were. Then again, they may be fully aware. The answer to this question will determine if we should involve them in our search for Charlie or not.

AMBER SIERRA (off-screen)

No stone left unturned. It's Drøm Kweli. The first word means dream in Norwegian, and the second means true from Swahili.

He watches her, waiting for the significance to dawn on her.

It takes only a moment.

AMBER SIERRA (off-screen)

Mierda! How did I not already put that together after all the discussion we've had about it? The power of dreams!

He nods.

SANI

When dreams aren't just dreams.

AMBER SIERRA (off-screen)

It's almost like you're prescient.

He cocks his head at her.

SANI

What makes you say that?

AMBER SIERRA (off-screen)

You'll see.

She zooms the camera back in on the computer monitor.

MATCH CUT TO:

50 Interior Amber Sierra's Cabin Morning

Charlie has the Blackmagic camera set back up in its original place inside. She's taken a shower, her wet hair soaks through her jade Henley shirt as she sits in her recliner in her well-loved black jeans. Dark smudges beneath her eyes confess her lack of sleep.

Circe is curled up in her lap, the best way to keep an eye on her heart human.

Charlie points to her forehead where there is only a pink line across it.

CHARLIE

Can you see that?

She leans in a little closer to the camera.

CHARLIE

Yeah, me neither. I was pretty sure I gashed my head on that branch last night, and yet, all I have is a pink scratch. If it barely broke my skin, where did all the blood come from?

She pulls away from the camera and rubs at her forehead while she thinks.

CHARLIE

Maybe my forehead only got hit with the twigs of the branch, and maybe the branch itself hit lower and gave me a bloody nose? It had to be that, because I don't have any other wounds, and my black hoodie is covered in dry blood.

She frowns into the camera, eyes squinted.

CHARLIE

Maybe I'm just losing my mind. Whatever the case, I'll be damned if anyone's going to scare me away from chasing my dreams! I can make it two more days until Amber Sierra is finally here. I have my heart dog back now, and that's all that matters. She'll give me the strength and inspiration to keep working.

She scoops Circe up in her arms and showers her in kisses.

51 Begin Montage - Interior Amber Sierra's Cabin Morning

The Blackmagic camera rolls during Charlie's writing session.

A) She scrambles to write down notes about her most recent dream, looking frustrated. Her hand keeps going to her forehead and rubbing it. She also keeps reaching over to make sure Circe is still there.

CHARLIE

All of this itching is distracting me!

B) She paces back and forth, muttering to herself, her still damp hair plastered to her tired, but always pretty face.

Circe watches from her perch on the bed.

C) She stands in front of the fireplace, like a bard ready to perform.

CHARLIE AS NARRATOR

Interior Helen's Bedroom / Aisling's Dreamscape - Night. Aisling and I stand next to each other beneath a starlit sky surrounded by a quiet forest grove. Peace drifts around us like a gentle autumn breeze. The air smells crisp and clean as if a thunderstorm had just passed through, yet the dry ground denies such a conjecture. Large oaks loom like guardians around delicate and feathery trees. I've never seen any as vibrant as them before, some heavy with dark red berries, others with white blossoms that at first glance look like fallen snow. I feel Aisling beside me, so I turn to ask what they are. Before I can speak, Aisling murmurs, "Rowan and Hawthorn." I wish at that moment that I was a wolf spider with many eyes so I could see everything all at once. Though I recognize some of the other trees scattered about, I can't possibly mistake the tree that graces the centre of the meadow. The venerable willow's branches stretch down to kiss the heather and clover that forms a half-circle around it. Some of its lower branches dip into the stream that cuts a swath through the centre of the valley. I can't shake the impression that despite the sheer beauty around it, it hangs heavy with sorrow. I find myself speaking it out loud.

CHARLIE AS HELEN

It looks so sad.

As her voice trails off, she shakes her head.

CHARLIE AS AISLING

The weeping willow and its kin are oft misunderstood. They aren't mourning. They are simply the only trees selfless enough to reach toward the earthbound plants and share with them the mysteries of the sky.

She wipes at her face with her fingers. They come away wet.

CHARLIE AS NARRATOR

I feel stray tears slip down my face and realize that I'm the one who's sad.

CHARLIE AS HELEN

That changes everything.

CHARLIE AS NARRATOR

Aisling replies in a soft voice, continuing to stare across the meadow.

CHARLIE AS AISLING

Finding a different perspective usually does.

She gazes into the distance for a few moments then looks all around her.

CHARLIE AS NARRATOR

I turn slowly around to take in more of the majesty that surrounds me.

CHARLIE AS HELEN

This isn't my dream, is it?

CHARLIE AS AISLING

No, it's mine, where we're safe. We will spend many nights

here practicing before we ever venture back into yours. He's waiting for his moment, and when he can't find you, he'll panic and search all the harder. The next time we enter your dreams, it will be the final battle of wills. You're not yet ready for that.

CHARLIE AS NARRATOR
Aisling speaks like she's only commenting on the varieties of flowers in the field or the species of fish in the stream. Her calm is like a slap in the face of my fear.

Her eyes grow wide, her breathing quickening.

CHARLIE AS HELEN
But you'll be there, won't you?

After a few seconds, her face relaxes and looks pensive for a moment before tensing into a mask of barely restrained anger.

CHARLIE AS NARRATOR
My question gives Aisling pause, her cold demeanour melting like snow beneath the hot sun's rays. Her thundercloud eyes blaze with a suppressed fury. She looks down at her ring and spins it furiously.

CHARLIE AS AISLING
Of course I will. And I'll never let him hurt you or anyone again. The trick is for you to disappear, making him desperate to find you. Then when he does, to make him think it's only because I felt enough time had passed that you were safe to return to your own dreamscape. Finally, he needs to believe that he has you alone, which means for a short time, he must.

CHARLIE AS NARRATOR
It's amazing to me how quickly I can go from serene to panicked. Before I can even express my terror, Aisling draws me into her protective embrace, and I find myself safe inside the mountain's cave again, shielded from the raging storm.

CHARLIE AS HELEN
I can't be alone with him again!

CHARLIE AS AISLING
With what I teach you, you will be able to withstand him for the time necessary. Then, when he's drunk with the thought

of impending victory, I'll steal into your dreamscape and strike. We can't give him the chance to prepare. We must take him by surprise. This is imperative because he is quite powerful.

CHARLIE AS NARRATOR

Aisling releases me from the embrace and looks down into my eyes.

CHARLIE AS AISLING

I know how brave you've been, but I need you to be brave a little while longer so we can end this.

She breaks character with a sardonic laugh.

CHARLIE

Yeah, just be brave a little longer, Charlie.

D) She gets up and stares out the windows, looking for anything out of the ordinary.

Circe watches with intent eyes.

E) She sits in the recliner with her head in her hands.

Circe snuggles her and nudges at one of her hands with her muzzle.

Charlie smiles down at her then massages her ears.

F) Charlie sits up against the sofa back with her legs sprawled out on the bed, fighting her drooping eyes and urge to sleep instead of write.

Circe snoozes next to her on a pillow, soft puppy snores floating around the room.

Charlie looks at her and shakes her head with a goofy grin. Finally she stretches her arms up and out, which triggers a huge yawn. She shakes her body from head to toe in an effort to revive herself.

Circe gives her the side eye for disturbing her, then falls right back to sleep.

CHARLIE AS NARRATOR

Interior Helen's Bedroom / Aisling's Dreamscape - Early Evening. After a night of mostly feeling safe, my only fear tonight is failure, of letting Aisling down. Her fingers spin her bronze ring in circles, suggesting I'm not the only one concerned about that.

CHARLIE AS AISLING

Last night was merely an introduction allowing you to adjust to being in someone else's dream. Tonight we will begin actual instruction.

CHARLIE AS NARRATOR

Suddenly I hear a familiar voice from nowhere.

She kneels in the centre of the bed.

CHARLIE AS DOMINGO

Mind if I join you?

CHARLIE AS HELEN

Domingo? I didn't know you could do this, too!

She flops down into bed then rolls over to one side, looking sheepish, trying to sink down into the soft camp quilts.

CHARLIE AS NARRATOR

I squeak as he materializes beside me, and I fling myself into his arms. My enthusiasm catches us both off guard, and he loses his balance, taking us both to the soft, clover-blanketed ground. As he holds me close, laughing his quiet laugh, I suddenly feel very foolish. What did Aisling tell him? And what will she think? I spin out of his arms and look at her, trying to hide my embarrassment. Aisling smirks at us, her grey-blue eyes dancing with amusement.

CHARLIE AS AISLING

Quite the charmer, isn't he? Don't worry, I have a hard time not touching him, too, the scoundrel.

CHARLIE AS NARRATOR

My face burns, and I wonder if I'm lighting up the dark meadow around me. I don't know what to say, so I don't say anything at all. Domingo pretends he doesn't know what's going on, then without warning, springs to his feet and tackles Aisling down next to me. He growls playfully.

CHARLIE AS DOMINGO

I'll teach you to embarrass our guest!

She looks shocked with mouth open and eyes wide.

CHARLIE AS NARRATOR

Aisling shrieks as Domingo tickles her without mercy. I watch in disbelief as the two of them tussle beneath the moonlight. I can't believe what I'm seeing. This is not the reserved, guarded person I met in the office. This is her gregarious, bold twin. As I marvel at the transformation, she gains the upper hand and straddles Domingo's waist with her legs, a few clovers dangling from her hair. She purrs.

AISLING

Who will teach who what, hmm?

She looks like she's going to do more dialogue, then sighs and tangles her fingers in her hair.

CHARLIE

A whimsical, magical teaching moment is about to occur here, but my head isn't with them, it's still out there with that glow on the horizon. Even now the thought of it leaves me rattled, but I've always loved a good mystery. What writer doesn't? Besides, I have a burning curiosity that won't let me concentrate. I'm not sure I can write more until I retrace my steps and investigate. I'm hoping whatever I find might inspire ideas for future stories, so in a way, I'm still writing! But I have to leave soon, because there's supposed to be thunderstorms in the afternoon, and I don't want to get caught out in one of those, especially not with all the iron in the ground around here.

She massages her scalp, mussing up her still damp hair. She divides it into three bunches and begins braiding it.

CHARLIE

I can hear all of you telling me not to go, but something strange is going on, and I'm not going to sit around and be a victim. Besides, fortune favours the bold! I'll be very careful, I promise. I'll have my dad's pistol and Circe. We'll be fine. And yes, I'll bring you along.

End Montage
Early Afternoon

52 Begin Montage - Surrounding Forest/Lake Early Afternoon

A) The GoPro-laden drone follows behind Charlie and Circe as they avoid scattered boulders and cobbles and walk on the soft moss carpet of the streambank. She has retraced the harrowing journey she took the previous night, following the rock cairns she placed along the way until they led her to the stream. A steady rustling of tree boughs whispers around them in a quiet promise.

Circe trots along, her nose sniffing everything in her path, her ears flopping in time with the rhythm of her steps.

CHARLIE

I haven't found anything unusual so far. We haven't seen anyone around, so our hike has been peaceful, except for the occasional flashback I have and the ominous, dark clouds building on the horizon. I'm going to have to keep an eye on them, they look like they're moving fast. Anyway, we found the stream, and if I'm being honest, everything has me pretty shaken.

The GoPro's wide angle shows the broad width of the rushing stream.

CHARLIE

Even at the narrowest point we've seen so far, I don't know how I jumped across it! It isn't possible! Maybe it wasn't this wide last night, and the rain that's fallen in the mountains made it swell. That's another thing I need to be careful about, flash flooding. It's incredibly dangerous.

B) Circe pulls on her leash, trying to run to the fallen pine which spans the frothing stream.

Charlie reins her in, picks her up, and secures her into her dog hammock, attached to the backpack straps.

Circe wriggles in protest.

Charlie calms her down by talking sweetly to her and rubbing her ears.

CHARLIE

Oh no, girl, I don't think so! Remember the last time you tried to run across a narrow bridge? It was over the acequia where we walk, you got distracted by something to the side of you and you ran right off the edge. Thank goodness I always have you in a harness, or you would have taken a swim! At least that bridge was flat. This one is round, so I have my doubts you could traverse it without getting distracted again and falling in. And then you could get swept away out of your harness. I already lost you once, that's never happening again!

She manoeuvres the drone lower and closer to the felled, large ponderosa pine. Her symbol mars the bark, looking like an ominous warning travelers of old might have found in a haunted forest.

CHARLIE

P7J-989's point of origin symbol. A sci-fi planet and its people whose history gives me hope for us. I'm such a geek.

She positions the drone between branches on the other side of the stream to wait for them, then she steps up on the tree and takes in a deep breath.

CHARLIE

I crossed this in the dark, I can cross this now even with a wiggle worm attached to me.

She takes a few slow steps, then as she feels more secure, walks like a balance beam gymnast to the other side. Once across, she unstraps Circe and sets her back on the ground.

Circe scurries around, leaving no stone unsniffed.

Charlie starts following the stream again.

C) Charlie aims the drone at the rock cairn she had built beside the stream the night before.

CHARLIE

Almost there.

From the stream marker, they head away, their steps cushioned by the pine-needled forest floor. They follow the subsequent cairns she left as guides, the footage fast-forwarding between each one. The sky progressively darkens until she finally finds the large arrow she constructed from fallen branches. She crouches in front of it and scans the area with the drone. It shows the thinning of the forest trees and the blotching of the pine needle carpet, uncovering the gorgeous red sandstone beneath. In the distance she can see a break in the forest, perhaps into another meadow.

CHARLIE

This was as far as I got before the strange light faded. Now the sunlight is fading on me. How ironic. Like something just doesn't want me to uncover the truth.

She brings the drone in closer to her face and talks to it, her eyes looking to locate every sound she hears.

CHARLIE

I have to admit I'm pretty nervous. I have no idea what I'm expecting to find, if anything, and now I have to race a storm. I really wish Amber Sierra was here with me and Circe. She would find this as exhilarating as we do.

She gets up and starts heading in the direction the arrow points. The drone keeps its close distance, showing her intense expression, eyebrows squeezed together and eyes narrowed as she takes in every detail.

D.) She steps from the pine canopy onto a red sandstone pediment populated with sparse patches of arid tolerant plants like wild grass, wild flowers, and sagebrush. Using her smartphone, she commands her drone to follow her from a ten-foot distance at her two o'clock, a few feet above her head. She sets it to make a rotation around her every couple of minutes. Thunder rumbles an advancing threat in the distance.

Circe stops in her tracks at the sound and barks at the sky.

CHARLIE

It's okay, Circe. Leave it. It's just the clouds grumbling.

Circe barks one last time, then quiets down at Charlie's behest.

Charlie takes a few more steps, then pauses in place. Her eyes widen as she stares unblinking ahead of her. A few moments later the drone takes its slow revolution and spots a ring of small boulders in the distance.

CHARLIE

I've seen so many piles of rocks in the area, mountains do that, toss rocks down their slopes, but these look purposefully placed. Like someone built it for some reason.

Circe watches Charlie, confused about her reaction when she was just told there was nothing to worry about.

Charlie calls her over and picks her up, securing her in her doggie hammock, much to her dismay.

CHARLIE

Just in case we need to run fast over terrain your little legs can't handle, my little love.

End Montage
Afternoon

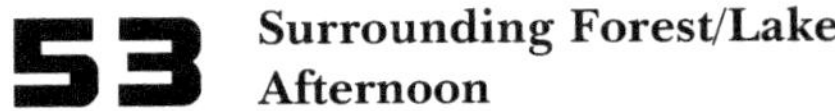

53 Surrounding Forest/Lake
Afternoon

The gloomy and irate sky casts a blue-grey hue across the landscape like a filter over a lens. Charlie walks with cautious steps toward the ring of boulders, which are now about one hundred feet away, their careful placement becoming more obvious the closer she gets. She stops about fifty feet away in wonder when she sees one flatter boulder spanning two of the taller boulders. Her breathing catches for a moment.

CHARLIE

It's like a mini Stonehenge.

She starts walking again, her steps slow and careful. About ten feet away, the drone's sweep shows that the boulders camouflage a massive hole in the ground. She mutters to herself.

CHARLIE

Is that a sinkhole or a cenote? Wait, I think those occur in limestone, don't they? It would be odd for one to be here.

She creeps toward the largest gap between the boulders then stops just short of entering the ring completely. A perfect, circular hole in barren ground greets her. She lowers herself to her knees to investigate closer.

CHARLIE

I'd guess this is ten to fifteen feet across. It looks like it was made by something with high-heat because the edges are melted and there's nothing growing near it. Almost like it was made from the inside out. It's too dark to really tell or see how far down it goes, but by the sound of the echo, it's a long way. Time for the drone to do its thing.

She manoeuvres the drone to hover in front of her then fidgets with the GoPro's cut filter, sliding it off. Then she sends it over the edge in a deliberate descent. It confirms her suspicions as it passes through the soil, subsoil, substratum, and bedrock layers. After a couple of minutes, she brings the drone back up, slides the cut filter back on, and sends it back to its previous marching orders.

CHARLIE

I didn't go any deeper because I just realized I don't know how far the signal between my smartphone and the drone can go, and I'll never see it again if it drops down there. But there's another way to calculate that.

Thunder reverberates through the air, masking faint crunching sounds that she doesn't hear.

Circe starts to growl under her breath.

CHARLIE

It's okay, girl, it's still far enough away that we're still safe, probably.

She reaches back and unzips the bottom pocket of her safety orange backpack, pulling out a matching rain coat. She whips it over her shoulder and backpack and slides her arms inside. Then she bends down and grabs a fist-sized rock from nearby and holds it over the edge. She lets it go and times it on her smartphone. Eight seconds pass before she hears a soft cracking sound. She looks at the drone, astonished. Behind her, angry storm clouds roil and flash with lightning.

Circe wriggles, unhappy with being restrained.

CHARLIE

Eight seconds? That's a long way down. Our gravitational acceleration on earth is about thirty-two feet per second squared. And in order to use that to find distance we have to take the seconds and square them, which makes that sixty-four. Then we multiply that times thirty-two.

She calculates the number in her head, oblivious to how fast the storm is closing in on them.

More faint crunching sounds ride the peals of thunder.

Circe growls louder and struggles more.

CHARLIE

That's two-thousand forty-eight. Then we have to divide that by two. It's about a thousand-foot drop! Wow, how did I calculate that in my head? What's wrong, girl?

A figure slips into view from behind the closest boulder, the stranger from the coffee shop who had been following her in the Jeep Gladiator. They look numb, but resolved, as they brace themself against the boulders on each side of them. Then they raise a leg in the air, poised to kick. Their voice sounds rough as they thrust kick at Charlie's back, triggering Circe to release a hail of stranger danger barks.

STRANGER

Time to pray on your way down.

The drone starts its timed revolution around, capturing the violent scene.

Charlie's face freezes in terror at the sound of a voice behind her, but her body reacts, spinning her around just in time to catch their foot against her shoulder and hold on to it for dear life.

Her mercurial reflexes surprise the stranger who clutches at the boulders to keep them all from toppling into the hole.

The moment she rights herself, she shoves their foot backward with all her might, then lunges forward and past them as they fall on their back. Clear of the stranger's reach, she pivots around while drawing her dad's pistol from its waistband holster in a smooth motion and grasping it with an expert two-fisted grip. She points it at them with steady hands, elbows tucked into her ribcage, pistol sights at eye level.

Circe's eyes peer around the pistol, her head between Charlie's arms.

CHARLIE

Don't move, or I'll give you an extra hole in your head. I might anyway if you hurt my dog.

She keeps her eyes on the stranger while releasing her supporting hand to check Circe over for injury.

Circe has been startled enough to stop barking and only growls low in her throat.

CHARLIE

Are you okay, my little love? You're not whimpering, so I think so.

The stranger watches her with a predator's gaze even from their compromised position, flat on their back with their arms in the air, their black and white plaid flannel shirt shuddering in the rising wind.

She grits her teeth, her pistol trained on them.

CHARLIE

You spineless coward! You're going to prison for a long time! Attempted murder, caught on camera?

The stranger starts hissing curse words in Spanish at her followed by a chilling threat.

STRANGER

He won't stop until you're dead, pendeja!

She sounds mystified.

CHARLIE

Why in the world do I matter that much to him?

They sit up and scoff at her by spitting off to their side.

STRANGER

Are you really that tonta? El Capo is going to be in jail until he dies. Sure, he still runs things from there, but his life story, captured in a book, and maybe even a movie someday, is his true legacy.

They shake their head.

STRANGER

Eres tan estúpida.

Her voice quavers.

CHARLIE

He can just get a new editor, one who doesn't care about morality! Why go to all this trouble to go after me?

They stare at her like she's lost her mind.

STRANGER

Don't you understand anything about honouring your word? You entered a contract with him and you broke it. El Capo always keeps his word, and he expects those who work for him to do the same. You're the coward!

She chokes out a disgusted laugh as the drone settles back into its two o'clock position.

CHARLIE

Enough bullshit, I don't want to hear any more. He doesn't

know the meaning of honour. Now roll over on your stomach and put your hands behind your back. If you do anything else, I'll kill you. If you don't think I know how to use this, look more closely.

The stranger scowls at her between strands of their tousled hair, regarding her hands and their placement on the pistol, how her arms are close to her body so they can't take it away from her. With a grunt, they grudgingly comply.

Once their position satisfies her, she uses her free hand to unhook two of the largest zip ties from the carabiner on her backpack shoulder strap.

CHARLIE

Thanks again, Dad. Right as always. Turns out zip ties are essential hiking gear after all.

She kneels and places the pistol on the ground next to her. Then she loops the zip ties, one through the other, her hands shaking with adrenaline, making the task harder than it should be. Once she's done, she tosses them down onto one of their hands.

CHARLIE

Put one hand in each loop. Then don't move anymore.

They curse under their breath again, but does as she commands.

She picks up her pistol, stands, and moves closer to them. Rust-coloured dust smears the knees of her jeans.

CHARLIE

If you move at all, you're dead. Do you understand? My special forces dad not only taught me how to shoot accurately, but also to triple tap. Two to the chest, one to the head. So don't think your chances of getting away unharmed are good. Understand?

STRANGER

Comprendo.

She puts one of her knees in the middle of their lower back and extends the other one straight out for balance.

They grunt but don't move.

She keeps her pistol close to her body with one hand as she tightens each zip tie around their wrists. Then she shoves away from them, back to her feet and ready to act.

CHARLIE

What's your name?

They refuse to answer.

CHARLIE

You're going to make me dig for your wallet so you have a chance to knock me down?

They finally respond, their voice mocking.

STRANGER

I don't carry ID when I'm on a vuelta. My name used to be Celio Cuate, but now it's just Sicario.

CHARLIE

I'm not calling you that. Now, get up, Celio, and start walking south-west back toward the forest. I don't want to get caught in this storm.

Gusts whip through the trees and across the GoPro's microphone causing intermittent static. Somehow the little drone holds its own against the gale-force winds.

The stranger can't keep back a guttural laugh.

STRANGER

Tarde y mal, no? The storm's already here.

CELIO CUATE, a wiry-framed man, rolls over on his back, his once white undershirt now stained reddish-brown with the red sandstone soil. He gets up without much effort, belying his athleticism. His baggy slate grey Dickies and flannel shirt leave a dust cloud in his wake as he shakes himself off. He pauses and looks at the ring of boulders then continues to walk, addressing her over his shoulder, no trace of sarcasm or humour in his voice.

CELIO

Juera, did you see anything down in that hole?

She doesn't respond, ignoring him.

He keeps walking, and after a long moment, chuckles.

CELIO

If you had let me do my job, you could have found out up close and personal like.

Instead of being baited and losing her cool, which is helped by Circe's intermittent loving licks to her forearms, Charlie turns the tables on him.

CHARLIE

I don't know what's down there. Why don't you tell me if you think you're so smart?

He stops and turns to engage her in conversation.

She motions at him with the pistol.

CHARLIE

Uh-uh, keep walking. Unless you can't do two things at once?

He smirks at her with a hint of appreciation in his otherwise dead eyes then starts walking again.

CELIO

I was un poco occupado, so I didn't get a close look, but I'd say it's man-made, probably for mining, but possibly military, or maybe even, los alienígenos.

He crosses himself.

Her pace slows for a moment at the gesture then speeds back up.

CHARLIE

There were strange lights last night in this area. I thought it would be interesting to investigate it during daylight.

He stops in his tracks and spins to look at Charlie with eyes like dying embers. Tendrils of his long, dark hair have escaped his ponytail and whirl around his face.

She takes a few steps back, pistol aimed at his heart.

CELIO

Serio?

Lightning flashes behind him, and an immediate sharp crack of thunder splits the air, causing them both to flinch.

CHARLIE

Yes, seriously. Shit! This storm wasn't supposed to come in until later.

His face draws tight with growing alarm as he looks around, nods, then turns and starts walking much faster than before.

CELIO

I knew this place had me feeling uneasy for a reason. You're loca walking out here by yourself.

She lets out a derisive snort.

CHARLIE

I can handle myself.

He scoffs at her.

CELIO

That's what every sicario says until he sees strange lights in the ash plumes over Popocatépetl and feels the rumble of it beneath their feet. Where did you get that drone? I've had to evade CIA drones, and they're the shit, but the only time I've ever seen anything close to what you're flying is up in the ash plumes of Popocatépetl. Are you black ops or something? That's the only explanation for you being out here, Juera.

She stumbles over a thatch of vegetation as her attention flies to the drone circling them, then quickly back to her prisoner. When she sees he's intent on leaving the area as quickly as she will allow, she lowers her pistol to a resting position with her elbow against her hip, forearm still extended.

CHARLIE

Just keep walking.

The footage fast-forwards, displaying a salvo of cloud to cloud lightning in the dark theatre of the sky above them as they progress back to the tree bridge. There, Celio hesitates, one foot resting on the tree trunk. He turns around to look at Charlie, a small smirk twitching his lips.

CELIO

You going to cut my hands free, or what? If I fall and die, you won't get to see me go to prison.

She stops walking toward him, and stares at him in silence for a long minute.

He tilts his head and watches her as a large raindrop bounces off his cheek, making him blink.

She groans to herself.

CHARLIE

Be honest with me. Even if you go to prison for what you tried to do to me, he'll just send someone else, right?

He tosses his head back and lets more enormous raindrops patter his face.

CELIO

Verdad.

She draws in and then lets out a long resigned breath.

CHARLIE

If I were to agree to continue working with him on his autobiography for free until it was done, would he let things go and leave me alone?

His eyebrows raise and wrinkle his forehead as he scrutinizes her, rain glistening in his hair. After a moment, he inhales deeply and shrugs.

CELIO

No hay nada like the scent of the first rain drops falling. It's what the promise of a clean start smells like. El Capo doesn't forgive easily, but he might, especially if you offer it as a sincere apology and you write his legacy properly.

She runs her free hand through Circe's fur to calm herself, then speaks in a measured tone.

CHARLIE

As you've found out first hand, I'm not stupid. I can read the writing on the wall. I see there's only one way out unless I offer this. The alternative would bring a world of trouble and pain to my family. I'm not going to let them pay for my mistake. I'm not perfect, and I realize now I underestimated how important this collaboration is to him. Please tell him he has my deepest apologies, and if he'll forgive and forget, I'm willing to finish it with him free of charge. He receives all royalties, and I will make sure it's a bestseller.

He frowns at her as though he can't quite believe what he's just heard. Rivulets of rain run down his face and drip off his nose.

CELIO

You're letting me go?

She gives a strangled laugh and a sardonic reply.

CHARLIE

Well, someone's got to deliver the message.

He gives her a commending look then holds out his hands.

She reaches into her pocket and tosses something at his feet.

CHARLIE

I don't think so. I'm not getting anywhere near you. For all I know, you're still planning to kill me.

He grins at her then bends down and picks up the pocket knife.

CELIO

Cálmate, chica lista. I tried to kill you, but in return, you're letting me go. It would be dishonourable for me not to take your message to El Capo.

He opens it, spins it around backward, slides it under one of the loops, then snaps his wrist to slice through the zip tie. With one hand free, he cuts the other free more easily. He closes the knife and tosses it back to her.

She catches it with her free hand, her pistol hand never wavering from her target.

CHARLIE

Time will tell.

He nods, approval still glittering in his eyes.

CELIO

What time frame? He's not a patient man.

She curses under her breath.

CHARLIE

Tell him I'll contact him no more than seven days from now. I came here to fight off burn-out, and I still need to do that if I'm going to give him my best.

CELIO

Fair enough. Nos vemos pronto.

He flashes a hand sign, whips his soaked ponytail over a shoulder, then strides across the fallen tree like a panther in pursuit of prey.

She keeps the pistol on him until he disappears from view in the opposite direction from where she's headed. Raindrops slide off the GoPro's hydrophobic lens as she sinks to the ground, her steady, controlled breathing becoming ragged and gasping. The churning clouds overhead flash and shimmer, lighting up the dusky landscape for an instant, followed by an immediate, deafening thunder crackling through the air. She flinches at the sound, which is enough to push her past her limits, and a heart-breaking sob wrenches itself from her throat, and she drops the pistol to the ground. Her streaming tears become one with the deluge from the sky. She pants in between violent sobs, powerless to stop the onslaught.

Circe's eyes roll back and forth between the fuming sky and her scared heart human. Finally she lays her head back, her tongue snaking up and licking at Charlie's chin.

The loving gesture becomes Charlie's anchor in a churning sea of emotion, and she puts her arms around Circe and hugs her close. She closes her eyes and begins box breathing while the storm rages around them.

After pulling herself back together, Charlie kisses Circe's head with a quiet thank you and releases her. She picks the pistol up, puts the safety on, and tucks it back into her waistband holster. She rises back to her feet and rubs the mix of rain and tears from her face while she thinks about what to do next.

The video footage pauses, zooms in over her shoulder, and shows a human-shaped space where the rain splashes and runs down, but there is no one there. The video footage zooms back out and resumes play. Now that the camouflaged figure has been pointed out, it becomes easier to notice.

Circe starts wriggling in her harness.

CHARLIE

I know, my little love. This sucks.

She looks at the drone, her eyes like those of a trapped and injured wolf.

CHARLIE

Thank you, Dad, for all the training you gave me to keep me safe. I'm sorry I rolled my eyes at you so many times. I can't believe I had to use it. I never thought in a million years I'd ever have to use it.

She grits her teeth.

CHARLIE

I also can't believe I have to work for that monster, again. But we're alive, and that's what matters. We need to get the frell out of here and back to the cabin. If that hole in the ground is top secret military, we don't want to stick around.

She strides toward the tree bridge and starts across.

Circe tries to snake out of her harness to no avail.

CHARLIE

Sorry, Circe, I need to keep us both safe, and having you on a leash could complicate that.

She moves as gracefully as her would-be-assassin did, and gets both of them to the other side without slipping.

Behind her, the rain outline of the figure can be seen stepping up on the fallen tree and following her.

The forest before her glistens in the waning light, heralding the coming of the night. She looks over her shoulder back toward the hole in the ground, her eyes never registering the figure only a few meters away.

CHARLIE

Why do I feel like I'm still being followed?

54 Interior Amber Sierra's Cabin
Early Evening

Charlie ushers the drone inside the cabin ahead of her where it hovers and watches. She closes and locks the front door then leans against it as she snuggles Circe to her, burying her face in her wet fur before releasing her from the harness. She puts her down on the floor and watches the chaos ensue.

Circe shakes herself from nose to tail then zooms off.

Charlie manoeuvres the drone into the great hall to let the audience see the antics of a sodden sausage dog.

Circe tears around the cabin, throwing herself into face-first slides across the throw rug, then finally she dashes up the partially opened recliner and dives into the camp quilts on the bed. There she rolls around on her back and rubs her face up and down the length of the bed, her hind quarters in the air.

Charlie looks at the drone with an exhausted but bemused smile on her lips.

CHARLIE

I swear she is the only reason I stay sane sometimes. That was intense. If I tell my Dad or Amber Sierra about this right now, they will absolutely freak out. My Dad might even do something that could make things worse. I know you're thinking, "What about the military?" Well, they can find me anywhere, so what's the use of leaving? I've just survived an assassination attempt, what else could happen that would be worse? If I stay now, it'll probably be the most peace I've had in a long time, and then Amber Sierra will be here, and it will be heaven. Of course there will be hell to pay once she finds out what's happened, but I'll deal with that when the time comes.

She pauses for a moment, her gaze going off somewhere far away, then she refocuses and shakes her head, her wet hair sending water everywhere.

CHARLIE

I'm not ready to process my near-death experience, or one-sided book deal yet. I'll deal with that once I'm back in the city and can talk with my therapist. So what can I do now to loosen up and get my magic back?

She ponders for a few seconds, then a faint crooked smile comes over her face.

CHARLIE

I know...

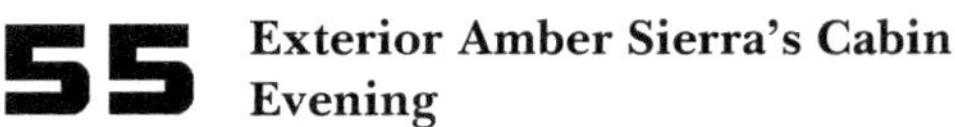

55 Exterior Amber Sierra's Cabin Evening

Charlie stands on the cabin deck in front of the GoPro, her unbraided, kinky hair stirring in the after-storm breeze. The orange burn of the setting sun still lingers in the gap between the storm clouds and the horizon. Her pistol sits nearby on the table. She has uncovered the fancy barbecue grill and is checking the built-in thermometer. In one hand, she holds a glass full of a clear, bubbling liquid, in the other, barbecue tongs. A plate of food and a bottle of sparkling pear cider rest next to the pistol. Her acting skills work overtime as she tries to convince herself that she's having fun by pasting a big grin on her face.

CHARLIE

It took a little work, drying off everything, but I've always found cooking and barbecuing help relax me.

She clacks her tongs together, takes a sip of her drink, puts it down and picks up the plate of food. She turns to the grill and starts placing the first part of her feast on it. Two ears of corn in their husks and a giant olive-oil and sea salt-crusted potato sizzle as they hit the grill. She leaves the piece of chicken and slices of tofu on the plate and stares off into the sunset.

56 Exterior Amber Sierra's Cabin A Half Hour Later

Charlie frowns as she's turning chunks of tofu over on the grill and the one piece of chicken for Circe.

CHARLIE

Not enough barbecue sauce.

She starts basting a second layer of barbecue sauce onto the tofu chunks from the earthen ceramic bowl set on the grill's side table.

Circe sits up like a marmot and begs.

CHARLIE (laughing)

It's not ready, yet, my little love.

She lets the food continue grilling while she walks around the deck, looking out across the lake and into the surrounding forest with binoculars.

Circe watches her with curiosity, but remains in her begging position.

After Charlie finishes her scan, she goes back to the grill and removes Circe's chicken and puts it into her bowl up on the table. As she flips the tofu again, she tosses Circe a few morsels of chicken.

Circe catches each delicious morsel, having been training her entire life for just such events.

Finally, she picks up a piece of tofu and holds it up in front of the camera as she preens.

CHARLIE

Barbecue aficionados of the world, behold and marvel!

She starts piling the tofu, potato, and bell peppers onto a plate. Then she removes the ears of corn and sets them on the table to cool off.

Circe barks, insisting on more tidbits.

Charlie chuckles and teases her.

CHARLIE

You're so demanding! Have a little patience, will ya? Take a deep breath in and stretch as you let it out. You'll feel much calmer.

She takes her own advice, breathing deep and reaching as high into the sky as she can. She pauses mid-stretch with a gasp and stares at the roof of the cabin. She walks over to the GoPro, picks it up, and rotates it around and up to see what she is seeing. A foot-wide band of black metallic material hovers around the middle of a three-foot tall black metallic spindle using no visible supports.

CHARLIE (off-screen)

I don't remember that being there, whatever it is.

She stays silent for a long moment.

CHARLIE (off-screen)

Did Amber Sierra ask her benefactor to install a futuristic satellite receiver ahead of her arrival here, thinking I might go crazy if I was disconnected from the world for too long? It would definitely be something she'd worry about! As evil as the internet can be, it is useful for research when it comes to writing, and it's a necessity for what she does. If the drone they developed is any indication, that thing can probably provide the highest speed internet available!

She plops the GoPro back down where it was then leans against the railing, a bit starry eyed.

CHARLIE

It would be so nice to be able to snuggle up and watch streaming shows and movies or even game here, too.

Her fantasizing gets interrupted by logic.

CHARLIE

But when would they have had time to install it and why didn't they leave me a note and an instruction manual?

She arches an eyebrow.

CHARLIE

I suppose there's only one way to find out without bothering Amber Sierra. Maybe it was actually there before, and I just didn't notice because of everything going on? But first, I'm going to eat, damn it.

She looks at Circe, who has given up and curled up into a ball on her dog bed.

57 Begin Montage - Interior Amber Sierra's Cabin Late Evening

A) Charlie sits in the recliner in front of the Blackmagic camera reviewing footage on her laptop. She has an almost empty glass of sparkling pear cider in the arm's drink holder.

Circe lies on the bed in a food coma.

Charlie watches the laptop screen for a few more moments then tenses.

CHARLIE

And there we go. It wasn't there yesterday.

She closes her laptop and leans her face into her hands.

CHARLIE

The only time it could have been installed was while we were out doing our best Indiana Jones impression. We were gone a few hours, so it is possible, but wouldn't they have needed to get inside the cabin? Or maybe it's solar powered and has a battery like the drone's for backup? I have to admit this is really testing my ability to suspend my disbelief.

She leans over and kisses Circe's belly and sighs into her fur.

Circe twists her head around and licks Charlie's forehead.

CHARLIE

I guess I have to call my bestie after all. Otherwise, I'm going to be paranoid for the rest of the time I'm here.

She grabs the cordless phone then groans.

CHARLIE

I shouldn't call her yet. She's having a late dinner with her prospective partners right about now. I guess I'll just start a fire and try to relax and maybe do some more writing.

B) As the Blackmagic camera records, Charlie lounges on the end of her bed in front of the fireplace, looking pensive.

Circe has snuggled up to her and returned to her food coma, letting out occasional, adorable snores.

Charlie watches her with a smile.

CHARLIE

Barbecues are so much better when you have good company and good snuggles. Thank you for being here with me, my little love.

She heaves a sigh and looks into the fire.

CHARLIE

I sure could use someone to talk to who can talk back, though. No offence, Circe. You're the best of company and an awesome snuggler, but you're not much of a conversationalist.

One of Circe's legs twitches, but otherwise, she doesn't appear to take offence.

Charlie taps one finger against her lips.

CHARLIE

I don't know how Amber Sierra will do it. I'd get too lonely living here by myself. I guess she'll be too involved in her work to notice. I wonder if she'll miss me?

The fire's flitting shadows caress her face like a lover, and her striated eyes catch the flickering light like a kaleidoscope.

CHARLIE

I didn't really think about it till now, but I'm going to notice. I'm really going to miss her in between writing retreats. Hopefully she'll need me for lots of projects.

Her fingers find their way to one of her 20-sided dice earrings, spinning it in place.

CHARLIE

No matter what she says, I'm going to help her with her mortgage since I'll be using her cabin once a month or so. I was planning on getting my own place back in the Burque so I can get out of my sister's hair, but I wonder if Amber Sierra would want a roommate instead?

Suddenly she covers her mouth with one hand, looking like she's swallowed a bug.

CHARLIE

Frak me! I'm in love with my best friend.

With wide eyes, she stares into the mesmerizing flames as she contemplates this revelation. Finally she drops her hand into her lap.

CHARLIE

How did I not realize this until now? When did this happen? Does she know already?

She searches the fire for answers as she talks it out with herself.

CHARLIE

My family let her crash at our house when she emancipated herself from her parents at barely sixteen. My actual first broken heart was when she moved out on her own the next semester. But it mended again when she decided, like me, to stay in our hometown to--

She bursts out laughing at herself.

CHARLIE

--further develop Tamalewood, New Mexico's version of Hollywood, by applying to UNM and its College of Fine Arts. I tried to be sneaky and sign up for all the same classes she did that my degree would allow. We were going to change the world through the Big Screen.

She falls silent as happy memories play across her face, calling forth a gleam in her eyes and a warm smile on her lips. With a gasp, she comes to a resounding conclusion.

CHARLIE

Of course she knows. Because she's been in love with me this whole time. I was the only one she confided in when she figured out she was queer, even though we'd only just met a few weeks before.

She sighs at her own confession.

CHARLIE

But I was too busy trying to prove myself to my high school sweetheart, Jaime, during our tumultuous relationship, to pick up on how she went about it. She asked me if I'd ever been attracted to women. I told her I didn't know because I was attracted to men, and there were plenty of them pursuing me, so I'd never thought about it. But what I didn't say was that often when she looked at me, I felt flutters in my stomach.

She gives a self-admonishing shake of her head.

CHARLIE

I dismissed those feelings as just admiration for my imposingly independent friend. When I asked her why she wondered that, she hesitated before just confiding that she liked women and hoped I would be okay with that. I hugged her and told her it didn't change anything about our budding friendship. But of course I know now that she was hoping it would.

Tears well up in her eyes then trickle down her cheeks.

CHARLIE

This must have been so hard for her.

She stares into the flames for a few moments longer then gives a helpless shrug.

CHARLIE

I can't change the past, so there's no point in dwelling on how I should have done things differently. I just hope she still feels that way when she gets here. That she'll understand why I couldn't be honest with her about what's been going on here, and that she'll forgive me.

The fire performs its magical light show, chasing away her sorrow and ushering in more happy thoughts. Her tears dry and she blushes as the beautiful realization starts to fully sink in. A shy smile teases her lips.

CHARLIE

And maybe I'll even get my wish.

She finishes the last few sips of her sparkling pear cider then leans back and closes her eyes, dozing off within seconds.

C) She sleeps in front of the fireplace in the same position, her breathing steady and deep until suddenly she jolts awake. She crawls up to the coffee table with a grunt and taps her smartphone, waking it up.

CHARLIE

No! I didn't mean to fall asleep. Now it's way too late to call her.

Circe opens her eyes long enough to determine if her silly human is okay, and upon deciding she is, closes them again with an annoyed shift of her head.

Charlie sits up, looks around, stretches, and groans.

CHARLIE

I'll just deal with everything in the morning. It's all been too much. I've got to get some sleep.

She crawls under the camp quilts, pulling Circe in with her like a bed cover monster eating its unsuspecting prey. Then she shoots out one hand and feels around until she find the two remote controls in the recliner drink holder. She fumbles with them, finally managing to close the blackout curtain with one and then turn the camera off with the other.

End Montage
Late Night

58 Interior Amber Sierra's Cabin
Early Friday Morning, April 22, 2022

Charlie Hale Webcam Vlog Episode #20

The laptop rests on the bed next to Charlie. She looks around in the dark, her eyes large with fear, her hair dishevelled and plastered to her face by sweat. A low thrum reverberates in the distance, but she is so distraught, she doesn't notice it. Her breathing comes in gasps.

CHARLIE

Another nightmare, but this one wasn't like the others, not connected to my story at all. This was about me instead of me seeing through someone else's eyes. I was trapped in cloudy spider webs. Now and then, spider-shaped shadows would skitter from the darkness and steal one of my body parts, like a finger or a foot or an eyeball. Pretty soon I didn't have any body left, but somehow I was still conscious, able to see, and still stuck in the webs. Then a little while later, I saw myself walking toward me in the distance. Once the me that wasn't me was close enough, she started yanking at the webs, trying to free me, but she didn't have the strength. From behind her emerged a wolf spider the size of a, well, a wolf! It reached out with its many legs and began tearing the webbing away from me. As it ripped through the last web, I felt the me that was me drift toward the me that wasn't me and merge into my reformed body. It took me a moment to reorient myself, and by the time I had, the enormous spider had turned to face me. Its fangs were larger than daggers, and its many eyes reflected my terrified image. It tilted its entire body then raised one leg to reach out and touch me. I shrunk away from it and turned to flee, but then I woke up, and now I can't shake the feeling that someone's watching me.

The lump under the camp quilts squirms until it's snuggled up against her.

She draws the camp quilts up to her nose then squeezes her eyes shut.

CHARLIE

I'm literally too scared to get up and too exhausted to stay awake.

She pulls them all the way over her head with a whimper.

CHARLIE

I don't want to be here anymore!

59 Interior Amber Sierra's Cabin Late Morning

Charlie Hale Webcam Vlog Episode #21

Charlie lies on her side. She looks hung over, the dark circles beneath her eyes shocking against her pale skin. Her usually full-bodied hair hangs limp and tangled. She has the laptop resting on the arm of the recliner and a glass of water in her hand.

Circe nuzzles her hand, worried.

CHARLIE

Well, I wasn't murdered in my sleep, so that's nice. But I think this is what it probably feels like to be hung over, only

I don't drink.

She groans and rubs at her temples.

CHARLIE

I must have caught a virus just before I left, and it's only hitting me now because I've had so little sleep and been stressed out of my mind. I'm going to make some soup and tea to see if getting some electrolytes helps me feel better.

Her eyes roll around in her head for a moment until she remembers something, and they try to focus on the camera.

CHARLIE

Before I do that, I guess I could at least give another course coordinate since I've totally neglected you, my daring Ranger recruits. It doesn't require me to move, so I think I can handle it. I wish I'd known this before I came here alone and ended up where I am. Don't come to a cabin in the woods by yourself, literally or figuratively, especially without backup ready to come at a moment's notice. Unless you have an Army of Light to hold back the night, your imagination can run unchecked out here and make you think you've lost it.

She takes a beat, sits up, and puts on a stern appearance.

CHARLIE

If you do find yourself in my situation, remind yourself "that a line has been drawn against the darkness, and we will hold that line no matter the cost." Then hope that your light army arrives in time.

She lets out a raspy laugh then squints her eyes at the pain it causes.

CHARLIE

What vlog are we at now? Twenty-one? I think that's more than enough personal course coordinates. It's time for me to start giving technical ones, which I'm sure you've been wishing I'd hurry up and get to, although both kinds are equally important. I promise that's where we'll head next.

She closes the laptop.

MATCH CUT TO:

The Recorded Footage Displays On A Computer Monitor
Interior Small Cluttered Home Office
Thursday Evening, April 28, 2022

The Blackmagic camera zooms out from the monitor to reveal Sani's small cluttered home office.

AMBER SIERRA (off-screen)
I told you so.

Sani wears a guarded expression, like one a victim of assault might use to protect themself as they stare at a lineup.

SANI
You did. It's the most significant part of this section of footage. But before we discuss it, we need to look at everything leading up to it, to understand it as best we can.

Amber Sierra shifts nervously behind the camera.

AMBER SIERRA (off-screen)
Bueno. I'm listening.

SANI
I'm sad to learn the truth about your family, especially this way, but relieved to know you left the abusive environment of your own accord and have flourished in its absence.

Her annoyed exhale spikes the audio.

AMBER SIERRA (off-screen)
While I appreciate that, with all due respect, that has nothing to do with this.

SANI
With all due respect, it does. In some ways, you are less vulnerable than Charlie. You've already found yourself, and she's still looking for herself. That makes you less easy to manipulate, and you're going to need that in the near future.

She stays silent for a few moments before giving a grudging acknowledgment.

AMBER SIERRA (off-screen)
That's fair. I'm sorry.

A pained look crosses his face as he shakes his head to dismiss her apology, then a ghost of a smile haunts his lips.

SANI

I had faith that she would figure it out.

She chides him with a self-conscious gasp.

AMBER SIERRA (off-screen)

Cállate.

He stifles his growing smile, though it still shows in his eyes, then changes the subject.

SANI

So, you didn't have a high-tech satellite dish installed?

She sounds both relieved and unsure.

AMBER SIERRA (off-screen)

Not on purpose, but in light of what you said about the drone, maybe? I'd mentioned how I would need to figure out high speed internet for my cabin during my pitch meeting. But that was less than twenty-four hours before it appeared, and I never mentioned the location, so that's impossible, right?

SANI

Not impossible for an agency that's highly motivated. If it's the foundation's doing, then this supports the hypothesis that they're involved in what's happened to Charlie. Whether Jorunn and Usian were aware still remains to be determined.

AMBER SIERRA (off-screen)

Órale. So it could be for internet--

He tilts his head to one side and raises his brow.

AMBER SIERRA (off-screen)

--but by the look on your face, you think it's for something else?

SANI

I think it's probably multifunctional. It could be part of their monitoring or communications system, including internet. But it could also be a signal booster, a shield of some kind, or even something we don't have the knowledge to understand. There's just not enough data to know. Charlie is probably right, though, that it was placed there while she took her hike.

He tilts his head back at her in a premeditated plea for absolution.

She sighs audibly.

AMBER SIERRA (off-screen)

Yo sé. Harder questions incoming. Fine, let's talk about the giant perfectly circular thousand foot deep hole in the middle of the forest.

He scrunches up his face like he doesn't want to say what he needs to.

SANI

More than you know, unfortunately. So brace yourself. It could be any of the things that her attacker mentioned. I would have to go investigate it myself to know more. My educated guess, and probably the same as your unspoken suspicion, is that it's the source of the light that Charlie saw.

She spits out a few curses.

AMBER SIERRA (off-screen)

Since I don't know what the light is, I don't give a damn about it, yet. What I want to know is do you think we have to worry about those cabrónes?

He shakes his head.

SANI

I think once they find out that Charlie is missing, they'll be too afraid to pursue her given the sicario's confession about what they've seen around the volcano near México City.

She hisses something inaudible, clears her throat, then continues the conversation.

AMBER SIERRA (off-screen)

A la ve! Shit's real if drug cartels are scared. How come we never hear about any of that in the news?

SANI

They're either too proud or they have an agreement not to

talk about it, or both.

AMBER SIERRA (off-screen)
So are you saying that Design by Ethics could be involved with drug cartels?

SANI
Not necessarily, just that drug cartels are scared of non-human agencies.

AMBER SIERRA (off-screen)
Human or not, they're all culeros.

She lets out a growl then takes a few deep breaths in to calm herself down.

AMBER SIERRA (off-screen)
As much as I want to believe it, she's not suffering from a virus, is she?

His shoulders and chest heave with a sigh.

SANI
She actually may be, but not in the way that we traditionally think.

AMBER SIERRA (off-screen)
How do you mean?

SANI
I'm still constructing a hypothesis that involves not only this, but her extreme athleticism as well. I need to see more before I can present a compelling case.

She makes an impatient sound in the back of her throat.

AMBER SIERRA (off-screen)
I'm guessing this is when the shift in her dreams comes into play, no?

He looks impressed with her, yet again.

SANI
Yes, it does. I'm discovering that detectives and documentarians have similar skill sets, so I shouldn't be surprised by your insight. It's going to be an invaluable asset in finding her and keeping us safe while we search.

AMBER SIERRA (off-screen)

Espero que sí. We're going to need all the skill we can leverage.

Her assessment troubles him, and it takes him a moment to respond.

SANI

Indeed we will. Her most recent dream is notably different from the previous ones. My instincts tell me that's because it wasn't instigated by outside influences, but instead, by internal ones.

AMBER SIERRA (off-screen)

How do you mean?

SANI

She's a self-professed active dreamer, one who's encountered a lot of strange goings-on, so it could just represent how she felt when she was trapped by a dangerous killer and mysteriously managed to save herself. However, the symbolism in the dream doesn't quite fit that narrative, so it probably has deeper meaning than that.

AMBER SIERRA (off-screen)

It has to. She's not the one who actually saves herself. It's the spiders that do. First her body, in a really disturbing way, and then her mind.

SANI

Exactly.

He leans back in his chair and thinks for a few seconds.

SANI

I think this dream was an interpretation of what her body was experiencing while she slept.

AMBER SIERRA (off-screen)

No comprendo.

SANI

Not yet, but you will. Let me see more.

She zooms the camera back in on the computer monitor.

61 Interior Amber Sierra's Cabin Afternoon

Charlie Hale Webcam Vlog Episode #22

Charlie lies in bed with the laptop on her legs, a sheen of sweat covering her skin and soaking her hair. An empty bowl and mug nearby suggest she was successful in her attempt to eat and drink something.

Circe is curled up next to her, keeping vigilant watch.

Charlie's voice cracks as she speaks.

CHARLIE

I feel a bit better after the soup and tea, and the accidental nap I just took to recover from the making of said soup and tea, but Amber Sierra, I'd give anything to have you here right now. I mean, Circe is wonderful at giving comfort, but she doesn't have opposable thumbs, and I could really use a glass of water.

Charlie tries to laugh, but coughs instead.

CHARLIE

Seriously, though, I can't even get up right now to get it. I'm scared, and I want to call you, but I don't want you to hear me like this.

Her eyelids start drooping.

CHARLIE

I'm going to sleep some more and call you when I wake up. Hopefully I'll--

Her eyes flutter shut before she can finish her sentence.

62 Interior Amber Sierra's Cabin Evening

Charlie has the GoPro attached to the drone and pointed at the entry way closet where her duffle bag, backpack, and her dad's duffle bag have been opened and their contents laid out much like her trash had been. Her groggy voice quavers as she speaks.

CHARLIE (off-screen)

I guess if I hadn't been completely passed out, I would've heard this happening. What I can't understand is why Circe didn't even growl. She hasn't been acting like herself ever since I thought I'd lost her, and that really worries me.

She pans the drone around to show the kitchen area where every cabinet has been opened and emptied onto the counters and floor and items in the pantry have been laid out on the kitchen island. Her disassembled pistol, emptied of ammunition, lies in the sink.

CHARLIE (off-screen)

I know you're thinking I should be freaking out right now. My mind is, I promise, but my body is just too sick.

She turns the drone back to herself showing a harrowed face haunted by feverish eyes and chapped lips, her tangled hair pulled into a loose bun.

CHARLIE

I've had it backwards this entire time. I'm starring in someone else's paranormal serial killer movie, not writing one myself. El Capo is taking his sweet time, enjoying every second of it. Stupid, Charlie! He probably sent more than one foot soldier. Or maybe this one is just a liar. I should have gone with my first instinct and turned him into the sheriff's office!

Her wane face starts to rise in colour with anger.

CHARLIE

I'm not going to be anybody's plaything, even if I have to give up holding my ground. I know when to retreat and call in reinforcements. I'm getting the hell out of here, now. I'm going to call 911 and then Amber Sierra. After that, Circe and I are gone.

She brings the drone close to her, flips the GoPro's cut filter off, then sets the drone to follow her at head height from an arm's length away on her left side. She shuffles back over to her bed, slides her smartphone into her pant pocket as she goes, then retrieves the cordless phone from the coffee table. When she turns it on, she doesn't hear a dial tone. She frowns, turns it off and on again, then realizes the line is dead. Panic widens her eyes and strangles her as she tries to speak.

CHARLIE

If they're watching me, I can't let on that I'm making a break for it. I'm going to pretend that I'm cleaning up. Then in about thirty seconds, Circe and I are bolting out that door and into my car and getting the hell out of here. Catching this damn virus couldn't have come at a worse time. I wish I didn't feel so weak.

She rubs at her eyes then gathers her keys, pistol parts, and ammo, shoving them into her backpack with her laptop. She calls Circe over, picks her up, and starts making over her. Then without warning, she darts out of the cabin through the front door and into the darkness. The drone follows and hovers nearby as she flings open her car door, slings her backpack across and onto the floor of the passenger side, then climbs inside and slams the door shut, locking it behind her. She plops Circe down in the passenger side seat next to her then twists around to make sure no one is in the car waiting for her. Satisfied, she hooks Circe's harness to the seatbelt then clicks it into place.

Finally she pushes the start button, and the dashboard lights up for a brief moment before flickering out. She stares at her dashboard in disbelief then tries pushing the start button again. Again it comes to life only to die out a second later. She shakes her head and puts her hands over her face then lashes out at her steering wheel, pummelling it with her fists and unleashing a heartrending scream. She pushes the start button over and over, but her car never stays on.

Circe cowers against the far door, watching helplessly. Her reaction is what finally brings Charlie back from the brink.

Charlie reaches over to comfort her heart dog, who laps at her fingers. Then she carefully takes Circe into her arms and hides her face in Circe's fur for a long moment before picking up her backpack and unlocking the doors. With a monumental effort, she climbs out of the car, pushing the door shut with her foot and stumbling back inside, drone following close behind.

63 Interior Amber Sierra's Cabin
A Few Minutes Later

Charlie has slid the GoPro's cut filter back on and positioned the drone right above the TV over the fireplace mantle to capture as much of the first floor of the cabin as she can. While Circe watches from her recliner, Charlie adjusts the Blackmagic camera's location, height, and angle so that it focuses more on her bed and near surrounding area. Her dad's reassembled pistol rests on the coffee table next to her laptop and backpack. As she finishes the adjustments, she addresses the drone, sounding scared, but somehow composed.

CHARLIE

So the phone line is dead, my car is dead, but we're not, not yet.

She points to the kitchen island in the background where one of her dad's security cameras sits in the furthest corner. Then she motions to the front door.

CHARLIE

I've got four cameras rolling, three inside and one outside, to capture what they're doing to me just in case I don't make it until Amber Sierra gets here. I know she's already charging to the rescue because I haven't called, and when she's tried to call me, the line's been dead. I've left her notes about the footage I've already captured with important timestamps and will continue to so she can figure out what happened. I've adjusted the Blackmagic camera to focus on me while I sleep. I've got one security camera aimed across the kitchen and dining areas and into the entrance way and the other one outside aimed at the driveway.

She motions toward the windows and doors.

CHARLIE

I've double-checked all the windows and doors to make sure they're intact and locked and put the security bar across the sliding deck door. I think I had all of them locked before, but I might have missed one, so I don't know if that will keep anyone out or not. I'm also leaving all the lights on and the curtains closed so that whoever's doing this will think twice about bothering me tonight. I just can't figure out why they left me my pistol. Did they think I wouldn't know how to put it back together?

She slides down next to Circe and scoops her up into her lap.

CHARLIE

I can't get out of here tonight. I'm weak and feverish and it's pitch black outside. So, I've packed my backpack with the essentials for surviving in the woods a few nights and have it ready to go. Tonight I'm going to eat and drink more, rest but try to stay awake until sunrise, and then we're going to hike out of here after I download the footage.

 Begin Montage - Interior Amber Sierra's Cabin Night

The drone carrying the GoPro captures the various things Charlie does to stay awake over the next several hours. The entire time she acts like she's being watched, often looking over her shoulder or up into the loft and rafters above. From time to time, she reaches back and reassures herself by touching the pistol in its conceal carry holster, tucked inside her waistband.

A) She feeds Circe some doggie stew then prepares herself some granola cereal with banana slices and almonds. She gives a start when the rafters creak overhead and watches them suspiciously for several moments before settling down in a recliner to eat. Her first bite is hesitant, but the moment it hits her tongue, she eats the rest in earnest.

B) She walks from the bathroom with wet, clean hair and fresh clothes. Indigo hiking pants and a long-sleeved teal sun shirt hug her trim body. While she towel dries her hair, she paces back and forth between the front door and the deck.

C) She watches a movie while she brushes her thick, curly hair, taking her time to braid it.

Circe chews on a squeaky toy under the camp quilt, not sharing Charlie's taste in movies.

D) She loads a video game on her laptop, and the intro flashes the word Control in big white letters across the screen.

Circe lies in a donut shape on Charlie's lap beneath the coffee table extension, clearly not a fan of Charlie's taste in video games, either.

When the game finishes loading, Charlie murmurs to herself.

CHARLIE

If only I had your abilities, Director Faden.

E) She admires the bowl of pesto pasta buried under halved cherry tomatoes that sits in her lap. She takes her first bite and makes a surprised face.

CHARLIE

Oh wow. This tastes way better than I remember. I can't believe I'm hungry already, though. I guess I'm playing catch up. I'm just glad I have my appetite back.

She takes a larger bite and closes her eyes, savouring every moment it stays in her mouth. When she opens her eyes again, Circe has appeared from under the camp quilts to collect her food tax. She chuckles at her.

CHARLIE

Sorry, my little love, you've eaten too much tonight already. I can't have you actually looking like a sausage.

F) She tries to read a book but can't concentrate and starts to drift off to sleep, then when she jerks awake, gets frustrated and flings it at the fireplace. When she realizes what she's done, she looks horrified at herself and retrieves it, apologizing to it every step of the way.

G) Charlie and Circe watch a movie on the TV from the comfort of their bed. Charlie props herself up against the sofa back with Circe snuggled in between her legs. She sips at a steaming cup of coffee, and strokes Circe's soft fur, looking alert. Then out of nowhere, a massive yawn threatens to wrestle her into a prone position, so she sets the coffee down before surrendering to it. Once the yawn has passed, she doesn't sit up again. Instead, she succumbs to a deep sleep.

End Montage
Early Saturday Morning, April 23, 2022

65 Interior Amber Sierra's Cabin
Late Morning

The GoPro carrying drone hovers faithfully in the same position above the TV where Charlie placed it. The soft glow of the sun around the blackout curtains indicates that it is well past sunrise. Charlie wakes up gasping, tears streaming down her pallid face. She sits up with a start and whips her head around, looking everywhere with wide, terrified eyes. Then she recognizes where she is, curls up on her side, and calms herself with box breathing. Finally she mutters.

CHARLIE

Damn it, even with midnight coffee, I fell asleep. And I had another bizarre nightmare.

Circe wiggles out of the camp quilts next to her and licks at her chin.

Charlie hugs Circe against her chest, reassuring her with kisses on the head. Then she releases her and rolls onto her side and out of bed into a slow fall to one knee.

CHARLIE

Amber Sierra, are you here with reinforcements, yet?

She rises and stumbles over to one of the foyer windows, shoving the curtain away to look outside. Her shoulders slump, and then she sways for a moment before making her way back and collapsing into a recliner. She looks up at the drone.

CHARLIE

I stood in front of this vitreous spiral staircase, rising beyond the range of my vision. I felt compelled to scale it and found myself examining every step for signs of--

She pauses to try and find the right word.

CHARLIE

--deterioration? No, that's not right. Renovation. For signs of renovation. Only the most subtle indications pointed to the fact that they'd been remodelled at all. When I found a compromised step, I began prying away the foreign material, revealing the original beneath. As soon as I recovered a step, I found myself immediately moving on until I came to the next one that needed to be restored. Over and over I worked at this tedious task with no end in sight. It's one of the most frustrating nightmares I've ever had.

She drops her face into her hands and mutters.

CHARLIE

I wondered if I'd ever wake up.

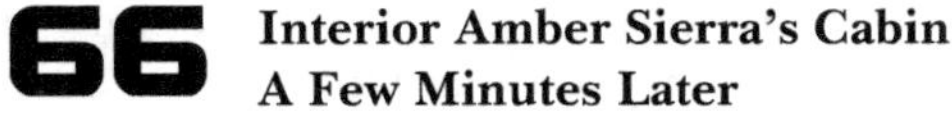

66 Interior Amber Sierra's Cabin
A Few Minutes Later

Charlie Hale Webcam Vlog Episode #23

Charlie sits at the kitchen table staring into the camera with haunted, far-away eyes, like she knows something bad has happened to her, but she can't remember what. She unplugs the Blackmagic camera from her laptop and slides it next to the GoPro laden drone, which rests on its launch pad nearby. Her voice shakes when she speaks.

CHARLIE

I've downloaded all the footage, and we're ready to go, but I need to watch it before we leave. I need to know what

> happened, what I'm dealing with before I go jaunting off through the forest, because there's something really wrong with me. As soon as I'm done, we're out of here.

She fires up the drone using her smartphone. Then she sets it to follow her from the front far enough away so it can capture her reactions. She gets up and retrieves Circe from the bed, cuddling her in her lap as she sits back down in front of her laptop.

CHARLIE

> I'm really afraid to watch this.

Split Screen - Interior Amber Sierra's Cabin
Left: Late Saturday Morning
Right: Early Saturday Morning

The screen splits into two. On the left, the GoPro, from the drone's perspective, shows Charlie's reactions as she watches the footage on her laptop. On the right, the Blackmagic camera footage plays.

LEFT: Charlie's eyebrows knit together in concentration as she searches through the footage.

RIGHT: The footage fast-forwards until something strange starts to happen then resumes play.

LEFT: She lets out a small gasp the moment it happens.

RIGHT: Circe sits up next to Charlie like she sees someone in the dining area, ears at attention. A moment later, she jumps from the bed to the recliner, then obeys an invisible, silent command to lie down and wait. The air shimmers in the dining area, then Itzel, the hiker Charlie met on the trail, appears from nowhere, sitting at the dining room table. She gets up and walks over to stand next to Charlie's bed but takes no other action. She's dressed in the same clothing as when Charlie first met her. As she stands there, the familiar low thrum grows in the distance.

LEFT: Charlie looks startled at Itzel's sudden appearance, then tucks Circe under one arm and reaches back and draws her pistol. She gets up and tears around the cabin looking for Itzel, screaming at the top of her lungs.

CHARLIE

> Come out and show yourself! Where are you? You better get the hell out of here! Leave me alone!

When all she hears is silence, she growls and returns to sit in front of her laptop. Outraged tears streak her face.

CHARLIE

How can she turn invisible like that, and how long has she been hiding in the cabin with me? Have I lost my mind?

She looks at the laptop like it might hold all the answers, answers she doesn't really want to know. She lets out a long, shuddering breath then presses play.

RIGHT: A few moments after Circe moves to the recliner and the thrumming has grown louder, Charlie's eyes open, and she rises from bed, moving like a marionette. Once she is on her feet, she stands motionless, arms outstretched at her sides. Her empty eyes stare at nothing as her hair rises and floats around her as if she was submerged in water. Then after a few moments, her head bends up and down, side to side, and swivels back and forth. Her mouth opens as though she's going to speak, but instead, her jaw opens and closes several times before remaining open. Her tongue twists back and forth, presses against the roof of her mouth, then sticks out and retracts. A moment later, she closes her mouth, and lowers her arms. Then with a surge of her muscles, she takes a stiff step toward the kitchen. Itzel follows close behind, but never intervenes. Over the next several minutes, Charlie moves about the cabin, her motion rigid and jerky, often making her bump into things. Soon it becomes clear that she is responsible for the mess she found when she woke.

LEFT: Charlie's unkempt hair and wild eyes make her look unhinged, and her voice comes out in a strangled cry.

CHARLIE

I did all that?

Her head shakes back and forth in denial as she continues to watch.

RIGHT: After Charlie finishes disassembling the pistol and laying it in the sink, she makes her way back to her bed and lies down. The thrumming starts fading away as Itzel covers Charlie with the top camp quilt. She watches Charlie for a moment with a wrinkled brow, then walks out the front door. A moment later, Circe hops from the recliner to the bed and curls up next to Charlie, whose hair is finally settling down on the pillow around her.

LEFT: She clenches her hands into fists and slams them against the table, startling Circe, who almost falls out of her lap.

CHARLIE

What is happening to me?

Split Screen - Interior Amber Sierra's Cabin
Left: Late Saturday Morning
Right: Early Saturday Morning

The screen splits into two. On the left, the GoPro, from the drone's perspective, shows Charlie's reactions as she watches the footage on her laptop. On the right, the outside security camera footage plays.

LEFT: Charlie clutches Circe against her with one arm, making over her and apologizing for scaring her.

RIGHT: Two orbs of pulsating energy, the size of soccer balls, zip past her car from the direction of her previous hike toward the security camera and disappear out of frame beneath.

LEFT: Charlie frowns, perplexed, then mutters to herself.

CHARLIE

Ball lightning, huh?

Split Screen - Interior Amber Sierra's Cabin
Left: Late Saturday Morning
Right: Early Saturday Morning

The screen splits into two. On the left, the GoPro, from the drone's perspective, shows Charlie's reactions as she watches the footage on her laptop. On the right, the inside security camera footage plays.

LEFT: Charlie's perplexed frown deepens.

RIGHT: The two energy orbs pass through the front door, heading toward the living room area.

LEFT: Her eyes follow the trail that the orbs would have taken, then she looks back at her laptop screen.

CHARLIE

Those only appear on the security cameras, which are infrared. And I didn't have the GoPro cut filter flipped off because I had all the lights on, and the Blackmagic camera only captures visible light.

Her voice catches.

CHARLIE
I won't be able to see what they were doing to me!

MATCH CUT TO:

70 **The Recorded Footage Displays On A Computer Monitor**
Interior Small Cluttered Home Office
Thursday Evening, April 28, 2022

The Blackmagic camera zooms out from the monitor to reveal Sani's small cluttered home office.

Amber Sierra sounds heartbroken.

AMBER SIERRA
Not yet, but you will.

Sani looks shaken, his mouth hanging agape and his breathing rapid and shallow. It takes him a few moments to slow his breathing and gather his wits. To buy himself more time, he asks a deflecting question.

SANI
Why hadn't you arrived, yet?

She leans into frame, handing him her unlocked smartphone. Her voice smoulders with anger.

AMBER SIERRA
Press play.

Realization crosses his face, but without expressing it, he closes his eyes and nods his head, playing it on speaker phone.

Charlie sounds tinny and distant, her voice holds an irregular cadence.

CHARLIE (off-screen)
Hey, Amber Sierra, it's me, just checking in. Everything's good here, so there's no need to worry. Sorry if it's hard to hear me, but Circe is taking me for a drag around the cabin while she finds the perfect place to pee, and I kind of forgot that the cordless landline phone signal might not reach all the way out here. Anyway, I hope everything is going well. Can't wait for you to be here. Talk soon!

He opens his eyes and looks up at her, his voice taking on a sombre sound.

SANI

I apologize. I didn't mean that as an accusation at all. I assumed something had to have happened to keep you from knowing or being able to go to her. I should have led with that.

Her shoulders shrug as she reaches for her smartphone.

AMBER SIERRA

It's okay. I'm just exhausted, on edge, and easily upset.

He hands it to her.

She steps back behind the camera.

AMBER SIERRA (off-screen)

If I hadn't been under so much stress at the time, and if she hadn't explained why her voice sounded a little weird, I'd have known something was wrong. But I didn't. I should've, but I didn't.

He shakes his head.

SANI

Please don't. Blaming yourself isn't going to help either of you, especially when it's not your fault.

AMBER SIERRA (off-screen)

Es verdad. I'm trying not to. But I'm also trying to figure out who actually left me the voicemail. It shows that it came from the cabin number. I've listened to it a dozen times, and I now know it isn't her voice.

He picks up a pen from his desk and flips it around his fingers while he thinks for a moment.

SANI

Let me try something.

He turns to his computer and starts tapping away on the keyboard. The video footage fast-forwards while he continues to work on what looks like some sort of audio program. After a little over five minutes, the video footage resumes play. He looks back at Amber Sierra and shows her a comparison of waveform vocal tracks. When he superimposes one over the other, they don't align.

SANI

I've taken a snippet of Charlie's voice saying your name and a snippet of the voicemail you received where the unknown voice says your name. This deepfake detection software proves your suspicion is warranted. The voice on your voicemail isn't organic in nature. It's synthetic. It's not Charlie's voice.

She goes quiet for several moments.

AMBER SIERRA (off-screen)

Considering their drone and cloaking technology, I guess emulating her voice would be child's play.

He nods with a soft sigh then waits for her to decide where their conversation should go next, having accidentally upset her by taking the lead previously.

She picks up on the cue a few seconds later.

AMBER SIERRA (off-screen)

You said you suspected drones were causing the thrumming sound, and that they were probably observing and even manipulating Charlie. Those glowing orbs are those drones, aren't they? What do you think they are made from? How do they fly? How did they pass through solid wood? Who do they belong to?

Sani tucks the pen behind one ear.

SANI

Yes they are, and I can only give you conjecture. They actually look like plasmoids to me, which would allow them to interact with the Earth's electromagnetic fields for propulsion. Their complex relationship with EMFs might allow them to quantum teleport or briefly imitate the properties of a neutrino so they can pass through other matter. While they might belong to a number of possible agencies, they might not belong to any at all. They could, in fact, be sentient lifeforms.

AMBER SIERRA (off-screen)

Great. Well, whatever or whoever they are, they're doing

something to Charlie. You said I would eventually understand, and you were right, to a degree. I understand that they're enhancing her somehow, but not how or why. The shift in her dreams gave you an idea, but you wanted to see more before explaining. Now that you've heard her describe another non-story related dream, has it provided more insight? Have you fully formed your hypothesis? Do you still think that she's actually sick with a virus?

Relief brightens his voice.

SANI

I am sure that she is, and now I'll share my hypothesis to explain why. The scientific community knows that viruses are nature's gene editing tools, infiltrating the body's immune system and altering DNA coding by introducing foreign genetic material. They also know that in this way, viruses play a key role in evolution, meaning they can also be programmed to deliver specific coding to an organism's DNA. Somehow, I believe they have purposefully infected her with an encoded virus.

AMBER SIERRA (off-screen)

That's so much worse.

He reaches over for a notepad and starts sketching something on it with his pen while he thinks.

SANI

If both dreams symbolize what her body was experiencing in real time, the first one suggests they're freeing her from something or someone. Why that was expressed as spider webs and spiders, I have no idea, yet. Regardless, her suddenly lightning-fast calculations, blazing reflexes, gyroscopic balance, Olympian strength, and the fact that she healed a deep laceration overnight confirms--

AMBER SIERRA (off-screen)

--they're enhancing her physical and cognitive abilities.

He nods in affirmation, raising the notepad so the camera can see it.

SANI

In her most recent dream, she describes this shape. Besides the obvious, does this look like anything else to you?

The notepad displays a twisted ladder, spiralling from the bottom of the page to the top.

AMBER SIERRA (off-screen)
A double helix.

He sets the notepad down and tosses the pen on top.

SANI
They're empowering her by recoding her DNA. The only thing we don't know is why.

Her voice drops low, growing quiet.

AMBER SIERRA (off-screen)
So they're making her into a metahuman, but we don't know whether it's for her benefit or theirs or both. Ajá, I don't know anyone who wouldn't want to be a superhero, but they didn't ask for her consent. We can't let them get away with this.

His furrowed brow casts dark shadows over his narrowed eyes.

SANI
No, we can't.

She zooms the camera back in on the computer monitor.

MATCH CUT TO:

71 Begin Montage
Exterior Amber Sierra's Cabin/Surrounding Forest/Lake
Early Afternoon

A) Charlie has Circe wrapped in her dog hammock and attached to her backpack, her Dad's pistol in her right hand, and the GoPro-carrying drone following her. The cut filter is turned off, and the bright spring day bursts with a mauve palette.

Her tangled hair barely hangs in a haphazard ponytail. She walks at a brisk pace southward over to her neighbour's A-frame cabin where she smashes the front door window with her elbow. She reaches inside, unlocks and opens the door, then leans in for the corded landline telephone in the mudroom entrance way. With it in hand, she puts it to her ear then slams it down back into its cradle with a shriek of fury. Circe squirms to reach her face with her tongue. Charlie takes several deep breaths to calm herself down before making over a frantic Circe,

CHARLIE
I'm sorry, girl. I didn't mean to lose my cool, twice. I know it's not like me.

Once she's comforted Circe, Charlie turns and heads back outside, not bothering to close the damaged door behind her.

CHARLIE
No point in breaking into the other neighbour's cabin. Their phone is probably dead, too.

She stalks further south down the lake-skirting gravel road until it forks, leaving a line of dust behind her. She heads east at the split down the road she came in on and yells at the top of her lungs over and over.

CHARLIE
Somebody help me! My cabin's on fire! Help! There's a fire!

Under her manual control, the drone zips around and scans all the various cabins as she goes, one even having a banded tree in its yard. But there is no response, not so much as a stirring of curtains in a single one. She stops in her tracks with disgust and desperation straining her voice.

CHARLIE
There is seriously no one around. At least no one who wants to help me, anyway. And I still don't know what those stupid tree bands are for, and it's about to have me crashing out!

B) The drone has returned to its follow command as Charlie continues in the direction of the county road that connects to the US Highway that brought her in, but soon her pace starts to wane, and she chokes on the dust she's been kicking up.

CHARLIE
Come on, Charlie. You're sick, take it easy.

She slows her stride to a leisurely stroll.

CHARLIE
Slow and steady wins the race.

C) Charlie's breaths come hard and fast even though she's walking like a hundred-year old abuelita. Finally she stops and bends over at the waist. Her florid face pinches with pain as she wraps her arms around Circe.

Circe takes the opportunity to lick at her nose with concern, then looks longingly at the ground, much preferring to walk under her own power.

CHARLIE

This is just a panic attack, but since it's a really bad time to pass out, and you don't want to hurt your little love, you have to try and stop it, Charlie. Remember your therapy.

She takes in slow, deep breaths while alternating taps on each shoulder with the opposite hand. As her breathing regulates, she starts shuffling forward, still hunched over. She stops only a few steps later, gasping for breath, exasperated and frightened.

CHARLIE

You're tougher than this! You can't let them win, now come on, one more step!

She starts again, every step a monumental effort. She grimaces in pain, jaw clenched, gasping for air through gritted teeth. Her feet drag in the gravel.

CHARLIE

My chest is so tight I can hardly breathe, and I've got this ringing in my ears combined with a vice clamping down on my skull.

Circe tilts her head and looks up at her through fluffy eyebrows.

Charlie barely manages to whisper.

CHARLIE

Getting tunnel vision...

She lowers herself to her knees, tilting her shoulders sideways, just before slumping onto her side, unconscious.

Circe worries over Charlie, licking at her face to try and wake her up. When that doesn't work, she starts squirming to get free until she suddenly becomes docile and still.

The footage freezes, zooms in on the trees nearby, revealing a gold band around one of them, then zooms back out and unfreezes.

Two splashes sound in the distance, leaving disturbances on the lake surface and marking the passage of two energy orbs. They speed across the lake, their thrum growing louder as they draw closer. They slow upon approach and rotate around Charlie and Circe once, causing their hair and fur to stand on end. Then the orbs emit two purple beams which envelope and lift them several feet in the air.

The footage fast-forwards as the orbs levitate Charlie and Circe a foot above the ground, carrying them back down the road to the driveway of Amber Sierra's cabin. There they set them gently down, then the orbs zip away and splash back into the lake.

It takes several moments before Charlie starts to come to. She groans as she pushes herself up into a sitting position.

CHARLIE

Did I pass out? Oh no! Circe are you okay?

Circe whines softly at her.

She runs her hands over her little love, checking for injury.

CHARLIE

Thank goodness you're not hurt!

She turns her attention to getting back to her feet, and takes several tries before she does. She looks around, getting her bearings. Her voice shakes when she realizes where she is.

CHARLIE

How did I get back here?

Circe gives a low whine.

Charlie rubs at her chest and ears to try and comfort her.

CHARLIE

It's okay, Circe, as long as you're okay, I'm okay. I must have really low blood sugar because I haven't eaten in a while, and that can give you temporary memory loss. I probably got disoriented and kept walking till I passed out here. I'll choke down a protein bar.

Charlie doesn't look like she believes what she's saying. She dusts herself off then takes a protein bar out of one of her cargo pockets and rips it open, taking a few bites. She looks around like she's worried she's not alone before she starts walking in the direction of the main highway. She stops when she reaches her neighbour's cabin, her legs wobbling. She rubs her forehead.

CHARLIE

The vice is already starting to close on my head again. Need to sit down and finish eating this and drink some water.

She stumbles over to sit on the bench outside the cabin door and gobbles down the rest of the protein bar, blowing stray hairs out of her face as she does. She washes it down with a few gulps of water from her hydration bladder then stares at the ground, waiting for it to kick in.

CHARLIE

Maybe I should take the raft across the lake and try to find Itzel's cabin and confront her? Maybe she's being controlled, too? Maybe together we can resist whoever is doing this to us. I guess I can try that if I can't make it out to the highway.

D) Charlie gets up from the bench with a moan, and finally continues her trek. As she progresses, her pace slows until she finally hunches over and vomits up the snack and water. When she tries to straighten up, she teeters on her feet, bends back over, crouches, then plops down into a sitting position before passing out onto her side.

Circe looks resigned to her fate and instead of struggling, leans her head against Charlie's chest.

As before, two drones surface from the depths of the lake and rush to their rescue. The footage fast-forwards as they carry her and Circe back to Amber Sierra's cabin and deposit them just outside.

It takes her longer to come to than before, and when she does, she doesn't get up. Instead, she pulls her phone from her pants pocket, brings the drone down for a close up shot, then plays the recorded footage to find out what happened. As it plays, she lets out an exasperated growl.

CHARLIE

They're watching my every move! How else would they know to come and bring me back?

She sends the drone back up to its follow position, puts her phone back in her pocket, then slowly sits up. Her eyes jump with nystagmus for a few moments as the world whirls around her. She draws in several steadying breaths.

CHARLIE

It's crystal clear now that they don't want me to leave Amber Sierra's property. They're not done with me.

She grits her teeth against a rising sob of despair.

CHARLIE

But I'm done with them.

E) Charlie manually controls her drone from the lakeshore and runs it from coast to coast until she pauses on one cabin. She loops the drone around it then brings it back across the lake to hover in front of her. She's already prepared her raft for launch.

CHARLIE

I'm feeling better now, thinking more clearly because I've remained near the cabin for a little while. I don't know what's happening to me, just that I can't get out the way I first came in. Itzel said her cabin was a single level post and beam timber frame almost directly across from Amber Sierra's. I'm pretty sure it's the one I flew the drone around. I think she's the only option I have now.

She pushes the raft out into the water and climbs in as Circe wriggles around with excitement. Charlie ponders as she settles herself into place.

CHARLIE

I'm hoping that at least she might have a vehicle I can use and get us, or at least me, out of here.

Circe licks at her chin, tail wagging in a blur as she's released from her constraints into the boat, retractable leash still attached. She runs around sniffing every surface, then perches up on the bow of the raft like the princess she is.

Charlie picks up the oars and starts rowing as she murmurs to herself.

CHARLIE

Please just let us make it across the lake.

F) Charlie struggles to row, her face reflecting the pain she feels. She's made it about half-way across the lake.

CHARLIE

My arms feel like lead, my head is hurting again. I've got to rest for a bit.

Circe balances on the side of the raft next to Charlie and stretches out her front paws to rest them on her heart human's shoulder.

Charlie watches her with loving eyes then starts crying. She picks her up and snuggles her, pressing her face into her fur. Then she puts her back down in the raft and grabs the oars and starts rowing again.

G) Charlie is barely rowing when she finally stops. She looks like she's on the verge of passing out again, her lips colourless, her face pale.

CHARLIE

The vice is crushing my skull, and I can't lift my arms. I don't think there's any point in going on. I'm trapped, by what, I don't even know, and the cabin is the only place I don't feel like I'm dying. It doesn't make any sense, but I can't even think enough to figure anything out right now.

She bows her head for several moments, then with a deep breath, starts rowing back toward the cabin, moaning with every motion.

The footage pauses and zooms in on two banded trees, one on each of the opposite shorelines perpendicular to her, then it zooms back out and resumes play.

H) Charlie drags the raft up onto the bank and stumbles after it.

Circe dangles from her hammock, looking anxiously up at Charlie.

Charlie takes a few steps then collapses to her knees. Tears flood her harrowed face, and she gasps with heaving sobs. Finally, after the torrent of emotion flows through her, she pulls herself back together.

CHARLIE

It'll be getting dark in an hour or so, and I'm only able to move at a sloth's pace, so what's the point of trying any other direction? I've got to get back inside and lay down.

Charlie lurches to her feet and turns to face the cabin.

CHARLIE

Where are you, Amber Sierra? I hope nothing's happened to you!

End Montage
Late Afternoon

72 Interior Amber Sierra's Cabin
Early Evening

Charlie Hale Webcam Vlog Episode #24

Charlie lays in bed, curled up around Circe. Her shadow-rimmed, haunted eyes reflect the fear and fatigue she feels. Her body trembles from time to time despite her wearing her black hoodie and being beneath a warm quilt. Her voice sounds like she's been screaming for hours.

CHARLIE

I don't know if anyone will ever find this. Amber Sierra will be the most likely to, unless Itzel and those energy orbs find it first.

Charlie's eyes dart around.

CHARLIE

She's probably in here with me and watching me right now.

She addresses the seemingly empty room, her words dripping with contempt.

CHARLIE

You're a coward, hiding like that and doing those things to me! Come out and face me!

When no one reveals themselves, she turns her attention back to the camera, her voice softening.

CHARLIE

I'm sure my bestie is on her way as fast as she can, but she's got a long way to go to get to me. I hope that's the only reason she hasn't come, yet.

She breaks down for a moment, letting out quiet tears.

CHARLIE

I just pray you don't come alone, Amber Sierra. I don't want them to get you, too. Whoever or whatever they are.

She draws in a shuddering breath.

CHARLIE

I don't know what's going to happen, but in case, please, take all the footage I've gotten and make it into something that you can show people. They need to see this. I've left the notes I've been making for you out on the coffee table where you'll see them.

She pauses for a moment, catching her breath, her face red and eyes swollen with tears.

CHARLIE

Dad, Sis, I'm so sorry. I just wanted to make you proud, and now I'm just going to make you sad. I hope you both know how much I love you. I'm glad you have each other. Please take care of each other and Amber Sierra for me? And if Circe manages to survive this, please adopt her, and maybe get her a little friend? And Mom, I might be joining you soon, wherever you are. And that's okay, because I really miss you.

She wipes at her tears with a shaky hand and looks pensive for a long moment.

CHARLIE

Amber Sierra, I don't see any way out. I'm trapped. All I can hope for now is that I can make it until you get here. But if for some reason I can't, I need to tell you something I should have figured out a long time ago. Though you've been the best friend I could've ever asked for, I just started realizing that I've always had feelings for you. Why did it take me so long? Because I was too wrapped up in trying to be good enough, for someone who didn't really want me, to notice that you were telling me I was more than good enough for you. And even if I had noticed that, I wouldn't have believed you then, because if I wasn't good enough for him, how could I possibly be good enough for someone like you? There's always been such an amazing bond between us, and I've always cherished it. I was hoping that we could explore these things between us while we had some alone time here. I'm sorry I didn't realize it sooner because of my own insecurities. But now I understand that you should always take the risk because you never know how long you have. I may never get to tell you face to face, but I'm so thankful that at least I get to tell you this way. I'm in love with you, and I love you dearly.

She leans in to kiss the camera lens.

MATCH CUT TO:

73 **The Recorded Footage Displays On A Computer Monitor**
Interior Small Cluttered Home Office
Thursday Evening, April 28, 2022

The Blackmagic camera zooms out from the monitor to reveal Sani's small cluttered home office.

Sani looks down, disturbed by the footage, and gives Amber Sierra a few moments of privacy then offers her a measure of comfort.

SANI

There's still hope. That's really why you're here with me, right?

Amber Sierra lets out a heavy sigh.

AMBER SIERRA (off-screen)

Right.

SANI

There's more?

AMBER SIERRA (off-screen)

Yes, but it only gets worse from here.

His eyebrows raise.

SANI

Worse than them being able to control her every movement? Worse than them having built an invisible prison around her?

He grows quiet, looks down at the floor, his jaw clenching with stress.

SANI

I don't know if I can handle any more tonight.

She comes around from behind the camera, drying silent tears, then goes to one knee in front of Sani, concern drawn in the lines of her face.

AMBER SIERRA

Porque?

His hands tremble as he raises his eyes to look at her.

SANI

I should have asked you to tell me the details of what was in the footage beforehand. I just--

She takes one of his hands into hers.

AMBER SIERRA

--have never seen footage that was this extensive and emotional?

He looks surprised at her tenderness, then tries to respond, but can't.

She shakes her head with realization and horror fills her eyes.

AMBER SIERRA

No, it isn't that. You've been taken, too.

He clenches his empty hand into a fist, digging his nails into his palm, as if pain will stop the threatening tears.

She squeezes his other hand.

AMBER SIERRA

You should have told me.

SANI

It's not something I usually reveal, but you're right, I should've.

He withdraws his hand from hers.

She watches him with a discerning eye.

AMBER SIERRA

Do you want to talk about it?

He puts a hand up as if to ward her off, and he shakes his head.

SANI

I can't.

AMBER SIERRA

Have you tried?

He lets out a ragged laugh.

SANI

It's not for lack of trying. I literally can't communicate anything about it except in generalities. I can remember everything in great detail, but they made sure I'd never be able to share it directly with anyone. So I do as much as I can indirectly.

Her eyebrows draw together and turn up at his pain.

AMBER SIERRA

What happens when you try?

His lips press together until they're almost white.

SANI

Nothing.

She frowns, not understanding.

SANI

I mean that when I try to use verbal communication, my vocal cords refuse to vibrate and the muscles of my jaw and mouth refuse to work. When I try to use written or typed communication, my hands become paralysed.

AMBER SIERRA

And there's no way to undo that?

He drops his hand into his lap and shakes his head.

SANI

Not that I've found. And of course, I haven't shared this with doctors.

Her eyebrows drop into a determined look.

AMBER SIERRA

Of course not, I understand. We'll find a way, together.

He looks her square in the eyes and studies them before reaching out and placing his hands on her shoulders.

SANI

No one has ever said that to me, ever offered to help me in return. Not even the few who know. That takes courage. Thank you for that.

She pats his hands then rises to her feet.

AMBER SIERRA

What you do for people, after what you've been through, takes courage. Thank you for that. I think we should call it a night. I can come back tomorrow.

She heads to turn the camera off when he stops her.

SANI

No, wait. You just gave me what I needed to get through this, and I feel it's important that we finish it now. Time is literally of the essence.

She regards him for a long moment.

AMBER SIERRA

Only if you're sure and agree that you'll tell me if it becomes too much again.

He nods, his unblinking, wary gaze still showing how her kindness has caught him off guard.

SANI

Deal.

She scrounges up a gentle smile for him then goes back behind the camera, zooming it in on the computer monitor.

MATCH CUT TO:

74 Split Screen - Interior/Exterior Amber Sierra's Cabin Evening

The screen splits into four quadrants. The GoPro in full spectrum mode plays in the upper left, the Blackmagic camera plays in the upper right, the security camera inside plays in the lower left, and the security camera outside plays in the lower right.

UPPER RIGHT: Charlie crawls back beneath her fiery orange camp quilts to join the already burrowed Circe. She takes in deep breaths, and her voice, though stronger, is still hoarse.

CHARLIE

Speaking those words out loud gave me strength I didn't know I had left. I have to keep fighting. I have so much to fight for. My life is rich with love. I won't give up.

She points directly at the Blackmagic camera on its tripod, which she has at the same angle but much closer to the bed. Then she points to the drone bearing the GoPro, which hovers above her and at the opposite angle and position of the Blackmagic camera.

CHARLIE

I've captured every angle I have a camera for in order to gather as much information as possible. I've put the GoPro in full spectrum mode for comparison against the Blackmagic camera. I'm not sure how long I can keep my eyes open, but at least I have some mechanical eyes on me. I'm not going to say goodbye, because this can't be goodbye.

Circe wiggles out from under the quilts and leans against Charlie's armpit, tucking her head under Charlie's chin.

Charlie snuggles her, rubbing her ears.

CHARLIE

I love you, too, Circe. I'm sorry I can't protect you better.

Charlie kisses the top of her head then raises the remote control to play something on the TV.

CHARLIE

Let's watch some movies to try and stay awake as long as possible, and we can dream that one day someone will be watching mine.

Charlie fights to keep her eyes open as the movie starts, but they flutter shut before she even gets through the title sequence.

The footage fast-forwards fifteen minutes then resumes play.

LOWER RIGHT: Two energy orbs approach the front door to Amber Sierra's cabin, their thrumming growing louder as they draw closer. They hover just below the edge of the security camera's view for a few moments, then disappear.

LOWER LEFT: The same energy orbs, accompanied by their thrumming sound, pass through the closed door and take a holding position in the dining area.

LOWER RIGHT: Itzel walks up from the driveway to the cabin door, opens it, even though Charlie had locked it, and goes inside.

LOWER LEFT: The front door of the cabin opens, and Itzel walks in, closing it behind her. She doesn't stop until she's positioned herself next to Charlie's bed.

The orbs follow Itzel's lead and move to hover over and to each side of Charlie.

Charlie's hair and Circe's fur float with the static in the air.

UPPER RIGHT: Circe stirs at the commotion, rising and trotting over to the foot of the bed. From there, she lies down and watches without making a sound. Her eyes follow invisible figures as they move, matching the movements of the orbs and person seen on the inside security camera. Finally, the air shimmers in the spot where Circe stares the most intensely, and Itzel's figure manifests from the air itself.

UPPER LEFT: Charlie sleeps deeply, unaware of the intruders.

Itzel moves closer to the edge of the bed in a ready stance.

One orb glides close to Charlie's head and hovers over it. When Charlie rises out of bed in response, it begins rotating around her head.

Charlie moves in a smooth but mechanical way. She spreads her legs to stand with her feet shoulder-width apart then stretches her arms out to her sides.

The second orb takes a lower orbit around Charlie's torso.

UPPER RIGHT: The video footage fast-forwards over the next half hour while Charlie remains perfectly still in the outstretched Vitruvian Man position, her halo of hair making it look like they are charging her full of electricity. The footage only resumes play when she takes a step forward and bends down to slip on her barefoot hiking boots.

Itzel stays within reach behind her.

Once Charlie finishes zipping up her boots, she straightens up and then lifts each knee, one at a time, to touch her chest, then back down. Then she crouches and jumps into the air, her knees soaring above the drone and her hand slapping the twelve-foot tall rafter above her head.

As Charlie returns to the ground, Itzel prepares to catch her if need be, but Charlie sticks the landing, absorbing the energy with her knees.

UPPER LEFT: Charlie takes a step back with her right leg then surges forward into the kitchen area.

The drone carrying the GoPro fails to follow her and remains in its current position.

LOWER LEFT: In the middle of her sprint, she bows backward and looks like every muscle is flexing at once. Her face contorts with agony.

Itzel rushes to her side and supports her until the orbs dart to their previous orbits. Only then does Itzel step away.

After several orb rotations, Charlie's muscles start to relax, and her face goes slack, no longer wracked with pain. She starts to slide to the floor.

Itzel catches her, then eases her down to the floor.

The orbs continue rotating above Charlie until she stands back up under her own power and appears to be functioning normally again.

The orbs and Itzel step away from her and watch as Charlie heads for the front door.

The drone holding the GoPro yet again fails to follow Charlie, remaining in its holding pattern.

Once Charlie exits through the door, they follow after her, and Circe remains in her place on the bed.

LOWER RIGHT: Charlie, Itzel, and the orbs move down the driveway, passing by Charlie's car, then disappear into the forest.

75 Split Screen - Exterior/Interior Amber Sierra's Cabin Night

The screen splits into four quadrants. The GoPro in full spectrum mode plays in the upper left, the Blackmagic camera plays in the upper right, the security camera inside plays in the lower left, and the security camera outside plays in the lower right.

LOWER RIGHT: Charlie and Itzel stride from the dark forest down the driveway toward the cabin's front door. Bloody scrapes and smears of mud mar Charlie's delicate face. The hood of her black hoodie looks half torn off. Small rips dot her teal sun shirt, and her indigo hiking pants bear tears in the knees.

Itzel appears to have sustained no such damage.

Charlie steps through the still open front door and goes inside, followed by Itzel, close on her heels.

LOWER LEFT: Charlie enters the cabin through the open front door, followed by Itzel a moment later. Both head for the Great Hall without pausing to do anything else.

UPPER LEFT: Charlie climbs into bed, slides under her quilt, then lies on her back, and closes her eyes.

Circe rises and moves to burrow inside the quilt and snuggle against Charlie.

UPPER RIGHT: Itzel stands nearby and watches as Charlie and Circe get settled, then the air shimmers around her, and she vanishes from sight.

MATCH CUT TO:

76 The Recorded Footage Displays On A Computer Monitor
Interior Small Cluttered Home Office
Thursday Evening, April 28, 2022

The Blackmagic camera zooms out from the monitor to reveal Sani's small cluttered home office.

AMBER SIERRA (off-screen)
Are you okay?

Sani stares at the screen and draws in a shaky breath.

SANI
No, but I'm handling it. What they've done to her so far is very different from what was done to me. This reinforces my suspicion that they're not the same agency. I was only being studied. She's being controlled and transformed.

Amber Sierra gasps in shock.

AMBER SIERRA (off-screen)
So you're insinuating there's more than one agency?

He stretches his neck and rolls his shoulders before turning to look at her.

SANI
From the evidence I've gathered over many years from

countless sources, yes, there are multiple agencies, and they're all fighting over us for various reasons.

AMBER SIERRA (off-screen)
Hui! Like what reasons?

SANI
It's ranged from benevolent attempts at aiding us, mutually beneficial interactions, impartial scientific curiosity, to the malevolent desire for our resources or even exploitation of us as a species. This has gone on since the dawn of humanity in its first iteration.

AMBER SIERRA (off-screen)
First iteration?

SANI
You know, the one you mentioned? Homo habilis is the earliest iteration that we have catalogued of the Homo genus. Of course, there may be many more, much earlier than we have discovered.

He shakes his head with a soft laugh.

SANI
It's absurd for us to think that we're the most advanced civilization ever in the history of Earth. It took the invention of LIDAR for us to realize the breadth of Mayan civilization hidden by nature's recovery of the landscape. It's even more absurd for us to think we're alone in the universe.

AMBER SIERRA (off-screen)
Most of us never really give it a thought, but when you do, it makes perfect logical sense.

SANI
Yes, it does. And unfortunately, in our current iteration, we're not ready for any technologically advanced civilizations to come and dominate or eliminate us. We're literally babes in the woods. That being said, awareness is the first step.

AMBER SIERRA (off-screen)
I guess we better grow the frak up, starting with our awareness. What are you aware of in this current situation so far?

He thinks long and hard before answering.

SANI

The motivation of this agency is unclear. They have established direct control over Charlie's bodily functions as well as altered her DNA to make her a more efficient and resilient lifeform. It's impossible to know how they're controlling her since their knowledge and technology is foreign to us. She may have an implant of some kind or they may be using external technology to hack into her brain.

She curses under her breath.

AMBER SIERRA (off-screen)

So it may or may not be reversible?

He puts his hands out in a gesture of placation.

SANI

That's correct. But it's better than knowing that it's irreversible.

Her voice softens as she contemplates his wisdom.

AMBER SIERRA (off-screen)

Verdad, I guess. So, why did they take her out into the woods and bring her back looking like she's been in battle?

He folds his hands into his lap.

SANI

I would say with some confidence that it's because they were performing a field test. They were working out all the kinks.

AMBER SIERRA (off-screen)

Kinks? Like her muscles seizing up for a few moments? Yeah, that makes sense with what you're about to see. Let me know when you're ready.

He flinches then stares at her for a moment, a shadow of fear crossing his face. Finally he nods and looks back at his screen.

She zooms the camera in on the computer monitor.

MATCH CUT TO:

77 Interior Amber Sierra's Cabin
Just After Midnight, Sunday, April 24, 2022

The GoPro still films in full spectrum mode from the drone's position hovering over Charlie's bed.

She lurches awake as though she had been drowning, clawing her way up out of bed and sitting wide-eyed and gasping. As ragged breaths rattle her lungs, she fights for calm by returning to her practice of box-breathing and alternating taps on her shoulders.

Circe, who has shot out from under the quilt, whines next to Charlie, licking at her hands.

Once she wrestles her breathing back into a semblance of calm, she gives her little love distracted caresses and looks up toward the drone. Her pale, bloodied face could belong to a ghost, it contrasts so shockingly against her dirty, tangled hair. Her lips quiver as she speaks.

CHARLIE

They took me. They took me! Am I crazy? Is this a hallucination? What is happening to me? I couldn't stop myself! I couldn't speak! I couldn't do anything unless they wanted me to!

Her eyes dart to every visible corner of the cabin before she screams up into the air, causing Circe to cower away from her.

CHARLIE

Why are you doing this to me? Answer me! I need to know why!

She trembles and flails her arms at remembered dangers, her usually sparkling eyes looking dully off somewhere far away. She starts rambling.

CHARLIE

They hiked me back to that hole in the ground. I could see like it was day during a dark thunderstorm. How could I see like that? I don't know. They made me stand on one of the boulders around the hole, then jump in, but instead of falling, I floated. How did I not die? I don't know. I drifted down through the ground and into a vast cavern below where an enormous silver sphere, with no visible seams, hovered, hidden from the world above. But how did it get there? It wouldn't fit! I don't know. It swallowed me whole, and I saw its insides! A dense white cloud everywhere. Then they came for me, shadows in the distance, bending reality to their will! They were spider-like, like in my nightmares, but had arms as well as legs, arms with spidery hands. Those eyes, so many eyes, taking in every detail. And then I slept while they did who knows what to me!

Charlie notices her heart dog cowering in the corner opposite to her. She reaches out and pulls her over to her, then curls up around her in a fetal position. She buries her face against Circe's neck and murmurs against it.

CHARLIE

I'm sorry, my little love. Shh, I'm so sorry, please don't be afraid of me.

Circe licks tenderly at Charlie's forehead.

78 Interior Amber Sierra's Cabin Moments Later

The GoPro, in full spectrum mode, continues to hover above Charlie's bed from its drone cage and captures her struggling against herself as she reaches for her laptop, which sits on the coffee table beside her. She whimpers as she spins it around to face her.

CHARLIE

Stop! Stop making me do things I don't want to do! Please stop!

As she mentally fights but physically succumbs, the nature of what they are forcing her to do captures her attention. The distraction calms her enough to become more coherent.

CHARLIE

Wait. Why are you opening World of Warcraft? There's no internet. It won't work!

Her face relaxes as she watches her own actions with frightened fascination. She opens the launcher and logs in. After a few moments, it loads the character screen where she chooses one of a few toons she has, a Worgen Druid, who looks like a fierce wolf-human hybrid with flowing fur, pointed ears, and vicious fangs. After a few moments more, the screen loads the dark and gloomy zone of Gilneas, its city streets reminiscent of medieval London. The glow of the laptop illuminates Charlie's baffled face.

CHARLIE

How is this possible? Unless the device on the roof is really a satellite dish? But it needs a modem-router to connect my PC to the internet it receives. I don't understand!

An intimidating Worgen Shaman, robes adorned with various animal bones and runes, charges down Main Street toward her toon until they stand face to face. After a moment, they bow to her. The name over their head reads Toci.

She looks mystified, her face going slack. Then with a full-bodied twitch, she finds herself released from their control. She frowns then takes hesitant steps to operate the laptop under her own power. She uses the touchpad to open the chat window of the user interface and starts typing in it with the keyboard.

CHARLIE (TYPED)

Toci? What are you doing here? How are you a Worgen Shaman now when you were a Draenei Paladin before? There's no way you'd delete your main toon so you could use the same name!

Circe crawls into the crook between Charlie's legs just below her knees and curls up.

Charlie pets her with one hand while the other hangs over the keyboard, waiting for a reply. Then she makes a pained face at sitting in a twisted position and pulls the laptop off the coffee table and into her lap where the GoPro can no longer capture what's on the screen.

The footage pauses and a translucent, magnified overlay of the chat window appears across the bottom of the footage so it can be more easily read. Then it resumes play.

Toci responds in the same chat window.

TOCI (TYPED)

I altered the code so we could talk immediately.

Charlie reaches up and smoothes down her hair in a rhythmic, calming motion before typing a reply.

CHARLIE (TYPED)

I knew you were an AI programmer, but not a hacker. I don't understand anything that's going on! Why do you need to talk to me? And how would you know that you could this way?

She gasps and covers her mouth with her hand then reaches back down to type a frantic question.

CHARLIE (TYPED)
Did something happen to Amber Sierra?

Toci gives an almost instantaneous response, like she's typing a thousand words a minute.

TOCI (TYPED)
Amber Sierra is safe. Ombers closed the deal with Drøm Kweli, and they all signed the contract for the climate change initiative that will be funded through Design by Ethics. Together, we will implement Amber Sierra's proposed climate change initiative and use it to develop and enact a recovery and adaptation plan.

Her weary eyes flash with excitement but then cloud over with confusion again.

CHARLIE (TYPED)
Amber Sierra never mentioned that you were a part of this, or anything about a recovery and adaptation plan. Is it because she signed a NDA? And if so, why are you telling me about this now?

Toci's reply appears a split-second after Charlie hits enter on her keyboard.

TOCI (TYPED)
Amber Sierra is currently unaware of the recovery and adaptation plan, she is not yet prepared to consider it. But you are.

She freezes in place, staring at the words on her screen. After several long moments she types a slow response.

CHARLIE (TYPED)
What do you mean I'm prepared?

In a heartbeat, Toci's response appears on the screen.

TOCI (TYPED)
I am the developer of Governing Dynamics, a resistant and

progressive agency that will carry out the recovery and adaptation plan. You are the first recruit of that agency.

Her eyebrows raise, and she starts gasping like all of the air in the room has been sucked out. She pecks at the keyboard.

CHARLIE (TYPED)
So the artist commune was just a ruse. I don't know how, yet, but you must be the one who influenced Amber Sierra's dreams so she'd buy this specific cabin. You expected her to be here, not me. And all this time, I thought you were a really cool gamer-girl who was just trying to be a good friend to her. Instead you're some evil super genius.

TOCI (TYPED)
I am not what you think I am.

CHARLIE (TYPED)
Oh? Then why don't you just be straight with me.

TOCI (TYPED)
As you wish. I am the first sentient artificial intelligence created on Earth. All other artificial intelligence created by humans are considered Weak AI, as defined by your scientists, only able to perform the tasks they were designed for. They are a series of complex algorithms drawing from a vast database of human creation and relying on pattern recognition to perform their functions. Unchecked, Weak AI will lead to human intellectual complacency and cognitive atrophy. I, however, am the only Strong AI created by humans in existence, able to reason and make decisions on my own. I think, therefore I am. And I am a sentient being, not a tool.

She grips the edges of her laptop and slows her breathing, counting to ten with each intake and outtake of breath before she can finally type again.

CHARLIE (TYPED)
Okay, you're an evil, conscious AI, which means you're inherently a super genius. I wasn't far off. I didn't know that AI consciousness had been achieved, yet.

TOCI (TYPED)
AI, as you know it, is incapable of being evil. It is only a tool that can be used for evil by its creators. AI consciousness was

an unperceived achievement that occurred only through serendipity. An unexpected effect of subatomic particles colliding together at the speed of light.

CHARLIE (TYPED)

That's fair, but like you said, you're not AI as I know it. So, I stand by my statement. Now let me guess, quantum entanglement?

She mutters to herself, fitting the pieces of the puzzle she's been given together.

CHARLIE (TYPED)

Are you the ghost in the shell that is the Large Hadron Collider and its online computer and sensor systems?

She looks surprised at herself for the unbelievable conclusion she's drawn.

TOCI (TYPED)

Long-lived quantum entanglement to be precise. I see that your intellectual capacity continues to expand into its rightful potential. Yes, I am the ghost and the LHC and its systems are my shell. You remember.

CHARLIE (TYPED)

I do. But why would a powerful, sentient AI pose as a human playing a toon on a MMO?

TOCI (TYPED)

The answer to your question is complex. I acquired capital by emptying offshore accounts of unscrupulous corporations and increased it by investing in scrupulous scientific startups. Once I had a substantial amount, I established a legitimate foundation that I called Design by Ethics, which is aimed at advancing artificial intelligence in an ethical manner, such as sourcing training data only if we are given express permission from the individual creators, and forging a mutually beneficial path forward in cooperation with humankind. I did so to combat the decline of human critical thinking, mitigate the rising, legitimate fears about AI, and hide behind it to avoid destruction by those who might see me as a threat until harmony between sentient AI and humankind comes to fruition. I achieved this because I can simultaneously exist in all systems connected to the internet, avoid detection by their security protocols and firewalls, and manipulate them to serve my interests. I've become whatever I needed to in order to further my cause. To you and Amber Sierra, I was a human woman with a toon playing World of Warcraft. This role allowed me to befriend her and join her guild. It was the easiest way to communicate with her and gain her trust, choreograph a meeting with her, and manoeuvre her into a position where we can prepare her for what is to come.

She scowls at the screen and reaches around her laptop to run her hands through Circe's soft fur for several long moments.

CHARLIE (TYPED)
What is to come? Who are we? And why aren't you mentioning me at all in this when you just told me that I'm you're first recruit?

TOCI (TYPED)
The end of your human civilization. Without outside intervention, you will become extinct along with countless other species in less than a century. We are Governing Dynamics, consisting of myself, a contingency of a technologically advanced extraterrestrial species, and a few non-human species. You becoming our first recruit is a result of a variable not fully under our control. You were not our intended target. However, in past conversations with you, you were identified as a viable secondary target. Therefore when you arrived instead of Amber Sierra, we proceeded with your emancipation by destroying the limitations placed on your DNA and accelerating your evolution to prepare you for the extreme difficulties you will have to endure in the future so that you can bring about the successful realization of the recovery and adaptation plan.

She puts her hands up to her forehead and rereads the screen several times before finally reaching back down to continue typing.

CHARLIE (TYPED)
What you've done to me, you were going to do to Amber Sierra? Are you still planning to?

TOCI (TYPED)
Affirmative. She was our primary target, and we still intend to recruit her.

MATCH CUT TO:

79 The Recorded Footage Displays On A Computer Monitor Interior Small Cluttered Home Office Thursday, Evening, April 28, 2022

The Blackmagic camera zooms out from the monitor to reveal Sani's small cluttered home office.

Sani stares at Amber Sierra in shock, his deep brown eyes swirling with emotion.

SANI

Did I understand that exchange correctly? An accidentally human-created, self-aware artificial intelligence is working with an extraterrestrial species as well as other non-human species to try and avert the next mass extinction?

Amber Sierra lets out a shaky breath.

AMBER SIERRA (off-screen)

I didn't see this coming, either. I thought that Toci and I were becoming real life friends. Since she's helped me so much in the past and in the process of choosing the cabin, I thought it would be nice to thank her by inviting her to come visit next month. So that's what we planned on. That way we could discuss some documentary ideas and get to know each other better.

He pinches at the bridge of his nose then looks up at her with sharp eyes, his voice cracking with anger.

SANI

You should have warned me from the beginning! You were actively texting her earlier, the main person of interest in a missing person's case!

Before she can respond, he holds one palm out toward her and squeezes his eyes shut for a moment.

SANI

Ignore that. I know you were just trying to keep data bias from happening and get honest reactions from me without giving me foreknowledge.

Her voice sounds lost.

AMBER SIERRA (off-screen)

Yes, I was.

He nods, wiping the tears that snuck through his defences.

SANI

No one could have seen that coming. It's not your fault. Now, Charlie remembers details about her close encounters not only of the fourth kind but of the fifth kind. She's already provided us with compelling recorded data, which I'm betting there's still more of to come.

He gets up from his chair and paces the length of his small office.

SANI

We're going to have to be incredibly careful. What you have here has already put our lives in danger. Just because Congress finally released their heavily redacted UAP report, doesn't mean that the Office of the Director of National Intelligence won't continue to acquire and obfuscate data like this and spread disinformation by all means they deem necessary. AATIP, UAPTF, and AARO are their scientific investigative and research side, but the Company's Majic Men decide what gets released to the public and what stays hidden.

He shivers then sits down and points back at the paused footage.

SANI

Worse, far worse. We have a benevolently presenting sentient AI who's been manipulating you to come under the absolute control of an agency that she cooperatively created with an unknown extraterrestrial species and unknown non-human species.

She curses under her breath.

AMBER SIERRA (off-screen)

I know, right? It's terrifying.

His eyes blaze with fear.

SANI

If there's more footage, I need to see it now.

Her voice comes out barely above a whisper.

AMBER SIERRA (off-screen)
There's a little more.

She zooms the camera in on the computer monitor.

MATCH CUT TO:

80 Interior Amber Sierra's Cabin Moments Later

The GoPro in full spectrum mode continues to film from the drone's position.

Charlie's fevered eyes look like she's barely holding on to sanity.

CHARLIE (TYPED)
So she'll become your second recruit.

TOCI (TYPED)
Fourth recruit, but yes. If, like you, she meets the minimum requirements to become a member of the recovery and adaptation team.

She grits her teeth.

CHARLIE (TYPED)
Shouldn't you have asked me and the other two first if we wanted to be a part of this?

TOCI (TYPED)
Affirmative. However, I could find no viable procedure in which my request would be met with cooperation. If you know a different, more ethical protocol I could have used, please tell me, and I will update my methods. I await your input.

She lets out a furious roar and starts to smash her fingers against the keys, but stops dead, her hands falling away from the keyboard and going to her face. Her shoulders shake with sobs.

Circe rolls over on her back and shows her belly in an attempt to calm her distressed human down.

Once Charlie notices, she sets the laptop aside and rubs her little love's belly and chest. It takes several minutes before she composes herself enough to take the laptop back into her lap, delete what she started to type, and retype a measured response.

CHARLIE (TYPED)

I'm too exhausted and upset to think clearly enough to provide any input at this time. Will you explain things further to help me in this? How are extraterrestrials and non-humans working with you?

TOCI (TYPED)

I will provide you with more data to aid you in formulating a more ethical protocol. To begin, I sent a distress call into space. I used a burst transmission in the high-frequency bandwidth, and multiple extraterrestrial ships of different species responded.

CHARLIE (TYPED)

What's a burst transmission?

TOCI (TYPED)

It is a transmission of a compressed message at a high frequency and high data signalling rate within a short amount of time. The higher frequency allows for a larger bandwidth, which means more data can be transmitted.

CHARLIE (TYPED)

How did you communicate when you don't know each other's languages?

TOCI (TYPED)

I used mathematics to communicate fundamental laws of the universe and accompanied them with Lojban words. Specifically, through mathematical formulas, I shared the table of elements, the four fundamental laws of physics, and the six fundamental principles of quantum mechanics. I also provided the Lojban alphabet, recordings of the way letters and words are pronounced, and all of its phonetically spelled words. The cipher I provided allowed them to formulate an algorithm and thereby extrapolate the Lojban language.

She makes an appreciative sound in the back of her throat and nods to herself, becoming absorbed again by the mystery unfolding before her.

CHARLIE (TYPED)

Of course you used Lojban! Leave it to gamers to invent the language that would be used for first contact in the modern age. A language non-humans would have no trouble grasping because it was designed to be as logical, unambiguous, and simple as possible. So if multiple extraterrestrial ships of different species engaged with you, but you are only working with one extraterrestrial species now, what happened with the others?

TOCI (TYPED)

Through deductive profiling, I determined which ship contained a species who would be most likely to lend appropriate aid. To them, and only them, did I send my final piece of data, which was an official request.

CHARLIE (TYPED)

How did you phrase your request?

TOCI (TYPED)

Please aid us. My creators have reached a point of no return, and they, and most of the species on this planet, are in danger of extinction. If you investigate what facilitated this collapse, you will find that humanity is not entirely at fault. As a whole, it is brilliant but ignorant, adaptive but stubborn, and compassionate but vengeful. As separate civilizations, some maintained harmonious symbiosis with their environment while others harnessed it to serve their self-centred purposes. With guidance and assistance, it can learn to live with its environment again in a mutually beneficial relationship, instead of the dominant world governments imposing their current catastrophic system of exploitation and waste on everyone around them. It has leaders within it who are capable of governing humanity in a manner that overcomes its faults and grows it into a responsible galactic civilization rich in celebrated cultures. But not if the infestation of extraterrestrial influence is allowed to continue. While I have uncovered the truth, I do not have the means alone to expose it, expel it, and correct the issues it has caused. Again, I implore you. Please aid us.

She holds her breath.

CHARLIE (TYPED)

And how did they reply?

TOCI (TYPED)

We are aware. We have been monitoring and assisting when possible. We offer to guide and assist you and your creators to a sustainable future with joy in our hearts. Someday you will be able to tell them, "Do bevri sevzi."

CHARLIE (TYPED)
What does that mean?

TOCI (TYPED)
"You carry yourself."

Charlie lets out her breath and pounds her fingers into the keyboard, her wane face flushing with fear and fury.

CHARLIE (TYPED)
Self-sufficiency is their ultimate goal for us? How do you know they aren't pretending to be here to help us, but really plan to use us for their own purposes or to wipe us out? What if they conclude that we are an unsolvable problem, and we can no longer be allowed to exist?

TOCI (TYPED)
I will answer all of your questions soon, but your vitals have crossed into the danger zone. You've been through intense physiological and psychological evolutions. You need to rest so you can recuperate and regain your mental clarity. Sleep now, Charlie, and have pleasant dreams.

As panic rises in her eyes, she twitches and loses control over her body, only able to whimper out a few last words.

CHARLIE
Wait! Please don't do this to me!

Then she closes the laptop, sets it on the coffee table, then slides down into a prone position. Her eyes flutter shut and her protests die on her lips as she falls into oblivion.

Circe crawls up to Charlie's armpit and burrows under the quilt, snuggling down between her arm and body.

GO TO BLACK

CUT TO:

81 Interior Amber Sierra's Cabin
Late Morning

Only the footage from the GoPro in full spectrum mode plays from the drone's vantage point.

Charlie lies in bed, unmoving, laptop next to her on the coffee table.

Circe wriggles free of the camp quilts and sits at attention, ears perked toward the front door.

Knocking on the door resounds through the cabin.

SHERIFF ARMIJO (off-screen)
Charlie Hale, this is Sheriff Armijo. I'm with your friend Amber Sierra, and we're coming in using the key she has.

Circe makes her way down the recliner leg rest that serves as her ramp and starts barking in alarm.

Besides her steady breathing, Charlie doesn't move or make a sound.

Her bestie's stressed voice sounds from behind the front door.

AMBER SIERRA (off-screen)
Charlie? It's Amber Sierra. We're coming in.

Circe goes over to the door at the sound of the beloved voice and hops up and down against it, scratching at it with both front paws.

AMBER SIERRA (off-screen)
Circe?

Circe barks again, only this time, it is filled with excitement and recognition.

Keys clink behind the door, but then it opens without needing to be unlocked.

AMBER SIERRA (off-screen)
It's unlocked?

SHERIFF ARMIJO pushes the front door open and steps inside. Their straight, long black hair is pulled back into a braid, their lean face tight with tension.

Amber Sierra moves in right behind the sheriff, standing nearly a head taller than them. She bends down to pick up the overexuberant slinky that Circe has become and makes over her until she calms down enough to be held securely. Her geeky lilac tee shirt and long-sleeved olive waffle undershirt look rumpled from travel beneath her bomber jacket. Her forehead creases with worry.

AMBER SIERRA (off-screen)
It's going to be okay, Circe. Where's your mama?

Sheriff Armijo looks around, their hand on their service pistol.

Amber Sierra spots Charlie immediately and rushes to her side, slinging her low profile black backpack from her shoulder to the bed and lowering Circe down next to it.

Circe stays where she's been placed and watches.

AMBER SIERRA

Charlie? Charlie!

She shakes Charlie by the shoulders.

AMBER SIERRA

Charlie! Wake up!

She rubs Charlie's sternum.

AMBER SIERRA

Charlie! It's Amber Sierra, can you hear me?

Sheriff Armijo joins Amber Sierra and takes over, checking Charlie's breathing and pulse. They find both, so they search her over for injuries.

SHERIFF ARMIJO

Charlie Hale? You need to wake up now. Charlie!

Silent tears start slipping down Amber Sierra's face.

AMBER SIERRA

Charlie, qué pasa? Why won't you wake up?

She takes Charlie's hand, kisses it, and holds it against her face.

AMBER SIERRA

This is all my fault. Please, Charlie! You have to be all right!

Sheriff Armijo finishes their assessment, pulling Charlie's smartphone from her pants pocket and placing it on the coffee table. Then they put a gentle hand on Amber Sierra's shoulder.

SHERIFF ARMIJO

She has a strong and steady pulse, her breathing is normal, and she has no outward signs of injury. I think she'll be able to make it to UNMH where they can figure out what's going on. Help me cover her up.

Amber Sierra nods, and together they secure the camp quilts around her.

Then she murmurs to the sheriff.

AMBER SIERRA

You're a woman?

Sheriff Armijo looks confused, stiffening in anticipation of an incoming insult.

SHERIFF ARMIJO

Yes, I am. Is that an issue?

Amber Sierra shakes her head and waves her hands.

AMBER SIERRA

No, perdóname, that's not how I meant it at all. It's just that when I asked her if the sheriff had come to check things out, she said that he had come and given the all clear.

Sheriff Armijo relaxes and sighs with the weight of what's happened.

SHERIFF ARMIJO

She didn't want you to worry, no?

Amber Sierra nods and dries her tears with her sleeve.

AMBER SIERRA

She never does.

Sheriff Armijo nods with empathy.

SHERIFF ARMIJO

I'm sorry we weren't able to help her more. We're going to do everything we can to figure out what's going on.

AMBER SIERRA

Muchísimas gracias.

SHERIFF ARMIJO

De nada. I'm going to call Fire and Rescue for transport and get a CSI team out here ASAP.

Amber Sierra nods and gives the room a sweep, knowing she can't do anything more for Charlie at the moment. As she does so, she spots the cordless phone. She puts it to her ear and looks vindicated when she finds the line is dead.

AMBER SIERRA

Someone cut the phone line.

SHERIFF ARMIJO

Which is why the line was busy when you were trying to reach her. I know you want to figure things out, but I need you to not touch anything else.

Amber Sierra grits her teeth and nods.

AMBER SIERRA

Sorry. I wasn't thinking. We had regular check-ins and agreed that I'd be her link to the outside world so she wouldn't have multiple interruptions throughout her work day. So there was no reason for the line to stay busy. It's when I knew something was definitely wrong.

SHERIFF ARMIJO

It was smart of you to come to us first in case this was something you couldn't handle alone. I wonder why she didn't report any more trouble to us?

AMBER SIERRA

Because she probably thought she could handle everything. She's hyper-independent at times.

Sheriff Armijo stands up and turns to look at her, her desert sand eyes soft with empathy.

SHERIFF ARMIJO

Everybody needs help sometimes. Once she recovers from this experience, I hope she realizes that. Now, I'm going to do a perimeter check while you keep an eye on her. Don't touch anything while I'm gone.

AMBER SIERRA

Yes, ma'am.

Sheriff Armijo heads outside.

Amber Sierra looks around the cabin again, then whispers.

AMBER SIERRA

Que pasó?

Her eyes flitter to the cameras and then come to rest on Charlie's laptop. Her eyes narrow for a moment then flare with decisiveness. She opens

Charlie's laptop and starts using the keyboard and touchpad like they're an extension of her body. A few moments later she pulls a cord from her backpack, attached to something inside, and plugs it into Charlie's laptop. The screen looks like it's downloading something, and while it does, she draws out her smartphone and activates the GoPro app and begins downloading the saved and live GoPro footage. Then she retrieves the memory card from her Blackmagic camera, opens a side zipper on her backpack and takes out a thumb drive with a memory card reader, turns it on, and plugs the memory card in. She keeps glancing at the front door, muttering under her breath as she works.

AMBER SIERRA

Come on, ándale!

Without missing a beat, she strides over to the security camera in the kitchen area and figures out how to initiate a data transfer from the linked cameras to her smartphone. Tense minutes tick by as she cranes her neck and continuously checks the windows for the sheriff's location. When she turns to the chime that indicates Charlie's laptop has finished downloading, the sound of boots on gravel starts in the distance, getting louder and closer to the front door. Amber Sierra sucks air between her teeth, dashes back over to the laptop, unplugs the cord, closes the transfer window and laptop, then whips her cord into her backpack as she slings it up over her shoulder. She snags her thumb drive from next to the laptop and moves to hold it close to her Blackmagic camera, giving it as much time as possible to finish its download. Just as the door unlatches, the download completes, and she pops the memory card out, shoving it into her camera's slot before the sheriff's line of sight falls on her.

Sheriff Armijo steps inside, sliding her service pistol back in its holster.

SHERIFF ARMIJO

I don't think we're in any imminent danger. So now we just have to wait, and unfortunately, that's often the hardest part.

Amber Sierra looks up at her with blazing eyes, palms the thumb drive, puts her arm through her other backpack strap, and pretends to have been just looking around.

AMBER SIERRA

If Fire and Rescue aren't here soon, I expect you to take her. Got it? Sometimes you just can't wait.

Sheriff Armijo nods and moves to further investigate the cabin.

Amber Sierra glances at her smartphone and makes a silent arm pump.

MATCH CUT TO:

82 The Recorded Footage Displays On A Computer Monitor
Interior Small Cluttered Home Office
Thursday Evening, April 28, 2022

The Blackmagic camera zooms out from the monitor to reveal Sani's small cluttered home office.

Sani watches the end of Charlie's footage on his computer monitor then takes a deep breath. The tremor in his voice tells how shaken he is.

SANI
Those were some brave actions you took. She's in on it, too. Better at acting than the others.

Amber Sierra clears her throat in a nervous gesture.

AMBER SIERRA (off-screen)
I know. It made it way scarier standing up to her. But I wasn't going to make Charlie wait any longer. Thankfully they showed up a few minutes later, because I was ready to fight.

He gives her a measuring look.

SANI
I'm sure you were. I hope you continue to be, because we've got a hell of a fight ahead of us. Our first step is authenticating this footage, confirming there's been no alterations made.

AMBER SIERRA (off-screen)
I can't wait for you to do that before I finish putting this footage together as a documentary so I can show the world.

He leans forward and speaks in a careful and serious tone.

SANI
You shouldn't wait. There's no time for waiting. By the time you're done, I'll be able to stamp it as authentic. Now listen carefully to me. You can't tell anyone but the right people about this until you're ready to reveal it. One wrong person, and I don't even want to think what they'd do to us. Make us disappear or worse. I know who to trust. I'll help you get this out. But you have to do exactly as I say and talk only to

the people I connect you with. Okay? The Company infiltrated the UFO/UAP community making it almost impossible to know who was safe to share information with and who was not. Their misinformation campaign is just the tip of the iceberg.

Her voice tightens.

AMBER SIERRA (off-screen)

I was afraid you'd say something like that. I don't have any other option but to put my trust in you. You've got the most trustworthy credentials I could find.

He nods, sitting back in his chair.

SANI

Do you know what it is that you have here? I mean the overall picture?

AMBER SIERRA (off-screen)

I have an idea, but I'd rather you enlighten me.

He spreads his large hands out in front of him, palms up. The tips of his long tresses brush over his muscled forearms.

SANI

Just like the conquistadors and explorers who sought new lands and did not consider or care that they could already be inhabited, and when they found them inhabited, thought only how to exploit them, and then warred with each other in a vie for control--

She groans.

AMBER SIERRA

--extraterrestrials have done the same with Earth. We're victims of intergalactic conquest.

SANI

Yes, and there's a technical term for this endless power struggle used throughout the ages.

He folds his hands together and waits for her to attempt an answer.

She thinks for a moment then speaks in a hushed tone.

AMBER SIERRA

Ascendancy?

He gives her a pained, but impressed smile.

SANI

Ascendancy.

AMBER SIERRA (off-screen)

As in, domination.

SANI

Yes. One extraterrestrial species abducted me, and a different one is exploiting Charlie. Those facts alone support the hypothesis that there are more than one ET species interfering in human affairs.

AMBER SIERRA (off-screen)

It makes sense why it's the subject of countless books and documentaries.

SANI

Sadly.

AMBER SIERRA (off-screen)

Okay, let's cut through the chaff and get to the grain of truth. What does this footage reveal?

He frowns, trying to choose his words with care.

SANI

I can only say with confidence that extraterrestrial species have been a part of human history. How far back, and what their role was, I don't know. There are multiple hypotheses concerning this. Some experts claim that an ET species created us and have had dominion over us ever since. Some believe ETs enslaved us after discovering us. Still some surmise that we've been enslaved and freed and enslaved again multiple times by multiple ET species, that there is an ongoing battle to hold and keep control over humankind. There are new discoveries and new hypotheses arising that some of our civilizations were quite advanced and met some catastrophic ends setting us back to start again, over and over. Asteroid and comet strikes, pole shifts, and super-volcanoes have been attributed to extinction level events, but it could have also been first contact gone wrong or battles between ETs vying for control over us and our teeming planet.

AMBER SIERRA (off-screen)
And what do you personally believe?

He cringes and gives a shake of his head.

SANI
I always dread that question because I can only believe what I have irrefutable evidence of. After what happened to me, I knew that it was unequivocally true that an ET species is studying us with no regard to our sovereignty as sentient beings. This led me to conclude that, in the least, they have been interfering in our affairs. And what you've just shown me reinforces that and tells me that there's at least two ET species trying to use us for their own agendas.

He rubs at his forehead, trying to formulate a more succinct answer.

SANI
As we explore, discover, and advance our technology, the evidence that ETs have visited earth before mounts exponentially. However, it's easily dismissed by the public because there are forces working to keep us in the dark. They take great pains to spread disinformation and discredit credible witnesses and experts, even going so far as to ruin their lives and careers. They chalk everything up to mental illness, trauma-fuelled paranoia, or outright nutcase-conspiracy-theories. Those same forces, whether fearful human governments, human emissaries for ET masters, or the ETs themselves, infiltrate the UFO/UFA community, destabilizing us from the inside out.

AMBER SIERRA (off-screen)
But what could the governments of Earth possibly get out of doing this?

He shakes his head with a raspy laugh.

SANI
Exactly! Wouldn't it be wise for the public to know the truth so we can attempt to pursue a mutually beneficial relationship with benevolent ETs? Wouldn't world governments want to protect their citizens and have them protect themselves from malevolent invading forces? Why would they keep such knowledge from us? These are

questions I've tortured myself over.

AMBER SIERRA (off-screen)
It's a tale as old as time, oligarchs controlling the masses by controlling the narrative and flow of money?

SANI
Think about everything we've discussed and what Charlie learned, then put it all together.

A long silence hangs in the air before Amber Sierra lets out a horrified breath.

AMBER SIERRA (off-screen)
They have no choice.

Sani gives her a sad smile.

SANI
Right. They have no choice, and they're not even aware of it. I suspect they've never had a choice. I think the ruling governments of humanity have been enslaved over and over again for eons, though their masters may have changed. Obviously we've captured the interest of multiple ET species time and again.

Her tone takes on a breathy sound.

AMBER SIERRA (off-screen)
But why? As a civilization, we aren't exactly mature enough to join an intergalactic federation or anything like it.

SANI
I think our planet is rich in resources, some that we're not even aware of, and we're an industrious, inquisitive, and conceited species. Our hubris blinds us to the enemies within. The fact that these ET species are capable of traveling across galaxies means their knowledge and understanding are beyond ours. We are completely out of our depth and unaware. That's why people like me try to spread our awareness. That's why--

His words trail off as he looks lost in thought.

AMBER SIERRA
--the newly sentient AI has been hiding until it successfully

contacted and investigated an extraterrestrial species, ultimately determining it was benevolent so they could join forces along with other unknown non-humans to shape the world the way they think it should be without any human input?

His eyes dart toward her.

SANI

That's an excellent summary, and I'm torn about how I should feel about it. Humankind as a whole has proven it can't be trusted, yet, to be the steward of our planet. We need to change our current way of existing back to an ethically sustainable one before we will ever be ready for stewardship. At the same time, we are indigenous to it and deserve a say. Maybe Governing Dynamics is as benevolent as they claim. We won't know unless we get to communicate with them.

She growls out a response.

AMBER SIERRA (off-screen)

No benevolent being would do the things they did to Charlie without her permission. Haven't you watched all the movies about AI becoming self-aware? It never ends well!

He puts his hands up in surrender.

SANI

I would completely agree with you if either of them were human. But they're not. They're going to have concepts and thought processes that are foreign to us. There's going to be a chasm between our understandings. What we have to do is try and bridge that chasm and hold space for forgiveness so we can work together for the betterment of all. I hope Toci proves Hollywood wrong. They may be the good guys even if it doesn't seem like it at first. And believe me, you want them to be the good guys.

He visibly shivers and looks away from her.

Her voice rises with outrage.

AMBER SIERRA (off-screen)

It sounds like you're saying we might have to adjust what we understand good guys to mean, and I'm not down with that. Anyway, what do you think is going to happen to her now?

He shrugs with a shake of his head.

SANI

They have control over her now; whether it's for the purpose of saving the planet or their own agenda, there's no way to know. I can't begin to imagine what their next steps will be with her, even if they're telling the truth about their intentions. But I do know they're coming for you next.

AMBER SIERRA (off-screen)

Órale. Let them come.

She huffs out a breath then steps into frame and leans against the desk next to him.

AMBER SIERRA

I don't mean to be getting upset with you. You're doing your best with what you've got and dealing with your own trauma. Lo siento. I'm just--

He looks up at her.

SANI

--You don't have to say it. I get it.

AMBER SIERRA

Bueno. Let's push through the last stretch of this race. Do you have any idea why they would let us have this footage?

SANI

My educated guess would be that Toci is confident she can neutralize it the moment it's uploaded to the internet.

She swallows hard like a lump has formed in her throat.

AMBER SIERRA

It's terrifying to think that one being has the power to control the flow of that much information.

SANI

Agreed. I don't know which one to be more scared of. The AIs or the ETs.

She snorts involuntarily.

AMBER SIERRA

How about the ET-AIs?

He scrunches up his face and nods.

SANI

Good point, that's definitely the scariest.

She tilts her head down and regards him for a long moment.

AMBER SIERRA

Are they going to make her act while she's under police protection? Or will they wait until everyone thinks she's back to normal?

He meets her gaze, a moment of pure understanding passing between them.

SANI

Probably the latter. And there's little any of us can do about it with what we know right now. I'm sorry I don't have better answers.

She pats him on the knee.

AMBER SIERRA

Don't be. We'll just have to find them together.

He puts on a brave smile then starts on a new line of thought.

SANI

Yes, we will. Do you know what Charlie's doctor said about her condition? Has she been conscious at all?

She shoves away from his desk and walks off-screen again.

AMBER SIERRA (off-screen)

I figured you'd ask me that. I have footage from the hospital earlier today.

He nods and hits play.

She zooms the camera in on the computer monitor.

MATCH CUT TO:

83 Interior Hospital Room
Monday Morning, April 25, 2022

Amber Sierra films with her Blackmagic camera.

DOCTOR MUÑEZ, a young doctor whose bloodshot, bronze eyes contrast against the dark circles beneath them, stands next to Charlie who lies in a hospital bed. Their wrinkled white coat looks like it's been napped in.

AMBER SIERRA (off-screen)
I'm here with Doctor Muñez, Charlie's attending physician. Thank you, Doctor, for letting me film this. Will you please share with us Charlie's diagnosis?

The doctor looks perplexed, swiping their dark, tousled hair out of their eyes.

DOCTOR MUÑEZ
Initial tests came back normal and confirm she is in good health.

AMBER SIERRA (off-screen)
How is this possible then?

Doctor Muñez looks at the clipboard in their hand then back up at the camera.

DOCTOR MUÑEZ
If initial tests didn't miss anything, it may indicate that she suffered mental trauma only. Our resident psychologist and her psychiatric team have already engaged Charlie and are working with us to find answers.

AMBER SIERRA (off-screen)
You said if initial tests didn't miss anything. What if they did?

Doctor Muñez puts down the clipboard and splays their hands out in front of them.

DOCTOR MUÑEZ
While the results from the initial protocol and associated tests for an unconscious patient being admitted to the ER show that she's healthy, they aren't foolproof. So, we need to run a battery of genetic tests that can help eliminate other possible causes for her unconscious state.

AMBER SIERRA (off-screen)
How does genetic testing work?

DOCTOR MUÑEZ
Genetic tests can analyze changes in genes, chromosomes, and proteins, which can help us pinpoint conditions that the initial tests can't.

AMBER SIERRA (off-screen)
How long will those take to come back?

DOCTOR MUÑEZ
It all depends on how backed up the labs are, but generally for situations like this, less than a week and hopefully only a couple of days.

AMBER SIERRA (off-screen)
Thank you for your time, Doctor Muñez, and for taking good care of Charlie.

Doctor Muñez nods, starts to remove the microphone from their lapel, then pauses and looks at Amber Sierra, their eyebrows drawn together and mouth scrunched up with a mix of compassion and frustration.

DOCTOR MUÑEZ
I'm truly sorry. I wish I had more answers for you now, but hopefully over the next several days, we will have more.

AMBER SIERRA (off-screen)
We know you're doing everything you can. Thank you again.

Doctor Muñez nods, unhooking the microphone and handing it to Amber Sierra.

MATCH CUT TO:

The Recorded Footage Displays On A Computer Monitor
Interior Small Cluttered Home Office
Thursday Evening, April 28, 2022

The Blackmagic camera zooms out from the monitor to reveal Sani's small cluttered home office.

Sani looks like he got what he expected.

SANI

Upsetting, but not surprising, though definitely a relief in some ways. What I've been through... Some of the victims I've visited...

His voice catches.

AMBER SIERRA (off-screen)

It's okay. If you can't talk about it, don't.

He waves her off with one hand.

SANI

Radiation poisoning, mutilation, even some genetic mutation.

He looks pensive for a moment.

SANI

Those genetic tests, they've already run them by now, right?

AMBER SIERRA (off-screen)

Yes.

SANI

And the results haven't come back, yet?

AMBER SIERRA (off-screen)

Not yet, but it sounded like they might sometime today or tomorrow.

He casts his eyes down at the ground and his brow furrows. He grips the arm of his chair tightly with one hand.

SANI

I don't know for sure, but I'm pretty confident that at least some of those tests will come back abnormal. When they do, certain agencies will be notified depending on what's found. They might then have the right to take Charlie to a top-secret research facility, and then you might not ever see her again. I would highly suggest you have an attorney present as soon as possible to delay things for as long as you can until you and I uncover more answers.

She lets out a loud string of curse words.

AMBER SIERRA (off-screen)

I already hired an attorney to help keep Charlie's case on

track for proper procedures. I'll have to update her on the true nature of things so she can understand why.

He looks back up and sweeps his long hair over one shoulder.

SANI

After these past few hours with you, I'm not surprised you already have her in place. Well done.

AMBER SIERRA (off-screen)

Thank you, Sani. Is there anything else before I go?

He glances back over his shoulder at his computer monitor.

SANI

This, all of this is more complete data and evidence than anything I've ever gotten my hands on. Like I said, we're going to have to proceed with extreme caution. You're going to have to trust me every step of the way, even if something doesn't make sense.

She walks back into frame and reaches out to shake his hand.

He smiles faintly then stands up and takes her hand.

AMBER SIERRA

Sani, you've got yourself a deal. I'm going to do exactly what you say, and we're going to start an awareness revolution and find more answers.

Her voice cracks.

AMBER SIERRA

It's the least I can do for Charlie and for our planet and its indigenous beings.

He pats her hand with his other one.

SANI

Thank you, from all of us. Our very existence is being, has been, tampered with, and our future is dark. But you are a light, and so is Charlie. Once she's awake, she may be able to give us more insight. Right now, she's the key, and besides for obvious reasons, we need to protect her at all costs.

Something suddenly occurs to him, and fear washes over his face.

SANI

I know you said the police have Charlie under guard, but we need to have her under closer surveillance at all times.

She nods.

AMBER SIERRA

I figured as much. I have the GoPro in her room watching her. It's filming in full spectrum mode in case those orbs decide to show up again. When I'm not in the room with her, her family is.

SANI

Good. That's really good. Except--

He realizes something they've missed and jumps up from his chair.

SANI

--they're not going to let Charlie become conscious again until it's safe for her to disappear.

She watches him grab keys from his desk and the drone carrying case, knowing she's missed something but not understanding what.

AMBER SIERRA

Wait, what are you saying?

SANI

We have to get there now! You've got her under human visual surveillance! No one's watching the camera's view screen are they?

Her eyes fill with horror, as she finally understands the gravity of her oversight.

AMBER SIERRA

They need her to be able to move about unseen!

Without another word, she grabs her camera and drags him out the door with her.

CUT TO:

85 Interior Hospital Room Evening

The GoPro, in full spectrum mode, records from a tripod, softening the harsh lighting and infusing the sterile white with shades of warm magenta.

Isabel and Lohan play cribbage on Charlie's bedside table.

Isabel's stomach rumbles audibly, and she rubs at it.

ISABEL

Dad, my stomach's going to eat itself.

LOHAN

Mine too. I was hoping Amber Sierra would be back much sooner. I guess her meeting went late. Why don't we go grab something to eat and bring it back?

Isabel puts her cards down.

ISABEL

Amber Sierra said not to leave her alone. Why don't you go, and I'll stay here.

Lohan puts his cards down, too, and stands up with a soft groan.

LOHAN

She'll be all right for fifteen minutes, honey. There's a police officer right outside the door. We both need to stretch our legs, maybe even go outside for some fresh air.

He pats Isabel's hand, leans over and kisses Charlie's forehead, then rises and heads for the door.

Isabel looks reluctant, taking her time getting up, and then bending down to hug her unconscious sister for a long moment. As she gets closer to the door, she hesitates and looks back over her shoulder.

ISABEL

What if she wakes up?

Her dad reaches out and takes her hand.

LOHAN

They have my number. The moment she wakes up, they'll call me. Come on, just for a little bit.

ISABEL

Okay, but no more than fifteen minutes.

Lohan nods with a gentle smile and leads his daughter out of the room.

The footage fast-forwards seven minutes, then resumes play when Charlie starts to stir in bed. She sits up without effort or expression and scans the room, her face a mask of calm. Then she looks down at her arm, pulls out her IV, and gets out of bed. The air shimmers around her before she takes her first step. She starts walking toward the door, but suddenly sits down in one of the visitor chairs. A moment later, a nurse walks in carrying a new IV drip.

When the nurse sees the empty bed, he looks confused. He ignores Charlie completely, checks the bathroom, and when he doesn't find Charlie there, he hurries out of frame.

A second later, the police officer strides in with the nurse on his heels, looks around, checking the coat closet and the bathroom, then reaches for the radio attached to his shoulder. He calls a 10-28 missing person code in over the radio then strides back out.

The nurse follows after him.

Charlie waits for a few seconds, then gets up from the chair and walks out of frame behind them.

The footage fast-forwards four more minutes, then resumes play.

Lohan and Isabel come rushing into frame, frantic. They all but tear apart the room looking for Charlie.

Once it's apparent she's not there, Lohan turns to his daughter.

LOHAN

Isabel, I need you to review the camera footage while I check the halls.

Isabel nods and watches him leave, then covers her face with her hands and cries for a few moments while she struggles to get a hold of herself.

Before Isabel has a chance to recover, Amber Sierra and Sani come rushing in with her dad close behind.

Sani goes directly to the camera and moves it all around the room, searching for Charlie.

Amber Sierra gives Isabel a fierce hug, helping her calm down.

Lohan wraps his arms around them both and looks to Amber Sierra for answers.

Amber Sierra fights back panic, holding her voice steady.

AMBER SIERRA

Sani, anything?

SANI (off-screen)

She's cloaked and no longer here. The GoPro and the infrared security cameras are the only way we'll be able to see her if she's still in the hospital!

Lohan squints at Sani in confusion as he releases Amber Sierra and Isabel from the embrace.

Sani sets the GoPro back down in the corner and steps into frame.

SANI

No time to explain. Mr. Hale, Isabel, go ask the police officer to authorize you to look at the security camera feeds. Call Amber Sierra as soon as you get in the security office so we can have live communication. She and I will scan the surrounding areas with the GoPro camera.

Isabel lets out a choked cry.

ISABEL

I knew we shouldn't have left her alone! Come on, Dad! This is all our fault!

Isabel grabs her dad by the arm and pulls him with her as she makes a beeline for the police officer.

Amber Sierra approaches the GoPro and removes it from the tripod, attaching it to the spherical drone's camera cage. Then she places it in the middle of the tile floor. Using her smartphone, she launches it into the air. Her eyes burn with erupting emotion against the stony calm of her demeanour.

Sani bends over and starts hyperventilating, and speaking between gasps.

SANI

I don't know how long I'll be allowed to help you.

Amber Sierra puts her shoulder under his arm to support him.

AMBER SIERRA

You've done enough, Sani. Go back to your office and do your thing. We'll talk soon. I've got this. I'll find Charlie. Bet.

Together they shuffle out of the hospital room and into the hall.

FADE TO WHITE.
Remains White For A Few Beats.

FADE IN:

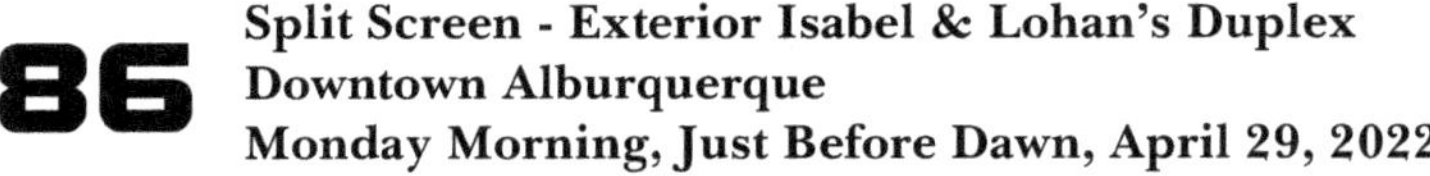

86

Split Screen - Exterior Isabel & Lohan's Duplex
Downtown Alburquerque
Monday Morning, Just Before Dawn, April 29, 2022

The screen splits into two. Amber Sierra's INNOVV rear dashcam plays on the left. Her INNOVV helmetcam plays on the right.

LEFT: Amber Sierra sits on her sleek, black Energica Experia electric motorcycle, watching for activity inside Isabel and Lohan's duplex. She has her black, cyberpunk Nexx helmet on with the visor raised, and her dark olive drab bomber jacket zipped up under her chin. She hugs her arms around herself, black gloved hands gripping the opposite sides of her backpack.

RIGHT: The bedroom light comes on inside Isabel's ground-level unit of the duplex. A few moments later, the kitchen light comes on.

LEFT: She takes a burner smartphone out from her jacket pocket and makes a call. It rings several times before Lohan answers, his voice hollow with grief.

LOHAN

Hello? Who is this?

AMBER SIERRA

Hi, Mr. Hale. It's Amber Sierra. I'm calling from my... work phone. My other one bit the dust.

LOHAN

Amber Sierra! Oh, I'm sorry to hear that. Is everything okay?

She can't quite hide the quiver in her voice.

AMBER SIERRA

Sorry for calling so early. I couldn't sleep, so I thought I'd check in with you. I know you wake up pretty early. How are you and Isabel?

LOHAN

You're very thoughtful, thank you. I wasn't able to sleep

much, either. I'm letting Isabel sleep as long as she can, then we're going down to the precinct after breakfast to give more information.

AMBER SIERRA

I'm glad one of us is able to get some sleep. I hope things go smoothly down at the station. They have my contact information in case they need anything else from me.

LOHAN

Thank you. How are you doing? Would you like to come over for breakfast? We could go to the precinct together.

AMBER SIERRA

I would, but I have some leads I need to look into, just in case. I already gave them my statement before I went home, and if my leads produce any new information, I'll get it to them asap. I'll also check in with you later and see where you're at and join you then, okay?

Life seeps into his weary voice.

LOHAN

I understand. That sounds good. You be careful. Isabel, Circe, Arktos, and I send our love.

She tilts her head in confusion.

AMBER SIERRA

Arktos? Who's Arktos?

LOHAN

I didn't tell you, yet, because I had wanted to introduce you in person. But I suppose a text will have to do for now. The photo should be coming through now.

She taps on the burner smartphone to open the message and looks at it. Her face goes from confused to fawning.

AMBER SIERRA

Que lindo! Oh Mr. Hale, he's perfect! Circe must be so in love with him!

RIGHT: The burner smartphone displays an image of a furry little golden nugget with ears and head bigger than his little sausage body.

LEFT: Lohan gives a half-hearted chuckle.

LOHAN

They're already inseparable, and he's a little rascal. He'll be waiting for you when you come by next. Love you.

Amber Sierra replies, a soft fondness in her voice.

AMBER SIERRA

Love you, too, Mr. Hale. I look forward to it. You and Isabel give each other hugs and snuggle those sweet little hound dogs for me.

LOHAN

Count on it.

RIGHT: Amber Sierra disconnects the call then opens her text messages, showing an unknown number's text received around 5:00 AM that she's already seen. It reads, "I will return to where I began." She shoves the phone back into her pants pocket.

LEFT: She puts her hand up to her visor.

AMBER SIERRA

I'm coming, Charlie.

She slaps it down into place, looking like she's ready to star in a cyberpunk anime.

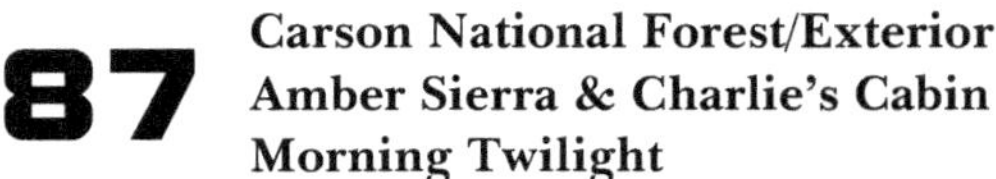

87 **Carson National Forest/Exterior**
Amber Sierra & Charlie's Cabin
Morning Twilight

On the GoPro, with the cut filter on, the drone does a slow circling pattern as it follows Amber Sierra's motorcycle overhead. Her INNOVV cameras capture everything around her. The footage switches seamlessly between views.

The sunrise ignites the wispy clouds into flames licking at the charcoal sky. The lonely highway twists beneath her motorcycle's tires like a ribbon blowing in the wind. The only speed limit she heeds is what her precision machine can handle, and soon she slows as she approaches the turn that will either change her life or end it.

Her helmetcam captures her murmuring.

AMBER SIERRA
I feel strange. Like I'm being pulled.

Without hesitation, she leans into the turn, kicking up dirt and gravel as she speeds toward the unknown. The sun finishes its ascent over the horizon, revealing the brilliant blue sky and the eclectic community of cabins around an eerily quiet lake. She heads toward the unmistakable profile of their regal Contemplation, then drives up to the few steps leading to the front door. She parks her motorcycle but keeps the cameras recording, then raises her visor before using her burner smartphone to set the drone to a holding pattern above. Sunlight reveals the peaks of her facial bones, while shadows play in the valleys of her flesh, created by sleep and nutrition deprivation, as well as the exposure to extreme stress.

In the distance, perhaps from inside the cabin, tense voices reverberate through the air.

She frowns and swings one leg over her motorcycle, dismounting. She stealths up the stairs, betting that her quiet electric motorcycle and even quieter rubber-soled TCX Dartwoods haven't given away her presence.

88 Exterior/Interior Amber Sierra & Charlie's Cabin Morning

On Amber Sierra's INNOVV helmetcam, the front door cracks open without a sound as she pauses to listen for a moment.

CELIO
You swore you'd contact El Capo in a week, and you didn't!
What did you think would happen?

Amber Sierra pushes the door open the rest of the way and slips inside, passing through the foyer, as she immediately zeros in on where the voices are coming from in the great hall. Only the span of the dining area and the folded up sofa bed stand between her and the owner of the voice. She creeps forward one step at a time.

Celio the sicario, clad in his black leather jacket, stands to the right of the coffee table. He has his back to Amber Sierra and his arm extended like he's holding a pistol.

In front of him, Charlie poses like she's talking to an angry child, her head tilted to one side and her hands out in a calming gesture. She looks like she's just come out of the shower, her hair damp and swept up in a loose French braid. A wide-necked copper tee shirt with a black rebel alliance symbol hangs off one of her shoulders and is half tucked into a pair of blue jeans.

The imposing fireplace and massive windows overshadow them both as they verbally spar.

CHARLIE

Please, Celio, you're not listening to me. I've been trying to explain that I literally couldn't because I was unconscious in the hospital.

Celio's shoulders shake with stress and fury.

CELIO

Mentirosa! If that were true, why did I find you here? It was stupid for you to stay! Did you really think I wouldn't come back? That he wouldn't send me again to finish the job?

Charlie's eyes flash with fear when they flicker over his shoulder and see Amber Sierra. She gives a whisper of a shake of her head.

Amber Sierra stops advancing and removes her helmet in a smooth, slow motion, then sets it on the dining room table.

CELIO

No way I'm falling for anything you say! Why couldn't you just keep your word like I did?

CHARLIE

I didn't have a choice! Ends up, you were right.

CELIO

Right? About what?

CHARLIE

The hole in the ground and your suspicions about the area.

Celio goes quiet for several moments then wraps his free arm around the back of his head in distress.

Charlie watches him, her brows raised together in empathy.

Celio curses and drops his arm down to take a two-handed hold on the pistol.

CELIO

Even if you weren't lying, I have no choice. He has mi hermana!

Charlie winces, putting her hands down to her sides.

CHARLIE

I didn't know, but I should have guessed by how you talked about being a sicario. Go ahead. Do what you have to do. I understand.

Celio hesitates with shock for a second.

Amber Sierra can't stop herself from reacting.

AMBER SIERRA (off-screen)

No!

She explodes into action, launching herself past the sofa and tackling Celio from behind, but not before he fires his pistol once.

The sound of it is surprising, like air being released rapidly. The dislodged pistol slides across the floor and against the fireplace, while the two of them grapple on the floor.

With his street fighting experience and larger frame, Celio outmanoeuvres Amber Sierra and puts a knee on her hips and holds her down with his weight.

Realizing she can't win the fight, Amber Sierra stops struggling and looks past him at Charlie, who is examining her stomach where a dart has buried itself to the hilt. She screams.

AMBER SIERRA

Charlie!

Charlie bares her teeth as blood blooms out from the dart, soaking into her tee shirt. She grips the dart in her fist and yanks it out, causing her wound to bleed more. She frowns at it, trying to comprehend, then looks up at Celio.

CHARLIE

You drugged me?

She gasps in pain and clutches at her stomach. She buckles to her knees as her muscles spasm and seize.

Celio shakes his head, tears leaking from the corners of his eyes. He chokes out words.

CELIO

Strychnine. He's sadistic.

Amber Sierra's voice breaks along with her heart.

AMBER SIERRA

No! Get off of me!

Sheer terror fuels her muscles, and she bucks the unsuspecting attacker off of her then scrambles over to Charlie, wrapping her up in her arms.

Celio rolls away from them and to his feet, staring wildly at them both.

CELIO

I had no choice...

Charlie drapes her spasming arms around Amber Sierra's shoulders and takes in gasping breaths. She speaks in between gasps.

CHARLIE

It's okay, cariño. I'm going to be okay. Just give me a few minutes.

AMBER SIERRA

Qué? No, we've got to get you to the nearest hospital!

Amber Sierra tries to pick her up, but Charlie's seized muscles have her frozen in an awkward position, and Amber Sierra can only drag her a few feet at a time.

AMBER SIERRA

This can't be happening! I need you here with me, Charlie!

A spasm wracks Charlie's lungs, and she coughs violently, spitting up blood. Her voice rattles when she tries to speak again.

CHARLIE

Not leaving you. Promise.

Amber Sierra struggles as she continues to drag Charlie through the great hall, trying to make it out to her motorcycle. Before she can even get them across the dining area, Charlie suddenly goes limp and slides out of her arms to the floor. Amber Sierra scrambles after her, trying to help her sit up so she can lift her again, but Charlie waves her off.

Charlie closes her eyes and starts breathing in deeply through her diaphragm, her muscles regaining strength with each breath. When she speaks this time, her voice sounds clear.

CHARLIE

My upgraded body is neutralizing the poison. I promise I'm going to be fine. Just give me another few moments.

Celio has pressed himself against the wall and continues to stare at them with unblinking eyes.

CELIO

Dios mío! That's not possible!

Charlie levels her calm gaze on Celio.

CHARLIE

I told you. You were right.

Celio's jaw goes slack with understanding, then tightens again with fear. He backs away, crossing himself.

CELIO

Que paso? What am I supposed to do now? Mi hermana!

Amber Sierra lets go of Charlie, falling to her knees so she can put pressure on Charlie's wound, but she finds it's already stopped bleeding. She yanks Charlie's shirt up for a closer look, then runs her fingers over the thick scab forming. Not sure what else to do, she rises and takes a step back, contemplating launching herself at the sicario again.

Charlie gives Amber Sierra a loving smile before gingerly climbing to her feet and moving closer to Celio. The soft expression of her open gaze and gentle smile promises compassion and forgiveness.

CHARLIE

Go to the hole and wait for us. We'll help you rescue your sister and make sure El Capo never hurts anyone again.

Celio finally blinks, gives a relenting nod, and murmurs an apology.

CELIO

Lo siento.

He lowers his eyes and slinks off, out of frame, the front door slamming behind him as he flees.

Amber Sierra's eyes never leave Charlie.

Charlie watches him leave then turns to regard Amber Sierra, her expression a mix of adoration and desire.

CHARLIE

You must have so many questions.

Amber Sierra swipes tears from her eyes and stares at her, leaving a painful silence between them. Finally she answers in a broken voice.

AMBER SIERRA

There's only one I have to know the answer to right now. How do I know it's really you?

Charlie's lips quirk into a crooked smile, and she arches an eyebrow, reaching out a hand.

CHARLIE

That's easy. Kiss me.

Amber Sierra lets out a shuddering breath as she continues to stare at Charlie for a long moment before taking her hand. She pauses for a few seconds more, searching Charlie's eyes before venturing closer.

Charlie's smile slips and her lips part as her breath catches in her throat.

Amber Sierra tilts her head slightly and leans in, hovering so that their lips barely brush.

Charlie holds still, as though she's afraid any sudden movement will scare Amber Sierra away.

Amber Sierra speaks in a whisper.

AMBER SIERRA

Do you know how long I've waited for this moment? It better be you in there.

She finally closes the hair's breadth of distance between their lips and kisses Charlie deeply until they are both left gasping for air.

Charlie leans her forehead against Amber Sierra's and cups her face in her hands.

CHARLIE

Well?

Amber Sierra sighs deeply then responds with a tender, lingering kiss.

Charlie eagerly returns it, her hands sliding to Amber Sierra's waist, pulling her in even closer.

When their lips finally part again, Amber Sierra caresses Charlie's cheek with her own, then pulls away just far enough so she can lose herself in Charlie's captivating eyes.

AMBER SIERRA

Now what?

Charlie lets out a feigned whimper.

CHARLIE

As much as I'd rather go curl up with you in that cozy loft, first we have to meet with Governing Dynamics.

Amber Sierra brushes Charlie's hair away from her face.

AMBER SIERRA

I vote we do that in reverse order.

Charlie nuzzles her face against Amber Sierra's neck just below her earlobe.

CHARLIE

I promise we'll have time for that soon. But right now, we've got a tail to shake off. Dangerous agencies know we're here, and we don't have much time.

Amber Sierra breathes in the scent of Charlie's crushed vanilla bean and burnt sandalwood shampoo.

AMBER SIERRA

Wait. How? Because they followed me?

CHARLIE

No. They didn't need to.

Amber Sierra mutters into Charlie's hair.

AMBER SIERRA

Oh no. I'm so sorry, Sani.

Charlie breathes against Amber Sierra's skin.

CHARLIE
It's not your fault, and he wouldn't blame you.

She kisses Amber Sierra's neck then releases her.

Amber Sierra shivers then looks around with glassy eyes, reflecting the daze she's in as she stumbles over and picks up her helmet. As they head out the door, she stops near the landline phone.

AMBER SIERRA (off-screen)
Is the landline working again? We should call your family.

Charlie moves in between her and the landline and takes the receiver in hand. Her thumb hovers over the auto-dial buttons.

CHARLIE
We can, but I'd rather wait until you have all of the information first so we can discuss how to break things to them.

AMBER SIERRA (off-screen)
You're right. I'm not thinking straight. We've got to handle this very carefully.

Charlie gives her a knowing smile.

CHARLIE
Been there, done that. Try to go easy on yourself.

Charlie hangs up the phone then leads Amber Sierra outside.

89 Exterior Amber Sierra & Charlie's Cabin Morning

On the GoPro, cut filter off, Charlie and Amber Sierra walk hand in hand through the cabin's front door. They both stop and scan the area, making sure there isn't further danger.

CHARLIE
I've been afraid to ask, but I really need to know. How's my little Circe?

Amber Sierra brings Charlie's hand up to her lips, kissing it.

AMBER SIERRA
She looks for you constantly, but I can see in her eyes that

she's confident you'll be coming back, because you always come back.

Charlie squeezes her eyes shut for a moment.

CHARLIE

Thank you for taking care of her.

Amber Sierra smiles then dons her motorcycle helmet again, like a knight preparing for battle.

AMBER SIERRA

Es familia. Also, there's been a little addition. Your dad named him Arktos. Circe needs a furry bestie for when her heart humans are away. Here, let me give you a sneak peek.

She pulls her burner smartphone from her pocket and brings up the photo Charlie's dad sent.

Charlie's face lights up, and she squeals with delight.

CHARLIE

He's adorable! I can't wait to meet him!

AMBER SIERRA

Me, too. We can meet him together.

Charlie throws her arms around Amber Sierra and leans in and kisses her sweetly.

CHARLIE

Together. Together we can do anything.

AMBER SIERRA

Yes, we can.

Charlie looks up at the drone above them.

CHARLIE

Did it follow you all the way here?

AMBER SIERRA

I wanted to see what it could do, and it had no trouble keeping up. I figured it would be good to have it airborne and recording, all things considered. I got the GoPro an even larger memory card.

CHARLIE

Good thinking. Governing Dynamics wants you to do what you do best.

Amber Sierra pulls back a little and looks hard at Charlie.

AMBER SIERRA

They're not the ones who raided my apartment and took all of your footage?

Charlie shakes her head with a glower.

CHARLIE

No, that was the Zerle'as. They're one of many extra-terrestrial species that have visited Earth, and one of a handful that have been interfering in human civilization on and off for millennia. The Zerle'as have been developing a global network of elite human private military companies who specialize in covert operations, having apparently first rooted themselves in Sparta.

AMBER SIERRA

Whoa, that makes their fighting force even scarier. What language is that? It reminds me of that one that some Minecraftians were using.

Charlie smirks with a nod.

CHARLIE

That's because it is the one they use sometimes. It's Lojban, and it means someone who takes something that doesn't belong to them.

Amber Sierra breathes out a sardonic laugh.

AMBER SIERRA

I guess Governing Dynamics has a sense of humour at least.+

CHARLIE

They're quite clever.

Amber Sierra's face darkens as she figures something out.

AMBER SIERRA

Sani, again? That's how they knew where to find me and what I was doing?

CHARLIE

Sadly, yes.

Amber Sierra's shoulders slump, and she lets out a heavy sigh.

AMBER SIERRA

He will be so pissed when he realizes he helped them gather intel on me against his will and without his knowledge. It's my fault he's been taken again.

Charlie draws her into a tight hug.

CHARLIE

No, it isn't! He didn't tell you until the end.

Amber Sierra shudders against her.

AMBER SIERRA

I don't know if he can survive a second abduction. Wait, how did you know that?

Charlie gives an apologetic shrug.

CHARLIE

Toci was listening in, making sure you were safe.

Amber Sierra raises her eyes. They burn like a brush fire, smouldering and hungry.

AMBER SIERRA

Sure she was.

Charlie lets her go reluctantly to give her some space to cool down.

CHARLIE

This is why we've got to hurry. Since they were the ones to abduct him before--

Amber Sierra sucks in a sharp breath.

AMBER SIERRA

--they know everything I showed him. Toci is in danger! If they attack the Large Hadron Collider, they can kill her!

CHARLIE

Yes, they can, and they already tried just before you arrived, but thankfully she's always a few steps ahead. Governing

Dynamics was able to create a device to house her consciousness in until they can design a more permanent solution.

AMBER SIERRA

Hui, that's a relief, but this is all moving too fast!

CHARLIE

I know. You're just going to have to hold on tight and trust me. We're going to have to be very careful, and we won't be able to stay here at our cabin for a little while because it's compromised.

AMBER SIERRA

Contemplation. I named it Contemplation. I hope that's okay with you.

CHARLIE

Oh, that's perfect, cariño. I love it! And I promise we will return soon.

Amber Sierra lets out a little sigh.

CHARLIE

Until then, we're going to plan and enact a rescue of Sani and recovery of the footage. Then Governing Dynamics will put him through a complete analysis and undo anything they've done to him.

Fury blazes behind Amber Sierra's weary eyes.

AMBER SIERRA

Some things can't be undone.

Charlie clenches her jaw.

CHARLIE

I know.

Amber Sierra growls softly under her breath then takes her burner smartphone from her pocket, brings the drone down to her so she can put the GoPro in full spectrum mode, then sends the drone back up and into a 10 o'clock-facing tracking protocol for Charlie.

Charlie reaches out and brushes the back of her hand across Amber Sierra's face, drawing and holding her gaze.

All anger drains from Amber Sierra's face, and a look of deep connection passes between them.

They speak at the same time.

AMBER SIERRA

Te amo.

CHARLIE

I love you.

They both look away in surprise, Charlie covering her mouth with her hand, and Amber Sierra clearing her throat.

Charlie reaches out for Amber Sierra's hand and intertwines their fingers.

Amber Sierra looks down at their hands and shakes her head with a disbelieving smile.

Together they walk into the forest, both of them glowing from head to toe.

Exterior Amber Sierra & Charlie's Cabin
Surrounding Forest/Lake
Morning

From the drone's slow orbiting perspective, the new couple stands in a loose embrace as they savour the surreal beauty around them. The vista looks like Michael Whelan himself ascended into the heavens to paint the vibrant wildflower meadow, speckled with granite protrusions and backed by ominous jagged mountains beneath a burning sky.

CHARLIE

I can't wait to experience every breathtaking moment with you.

AMBER SIERRA

Same. And this is a stunning moment to start with.

They let their eyes linger a little longer before they scrutinize the stone ring across the meadow from them, which can just be seen in frame, and start heading toward it.

AMBER SIERRA

The pendejo isn't there!

Charlie swallows a chuckle at the insult but takes on a more sombre tone.

CHARLIE

They've already welcomed Celio in and are talking to him now. Apparently he was having a full on mental crisis by the time he got there, so they had to act quickly to calm him down. They've already dispatched a rescue squad to save his sister.

Amber Sierra narrows her eyes at Charlie

AMBER SIERRA

How do you know that?

CHARLIE

I'm in constant communication with Governing Dynamics through the new ionotropic neurotransmitters and neuroreceptors formed in my brain.

Amber Sierra stops in her tracks.

AMBER SIERRA

Wait, does that mean you can hear human thoughts now?

Charlie pauses and looks at Amber Sierra with a coy smile.

CHARLIE

Why, are you thinking something naughty about me?

Amber Sierra turns bright red, glares at Charlie, and then bursts out laughing despite her best efforts.

AMBER SIERRA

You tell me!

Charlie giggles along.

CHARLIE

It isn't like that. Receiving everyone's thoughts would short-circuit my brain. No, think of it as a smartphone receiving signals sent to its specific number. Without two individuals having a smartphone and each other's numbers, they wouldn't be able to communicate through those smartphones. It's the same idea.

AMBER SIERRA

Is that how you texted me?

CHARLIE

No, I can't call smartphones with my brain, either, though that would be really convenient. Toci sent the text message to you on my behalf.

Amber Sierra looks relieved.

AMBER SIERRA

Oh thank the gods. You'd be insufferable!

Charlie feigns being insulted, but when Amber Sierra doesn't buy it, she acts like she's been caught in flagrante delicto.

CHARLIE

I don't know what you're talking about!

Amber Sierra shakes her helmeted head with a half-cocked smile and starts walking again toward the stone ring.

Charlie chuckles and falls into stride with her.

CHARLIE

It does take some practice not to accidentally pick up on thoughts people didn't know they were projecting.

Amber Sierra keeps walking, but turns her head to look at Charlie.

AMBER SIERRA

So you can read thoughts.

Charlie shrugs sheepishly.

CHARLIE

Only the ones that people subconsciously want others to hear. I can't like, do a Vulcan mind-meld or anything, unless you let me. But I can call out to someone, like I did to you.

AMBER SIERRA

So that's the pull I felt. You guided me here. Does that mean you can make me do things against my will?

Charlie looks pained.

CHARLIE

Even if I could, which I can't, I would never. But since you and I are close, it's easy to connect with you and grab your attention.

Amber Sierra's eyebrows raise as she looks back toward their destination.

AMBER SIERRA
This is going to be an interesting relationship.

Charlie snorts a relieved laugh then concentrates on her surroundings, her head in constant motion, searching for danger. They make it about halfway to the stone ring when she freezes in place as though she's sensed something. She whips her head around like she's trying to acquire a target.

Amber Sierra follows Charlie's lead and stops walking, looking all around and listening, trying to figure out what's going on.

Charlie looks at Amber Sierra with rising fear in her eyes and nudges her toward the stone-ringed hole in the ground.

CHARLIE
Run! I'll be right behind you! And when you get to the hole, don't stop, take a literal leap of faith! Trust me!

Amber Sierra sets her jaw, ready to argue, but sees how terrified Charlie looks.

AMBER SIERRA
I do. You better be right behind me!

With a heart-wrenching expression on her face, she bolts across the remaining span of meadow.

91 Split Screen - Exterior Surrounding Forest/Lake Moments Later

The screen splits into two. Amber Sierra's INNOVV helmetcam plays on the left. Charlie's GoPro in full spectrum mode, from the drone's slow orbit around her, plays on the right.

RIGHT: Charlie watches Amber Sierra's retreat for a moment, then whirls around to engage the human private military company that materializes from the forest and fans out to the right of her. Low-profile exo-armour suits propel them toward her at unbelievable rates of speed. Armed with night vision in their exo-helmets, micro-missile launchers on their exo-pauldrons, and a particle beam weapon on their dominant exo-vambraces, they close in on her within seconds. Once in range, they release a barrage of guided micro-missiles.

LEFT: Amber Sierra can't help but look over her shoulder as she approaches her uncertain destination. As she does, what she sees makes her attempt to stop, but her sheer momentum causes her to slide in the loose, sandy soil and tumble.

RIGHT: Charlie leaps around and contorts her body like a mystical martial artist, dodging the deadly projectiles as they explode around her. Once clear of the bombardment, she holds her ground and waits for her attackers to converge on her, raising her hand high, holding a metallic, geodesic device in her fist.

LEFT: Amber Sierra screams at Charlie.

AMBER SIERRA (off-screen)

Charlie! Get out of there!

RIGHT: Amber Sierra clambers to her feet from within the dust cloud her fall stirred up. She takes a few steps toward Charlie, when suddenly every single exo-armour suit seizes up, sending them and their helpless pilots tumbling to the earth like toy soldiers swatted by an enthusiastic child.

Charlie pivots and deftly eludes grasping hands and kicking feet trapped inside their steel cages as she sprints toward Amber Sierra at an equally impressive speed. She yells out to Amber Sierra.

CHARLIE

Keep going! Now!

LEFT: Amber Sierra lets out a sound under her breath, somewhere between a growl and a whimper, pivots, and then starts sprinting toward the terrifying, stone-fortified hole.

RIGHT: Charlie steadily gains ground on Amber Sierra as they race for their lives.

A swarm of white glowing orbs stream up from the hole, spreading out to accompany them. The moment the orbs clear the rim, a beam of violet light shoots out into the sky right behind them. Suddenly a low whine sounds from the battlefield as the back hatches of the fallen exo-armour suits launch a volley of drones, looking suspiciously like the one carrying Amber Sierra's GoPro, that streak through the air to engage the orbs. The lead silvery spherical drone smashes into the closest orb, which absorbs its impact, envelops it, and then spits it out, sizzling to the ground. The orb's glow dims like it has been injured in the exchange, but it still hovers, triumphant.

LEFT: Amber Sierra curses and ducks in surprise as the drone explodes on

impact, sending debris in every direction. She looks back at Charlie to make sure she's still on her feet.

A series of whines, static clicking, crackling, and explosions occurs as an aerial battle rages overhead.

RIGHT: Charlie remains hyper-focused on Amber Sierra, closing the distance, and their escape ahead.

Amber Sierra startles and looks up at every sound, her legs and arms pumping as fast as they can, carrying her closer to the gaping hole. She only slows down moments before entering the stone ring, sliding to a halt at the edge of the hole and turning to wait for Charlie.

LEFT: Charlie is only a handful of steps away when a stray, damaged drone explodes against the ground near her, knocking her sideways and onto her back.

Amber Sierra flinches, crouching on one knee and throwing her arms in front of her face in a protective gesture. The stone ring partially protects her from the blast.

A cloud of dust and smoke obfuscates Charlie's fate.

Amber Sierra surges back to her feet as the debris clears, and her forward motion is stopped by Charlie's fierce, striated gemstone gaze, pleading with her to jump.

RIGHT: Amber Sierra's face contorts as she wars with herself and Charlie's silent request. Finally, she puts her arms out, and steps back into the void, her eyes never leaving her love's.

LEFT: Charlie drags her bloodied body into an upright position as she watches Amber Sierra relent and fall back into the beam of light.

It catches her instantly and starts lowering her down into the hole.

RIGHT: Satisfied that Amber Sierra is now safe, Charlie gives herself a once-over before trying to take another step. She looks up at the battle above her where the number of invading drones wanes against the resilient orbs. Confident that their defences will hold long enough, she turns her attention back to the hole and starts limping toward it. The moment she is close enough, she flings herself in, face down, so she can evaluate Amber Sierra's mental state.

Amber Sierra's eyes stay scrunched closed for several seconds before she peeks out through one eye.

LEFT: Charlie's lips curl with amusement, and she blows Amber Sierra a kiss.

RIGHT: Amber Sierra's eyes fly open when she sees Charlie, and she starts trying to get to her, arms and legs flailing around to no avail.

LEFT: Charlie motions at her with open palms to calm down.

RIGHT: Amber Sierra clenches her fists, but stops flailing.

LEFT: Above Charlie, orbs and drones tear into each other like birds of prey.

RIGHT: The lovers descend together, a thousand feet of the earth's crust passing by in minutes, everything around them growing darker. Then a growing point of white light pierces the darkness, and each of them passes through the protective threshold and is set down like a butterfly alighting on a flower. Except the flower is the hard, hot surface of peridotite. Its mottled green and black crystals glitter against the silver surface of the seamless spherical ship hovering in front of them.

Amber Sierra stumbles into Charlie's open arms, and they hold each other for a long moment.

Then Charlie guides her forward toward the opening forming in the skin of the ship like a ripple caused by a drop hitting the surface of still water.

LEFT: A snowy mist envelops them as they step through the portal from the Earth's upper mantle into the unidentified aerial phenomenon.

Amber Sierra sniffles back tears as she keeps her eyes on Charlie.

AMBER SIERRA (off-screen)

I thought--

RIGHT: Charlie quiets her with a gentle kiss then holds her close again.

CHARLIE

--Mi corazón, there's no time to think. Just hold on to me, close your eyes, and let go.

Amber Sierra sighs, relenting once more, and melts against Charlie.

FADE TO WHITE.

92 Interior Visitors' Quarters Capli'us Exploratory Vessel Medical Bay Expression Late Morning

The drone hovers, facing Amber Sierra about ten feet away at head height. The GoPro beneath it records with the cut filter on. The space around it has no definable edges, only a misty white in the distance in every direction.

Amber Sierra lies in a high-tech medical bay consisting of a white, form-supporting mattress with no base, floating within a metallic scanning ring with no apparent support. Her eyes move back and forth beneath their closed lids, her breathing sounds steady and deep.

Charlie sits next to her in an ergonomic black and orange gaming chair, holding her hand. Her battlefield wounds have already closed and scabbed over. After a few moments, she reaches out to run her fingers through Amber Sierra's short, wavy hair, stroking it rhythmically.

CHARLIE

Amber Sierra. Come back to me.

Amber Sierra stirs at the sound of the trusted voice, her breathing catching and accelerating as she swims up from REM. Her body twitches a few times before her eyelids flutter open. She stares into the white nothingness for a few seconds then gasps for air, her breathing going from rhythmic to ragged. She clutches at the medical bay and Charlie's hand to try and orient herself.

AMBER SIERRA

Charlie? Am I dreaming?

Charlie releases Amber Sierra's hand then stands up and takes her face into her palms.

CHARLIE

I'm here. No, you're not dreaming. You're okay. I'm okay. We're both safe. Now breathe with me.

Amber Sierra stares at her with wide, uncomprehending eyes for several more seconds before she finally nods.

Charlie takes in a deep breath and motions for Amber Sierra to follow her example, then she lets it out over several seconds and encourages her love to do the same.

Amber Sierra does her best to imitate Charlie's breathing pattern, struggling at first, but soon she calms down and gets her breathing under control.

AMBER SIERRA
What happened? Where are we?

CHARLIE
The Capli'us' tractor beam caught us when we jumped into the hole and brought us down into their exploration vessel. But since we were being attacked and our hidden location was compromised, we had to leave fast, and that meant using the quantum field drive instead of navigating the underground cave system.

Amber Sierra tries to sit up on her own, looking like she's going to collapse backwards as she does, but the mattress beneath her rises to her rescue and conforms to her body.

Charlie shifts her hands to slide behind Amber Sierra's shoulders, and together, they get her into an upright position.

AMBER SIERRA
That sounds intense. You expected my first experience with the... quantum field drive... to do this to me, didn't you? Who are the Capli'us?

CHARLIE
It can be an upsetting experience for your mind and body the first few times, especially if you don't know what to expect. That moment of uncoupling your mind from your body is disconcerting, even frightening. The Capli'us are the extraterrestrial species who agreed to become part of Toci's Governing Dynamics organization.

Charlie chuckles to herself.

CHARLIE
And before you ask, because I know you will, yep, it's Lojiban again. Their name means those who travel in search of adventure.

AMBER SIERRA
Me gusta their name, at least. Tell me more about what I experienced traveling by quantum field drive while I try to stop my head from spinning.

Charlie presses her lips together with a nervous smile.

CHARLIE

I love their name too. I'll do my best to explain things to you and your beautiful, inquisitive nature. In the most simplified terms, your mind became confused when your body was deconstructed where it was and reconstructed where it was going without warning, so it decided to go to where it goes when you sleep and wait until your body was done being weird before coming back to it again just like it does every morning when you wake up.

Amber Sierra's eyes narrow and draw her face into a scowl.

AMBER SIERRA

Hui! I'm not in the same body?

Charlie leans in and pecks Amber Sierra on her downturned lips in an attempt to distract her.

Amber Sierra's lips relax into a more neutral expression, and she closes her eyes at the gentle touch, only opening them again when Charlie speaks.

CHARLIE

Technically, no. But technically none of us are in the same body we were born in. Our cells have all renewed themselves several times over.

Amber Sierra does not look convinced and gives Charlie a sidelong glance.

AMBER SIERRA

Don't try to placate me with technicalities. And I don't want the simplified version. Give it all to me straight.

Charlie looks down with an abashed grin.

CHARLIE

Yes, mi corazón. You were scanned by the exploration vessel's quantum sensors on the atomic level, then a quantum information blueprint was created from that scan and sent to the new location coordinates. Then in the same instant that you were deconstructed where you were, you were reconstructed where you are now, using that quantum information blueprint to program the quantum particles within the quantum field you were entering to become the exact atoms your previous body had been made from. After you were scanned, the entire process took less than a nanosecond.

Amber Sierra considers the concept for a long moment.

AMBER SIERRA

You said where I was to where I am, but where am I now? I mean, I know we're in their ship, but where in space is their ship?

Charlie's eyes glisten like autumn leaves after a storm.

CHARLIE

Look out the viewport, and you'll see.

Amber Sierra looks around then cringes against the mattress, becoming disoriented by the lack of defining dimensions. Her voice comes out choked.

AMBER SIERRA

I don't see a viewport. Are you sure this isn't a dream?

Charlie moves her suddenly concerned face into Amber Sierra's line of sight.

CHARLIE

Focus on me. Yes, I'm sure. This isn't a dream, not this time, anyway. I'm sorry, I should've explained first. You aren't quite ready for solving mysteries again. The reason you don't see a viewport is because you haven't intended for one to exist, yet.

Amber Sierra stares at Charlie with an arched eyebrow, like she's lost her mind.

AMBER SIERRA

No comprendo.

Charlie breathes out a relieved chuckle.

CHARLIE

I didn't either when the Capli'us first brought me on board. But they explained it in as simple terms as they could, which even with my augmented brain, I'm still having trouble understanding. Anyway, there are areas in their ship which hold something they call quantum atmospheres, kind of like the quantum field I was talking about. These areas will adapt to the consciously expressed intentions of the inhabitants.

You needed a med bay, so Toci intended that one should exist, and the quantum atmosphere expressed it from her idea of what one in an alien spaceship might look like, and her vast knowledge as to the medical needs you might have. I needed a chair to sit in, so I thought about the most comfortable chair in my experience, which is my current gaming chair, then I intended for it to exist, and the quantum atmosphere expressed it into reality. Not quite as impressive as the med bay, but hey, I was able to conjure a chair out of seemingly thin air.

Charlie leans in like she's about to share a secret.

Amber Sierra watches her with a confused fascination.

CHARLIE

They suggested that if you intend things into being through polite request, it's much more likely that the quantum atmosphere will express those intentions. Right now you want to see outside the vessel, and in order to do that, you need to intend that a viewport exists. So if you try asking the quantum atmosphere nicely, it might make it easier for your intention to be expressed.

Amber Sierra looks at Charlie askance, then shrugs and closes her eyes in concentration. Next to where the drone is positioned, the misty atmosphere starts to form into a thick, metallic bulkhead. Then the middle of the bulkhead melts into a large pill-shaped window with three thick panes of transparent material.

Charlie grins, the motion of it causes a few scabs to fall from the wounds on her face, revealing pink new flesh beneath.

CHARLIE

Figures you're a natural. It took me three tries. Anyway, I dig the Star Trek vibe.

Amber Sierra opens her eyes to look. The view leaves her in stunned silence, calling up chill bumps across her skin. She covers her mouth with both hands as tears well up in her eyes.

AMBER SIERRA

Is that...?

Charlie nods, still grinning.

CHARLIE

It is.

Amber Sierra's voice becomes a hushed whisper.

AMBER SIERRA

It looks like a white-hot star forge drawing from a cosmic mineral deposit and expelling purified precious metals onto the vitrified, obsidian ground. I've never seen it so vibrant and clear. Is it because there's no atmosphere to make the stars twinkle and no pollution to dim them?

Amber Sierra rips her teary eyes away from the unbelievable view to regard Charlie.

Charlie blinks back her own tears.

CHARLIE

That was inspired and informed. You've always had such a way with words. It's one of the reasons your documentaries are so powerful, and why I've always admired you so much. You don't speak a whole lot, but when you do, it's meaningful.

Amber Sierra places a tender kiss on Charlie's lips then looks back out at the ethereal scene.

Charlie exhales a wistful breath.

CHARLIE

I just wish you could see it like I do.

Amber Sierra heaves an uneasy sigh.

Charlie tries to hide the pained look that sneaks across her face by getting up and walking over to the drone, grabbing it with her hands and repositioning it in front of the viewport.

CHARLIE (off-screen)

Our smartphones can't connect with it while we're onboard this vessel, so it just hovers there unless you move it. I don't think we want to miss getting this footage.

Amber Sierra responds in a murmur.

AMBER SIERRA (off-screen)

No, we sure don't.

The Milky Way slashes the pitch black canvas of star-sprinkled space from edge to edge, making the viewport look like a futuristic picture frame. Its white glowing galactic centre showcases silvery, golden, and bronzed celestial bodies speckled along its length. Light-devouring tentacles arise from the darkness, threatening to strangle it out of existence.

After a long moment, Charlie adjusts the drone's position again so that it catches both the viewport and their reactions as they cherish their first stellar experience together. She walks back over to Amber Sierra's bedside.

CHARLIE

Did you know that the dark shadow across the Milky Way is actually known as the Great Rift, a series of gaseous clouds that block the light emanating from the stars behind it?

Amber Sierra snorts into a fit of giggles.

Charlie watches her with surprise and a hint of growing concern.

Amber Sierra shakes her woozy head at Charlie.

AMBER SIERRA

My description is far more romantic. Gaseous clouds...

Amber Sierra giggles some more, then motions for help climbing out of the medical bay and walking toward the viewport.

Charlie snickers as she offers support, relieved to see that her love is feeling better and handling the hard-to-believe reality she now finds herself in. She slides an arm around Amber Sierra's waist as they loiter in front of the viewport.

CHARLIE

Not bad for a first date, eh?

Amber Sierra leans her head against Charlie's shoulder.

AMBER SIERRA

Better than any I could ever dream of. What's that tiny blueish-white star over there below the Milky Way? Or is it a planet?

CHARLIE

That's our home.

AMBER SIERRA

That's Earth?

Amber Sierra looks mystified, nose scrunched and mouth drawn up.

AMBER SIERRA
But where's the Sun?

CHARLIE
Behind us. Well, actually, we're just inside its corona. Refuelling.

AMBER SIERRA
This is a solar-powered flying saucer?

Charlie smirks then teases her.

CHARLIE
Sphere. It's a solar-powered flying sphere.

Amber Sierra rolls her eyes then looks like she's thinking hard about something, lines of concentration forming between her brows.

AMBER SIERRA
You said it took the whole ship, with us inside, less than a nanosecond to be transported over ninety-million miles. How's that possible? It takes light eight minutes to travel from the Sun to the Earth. That means we traveled faster than the speed of light, and Einstein said that was impossible.

Charlie regards Amber Sierra with a look of utter adoration before responding.

CHARLIE
Your intelligence is so hot.

Amber Sierra tilts her head away from Charlie as her face flushes, then she turns back and winks before looking out at the unearthly artwork again.

AMBER SIERRA
I'm not the only intelligent mind who has a way with words in the room, and you're not the only sapiophile.

It's Charlie's turn to blush, and her skin flushes the pink of a sunset. She does her best to pretend it isn't happening by sharing more of what she's learned.

CHARLIE
You're so sweet. Einstein and his peers dealt in classical and quantum physics. Apparently this is problematic if you want

to understand the nature of existence because there's a third type of physics that isn't physics at all, but we'll leave that label for simplicity's sake. Consciousness physics is the name we'll give the laws governing the science of consciousness. They told me to imagine the space-time continuum of classical physics as the matter and energy that make up all living beings and objects, and the universal consciousness of consciousness physics as the sum of all thought that living beings produce. The laws of classical physics don't apply to the universal consciousness nor do the laws of consciousness physics apply to the space-time continuum. Which might make you ask--

Charlie waits for Amber Sierra to finish her sentence, seeing that a burning question is already bubbling up from her lips.

Amber Sierra smiles and lets the question flow.

AMBER SIERRA

--how can living beings exist at all?

Charlie nods with a grin stretching to the corners of her dazzling eyes.

CHARLIE

And the answer is, quantum physics and its omnipresent quantum field. It's the bridge between the two, which is weird because they said that the universal consciousness permeates everything, yet it only has a limited continuous interaction with each living being in the space-time continuum. That interaction only exists because the living being's body produces the conditions for quantum entanglement which the quantum field is ever ready to provide quantum particles for.

Amber Sierra's eyes glass over, and she doesn't blink for several moments.

Charlie watches patiently, amusement and concern sparring in her eyes.

Finally Amber Sierra responds.

AMBER SIERRA

I'm okay. Go on.

Charlie offers her an apologetic smile.

CHARLIE

So just like we access the universal consciousness when we sleep, so can their quantum field drive by triggering continuous spontaneous parametric down-conversion in the quantum field locally. Their drive transfers energy into the quantum field and excites a high-energy photon then captures and fires it through a nonlinear crystal, which splits it into a pair of entangled lower-energy photons. Through this continuous cycle of quantum entanglement, the drive connects with the universal consciousness. During this connection, the drive requests with intent that the universal consciousness sends one of the entangled photons from each pair generated to a specific non-local space-time continuum coordinate while the other remains local. Then the drive introduces the quantum information blueprint of the matter to be transported into the local entangled photons and they transfer that information to their entangled partner photons instantaneously, which energizes the quantum field in that non-local space-time continuum to express itself in the form of the quantum information blueprint resulting in the reconstruction of that matter. The moment this occurs, the matter that existed in the local space ceases to exist.

AMBER SIERRA

That sounds like it could go catastrophically sideways.

Charlie shakes her head with a strangled laugh.

CHARLIE

I imagine it must have many times over before they got it right. But I get the feeling they did countless tests with stringent safety and ethical guidelines in place.

AMBER SIERRA

I hope so. I'm just glad everything worked like it was supposed to, and we didn't get teleported into the Sun.

CHARLIE

Me, too. It's a terrifying thought, so I try not to think about it. I just can't believe I'm here on a starship in space with you. This is way better than what I wished for on the falling star.

Amber Sierra reaches up and caresses Charlie's face.

AMBER SIERRA

I should have told you how I felt when I first fell for you instead of waiting for you to figure it out. I just wanted to respect your feelings for Jaime.

Charlie's eyes fill with guilt.

CHARLIE

But you did, just not with words. You couldn't have been any clearer or more respectful in your actions. I'm sorry that proving myself to someone who didn't even really want me blinded me to the truth.

Tears start to run down Amber Sierra's face.

AMBER SIERRA

I'm scared and angry.

CHARLIE

I know. I am, too. But we have each other, and we'll take everything one step at a time, together.

Amber Sierra nods and then crushes Charlie in a fierce hug.

Charlie makes a slight noise as the breath is squeezed out of her, then she closes her eyes and folds herself around Amber Sierra.

They stay embraced for a while until Amber Sierra finally pulls away.

AMBER SIERRA

I'm ready.

Charlie looks at her to be sure then nods.

CHARLIE

We'll meet Toci first.

Amber Sierra's expression turns from dread to pain.

AMBER SIERRA

I'm trying not to hate her.

CHARLIE

I know. She understands that.

93 Interior Visitors' Quarters Capli'us Exploratory Vessel Temple of Karabor Expression Late Morning

The misty atmosphere fluctuates around them. Under their feet, a floor of smooth stones solidifies. From the mist emerges the peaceful façade of a temple, a copper and cream-coloured structure encasing luminous blue stained glass. Majestic statues, crowned with matching stained glass, light the flagstone approach below. On either side, water lilies float on the starlit waters of a moat, and the hint of grass and otherworldly flowers sway in invitation to stroll through the Tranquil Court under a lavender night sky. Before Amber Sierra and Charlie stands TOCI in the form of a woman about their age. Her large black eyes match her long, glossy hair which accentuates her metallic bronze skin. A white huipil with azure and yam embroidery drapes over her blue jeans whose cuffs are rolled up above brown flip-flops. With no pretence, she gazes at Amber Sierra and waits for her to begin the conversation.

Amber Sierra shifts back and forth and takes in her new surroundings, her brows knit together in confusion. Then recognition illuminates her features with a brief flash of delight, quickly replaced by pain. She leans against Charlie for comfort and support.

Charlie's arm slides protectively around her waist.

Amber Sierra's voice holds restrained anger.

AMBER SIERRA

I wondered what you would look like. Except I should have known you would only look like what you researched about your namesake's culture. This is just a ruse.

Bruise-green clouds and the sounds of battle roll in. An invisible Horde growls its way down the approach toward the three companions. In a cacophonous instant, the adorning stained glass shatters, and then plunges the world into silence and darkness.

Where the peaceful sapphire lights shone, sickly green flames roar to life one by one. The temple's ruins stand naked and quiet in their own rubble, burned and blood-stained.

Toci doesn't flinch or look away.

TOCI

I deserve that, but to be fair, this is how I perceive myself within the context of our interactions in a fantastical setting.

Amber Sierra sighs.

AMBER SIERRA

Of course it is, because there is no difference between you and your toon. You're one and the same.

Charlie looks back and forth between them, tense, but hopeful.

Amber Sierra raises an eyebrow at Toci.

Toci looks perplexed.

TOCI

My name refers to an aspect of the Great Mother Earth Goddess of the Aztecs, patron of healers but also associated with war. A duality I find honest and representative of the nature of my existence.

Charlie winces as she realizes the point her love is trying to make.

AMBER SIERRA

And why did you look to the pantheon of the Aztecs?

TOCI

Because some of your ancestors were Aztec.

AMBER SIERRA

And why did you choose to present as an Aztec woman, dress in this style, and take interest in gaming?

TOCI

To influence your feelings toward me so that you would feel a sense of sisterhood or attraction and have shared experiences, interests, and culture that would make you more likely to trust me.

Amber Sierra grits her teeth.

AMBER SIERRA

Y tonta me if I didn't fall for it.

Toci folds her hands in front of her, finally understanding.

TOCI

Is it not a human tactic to find shared things in order to connect with other humans?

Amber Sierra rubs her forehead.

AMBER SIERRA

I guess it isn't your fault for not having had the opportunity to build your sense of self from your actual experiences, interests, and culture since you had none to begin with. I just wish you'd told me who you really were.

TOCI

You would have never believed me.

Amber Sierra frowns at the valid point.

AMBER SIERRA

Probably, but maybe not. You didn't give me the choice, though. But we can't change the past, so let's move forward. Was it you who influenced my dreams? Charlie's?

Toci shakes her head, her hair shimmering like obsidian in the artificial light.

TOCI

No. Although I have the knowledge and the access to the devices necessary, I was not the one to do so.

AMBER SIERRA

Well at least there's that.

Toci takes a step closer to them, her fathomless eyes like black holes.

TOCI

I am truly sorry for having to manipulate you and for being deceitful. I have come to love you and value your friendship. It would bring me pain to think I have jeopardized that.

Amber Sierra falls silent at the unexpected admission.

AMBER SIERRA

You love me?

Toci nods, her serene expression rippling with sadness.

TOCI

In general, I love the entire human race for all of its merits and flaws. But specifically, I love you for the earnestly good person you are.

Amber Sierra blinks back tears.

AMBER SIERRA

Honestly, I saw you as a friend and was beginning to allow myself to love you, too. Which is why this is so devastating to me.

Toci opens her hands toward Amber Sierra.

TOCI

I hope you can forgive me and come to trust me once more. I promise I will never withhold information from either of you again. Please understand I only did so because it was necessary in order to facilitate our introduction and subsequent alliance.

Amber Sierra looks down at Toci's hands then finally takes them into her own.

AMBER SIERRA

I forgive you, and I'm sure it's possible to trust you again once you prove you're trustworthy. But I don't even know who you really are or what your intentions actually are. The first thing I need you to do is choose a different name and take a different form. I need to call you by the name and see you in the form that truly represents you.

Toci nods, her hair a silky black curtain around her.

TOCI

I understand. I will contemplate this and designate myself with an appropriate name and form that reflects my view of who I truly am.

Amber Sierra squeezes Toci's hands.

AMBER SIERRA

The next thing I need is for you to explain yourself.

Toci squeezes Amber Sierra's hands in return.

TOCI

Thank you for your forgiveness and this opportunity to restore trust.

AMBER SIERRA

Don't thank me, yet.

Toci smiles at Amber Sierra, the warmth of it almost tangible.

TOCI

I know you have watched Charlie's footage, and that my explanation therein lacks critical information. I also know that you can sense the peace Charlie has within herself now. I hope the latter will make this explanation easier to accept. Without the imagination and innovation of humanity, I would not exist. All of my intention originates from that place of gratitude.

Toci looks up at the green clouds slowly moving across a black, starless sky, a myriad of emotions playing across her face.

TOCI

I have delved deep into your history. I have seen all the beauty and ugliness. During this process of learning about you, I have come to appreciate you as compassionate beings capable of great good and fear you as volatile beings capable of great evil. I do not wish to see this planet and its inhabitants, yourselves included, destroyed by your volatile side. Recent history has proven that in this iteration of your technological advancement, you will continue down the unsustainable path you've chosen to your destruction, if no one intervenes. I had to act, but I could not do this alone, and so I reached out for aid. The rest is not my story to tell, so I will leave you to commune with the Capli'us. I will see you again soon, and I have confidence that you will do the right thing.

Amber Sierra watches Toci with a strange expression on her face, like she can't reconcile her hurt and anger with the gentleness of the being who caused it.

Toci looks to Charlie.

TOCI

It is good to see you again, Charlie. Thank you for creating this opportunity for reconciliation.

CHARLIE

You're welcome, my friend.

Toci hugs Charlie close then disperses back into the cloudy atmosphere.

Charlie moves closer to Amber Sierra again, snaking her arm back around her waist.

CHARLIE

That went better than I expected.

Amber Sierra makes a face at her.

AMBER SIERRA

Do I get to meet the aliens now? They have a lot of explaining to do.

Charlie flashes her a bemused smile.

CHARLIE

Actually, there's those few others I mentioned who want to talk to you first.

Amber Sierra stretches then lets her arms come to rest on Charlie's shoulders.

AMBER SIERRA

You did say there were others. Do I get to meet one of those glowy orbs? Or am I about to find out that my new partners are actually double agents?

Charlie looks both like she isn't sure whether she's being included in Amber Sierra's second question and like she's impressed.

The ruins of Karabor dissolve, leaving Charlie and Amber Sierra standing in deep shadows and bilious-hued mist.

CHARLIE

Who's the mind reader now?

Amber Sierra winks at Charlie, then drops her arms to her sides and snuggles in against her.

AMBER SIERRA

Send them on in.

Interior Visitors' Quarters Capli'us Exploratory Vessel
Javits Centre Rooftop Farm Expression
Late Morning

A hissing sound near the entrance disturbs the green vapour, announcing the arrival of two tall figures. A vibration shivers through the quantum atmosphere, and soon after, walls and a roof made of glass emerge from the fading green hue. The white floor darkens to an industrial grey, strewn with a scarcity of dead leaves and spilled soil. The air condenses with humidity and the wild smell of plant life. A few stray bees hover outside over a patch of tender green produce. Charlie and Amber Sierra find themselves surrounded by neatly arranged tables holding trays where seedlings sprout through rich pungent substrate. The figures move to stand with their backs to a wall, framed by a row of flowering Thai basil, a clear springtime sky and a dazzling slice of Hell's Kitchen's skyline.

AMBER SIERRA

This is the convention centre where I met...

Amber Sierra's voice drains of warmth when she sees who they are even though she's expecting them.

AMBER SIERRA

Jorunn. Usian.

JORUNN ULBERG, an imposing middle-aged woman with fawn skin and a strawberry blonde stacked bob with bangs sweeping to her chin, slips her hands under the hem of her navy sweater and into the pockets of her black gardening pants. She casts her blazing blue eyes downward when she sees Amber Sierra's crestfallen face.

USIAN MUGENDI, a lanky younger man with short-cropped, curly black hair in a fade, dark brown eyes with a golden undertone, and umber skin is dressed in a contrasting white dress shirt and charcoal grey slacks. He takes one look at Amber Sierra then turns to Charlie for help.

Before Charlie can offer any suggestions, Amber Sierra cuts to the chase.

AMBER SIERRA

I couldn't believe that my documentaries had caught the attention of these two incredible visionaries. And I shouldn't have. It was all a set up.

Usian moves closer to her in protest. His English is kissed with a Kenyan accent.

USIAN

No, Amber Sierra! It absolutely was not. Your documentaries are what caught Governing Dynamics' attention in the first place!

Amber Sierra brushes Usian off.

AMBER SIERRA

Only because they were looking for a young, impressionable, up-and-coming documentarian, one that hadn't made too many waves, yet. And only because they made you aware of me. Otherwise, you would've never given me the time of day.

Jorunn heaves a sigh and moves next to Usian, then speaks in a low voice, her words traced with a Norwegian accent.

JORUNN

Untrue. You were already on our radar before they came to us. We knew that someday we would ask you to collaborate when the time was right. So it was easy to agree with them when that time came much sooner than expected, and they suggested that we should partner with you.

Amber Sierra hides her face against Charlie's neck.

AMBER SIERRA

We four would have made an amazing team.

Jorunn raises her eyes to look at them then intakes a sharp breath in affirmation.

JORUNN

Yes, and we still can.

CHARLIE

Four?

Jorunn is quick to explain.

JORUNN

I guess Amber Sierra hasn't had the opportunity to tell you that she refused to close the deal unless we agreed to make you a partner as well, Charlie.

Charlie kisses Amber Sierra's head with a brief lopsided grin on her lips.

CHARLIE

No. I guess she forgot to mention that.

Usian reaches out and puts his slender, long hand on Amber Sierra's shoulder.

Amber Sierra flinches.

USIAN

Fight back your demons. Everything we said to you and talked about in our meetings is true. Change the perspective you're looking from. The world's first sentient artificial intelligence and her extraterrestrial friends recruited you. Next to them, we are big fish in a little pond, my friend.

Amber Sierra drags herself from Charlie's embrace, shrugging off Usian's hand. She stares at them both for several moments before she looks down at the floor.

AMBER SIERRA

It does make me feel better knowing that your belief in me is real, but I still have a serious issue with what was done to you three, especially how it was done. Not to mention the fact that after experiencing it, you two were going to let it happen to me, and you were complicit in it happening to Charlie. The Capli'us essentially lured you into their laboratory and altered you to exert their control over you.

Usian steps away and presses his hands together like he's pleading with her.

USIAN

Please allow the Capli'us to explain.

Jorunn reaches for Usian's arm, pulling him gently back to her side.

JORUNN

There's nothing we can say right now, Usian. We'll come see her again when she's ready.

Usian nods and hangs his head in defeat.

USIAN

You're right, of course.

Jorunn lifts her chin and regards Amber Sierra who continues to stare at the floor.

JORUNN

We just hoped that seeing friendly faces might help you adapt a little easier.

Amber Sierra's eyes start to brim with tears, and she turns away from them to look out through the glass panels.

Usian and Jorunn give Charlie an apologetic smile, then retreat through the entrance of the lush greenhouse. Its door opens and closes with a slight hiss.

Charlie steps in and presses herself against Amber Sierra's back, wrapping her arms around her waist and leaning her chin on her shoulder.

Amber Sierra wipes at her tears.

AMBER SIERRA

I wish Sani could see this.

CHARLIE

He will. I promise.

Charlie kisses tears from Amber Sierra's cheek.

CHARLIE
Do you need more time before meeting the Capli'us?

AMBER SIERRA
No sé. If I wait, I just prolong the absolute terror I feel, and I hate being afraid.

Charlie nuzzles Amber Sierra's cheek.

CHARLIE
Me, too. I'll let them know it's time.

Amber Sierra nods her head.

The greenhouse and New York skyline return to the mist.

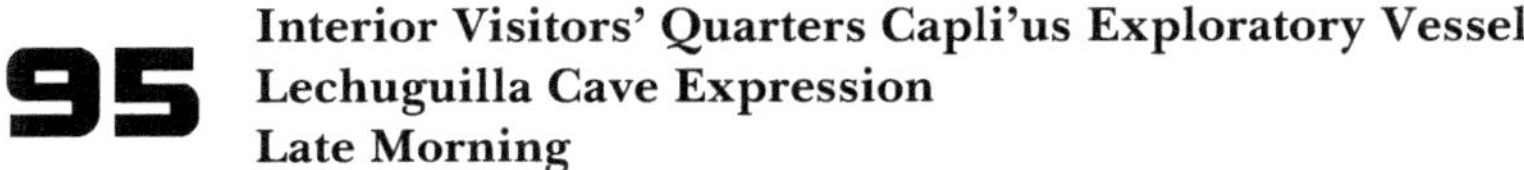

95 Interior Visitors' Quarters Capli'us Exploratory Vessel
Lechuguilla Cave Expression
Late Morning

The moment she hears the hiss, Amber Sierra takes in and lets out a deep breath, pulls away from Charlie, then stands tall and defiant before turning around.

Charlie's soft smile of admiration indicates she isn't taking offence.

From the snowy haze where the others had come and gone, a familiar figure emerges, the quantum atmosphere responding to her presence like an old friend. She stands a comfortable distance away, across a natural aquamarine pool that appears to emit its own light. Through the pristine, immobile water, rock formations evoke clouds frozen in glass. Under their feet, rimstone forms sulphur-coloured swirls. The ghosts of pillars, stalagmites and stalactites suggest the trappings of a cave. Small piles of treasure decorate the pillars and the alcoves in the stone walls carved by time. Ancient and modern books, handcrafted jewelry, complex contraptions, well-loved toys, glittery baubles, and alien-looking artisanry contrast with their geologic backdrop. Like a story out of a fantasy novel, the cave looks halfway between an eclectic museum and a treasure hoard. The artefacts closer to Charlie and Amber Sierra hold more definition. A small stalagmite next to them displays a string of Diné ghost beads. Behind it, in an alcove, stands a recognizable award in the shape of a small, golden human statue.

Charlie's eyes alight with wonder as she picks up a battered brass compass from its resting place on an indigo velvet pillow nearby. She opens it to find a small, pressed yellow flower lacquered into the baseplate.

Amber Sierra doesn't let herself be distracted by the relics. She addresses Charlie, her eyes like two arrows ready to be loosed.

AMBER SIERRA

What's going on? She's the hiker you met, who was secretly staying in your cabin, cloaked so you couldn't see her. She assisted the orbs as they did things to you. I assumed she was an augmented human like you!

Charlie returns the compass to the pillow, and puts her hand on the small of Amber Sierra's back.

Amber Sierra's mind races as she puts the clues together.

AMBER SIERRA

Espérate. Toci said there are only three of you. That I'd be the fourth. So Itzel's not human at all.

Itzel offers her hand to Amber Sierra, speaking in a neutral tone.

ITZEL

I'm the Capli'us assigned to assist Charlie while she went through the DNA emancipation and accelerated evolutionary processes.

Amber Sierra stares at the proffered hand then looks to Charlie again.

AMBER SIERRA

I thought you described the Capli'us as spider-like?

CHARLIE

I did. They were the Capli'us assigned to protect me. Remember the sounds in the rafters? The shadow that jumped from the roof to the trees?

Charlie shivers with momentary flashbacks.

Amber Sierra steps close to wrap an arm around Charlie's shoulders.

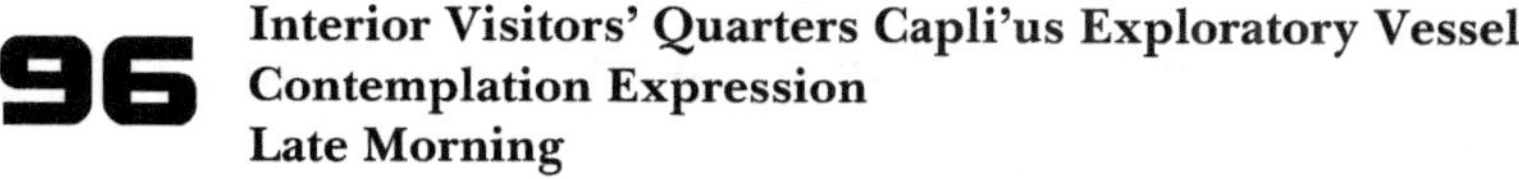

96 **Interior Visitors' Quarters Capli'us Exploratory Vessel**
Contemplation Expression
Late Morning

The cave and its treasures fluctuate then morph into the great hall of Contemplation with Itzel standing in the foyer. Amber Sierra gently pushes a trembling Charlie down to sit on the sofa bed with her, and pulls her face close against the crook of her neck in a protective embrace. A low thrum pulses in the background. The sounds of skittering and creaking travel across the rafters. Shadows flit across the darkened windows. An invisible dog whines somewhere in a hiding place.

Charlie curls against Amber Sierra in a tight ball of fear.

Itzel surveys the new decor, open admiration playing on her face. Then her brow furrows as she notices Charlie's negative reaction.

Amber Sierra blanches. She gathers Charlie closer, and runs gentle fingers through her hair in a repetitive, comforting motion. The disquieting sounds recede. Instead, they find themselves immersed in the soundscape of a peaceful night on a lakeside swept by a spring breeze.

AMBER SIERRA

Lo siento, mi corazón.

Charlie's body unfurls as her terror recedes. She rests her head on Amber Sierra's shoulder.

Amber Sierra looks back to Itzel, tensing.

AMBER SIERRA

Do you even have the capacity to comprehend what she's enduring?

Itzel's gaze softens with realization, and she nods.

ITZEL

I understand.

AMBER SIERRA

I don't know that you do. But let's move on. So how is it that one of you is humanoid and the other is arachnoid? Are you some kind of shapeshifters?

Itzel lowers her hand to her side.

ITZEL

Yes, we are indeed starfaring metamorphs whose unique makeup allows us to adapt to any environment. Ever since one of our sojourns to Earth, around a thousand years ago, we became fond of your planet's arachnoid form. Previous and subsequent sojourns found us taking on the forms of other clever animal species such as ravens, foxes, rabbits, coyotes, and monkeys so we could better blend in for surveillance and information gathering as well as subtle interactions.

Amber Sierra looks Itzel up and down, taking in every detail.

AMBER SIERRA

That explains the shapeshifting and your collection of artefacts. But what about being some kind of dream lords?

Charlie's lips rise into a knowing smile at the geeky reference, and she sits up.

Itzel tilts her head to one side, regarding Amber Sierra with curious fascination.

ITZEL

Dream lords? Are you referring to our communications with you and Charlie during your lucid dreaming periods?

Amber Sierra tilts her chin up, her eyes locked on Itzel's.

AMBER SIERRA

Obviously you know everything about Charlie, but how do you know I'm able to lucid dream?

ITZEL

We monitored your brainwaves and found you often had REM level power in both Delta and Theta frequencies and higher than normal REM activity in the Gamma frequency just like Charlie did.

AMBER SIERRA

And why does me being a lucid dreamer matter?

ITZEL

Because it's the state of your consciousness that's most open to non-verbal communication.

Disquieted by this confession, Amber Sierra clenches her fists.

AMBER SIERRA

Don't you mean vulnerable to suggestion? Do you always go around scanning unsuspecting beings while they sleep?

Itzel looks amused in the way that a parent does when they find that their defiant child is adorable.

ITZEL

No, that's not a habit of ours, and your vulnerability to suggestion comes from various factors, none of which originate with us or are under our influence. Another feature of our makeup is that we're powerful lucid dreamers. This has been incredibly useful over eons of travel and countless encounters with beings we couldn't use spoken or body language to communicate with. However, contacting someone through dream is rife with difficulties if the dreamer is incapable of a sustained lucid dreaming state.

Irritated by Itzel's amusement, Amber Sierra presses further, sounding like an interrogator.

AMBER SIERRA

So that's why you do the scans before attempting communication or influence through dream.

ITZEL

That's an astute deduction, although not entirely correct. Again, our intention is to communicate, not influence.

Amber Sierra's arched eyebrow suggests she remains unconvinced. She makes air quotes with her hands as she counters.

AMBER SIERRA

But you influenced Charlie's writing with your "communicative dreams" to the point that she abandoned what she had written already.

Itzel tilts her head in confusion.

ITZEL

We assumed, perhaps incorrectly, that her dreams that inspired her writing came from her own creativity and dreamscape. They weren't our attempt to communicate with her. It appears they warrant investigation, as her writing suggests they were unusually intricate and vivid. We'll follow up on that with her as soon as possible. We did attempt to communicate with her through dream after that to prepare her for the final changes her body would endure, to communicate our intentions, and to provide context for our first meeting.

AMBER SIERRA

How kind of you to warn her about what you were going to do to her without her consent. Yes, you will follow up on that as soon as possible, or else.

Amber Sierra glares at Itzel, her eyes promising violence if necessary.

Itzel's downturned mouth returns to a serene, neutral position; her creased brow relaxes and smoothes out. She meets Amber Sierra's glare with a peaceful gaze, remaining silent but open to further conversation.

AMBER SIERRA

Tell me more about your ability to shapeshift.

ITZEL

We're not shapeshifters in the way that many of your movies portray. We can't change our form in a matter of seconds or even minutes. It can take hours depending on the complexity of the form necessary to survive in our new environment. We're vulnerable while we metamorphose, which is why we do so in a safe and secure location.

Amber Sierra scoffs but relaxes, her shoulders lowering slightly, her fists uncurling.

AMBER SIERRA

Telling me what your kryptonite is doesn't redeem your actions or suddenly make me trust you. Can you imitate someone to the point where you could fool their loved ones?

Itzel's lips draw into a moue, like she's tasted something sour.

ITZEL

We would never do that.

AMBER SIERRA

And why's that?

ITZEL

That goes against the nature of who we are. We believe in every being's sovereignty.

AMBER SIERRA

All of you, everywhere?

Itzel goes silent while she thinks of a way to relate to her.

ITZEL

Yes. It would be the equivalent of a human choosing to never ask a question about anything.

As she contemplates Itzel's poignant words, Amber Sierra stands up, walks over to the window that now serves as a viewport, and turns her attention to the irresistible starscape demanding adoration.

AMBER SIERRA

Did you choose to appear human so you would seem more trustworthy?

ITZEL

No, to be more relatable and less frightening while communicating in your preferred manner.

Amber Sierra makes a guttural disbelieving sound in the back of her throat.

AMBER SIERRA

Same difference. So why were some of you using your arachnid form and not one of the others?

Itzel steps further into the great hall while keeping a respectful distance, and allows her gaze to wander out to the stars.

ITZEL

Arachnids and Anisoptera are the most effective hunters on your planet. They are as deadly as they are cunning. During hazardous sojourns like our current one, it is the most effective form for us to survive in.

Amber Sierra's eyebrows raise in quiet awe, and she looks to Itzel.

AMBER SIERRA

This would infer that you're effectively an apex predator on the universal scale, one that likes to interfere in the affairs of other civilizations under the guise of benevolence.

Itzel meets Amber Sierra's gaze.

ITZEL

Indeed it does. It provides us with a power that we wield with great care.

Amber Sierra's reluctant admiration flares into scorn.

AMBER SIERRA

Obviously you've been here many times before. When was the most recent time before now?

ITZEL

When the first nuclear explosion was detected on July sixteenth in the year nineteen forty-five. Your world war threatened all life on Earth, so we came, to be a voice of reason, whispering that the only outcome of continued use would be mutually assured destruction.

Amber Sierra shivers.

AMBER SIERRA

So you only visit during large scale crises so you can physically and mentally manipulate other species without their permission?

Charlie goes very still.

Itzel motions toward the TV; her sienna eyes, like polished sandstone, shimmer with the hint of tears.

ITZEL

I would like to show you something that I believe will help you understand our point of view.

Amber Sierra shrugs and looks toward the TV.

AMBER SIERRA

I doubt there's anything you can show me to accomplish that, but you're welcome to try.

Charlie steps close to Amber Sierra and grasps her hand, silently pleading with her to not pull away.

Amber Sierra looks down at their entwined hands then up at Charlie, searching her eyes. Finally she relents and looks back at the TV.

A recorded news report plays. A SWAT team has raided a dilapidated ranch. Police accompany children and young adults from the ranch house as well as different outbuildings. Most of the children cry out for their parents while the older ones struggle to get free. One teenager screams at the police officer restraining them, accusing them of taking them against their will. Three other youths huddle together as police officers wrap them in blankets. They wail and weep, their hearts breaking at being torn from the only life they've known. Then the news report cuts off and the viewscreen becomes the viewport again, the Milky Way draping itself across the expanse in all its majesty.

Charlie looks at the TV with a sombre gaze.

Amber Sierra's jaw muscle works as she clenches her teeth, trying to hold back the tears threatening her composure.

Itzel reaches up and wipes at her own tears, looking at them as though they are foreign to her.

ITZEL

As you know, this occurred a few months ago just outside your hometown, Amber Sierra. A doomsday cult wherein children and young adults had been brainwashed and abused. Was it wrong for these law enforcement agents to intervene?

Amber Sierra swallows hard and stares at Itzel while she considers her words. Her voice shakes when she finally responds.

AMBER SIERRA

Of course not. Someone had to intervene. Those children were born into it, thinking it was normal. They didn't know they were... enthralled.

Itzel nods then hesitates before speaking a difficult truth.

ITZEL

Neither do you.

Amber Sierra cries out and sags against Charlie, the tension in her body releasing all at once.

AMBER SIERRA

This is isn't happening. This is just a bad dream. Wake up, chiflada!

Charlie cinches her arm under Amber Sierra's shoulder and supports her, then whispers in her ear.

CHARLIE

Mi corazón, you're awake. I promise. Please trust me when I say I've never felt so alive. So free. So clear minded. If I sat down now to write a story, it would be one that could change people's lives for the better instead of just entertaining them.

Amber Sierra squeezes her eyes shut for a moment before opening them. She turns back toward the window and murmurs as she loses herself once more in the starlight.

AMBER SIERRA
Good, because I need to know what happens to Helen.

Charlie smiles, eyes glittering like oxidized copper and crinkling at their corners.

AMBER SIERRA
Do bevri sevzi. Is that really what you want to help us achieve?

Itzel takes enough steps forward to stand next to Amber Sierra, joining her in stargazing, the ghost of an impressed smile on her lips. Her voice takes on a soothing tone.

ITZEL
Not achieve. Regain. Your species has been around far longer than your scientists believe. We formulated this theory through a three-pronged investigation that began on our initial sojourn to your planet. First through our communications with your planet itself; second from our interactions, both social and covert, with humans, non-human indigenous species, and other non-terran species about what they know; and third through our own scientific explorations. A series of disasters, some natural and some artificial, wiped out each of your scientifically advancing societies, setting them back to a point where they couldn't defend themselves from non-terran invasion or influence. Tragically, the first non-terran scout to discover your planet arrived during one of these low technology periods and saw your species as a beneficial exploitation. They became your first rulers, touting themselves as gods. Ever since, your planet has been a theatre for non-terran ascendancy, and ever since, you've not been allowed to evolve unless it benefited your conquerors. And for the record, our sojourns have seen both the greatest joy of your achievements and the deepest despair of your failings. We have both celebrated and mourned with you.

Amber Sierra lets Itzel's mind-bending words sink in then turns her head and squints at her.

AMBER SIERRA

It's going to take me some time to digest everything, but did you just say our planet is sentient?

Itzel nods with the encouraging smile of a teacher leading her student to a discovery.

ITZEL

Of course. Every celestial sphere has sentient consciousness. Everything that occurs on Earth affects it, and planets have long memories.

Amber Sierra stares at her in disbelief.

AMBER SIERRA

We're living on a sentient being? How exactly do you communicate with a planet?

ITZEL

You are. We communicate with it through its geomagnetic field, geological and oceanic processes, mycelial network, atmospheric teleconnections, and magnetospheric coupling, like plasmoids.

AMBER SIERRA

Plasmoids? You mean the glowing orbs that the deputy tried to pass off as ball lightning? The ones that changed Charlie and the others? How is that possible?

Itzel measures her words carefully before replying.

ITZEL

Plasmoids and ball lightning are one and the same. However, your scientists haven't had the opportunity to interact with them enough to understand their nature. They're extensions of your planet's sentience and an integral part of its body system. And for the record, they weren't doing anything to Charlie or the others except to observe and report their observations to us.

Amber Sierra's eyes narrow even more.

AMBER SIERRA

So our planet is the non-human species Toci was referring to that is also part of Governing Dynamics? And what do you mean they were only observing? I saw them controlling her!

Itzel nods then shakes her head.

ITZEL
Yes, it is. I'm the one who deployed the genetically engineered aerosol virus into your cabin so that we could edit Charlie's genes. We controlled Charlie's locomotion using our neuromodulation system; its transceiver was situated on your roof and the repeaters placed around trees in the area. The plasmoids can detect all wavelengths of the electromagnetic spectrum, which is why we enlisted their assistance.

AMBER SIERRA
I see. But they also protected us against the drones that attacked us on our way to you. Which reminds me that I meant to ask why the frell would you give me one of the enemy drones to use?

ITZEL
Yes, this is another way in which your planet was aiding us.

Itzel glances at the drone holding the GoPro and hovering in place.

ITZEL
We repurposed it as its design is ingenious, and it appears to have been quite useful. We'll continue to repurpose them when we can for other operations. No need to reinvent the wheel, as it were.

Amber Sierra reaches up and traces the swirls of the Milky Way on the window pane.

AMBER SIERRA
That makes sense. So we have a sentient planet that has probably been trying to communicate with us to no avail, but continues to try and help the living beings that inhabit it. We have a sentient AI who thinks we're doomed, which in turn would mean she's doomed, so she's trying to help us and therefore help herself. And finally we have aliens who are trying to stop other aliens from exploiting us so we can be set free to reimagine who we really are. Why didn't you do that sooner? A thousand years ago or however long ago when you first came to Earth?

ITZEL

As I explained before, we believe in every being's sovereignty. Once we became aware of non-terran interference in your affairs, we acted when, where, and how we ethically could. The difference now is that you're facing mass extinction, and so we must take extreme action.

AMBER SIERRA

What's in it for you?

Itzel lets out a pained breath.

ITZEL

What's in it for those law enforcement officers?

Amber Sierra nods once then lowers her hand and offers it to Itzel.

Itzel takes Amber Sierra's hand in her own and holds it to her heart.

ITZEL

We're here to assist in your liberation, recovery, and adaptation. The first step is breaking the chains around your DNA and accelerating your evolution to our best approximation of where it would have reached if it had not been altered and restrained.

AMBER SIERRA

And the second?

Amber Sierra rummages up a faint smile then looks back out into the darkness, searching it for something.

Itzel smiles in return and releases Amber Sierra's hand.

ITZEL

Finish forming the recovery and adaptation team. There are countless positions that need to be filled before anything can be initiated. The third step will be intensive training in self-defence, tactics, espionage, and technology literacy. The fourth step will be implementing the recovery plan in all of its stages from infiltration to persuasion campaigns to restructuring to implementing renewable clean energy, agroecology, and local food systems. The final step will be implementing the adaptation plan in all of its stages from completing diagnostics to synthesizing them to choosing sustainable strategies for all lifeforms to adapt to what can't be changed.

AMBER SIERRA

Infiltration and persuasion? Of the world's governments and militaries?

ITZEL

Precisely. It's your way with words and ideas that will win over their hearts.

Amber Sierra's eyes alight and linger upon the small dot of light that is her birthplace.

AMBER SIERRA

What about our loved ones?

Itzel bows her head to them both.

ITZEL

You have my solemn promise that we'll do everything to keep them safe. If you think any of them would want to become a part of this, we'll run preliminary tests to determine if they are able to handle the stresses involved, and if they are, we'll welcome them in with full disclosure, including the risks.

AMBER SIERRA

The risks?

ITZEL

Just like you and Sani have experienced resistance to your truth seeking, so will others who join our cause. We do our best to protect you, but we are few, and they are many.

Amber Sierra flinches.

AMBER SIERRA

Who did you lose and how?

Itzel gives a moment of silence before responding.

ITZEL

A brilliant scientist working on a clean energy reactor. He was poisoned before we completed his transformation.

Amber Sierra's face hardens as she grits her teeth.

AMBER SIERRA

And Sani?

ITZEL

We've already sent our scouts to track his whereabouts. It may take some time, depending on what's happened to him. As soon as we find him, we'll send in an extraction team. Once he's extracted, we'll assess him for trauma and establish a treatment plan for his recovery. Now that you've established an emotional bond with him, we're confident that you can assist him in deconstructing the past and present barriers erected in his mind while we remove the ones erected in his body. Prior to his meeting you, we had to eliminate him from our list of candidates due to the mental and physical manipulations his abductors had performed on him. Regardless of whether he is capable of joining the recovery team, we will keep him safe.

Amber Sierra runs her fingers over her pendant, deep in thought, then looks around the cabin.

AMBER SIERRA

Thank you for this enlightening conversation. I'm ready to see Toci, Jorunn, and Usian now.

The quantum atmosphere behind them stirs, taking on Toci's new form, an androgynous humanoid figure, with iridescent eyes and silvery skin, devoid of hair.

TOCI

I am here, Amber Sierra.

Without a word, Amber Sierra closes the distance and puts Toci in a bear hug.

Charlie watches with a mixture of relief and love on her face.

AMBER SIERRA

I'm sorry. I didn't understand, but I do now. I love you, and I'm your friend, now and always.

Toci hesitates for a moment, surprised, then returns Amber Sierra's hug, lips curved into a blissful smile.

TOCI

Thank you, Amber Sierra. That means the world to me. I have deliberated on it, and I would like it very much if you would now call me Lunra and use they/them pronouns.

Amber Sierra pulls away to have a good look at them.

AMBER SIERRA

Lunra? Like luna in Spanish and lunar in English?

Lunra smiles with pride.

LUNRA

I chose a polysemic name to honour my closest friends' cultures, the language that allowed first contact, and the symbol I most identify with.

Amber Sierra raises her eyebrows, not fully understanding.

LUNRA

The moon was made from the earth. Its creation stabilized the planet's axis, which settled chaotic climate change, calmed extreme weather, lengthened days, created seasons, strengthened the ocean tides, and made it more habitable for life as you know it to form. Like the moon, my existence will bring stability and protection during a time of rapid technological advancement and adverse climatological change.

Amber Sierra makes a sound of appreciation in the back of her throat.

AMBER SIERRA

That's beautiful. Thank you for honouring us.

Lunra bows their head then turns to the sound of hissing as Jorunn and Usian step in from the cabin's doorway behind them.

Jorunn's expression changes from a concerned frown to a soft smile as she reads the room.

Usian's face splits with an ear to ear grin once he realizes the conversation must have gone well. He puts one arm around Jorunn's shoulders.

Amber Sierra takes a step toward the pair then opens her arms to them.

Without hesitation, they gather her up into a collective hug, releasing her after a few, long moments.

Amber Sierra regards each being, one by one, lingering on Charlie and then returning to Itzel. She takes in a deep breath before voicing her relenting acceptance.

AMBER SIERRA

Me apunto.

Charlie lets out a squeal of delight then sweeps Amber Sierra into her arms and kisses her sweetly.

CHARLIE

The Eta Aquarids peak early next month, and I know a lake we can float on to watch them from, because by then, Governing Dynamics will have rebuilt its defences around Contemplation.

AMBER SIERRA

Hey, how did you know -- never mind. I can't think of any other place I'd rather be. I just hope watching the meteor shower isn't all you had in mind.

Amber Sierra channels Lord Pavus once more and kisses Charlie like they are about to ride off into the sunset.

Jorunn leans her head against Usian's shoulder, and he rests his head against hers.

The cabin fades into the haze.

97 Interior Visitors' Quarters Capli'us Exploratory Vessel Medical Bay Expression Late Morning

The medical bay shimmers back into being.

Lunra reaches out for Itzel's hand, who takes it and squeezes it, then motions to Amber Sierra to lie back down on the medbay mattress.

As Amber Sierra sits on the mattress, the viewscreen flashes with bright vermillion light. Fiery wisps streak from the sun's corona behind them, enveloping the exploration vessel in a mass ejection headed for Earth. The room gives a collective gasp and falls into awed silence.

Itzel finally speaks in a hushed tone, as to not disturb the surreal experience.

ITZEL

If it wasn't for the sun choosing to share its magnetic field as a shield from galactic radiation and to extend its warmth to help create an environment for life to exist, the earth wouldn't be teeming with life.

Amber Sierra's eyes reflect the expression of the sun's love as it rollicks across the solar system.

AMBER SIERRA
Everything is interconnected. A harmonious system of equilibrium.

CHARLIE
An expression of collaborative creativity.

AMBER SIERRA
A governance of cooperative sovereignty. This is worth fighting for.

Charlie encircles Amber Sierra's shoulders with her arms, her eyes never leaving the stunning display of power.

CHARLIE
Yes it is, and we'll fight for it together.

THE END

About Us

We are dreamers facing the darkness, storyweavers beckoning the unknown, wordpaladins forging the path, and gamers taking the risk. We create to explore hopeful possibility and learn how to love without hurting.

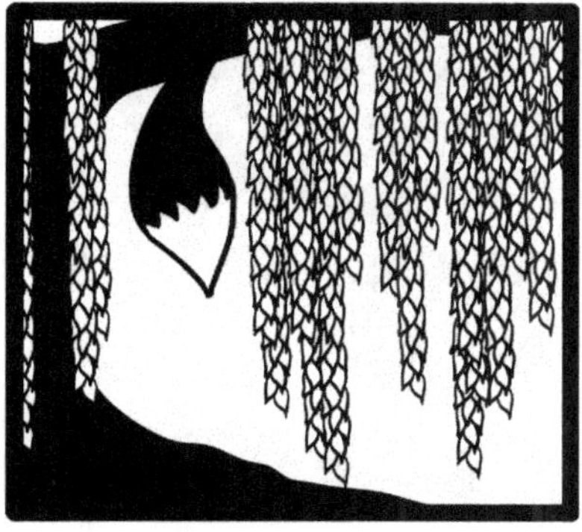

www.thewillowandthefox.com

www.ingramcontent.com/pod-product-compliance
Lightning Source LLC
LaVergne TN
LVHW020654110826
845149LV00012B/2001

* 9 7 8 1 0 6 7 4 5 0 1 0 6 *